The *Gawain* Legacy

The *Gawain* Legacy

Jon Mackley

Winchester, UK
Washington, USA

First published by Cosmic Egg Books, 2014
Cosmic Egg Books is an imprint of John Hunt Publishing Ltd., Laurel House, Station Approach, Alresford, Hants, SO24 9JH, UK
office1@jhpbooks.net
www.johnhuntpublishing.com

For distributor details and how to order please visit the 'Ordering' section on our website.

ISBN: 978 1 78279 485 1

A CIP catalogue record for this book is available from the British Library.

Design: Stuart Davies

Printed in the USA by Edwards Brothers Malloy

For Zoë

My precious perle wythouten spot

Ƿ byþ ðerlé scearp

~Thorn is very sharp~

As þou foly hatz frayst, fynde þe behoues

~ As you have sought folly, you deserve to find it ~

Gawain and the Green Knight, l. 324

Author's Note

In the late fourteenth century, an anonymous Cheshire poet wrote a poem which subsequent editors have titled *Gawain and the Green Knight*. The manuscript is bound with three devotional texts and kept in the British Library.

Gawain and the Green Knight tells of King Arthur's court at Camelot. A strange knight, dressed entirely in green with green skin and hair, declares he will receive a blow from his mighty axe and, a year later, he will deliver a return blow. Gawain decapitates the Green Knight, but the knight picks up his head, which reminds Gawain to look for him in a year.

Gawain leaves Camelot in search of the Green Knight's chapel. On his journey he finds a castle: the host welcomes him, telling him the Green Chapel is nearby and offers Gawain a bargain: he will hunt in the forests and give Gawain whatever he kills. In return, Gawain should remain in the castle and hand over anything that he 'wins'.

Over the next two days, the host's wife flirts with Gawain. She becomes more overt in her advances and only leaves once Gawain has given her a kiss, which Gawain, in turn, gives to his host.

On the third day, realising she will not persuade Gawain to sleep with her, the lady offers him her girdle. Gawain takes it, not as a love token, but because she promises it will make him invulnerable to the Green Knight's blade. That evening, Gawain gives his host three kisses, but conceals the girdle.

The following morning, Gawain travels to the chapel where the Green Knight is waiting for him. Gawain bares his neck, but twice the Green Knight feigns the blow. On the third attempt, Gawain receives a slight nick in the neck. The Green Knight explains he had been Gawain's host in the castle and knew everything that had occurred with his wife. Each attempt with the axe represented a day in the castle. On the first two days, Gawain had been honourable with the host's wife. On the third day he had kept the girdle, but his intentions had been self-preservation, rather than sexual, so there was only a minor blemish on his character.

Humiliated, Gawain returns to Camelot and tells King Arthur of his trial. He sees the girdle as a sign of his humiliation, but the court wears it as a badge of his honour.

The tight structure, the author's use of locations that are familiar to his audience and the repetition of numbers and alliterative letters, have led readers of *Gawain* to search for hidden codes including the author's name; and who knows what else is hidden in *Gawain*'s legacy?

1

For Lara, the fact she was leaving her husband wasn't so bad as the bus being late.

The deep blue hues in the sky were fading in the east. A single wispy cloud floated above, tinted black in the January night. The morning star glittered, watching her. She dragged her coat tight around her slim frame against the chilling wind.

Distant shimmering lights led to the nearby train station. The glow seeped through the morning mist around the platform. A few figures stood waiting to catch early trains like freezing caricatures from a Lowry painting.

The painting … the painting had been the final nail in the coffin of her relationship with Michael. It seemed petty now. Even now, despite her desperation, despite her fear, her resolve had almost broken. She could still return before he woke and he would be unaware of her intentions.

But nothing would have changed except her diminishing self-esteem. He'd continue tormenting her and she might never again find the strength to leave.

She could, of course, catch a train from here. An early commuter train would take her to Birmingham, or to London. From there she could travel to anywhere in the country; hell, she could get to Europe if she wanted.

A man walked past with a dog, which sniffed at her holdall. The owner grunted a 'good morning'. He dragged the dog away, not looking at her.

The light bleeding across the sky had eclipsed the morning star; the clouds were tinged with salmon. The concealing darkness was exposing her to the terrors of the day.

She stared at the Lowry caricatures again, wondering if they could see her, as she saw them. She should have taken off her glasses before she started, then she wouldn't have known about them: blissfully ignorant in blindness.

She removed the glasses, carefully folding the arms down. She could see clearly enough without them, but in this half-light, distant things became blurred.

If eyes are the windows to the soul, I don't want anyone looking into mine.

Without her glasses, the world blended into an anonymous blur of colours. She only needed the glasses for driving and reading, but tiredness had enveloped her and the world faded away to a hazy nothingness.

If I ever leave my husband again, I'll go when I'm less tired.

But there wouldn't be a next time, she thought, unconsciously crossing her fingers. Standing here, waiting for the bus, marked the end of that relationship. And all the time, her father's quotation from *Twelfth Night* on the day she had announced her engagement, rang in her mind: *Many a good hanging prevents a bad marriage.* Had he seen something wrong in their relationship when she had been blinded by love?

And it wasn't even a nice *painting,* she reminded herself. But Michael had decided it suited the bedroom wall and, because Michael was always right, it had gone up. Six months later, it had fallen down again. Gravity had chosen five o'clock in the morning to remove the painting from its seat of glory. The ensuing argument had forced her to the end of her tether: Michael had found a way of making it her fault. Already, she had been unconsciously planning her escape. Now, less than twenty-four hours later, she had walked out. Her heart had hardened, even though she was still brushing tears away.

And even though she was devastated by grief because everything had ended, and she was crushed by the uncertainty of the future, there was another, stronger, overwhelming emotion.

Relief.

She glanced over her shoulder. The rising sun paled in the mist. Even without her glasses she recognised the familiar landmarks of "home": the river Welland and the bridge, the wooden archway of the George, the yellow limestone and timber-framed buildings. She needed to leave them all behind her now.

Shivering, she realised her teeth were gritted. She tapped her foot in irritation, praying the bus would arrive soon.

She looked back at the train station. Her first awareness that something was wrong was pure instinct. It was the same pervading fear that ate into her gut when she heard the key scraping in the lock as Michael came home from work. The sensation was so familiar that, at first, she thought he had found her, that he had woken early, found her note and had come to drag her back.

A movement, almost imperceptible.

She put her glasses on again and looked down the bank, past the discarded shopping trolleys, to the train lines.

Swathed by the morning mist, she saw a figure standing, Christ-like, arms outstretched, his overcoat hanging loose around him. Standing on one of the sleepers between the silver of the railway lines.

As she watched, he knelt down, his arms suspended in a parody of the Crucifixion: resigned to his fate.

The mist had almost swallowed him. In the distance – a mere pinprick in the curtain of the night – she saw the light of the oncoming train. The Jesus character had worked out this train wouldn't stop, wouldn't even slow down for the platform. And there was no way the driver would see him in time, even if she could.

Another movement. Further down the lines, in the path the train would take, she saw lights in the distance, torch beams spearing the mist. Dogs barked. Her mind tried to connect the images: man running away from men with dogs. Did he hope the train would get him before the dogs did?

She wasn't usually blessed with a vivid imagination, but her mind was saturated by the image of a body after impact.

The train continued: a weapon of suicide.

She wasn't aware of moving, didn't know where the reserves of strength came from. It was like watching someone else when she hauled her bag over the iron railings. A myriad of thoughts struck her; the most forceful was a chiding voice inside her head: *It's better to try and fail than to not try at all and live with the consequences.*

Then she was lifting herself on to the railings. Her holdall rolled away down the embankment. She shuddered. If she fell, she could tumble uncontrolled down the side of the bank, perhaps skewering herself on the debris waiting at the bottom like a crocodile's teeth.

She heard the hum of the train on the lines; the sound of the engine was carried by the light breeze. She let go of the railings and slipped down the bank, scrabbling for grasses and roots. She landed down alongside her bag.

The rattling train drew closer. The light pierced the darkness and behind her, torch lights swung closer.

She ran across the train tracks, tripping, stumbling, but caught herself before she fell.

The Jesus character was standing in front of her, a shade among a multitude of shadows.

Her body no longer responded to rational thought. She was either going to help him or join him.

She tripped again, then ran, finding a rhythm to avoid obstructions in her path. The train bore down on her like a predator alighting on its prey. It was on top of her.

She wasn't going to reach the man in time.

The screams of the train were deafening, like standing in the heart of a volcano. Lights blazed. Ozone burned. Suddenly, adrenalin surged through her, filling her with inhuman strength.

She leapt, already knowing she was going to miss the man and be hit by the train herself.

I'm too late, she told herself. *He's dead.*

Her hands connected with solid muscle. She hadn't tensed her arms. They buckled against him. The man hadn't been prepared for a 'rescue'. His body crumbled. Her jaw connected with his shoulder. Her teeth snapped together. Blood filled her mouth. Her head swam with the shock. She curled her feet underneath her, pulling them from the path of the train.

The world erupted. Wind was dragged out of her. Her spirit felt like it was being sucked out of her eyes. The vortex dragged her towards the train, as unforgiving as a demon.

In eternal moments it was over. The train had gone. She clawed at the earth, fighting for breath. Behind her, the torches had scattered but dogs barked, picking up the scent. They were close. Beside her, the man was crying.

'You should have left me.' His voice was child-like. 'It's got to end now.' He looked around, as if trying to find the next train. 'They'll find me,' he whispered.

Ungrateful bastard, Lara thought. She stared behind her. The torchlight moved closer. The men had regrouped. The barking was muffled; the man's scent was masked by the stench of the train.

'Get away,' the man said, looking down on her. Even in this half-light, she could see his eyes were slits, his top lip curled, baring his teeth and his contempt. 'Get away now, before they see you.'

'What?' Lara started.

The man turned, hauling himself from where he had fallen. He grabbed her by the wrist. 'Too late.' His voice was forlorn. 'They'll find you too, come on.'

Lara was stunned. That morning she had planned to get away, laying a false trail. Did it matter if she went by train or by bus? Wherever the man was going was just as anonymous as anywhere she had planned. 'My bag,' she gestured feebly.

'No time.' He pulled her with him, dragged her. She

stumbled. He glanced at his watch. Now they were running along the sleepers, towards the station.

'Platform two; train to Birmingham,' he said. 'Which is it? Left or right?'

'Right,' Lara said. She peered over her shoulder. She felt that if the torches swung in the right direction the beams would burn her, like a vampire in sunlight.

She blinked in the bright station lights. The man lifted her on to the platform. She started to run as he pulled himself up behind her. A momentary strand of reason threaded in her brain. The men following him were probably police. This man could be a criminal. If she was caught, she'd either be considered an accomplice, or fined for trespassing on the train tracks. No good turn goes unpunished.

She wanted to get away, but the man had caught up with her. He placed a hand on her shoulder. His grip was firm and strong. Uncomfortable. She wouldn't be able to pull away, even if she wanted to.

The tannoy crackled: *The train now approaching platform two is for Birmingham New Street.*

The train came to a halt. The few people on the platform stepped forward. Lara and the man became part of the crowd, swept towards open doors.

She looked behind her again. The lights of the station muted the torches. 'Come on,' he said, shoving her into the carriage. There was a kind of forlorn anger in his voice. He almost pushed her into a seat a few places up from the door. 'Turn away from the window,' he snapped, sitting down opposite her. 'Don't let them see you.'

The train was hot. Sitting down, she realised perspiration was dribbling down her cheek. Her lungs were burning and her heart pounding. While the adrenaline had been pumping, she had not noticed how tired she was.

She watched him resentfully. He had pulled his collar up. If the other men were the police, then they'd have the authority to search the train, carriage by carriage until they found their quarry.

She was suddenly anxious. 'Let me go,' she whispered. 'This is nothing to do with me. I won't tell anyone about you.'

He shook his head despondently. There was a hydraulic hiss of closing doors. Lara wondered if any of the men had come on board: how many of them were looking for her, even now? 'You're not a prisoner,' he said. His voice was soft, distant. 'But the dogs'll have your scent. They'll find you.'

'How? They don't know me.'

'They always seem to,' he said, almost wistfully.

Lara unconsciously touched her face, making sure she still had her glasses. The realisation fell upon her. When dawn spread her fingers across the line they would find her holdall, which would have something to identify her. They could trace her to Michael, find out her details.

The train pulled away. Lara peered into the darkness. The man turned her head away from the window with a strong finger under her jaw. In that brief moment, she had seen men … and perhaps a woman … some of them were in grey trench coats, looking like First World War officers. Perhaps she had made eye contact with one of them, a stern-looking man with round glasses …

She sat back, watching the other passengers. Then she stared at the man, perhaps seeing him for the first time. His eyes were closed. His face had changed. The furrowed concern had melted, replaced by a mask of serenity. He was unshaven, but he had an angular face, noble and refined, with the ruggedness of an actor. His hair was swept back. It reached down to his shoulders.

She drew in a breath, but the man opened his eyes and silenced her with a raised finger. His eyes flicked to the other passengers. 'Not here.' He leaned back and closed his eyes.

Lara slumped back, frustrated. 'Where are we going?' she

asked.

An uncomfortable few seconds passed before the man opened his eyes – piercing blue – and regarded her. She wondered what else was in there: what pain was searing through his heart?

For a while he remained silent. When he finally spoke, the lines of concern scored his face again and his voice was filled with sorrow. 'It was almost over. They would have left it …'

'What?'

The man looked away.

'Don't I deserve an explanation of where we're going?'

'Where *we're* going?' the man said. A wry smile touched his eyes. 'Why do you think *we're* going anywhere?'

Anger flared inside her. 'Damn you! Why are you so enigmatic? Don't I deserve a word of thanks for risking my neck?' Tension locked her shoulder muscles, but curiosity overrode her indignation. 'Don't I at least deserve a name?'

He studied her for a moment and then whispered, 'Will.'

She shot him a caustic smile. 'That's a start. I'm Lara …' Her teeth clamped when she realised she didn't want to give her married name. That part of her life was over. 'Halpin,' she added.

Will nodded. He offered no more information and asked nothing.

'Where are we going?' Lara pressed.

Again, the painful silence as Will thought through his answer. 'Away from here. Does it matter?' He saw the agitation in her eyes. 'To Birmingham for now. After that …?' He mouthed something, almost inaudible. 'Where would you go?'

The train slowed and pulled into the next station. A man sitting across the aisle got up and left. Will watched him apprehensively. He waited until the man had gone and then fixed his gaze back on Lara. She shifted uncomfortably, trying to read his expression. She tried to speak, but no words came out. Instead she just shook her head. When the train pulled away, he spoke again.

'What about you?' he wondered. 'You're running, just like me. But you're not focused. Regrets already? Or did you just want to get out of Stamford and make it up from there?'

Lara tried not to recoil under his sarcasm, she couldn't meet his gaze. Was she so easy to read? Although she'd thought about Michael, she still couldn't grasp that she was away from him. Not free, but away. And then there was the whirlpool of emotions. She had expected to grieve for the passing of a relationship, but there were no tears left inside.

'You do have regrets,' Will said. Something danced behind his eyes.

Lara shook her head. 'Memories, some good, some bad. A few realisations, nothing else.' She stood up. 'Excuse me.'

He placed a hand on her arm. 'Where are you going?'

'To the loo,' she said bitterly. 'That's all right, isn't it?'

His shoulders slumped. He closed his eyes again, not willing to be drawn.

She made a shaky path along the train, away from him.

There was solace in her brief isolation. The small cubical reeked of bleach. She quickly checked her pockets: money that was the important thing, and her passport – she had both of them.

She wiped the seat and flushed the lavatory before sitting down. Sitting there, she focused her mind away from the problems taunting her. In the relative stillness she realised for the first time that she was on a train, away from Stamford.

She was free.

It was impossible to truly believe it. She'd lived so long with the chains of marriage strangling her. She wondered if she had ever been in love with him, or whether it was the *idea* of being in love that had seduced her.

She tried to tell herself everything would have been all right if Julia had lived. Julia, the daughter that never was, the child strangled by her own umbilical cord as she struggled her way into life. When Lara had fallen pregnant, she'd hoped a new focus would unite the pair of them.

Tears brimmed, then spilled. She always cried when she thought of Julia. She cried for her own loss and the love she would have been able to give. But also because it would have been unfair to bring a child into a relationship like theirs. Although she'd hoped Michael would have mellowed with fatherhood, the more she thought about it, the less likely it seemed.

He'd not been present at the birth; not been with her when she'd discovered Julia had died. When he eventually saw her, he had sat glaring at her, his silent brooding making her feel that Julia's death had been her fault.

That had been eighteen months ago. While she recuperated, she'd endured his snipes about how lazy she was, her body became numb to the emotional pain he inflicted. Then, largely to get away from him, but also to subsidise his evening drinking, she took a part-time secretarial job. It was boring, repetitive work and she was nowhere close to achieving her potential, but Michael was insistent that she was at home when he returned; he barely gave her any freedom.

No more, she told herself. *I'm free.*

But would Michael ever let her be totally free? Would he find her and drag her back by the hair? Would he tell the authorities she'd stolen something? She smiled inwardly. All she had taken were the clothes in which she sat and a small amount of money, a nest egg she had protected from Michael's drinking; the secretarial job had provided her with only a small amount to get away.

She washed her face, hoping her rheumy eyes and tear streaks would fade. She couldn't stay around this 'Will' character, whoever he was: whatever his misdemeanours, he was clearly suicidal.

At the same time, she wanted to help him. Perhaps that would be the first step on the road to redeeming herself?

That's Michael talking again, she realised. *Making me feel guilty. Making me feel it's my fault.*

Isn't it? a cold voice chided her.

If Will was suicidal, then he was dangerous. He might try again, and maybe not care who he took with him.

She took a deep breath, closed her eyes, then exhaled slowly. She'd try to get him to talk. That was all. If it didn't work, well, walk away ... fast. But at least Will had a direction, which was more than she had. He was right: she hadn't thought this through. She could follow for a while, at least.

Steeling herself, she wove her way back along the carriage to where Will was waiting. He nodded an acknowledgement, but did not smile.

'The conductor came round, so I paid for both of us.'

She sat down. She was tired and hungry. She said nothing. Just like with Michael, all her resolution drained away.

Will's eyes narrowed. 'D'you do a lot of this? Wandering around in the early hours? Pulling people away from oncoming trains?'

'Only as a hobby,' Lara said acidly. "Thanks" would do.'

Will sat back in his seat, saying nothing.

'Where are we going?' Lara asked.

'We?' Will cocked his head. 'I'm going to Chester, eventually. You could leave at Birmingham. Go somewhere else? Or go back to wherever you came from.'

Her heart dropped. 'Chester,' she repeated uneasily. 'Why?'

'Because it's there.' His eyes had started to crinkle. It was the first sign of happiness she had seen in him. 'History, architecture. And shops. You'll need new clothes. Is there a problem with Chester?'

'Only the ghosts.'

'No such thing as ghosts,' Will said sharply. He stared out of the window. 'Birmingham International,' he said. 'New Street soon.'

Passengers collected bags and coats. Lara sat still, waiting for Will to speak. He chose not to. His eyes flicked from buildings to roads. When the train slid to a halt, he waited for the other passengers to disembark before nodding to the door.

She followed him, away from the platform, up the stairs, through the ticket barrier and into the main foyer, packed with morning commuters. The smells from the multiple eateries crashed against her senses.

Will glanced over his shoulder as he passed underneath the displays announcing the arrivals and departures. While he scanned them, she watched a huge screen broadcasting Sky News, half expecting the lead story to be that she had left.

'Ninety minutes until the train,' he said, breaking her thoughts. 'Change at Crewe.' She was about to speak, but he was already hurrying away like a frightened mouse. He joined a short queue.

Chester, Lara thought. *If I'd left home, would I go back to where I'd lived before? Wouldn't that be the first place Michael would look for me?*

Was she focusing too much on Michael? The way he had treated her: not love, not even affection. He needed a servant, not a wife. Surely, he'd see there was nothing worth salvaging in the relationship and let her go. She closed her eyes. A part of her was scared – very scared – that he'd chase her to the ends of the earth, not satisfied until she was back in his possession.

When Will opened his wallet, Lara saw it was bulging with banknotes. Evidently he believed he'd take it with him when he crossed over to the other side, or maybe the ferryman of the river Styx didn't accept credit cards.

'Hour and a half,' Will said, looking at his watch. He peered around apprehensively. 'Birmingham's changed a lot since I was last here.' He pointed to a pub on the concourse. 'You ought to get some breakfast. You look like you'll fall down any minute.'

He led her away from the growing crush of commuters and

the harsh station lights to the subdued lighting of the pub. He strode confidently into the wide bar room: the bar was in the middle of the room. The young barman was well dressed. This was the kind of place where businessmen would have their lunches. 'Full English breakfast and a couple of cups of coffee,' he said.

The coffee was poured. Will carried it to a table at the side of the room. Lara sipped gratefully. The coffee provided a link with reality, a tangible moment which forced the morning's events into the dawn's fog. Perhaps she'd wake up and discover it was all a dream. When she woke would she find herself still in Stamford?

'Do you have a mobile?' Will asked.

Lara instinctively tapped a pocket, then shook her head. She'd deliberately left it at home.

'Good,' Will said. 'They'd trace you with a mobile.' He glanced up. The barman arrived with her breakfast. Lara's head reeled. The smells were overwhelming. She had not realised how hungry she was. She devoured it quickly, looking up at Will occasionally. He sat back in his seat, eyes closed. Marks of consternation etched their way into his face.

'All right,' she said when there was nothing else to eat. Her voice was quiet and calm, 'Will you tell me what's going on?' He said nothing. 'Surely nothing's so bad you have to end it all?'

He didn't look at her. His eyes were vacant. He stared at his cup as if the grouts of his coffee would yield answers to unspoken questions. 'You'd never believe it.'

'Those men,' she said. 'Why were they looking for you?'

'It's a long story.'

'We have time,' Lara said, but her eyes flicked nervously to the door. Part of her expected it to burst open. She shuddered, realising she was adopting his paranoia. Her gaze returned to Will and her eyes narrowed. 'Look, I'm not prying. There's a fine line between concern and intrusion, but nothing's worth giving up absolutely. Surely?' That was a lie and she knew it. If nothing was worth giving up then why was she here and not with Michael? *Only words*. She was telling him what she needed to hear; offering platitudes, hoping to make her own pain better. 'Will,' she whispered. 'Please, you don't have to tell me anything, but maybe we can rake through the ashes of your troubles and find something worth salvaging.' She wanted to reach out, place her hand over his, but felt the intimacy of touch might bring reality to what might still be a dream.

For the first time, he looked up at her with a penetrating stare. There was a depth to those eyes suggesting an "old soul". Lara wondered if he had truly noticed her since they had met. She smiled gently, a comforting, sympathetic smile, rather than trying to make him feel like a lost puppy.

'Lara,' he said, nodding. His acknowledgement implied everything was all right. His jaw clenched. 'You look like her … a bit.'

She did not ask whom he meant – his lost love, she guessed. She felt a sting of guilt. Was this what Michael was going through at the moment?

'She left, is that what happened?'

'Leaving wasn't the problem.' Will shook his head. 'It was when she came back.'

2

Will regarded her carefully, seeming to scrutinise her face for traces of malice. When he found none, his shoulders sagged. He closed his eyes. 'I guess,' he started, but his voice cracked. He cleared his throat and started again. 'Once upon a time, I had everything I wanted. I was a history teacher. I could make it come alive because I could *see* what I was teaching. Sure, the job was frustrating when my hands were tied with admin, but there were moments … and then there was Janet. She was my world.

'I don't know when it started to go wrong. They say you know the moment you first fall in love, but you never know when you lose it.

'Janet …' he stumbled over the name. 'She still lived at home. She stayed with me sometimes – we'd talked about her moving in – but, then, something … I don't know. Her mother fielded my calls, telling me she was out. Eventually, Janet saw me; told me she wanted a new life, away from Norwich … away from me. She couldn't tell me what was wrong with us, only that she didn't love me in the same way as before.' His eyes expressed more challenge than curiosity. 'Are blokes too insensitive? Should I have seen it coming? I keep telling myself I should've, but I wasn't looking for the signs.'

Lara watched him. He had paused. She didn't know if he wanted an answer. 'People change, Will,' she whispered. 'Relationships change.'

Will lowered his eyelids, perhaps so he could see out, but no one could see in. 'That's pretty much what she said, too.' When he looked up again, his eyes were misty and distant, staring across the bar and across eternity at the same time. 'I cried. I don't know how long for. It was dark when she left. I was still crying at dawn.' His cheeks burned with remembrance. 'I'm not a romantic, but I believed her when she'd said she wanted me forever. I thought I'd treated her well. I wasn't promising a brilliant life, but people will always need teachers.' He gave a sad sigh. Lara wondered if, even though he'd spent an age soul-searching, this was the first time he had asked himself the right questions.

'After she went ... when I wasn't at school, I found oblivion in drink. But alcohol didn't intoxicate me. It just made me sleepy and I dreamed of what might have been. I drowned myself in work when I could, but the cracks were showing. I couldn't hide what was happening.' Now his eyes seemed to beg for absolution. 'I tried to concentrate on anything but her, but I never could. I saw those flashing grey eyes everywhere.' His eyes were remote. 'She could have been a romance heroine.' He clasped his hands together and his voice lost its animation. 'The thing about romance heroines is that they're supposed to be put on a pedestal and worshipped. Never touched.

'I didn't give in gracefully. I texted and emailed, hoped she'd respond. It's the paradox of falling out of love. I wanted her so much, but wanted to reject her. And she didn't take kindly to being harassed by a drunk.' He ran a finger around the lip of his empty cup. Lara made no move to get another and neither did he. 'I waited by the phone, in that buzzing twilight of despair, didn't know if she'd call or whether the last thing she'd say was that bitter goodbye. I would feel my vision blackening, my grip on reality slipping.' He glanced across at her. 'There's months of my life where I don't know what I did.' He laughed, but there was no humour in the sound. 'That happens sometimes when you're a teacher. The weeks blend into each other. But, I once woke on a station platform in London. I didn't know how I got there, all I knew was I had to get back to Norwich before 9.15. The kids didn't get their homework marked that day. The head teacher called me in. "Blah, blah, blah, standards are slipping; blah, blah, blah, expect better, blah, blah." Wasn't interested in anything I had to say. Why would he be? I was a liability. He wanted me to deny anything was wrong. I needed to scream out I'd been beaten and I needed help.

'Things didn't get better. I was told to find a new position at the end of term.'

He waited for Lara to say something. She felt awkward under his stare. She felt he wanted her to yield answers for which there were no questions. She shifted uncomfortably. 'Sorry,' was all she managed.

Fire flashed in his eyes, violent and dangerous. 'I don't want pity,' he snarled and she recoiled at the venom in his voice. 'D'you think a *stupid* platitude can solve everything? It's too late for that.' Lara wondered if she should get away from him now, but the anger was gone as quickly as it arrived. He stared mournfully into his empty mug. 'It was always too late.'

His eyes became stony. 'What hurt the most was there wasn't any support. Everyone's been through a break-up. Why should mine affect me so badly? I wanted help, wanted to break away from the self-destructive cycle and no one wanted to listen.'

Lara nodded. She knew exactly how that felt. 'I still tried to speak to her,' Will continued. 'Her mother permanently guarded the phone. Told me to leave her alone. She'd found someone else. She was starting a new life with him. How much time had passed? Months? Years? The fact she'd moved on and I was still in the same place as when she left ... destroyed the last of my self-esteem. I told the school I wasn't coming back. They probably said "no great loss" and got a supply teacher.'

He stared down at the coffee cup, then glanced at Lara. 'Do you want some more?' She shook her head, not wanting to break his stream of thoughts, but he sauntered away and returned a few moments later with another cup. One of the bar staff followed him and cleared away the dirty cups and plates.

'My memory ... it's blacked out most of what happened,' Will explained as he sipped the coffee. 'It's hazy. A dream. But if I concentrate I can remember small details. I escaped into fiction.

I don't know how many books I read. I was just picking them up off the shelf, reading them, putting them back, then picking up the one next to it. I don't remember much about what I read: it was *War and Peace* at one stage, but the only reason I know is because the spine's bent.

'Sometimes I'd pray Janet would come back, others I prayed she never would.' His voice became grave. 'I should've learned there's no point in trying to change what's already happened.'

'But she came back,' Lara prompted.

'Oh yeah, she called. Said she'd been mistaken about her fiancé. She regretted everything, needed to talk to me. I was mad ... furious *and* insane. But she was desperate. She needed the same help as I did, and I wasn't going to refuse. But I also wanted her to see what I'd become, what she'd done to me.

'She came back. It would have been better if she hadn't. She didn't mean to, but it was like rubbing salt into my wounds. Everything had been a horrible mistake. She said she was sorry. If there was any love left in me, I'd forgive her.' His jaw tightened, his eyes were bitter. 'She put the onus on *me* to forgive *her*, like it was my responsibility. I'd lost everything. So had she, but she'd had a choice, in both relationships. She chose to walk away from both of us.

'And now she wanted to come back. The grass really wasn't greener. She saw I needed help. I wasn't going to get better overnight. She'd be there to help me through it.

'I was a fool. No, I was *desperate*. I let her come back.

'We spent the night together, both uncomfortable with the familiarity, but a part of it was like we'd never been apart. She knew my ways, I knew hers. It's impossible to break that intimacy.

'She left that morning to tell her mother she was moving in with me. She'd take no arguments. She said I needed someone to be there.'

He took a mouthful of coffee and paused, uncertain whether

to swallow it or not.

'She never made it home,' Will said finally. 'I got a call. There'd been a car accident. That wasn't the worst. Her mother held me responsible. Irrational, but she needed someone to blame. I tried to go to the funeral, just to say my goodbyes, but I wasn't allowed to be there. Her father saw me off.

'That was the last thing I knew. I wandered. I'd no intention of going home. I had my bank card, I could have wandered as long as I wanted. I walked. I don't know how long I walked, or where. There were nights I slept under bridges, drunk, unable to face anyone.' He let out a long exhalation. 'This is the first time I've talked about this.'

'What about those men?' Unconsciously, Lara motioned towards the door. Will's eyes darted there nervously.

'They never talked to me,' he said in a caustic tone. 'They might if they'd caught me. Well, maybe not "talk", maybe "interrogate".'

'What do they want?'

Will didn't answer for a long time. When he finally spoke, his voice was low and serious. 'When I looked for shelter, I found a maze of tunnels, just outside Bath.' Now his voice had become a conspiratorial whisper. 'There are places in this country we aren't meant to know about. It was a storage area for ammunition used on D-Day. It's supposed to be for storage now, but only a small bit is used commercially.' He stared past her, remembering. 'It's hard to map. I think I found the back door. There weren't many people there. Manual workers, a few security guards, except they weren't regular security: they had guns. I stayed away from them, like Gollum, except I didn't have the ring to make me invisible.'

He picked up his coffee cup again and glanced at his watch. 'I should stop. Train'll be here soon.'

'Half an hour,' Lara said defiantly. 'Carry on.'

Will made a noncommittal gesture. 'I got hungry. I got daring, looking for guards' sandwiches. Instead of finding a mess hall, I found a storage chamber, except this wasn't something you'd leave *Securitas* in charge of.'

'What was there?' Lara asked, breathlessly.

'Ancient papyri. There were maps of Iraq showing where Babylon once was. There were medieval manuscripts of Gnostic gospels – books that never got into the Bible – and scrolls from the library at Alexandra.'

Lara held up her hand. 'I don't follow. What's so special about them?'

Will stared at her quizzically. 'The Alexandrian library had the most advanced collection of manuscripts for its time. It put the British Library to shame.'

'So?'

'It burned down a couple of thousand years ago and all the manuscripts were destroyed with it.'

'So the tunnels contained rare antiquities? Maybe they were being catalogued?'

He shook his head. 'Another thing – the bindings were in modern German.'

'They'd been brought from a German museum?'

'No. There's a story that Hitler was mad about the occult. He thought supernatural powers might help his war effort.' He glanced at his watch again. 'I think this store room might have held some of the things Hitler found.'

'So why are they following you? Do they want to know what you found?' She shook her head. 'No, this isn't real. This sounds like a conspiracy, a corrupt and secret organisation ...'

'But that's what it *is*. I saw some of the manuscripts. They weren't supposed to exist.'

'What did you see? What was so important?'

'The completed *Canterbury Tales*,' Will started. 'Only one tale for each pilgrim, but it includes "The Ploughman's Tale", and tales from the Guildsmen, as well as what they did when they reached Thomas à Becket's Shrine in Canterbury.'

'What did they do?'

'Got pissed, just like in the rest of the tales. And the Wife of Bath chose Harry Bailey as her sixth husband.'

Lara stifled a laugh, but then her face grew serious again. 'How d'you know it wasn't a forgery?'

'If it's a forgery then I'm Prince Edward,' Will snapped. 'Normally Chaucer's scribes copied the manuscripts for him. He never wrote any in his own hand, except this one. I've seen his signature on the account rolls of the Smithfield Tournament of 1390. The writing is identical, even down to the nib he was using.'

'That doesn't explain why you're being followed,' Lara said, but then realisation dawned. 'You *took* one!'

Will nodded.

'Can't you take it back? It's not a crime to be better read in Chaucer than your average scholar. What did you take to make you a danger to National Security?' When Will raised an eyebrow, Lara continued. 'You must have something vital to them. That's it, isn't it? They don't chase you with dogs because you've got an overdue library book.'

Will nodded. 'It's a manuscript, like everything else there.' He reached into his coat. There was a large inner pocket. From this he withdrew a small battered codex. The cover was cured red leather; the folios cut from uneven sheets of vellum. Will held it like an over-protective parent.

'What is it?' Lara wondered.

'A fourteenth-century poem called *Gawain and the Green Knight*. It's a second copy of the text.'

'What does that mean? What happened to the first copy?'

'It's in the British library. It's so rare, you practically have to sign in blood to see it.' He tapped the cover. 'This one is pretty much identical. A second copy.'

'Why's it different from what I read at school?' she asked.

'You read *Gawain* at school?' Will was surprised.

'And Geoffrey of Monmouth,' Lara added.

'I'm impressed,' Will said, opening the manuscript. Lara stared at the letters. They were a faded scrawl across browned pages, almost unreadable. Some of the characters were part of an alphabet she didn't know. The version of *Gawain* she'd read was nothing like this: she'd been able to read that! She stared at it in frustration, trying to re-focus her eyes to see the writing. 'This is definitely *Gawain*,' Will said. He opened the manuscript carefully, the vellum strained, threatening to crack. Eventually, he found the place he wanted to read. '"Siþen þe sege and þe assault watz sesed at Troye,' he recited proudly. Looking at her he said: 'That means "Since the siege and the assault was ceased at Troy". It's easier when you recognise the characters.' He reached into the inside pocket on the other side of his coat and pulled out a small notebook. He wrote on a fresh page: *Gawain and þe Grene Kniȝt*.

Lara stared at it and started to read out loud. 'Gawain and …' she paused and stumbled over the next word. 'Per?' she asked, looking up at Will like a schoolchild expecting the teacher to tell her the answer.

'The letter's called "thorn". They stopped using it in the fourteenth century. "Th", like the beginning of … well "thorn".' He gave her a gentle, encouraging smile. 'See? "Sithen the sege". It's not hard. Anyway, you can get past the next word. What about the last one?'

Lara sighed stoically. 'It's got to be "knight" by association. I don't think the poet called his masterpiece, "Gawain and the Green Aardvark!"'

'The letter's called yogh. Pronounced "ch", like in the Scottish word "loch".' He smiled, then concealed the manuscript back in his pocket. 'So much for linguistics. We ought to get that train.' He started to get up, but then he paused, glancing at her. 'You don't have to come. I've not kidnapped you. You can go anywhere you want.' He patted his pocket. 'But this is more than a book with fancy letters. I think there's a trail to follow. The more I read it, the more I think the poet left codes. I think this might lead to something that's been hidden for six hundred years. That's why Hitler had it; if he'd invaded England he'd have set his troops to find whatever's at the end of this trail and use it against America and become emperor of the world.'

'Isn't that melodramatic? Aren't history teachers supposed to look for the truth?'

'Truth is for philosophers. History's written by the winning side. I want to know why this poem has been tied in with the linguistics.' He shook his head. 'It's perfect, it's too perfect. It's like this text's been divinely inspired.'

'Now that *really* sounds melodramatic!'

Will regarded her coldly. 'Maybe. But everything that's happened today's been melodramatic.' His gaze was steady. 'They almost caught me. Now I've got away, I've got time to work out why there's another copy of a supposedly unique manuscript.' He looked at his watch. 'My train to Chester leaves in ten minutes.'

'Why Chester?'

'The poet came from Chester. He was writing about what he knew.' He chewed his lips. 'I don't have time to convince you about it all. Nor why those men might think I've cracked the code.'

'Have you?'

'Not yet, but I'm close.'

'Then why should I come?'

'Maybe because you've nowhere else to go? I'm running. I'm going to keep running until I've found out what's behind *Gawain.* This is something someone's been trying to cover up. Maybe they burned down the Cotton library just to stop this manuscript from being seen again?' He glanced at his watch again. 'I really do have to go now, Lara. Whatever *you're* running from, they won't find you if you keep moving. But maybe you *might* want to stay in Birmingham. There are worse places.'

Lara grimaced. 'Not many.' She shook her head. 'Too close to Stamford. I need to get further away.'

'Not too far away though,' Will advised. 'Whoever it is will look for you locally, then jump to quite a distance, hopefully missing you in the middle.'

Lara nodded. 'All right, I'll come. For a while, at least. But if you're headed to Chester, won't those men know that?'

'No,' Will said. 'They're grunts, soldiers paid to accept orders and not think for themselves. They can't read this. They've no idea about the history of the manuscript or why I'll go to Chester. But it doesn't matter. They'll find me eventually. They always do.'

3

Will had said nothing on the train as far as Crewe. Lara sat facing him. His dark-ringed eyes were closed. He was pale. And she drifted into memories of her childhood.

'Regrets?' Will said suddenly.

Lara started, surprised he was looking at her. 'Not yet,' Lara snapped, then flushed. 'Sorry, that was rude.'

'Not at all,' Will said passively. 'They're your thoughts.'

He closed his eyes again. Lara watched him. She thought it was strange that he had spoken, and then avoided looking at her. But then, a lot about him was strange. He didn't look like someone who'd been standing on a railway line only hours before. But then, what *did* someone with suicidal tendencies look like? 'I was thinking about my father,' she admitted eventually.

'Aren't you a little old to be running away from home?' Will said without opening his eyes.

'Not running away,' Lara said. 'Going back. 'I was born near Chester, in a village not far away. A village called Beaded. Hardly a village. It's so small it isn't on most maps. SatNavs have a problem finding it.' She shivered involuntarily. 'Its only claim to fame is its thirteenth-century church.'

'I thought you were looking edgy. Explains what you said about facing ghosts.'

'I don't have many happy memories of the place. My father still lives there.'

'Just your father?'

Lara nodded.

'No mother?'

Lara shook her head. 'She died when I was born. My father never spoke about her, never showed me photographs. They were both older than my friends' parents.' She realised she was blushing, as if her parents' age was a crime.

'What did your father do?'

'For a living? Teacher.'

Will smiled. 'Now you're talking shop.'

'He was a good one, I think. Traditional. But he retired and practically became a hermit when my mother died.' Her eyes glazed over; she almost felt she could look through the mists of time. 'I remember sitting on his lap and he read me stories. Not adventure stories that my friends read, but Shakespeare. He was fond of *Twelfth Night* and *The Comedy of Errors*. So fond of *them* that I wasn't allowed to read any others.' She smiled. 'I could recite them by the age of ten. But my father had a wonderful soporific voice. He used to play all the characters himself.' Her face suddenly clouded over as if remembering a bitter memory. 'Funny, those were the only plays he ever read to me. He almost went mad when I read *Hamlet*. He said it was too violent.'

Will said nothing. Lara laughed uncomfortably. 'Well, enough trivialities. Tell me more about *Gawain*.'

'What do you want to know?'

'What happens? It's a long time since I read it.'

Will nodded. He brought the manuscript out of the inner pocket, opened it and showed it to Lara. She stared at the words on the page, peering at them as if that would help make sense of the language. 'The version I read was very different. I could read that. This is all Greek to me.'

Will smiled. 'Actually, it's Middle English.'

'Doesn't matter. I still can't read it.'

Will leaned back. 'It's set when Camelot's in its infancy. It's Christmas. Arthur's put a downer on the evening. He won't eat until he's heard a tale of valour or seen a battle to make his blood run. Anyway, a Knight rides in. His clothes, skin and beard are all green. He's handsome and terrifying, carrying a massive axe. The Green Knight challenges Arthur; he says Arthur can hit him as hard as he likes with the axe and he'll match that stroke a year and a day later.'

'Sounds daft,' Lara said. 'Why'd he do that?'

'A show of power. After all, no one thinks he's going to deliver the return blow. Not if he's dead. So, it puts the fear of God into them. Then Gawain steps in and cleaves the Green Knight's head from his shoulders.'

'Primitive, but effective.'

'Absolutely, or so Gawain thinks. The Green Knight picks up the severed head, which speaks to Gawain and tells him to look for him in a Green Chapel to receive the return blow a year later.'

'Not Gawain's day then,' Lara said, smiling. 'I bet he wasn't expecting that.'

'I bet he wasn't,' Will said, returning her grin. 'So off rides the Green Knight. A year later, Gawain sets out to find the Green Chapel. He travels through Wales and Northern England until he sees a castle. The Lord makes him welcome, tells him to stay a while: after all, the Green Chapel is only a couple of hours ride away. Then the Lord offers Gawain a challenge: the Lord will go hunting in the forests and give his spoils to Gawain, while Gawain stays in the castle and Gawain will give whatever he receives to the Lord. Gawain agrees.'

'Sounds too good to be true. You'd have thought he'd've learned from the first challenge.'

'Rule of thumb in Medieval England: if something sounds too good to be true, it probably is, so never accept challenges. You might be called a coward, but you might keep your head on your shoulders.' Will smiled again. 'Anyway, the following morning the Lord hunts a pack of does. Gawain has a lie-in and is woken by his host's wife. She tries to seduce him. Gawain shies away from his reputation of shagging anything in a skirt and seems embarrassed by the situation.'

Lara raised an eyebrow. 'Sounds like every man's dream. To be seduced and not do any of the work.'

Will ignored her. 'Eventually he concedes the lady a kiss, and when the lord returns, Gawain gives the kiss to him.'

Lara choked back a laugh. 'He kissed the Lord? What kind of writer was this medieval creep?'

'It's called the Exchange of Winnings. Gawain kept his word and gave up everything he received during the day; but he didn't have to explain where the kiss came from. It's the same the next day. The Lord hunts a wild boar, and the Lady's advances become bolder. She persuades Gawain to give her two kisses, which are given to the Lord on his return.

'By the third day, the Lady realises Gawain isn't going to take advantage of her body, so she gives him a silk girdle. Gawain only accepts it because the Lady says it'll make him invulnerable to the Green Knight's blade. It's not a love token. Meanwhile, the Lord is out hunting a fox. Gawain doesn't surrender the girdle in the final exchange of winnings; it'd be dishonourable to tell the Lord his wife was giving out love tokens and contemplating adultery. Instead he gives the Lord the three kisses he won from his wife.'

'Sneak,' Lara said. She considered this, 'Priceless silk would've trumped the dead fox. Gawain conceded the game?'

Will nodded. 'The following morning, Gawain sets out to the Green Chapel. The Green Knight is waiting for him. Gawain accepts his Fate and bares his neck for the axe. Twice the Green Knight feigns the blow and the third time Gawain receives a slight nick in the neck. The Green Knight explains each attempt represented a day Gawain spent in the castle. For two faultless days Gawain resisted the Lady's temptation, but on the third day he concealed his prize, not a love token, but an attempt to save his own life.'

'That doesn't sound very fair,' Lara said. 'Sounds like Gawain was trapped between the Devil and the Deep Blue Sea.'

'That was the point. Gawain couldn't abuse his host's hospitality, and it would be discourteous to offend his host's wife. Handing over the silk girdle might have meant the Lord could have killed his wife for contemplating infidelity.'

'Sounds like *she* wouldn't get a good deal either.'

'The Lord knew what she was up to. *She* was part of the plan. Gawain might have lost the challenge, but he's older and wiser because of the test.'

'He probably knows better than to take up daft challenges,' Lara said.

'The Green Knight turns out to have been Gawain's host all along. He praises Gawain for his handling of a delicate situation, but Gawain only sees his shame. He wears the green girdle for the rest of his life as a symbol of dishonour, but, when he returns to Camelot, the whole court wears the green girdle to honour his adventure.'

'So they all lived happily ever after?' Lara sounded cynical.

'Well, I doubt Gawain liked being reminded he cheated his host. And then the court fell apart with war, treason, adultery and the battle between Arthur and Mordred.'

Lara smiled up at him. 'It's a nice story, but it doesn't explain why Hitler was interested in it, or why *you'd* die before giving it up.' She looked away, 'Unless you think standing in front of a train represents a feigned attempt with the axe.'

Will tapped the cover. 'There's power here,' he explained. 'There are too many coincidences: the number of times the number three is mentioned. Or two for that matter. Or four. Or five. There's another poem in the collection called *Pearl*, with one hundred and one stanzas, exactly the same as *Gawain*.'

'Maybe that's all the poet could count up to,' Lara said flippantly.

'Maybe. But maybe the numbers are significant. It's like signing a letter. We know nothing about the author. But the poem's got secrets in it. The clue's in the numbers. That's why I'm going to Chester. I'll start with what the poet would've seen.'

'It could be anything,' Lara protested. 'Also, it could have been destroyed since the poet died. There's been a lot of wars, and what happens if they've put a road through the poet's favourite hill?'

'I guess we'll just have to wait and see.'

'And another thing. Those men … if they know you've got the book, then they'll look wherever they think the trail's leading you.'

'The poem's been around for six hundred years, Lara. No one's found the answers in that time. Why should they start now?'

Lara nodded. 'And why should *you*?'

Will stood up. 'This is Chester. Time to go.'

*

'Do you know Chester at all?' Lara asked as they came out of the station and walked towards the city.

'Not very well. I had an aunt who lived near here, so my mother brought me every once in a while. We saw the same things: the Roman amphitheatre, the Rows, the Guildhall Museum, the Cathedral. Not much more.'

'What a shame,' Lara said earnestly. 'How long ago?'

'Fifteen, twenty years ago?' He marched purposefully past the city walls. In the distance, looming over the houses like a guardian, the cathedral glowed with the tinge of red sandstone.

'What are you looking for?' Lara asked.

'Somewhere to stay. We're not sleeping rough tonight.'

She felt a sudden chill. 'Will, I'm not sure I can afford that. My savings …'

'Don't worry,' Will said with a wry smile. 'This is *my* nightmare, so while I'm dragging you along, I'll cover for you.'

'There's loads of Bed and Breakfast houses and hotels here,' Lara said pointing.

'I know, but they're all too big. Anywhere with more than a couple of rooms and someone might know us.'

Lara considered this. 'You're worried about meeting someone we know in a place neither of us has been for years? That's really paranoid, Will.'

Will grimaced. 'Let's just say the world's a small place.' He turned into a residential street and walked quickly along the road. He stopped outside a modest black and white timber-framed house with a laminated sign stating 'Vacancies'. Aside from the sign, there was nothing to show it was a business of any sort, no enticing house name: Lara had expected it to be called 'Cathedral View' or some such thing. It didn't say how many rooms there were, or what facilities were available.

'This is what we want,' Will said. 'Not far from the Cathedral and quiet as well.' He looked at Lara. 'I want an early start tomorrow.'

'Will, it's just gone two thirty. There's still things we can do today.'

Will nodded. 'We need lunch first. I can't think on an empty stomach. Then we need some clothes and a bath.' He wrinkled his nose. 'I feel like I haven't had a bath in years.' He placed a gentle hand on her shoulder. 'And I don't need to be Einstein to see you're exhausted. You need sleep.' He glanced around him. Daylight had never really broken through the overcast winter sky. 'Darkness is oppressive. It conceals. Useful for us, but I also don't want to be walking when I can't see who's following me.'

'You really take this seriously, don't you?'

'Only because I have to.' Will marched forward and knocked on the door.

The door was opened by a middle-aged woman with snowy hair. She would have been pretty once, Lara thought, but age had etched itself into her face. She smiled welcomingly 'How can I help you?'

'I'm Will, this is Lara. We need a couple of rooms.'

The woman seemed to hesitate. *She knows,* Lara thought, *knows that we're running.*

'I have a double room,' the woman said. 'The other rooms are being decorated,' she added apologetically. Lara was about to protest, but Will was already shaking his head. 'Lara and I are friends,' he explained. 'Perhaps we should go somewhere else.'

The woman hesitated again, seemingly struggling with a dilemma. Then, seeing Lara, her face, already welcoming, softened further. 'My daughter's bedroom ...' she said gently, to Lara, not to Will; there was a faint stammer in her voice. 'You could stay there.' She seemed to need to provide an explanation. 'She ... I keep forgetting I can use that room as well.' She smiled again, but this time Lara felt uncomfortable.

The woman seemed to compose herself. 'I'm Elaine Victor,' she said, shaking hands with Will. 'Welcome to my house.' She led them upstairs. 'Bathroom's here,' she said, indicating a door identified with the sign 'Yer tiz'. Lara groaned inwardly at an older mentality where 'lavatory' was replaced by euphemisms.

She led Will to a room at the end of a corridor. It was sparsely decorated in pastel colours. There was a cupboard and sink against one wall and a double bed against another. A kettle and sachets of tea and coffee sat on a bedside cabinet beside the bed. Will thanked her and dropped his bag on the floor. 'We'll head out soon,' Will said to Lara. 'I need to freshen up first.' He smiled at Mrs Victor and indicated down the corridor. 'The loo's down there as well, is it?'

Mrs Victor nodded, embarrassed. 'Come on, I'll show you to your room,' she said to Lara, as Will advanced down the corridor. Lara nodded and followed.

It was a large room; a single bed rested against one wall. Orange and blue material covered the ceiling, concealing four spotlights which bathed the room in subdued light. A large oval wicker-framed mirror stood in one corner. Behind it was a hanging basket of flowers, while on the frame was a white mask and a Peruvian hat. Opposite the bed was a black and white picture from *The Third Man* and two pencil drawings of young girls: they were either sisters or the same girl aged six and ten.

She realised she was staring, analysing the decor, and Mrs

Victor seemed embarrassed by the attention. 'Did your daughter decorate this all herself?'

Mrs Victor nodded, but said nothing.

'She must be very talented,' Lara said.

'She was,' was Mrs Victor's solemn reply. She retreated from the room mumbling a vague apology, leaving Lara feeling she had made a tremendous *faux pas*.

Twenty minutes later, Will knocked on Lara's door. His hair was still wet from the bath. 'I want visiting rights to that towel,' he said, smiling. 'I didn't want to leave.'

'What good was a bath when you changed back into the same clothes?' Lara asked.

'I *feel* clean now, even if the clothes are dirty. It makes all the difference. Anyway, let's get some food and some shopping. Then we can plan for tomorrow.'

'We won't be too late back,' Will said. 'Probably not much after six, so we won't trouble you for a key.'

Mrs Victor smiled and nodded. Lara smiled uncertainly, but whatever error she had made seemed to have been forgiven.

As they went outside, Will glanced disdainfully at the darkening sky. 'What do you want first, food or clothes?'

Hunger pangs mixed with anxiety had been attacking Lara all day: 'Food.'

*

'The good thing about eating at this time of day is no one else wants to,' Will said, leading her into a modest restaurant with a mock Tudor façade, near the Rows. It was dimly lit, with mauve curtains at the window. The music was gentle, almost inaudible.

The waitress seated them at a table in an alcove. Will peered over his shoulder at the cathedral outside. 'Magnificent, isn't it?'

Lara said nothing. She was too tired to admire the architecture. Will smiled. 'Poor little button, you're shattered, aren't you?'

The waitress arrived with a couple of menus. 'Have whatever you want,' he said.

Lara glanced at the menu. 'Steak,' she said with a wry grin.

'Good idea!' Will said. He caught the attention of the waitress and ordered two steaks.

'I was kidding,' Lara protested.

'Be careful what you wish for, it might come true,' Will said and thought for a second. '*I am a great eater of beef and I believe that does harm to my wit.*'

'You really know your Shakespeare, don't you?'

Will waved his hand noncommittally. 'Sometimes I had to stand in for the English teachers.' Realising the waitress was waiting for a drink order, he asked for two cups of coffee. The waitress returned a few moments later.

'Do you drink anything except coffee?' Lara asked.

'Sometimes. Caffeine's as much a drug as alcohol, but I prefer to keep my senses sharp.' He looked away. 'I drank enough alcohol to last me a lifetime. Now I need my wits about me.' He seemed to sniff the air. 'They're close,' he said. 'They may not know we're in Chester, but they'll find a way to smoke us out.'

'So we'd better put a move on, what can we do tonight?'

Will turned, gazing at the cathedral. It had been illuminated, both inside and out. The lower part of the building was highlighted, the upper sections bathed in shadow. The lights inside emphasised the shapes of the mid-Gothic windows. 'The cathedral will be closed tonight. I think that's where we'll find … something. Of course, we don't actually know if the cathedral *is* the right place. The poet could have seen something in the Roman ruins. Impossible to say.'

'And once we get inside, what are we looking for?'

'There's a passage in the poem. I think it's part of the code. You should take a look.'

Will took the manuscript from his pocket and flicked through the pages. He opened it at a paragraph with an illuminated letter. 'These letters are scattered through the book to mark the four different sections,' Will explained. 'But, in some places, smaller letters are used. I think it draws attention to the stanza.'

The words wove in front of Lara like a magical charm:

And quy þe pentangel apendez to þat prince nobel
I am in tent yow to telle, þof tary hyt me schulde:
Hit is a syngne þat Salamon set sumquyle ...

Lara shook her head. 'I've told you. I can't read this.'

'I hadn't forgotten,' Will said. 'I wanted you to see the illuminated letters.' He pointed to the top of the paragraph. 'It says here,' he paused while translating it in his head. '"Then they brought out a shield that was of bright gules ..."'

'Bright what?'

'Red,' Will said. 'Don't interrupt. "With the pentangle depicted in pure gold hues".' He jumped a few lines. '"And why the pentangle belongs to that noble prince, I intend to tell you, though it will delay me. It is a sign which Solomon once set as a token of truth, for it is a figure which has five points, and each line overlaps and locks with the other, and everywhere is its endless and the English call it, all over the place, as I hear, the endless knot."' He tapped a word. 'The pentangle – he spells it "Pent-Angel" – is like putting an asterisk at the top of a page to remind yourself it's important.'

'And that's your theory?' Lara shook her head in disbelief. 'Gawain's shield has an arrow pointing in five directions. How do you expect to follow a map from that?'

Will smiled. 'The shield is the marker. This is the first time in English literature that the Seal of Solomon is mentioned. The poet goes to great lengths to explain the details of the shield. His audience wouldn't have heard of it before.'

'And ...?' Lara realised she was leaning forward in anticipation.

'At any time before this poem, someone might have thought

of Jewish mythology where the star has six points.'

'So maybe the poet didn't do his research properly?'

Will shook his head. 'He knew what he was doing. The positioning of the star was equally important. He says, *It is a sign that Solomon once set* It's the first time Solomon is mentioned. That's at line 625, which is 5x5x5x5.'

'How do you know that?'

'I counted. Then I started to think about how I'd disguise a code if I were writing the poem. I thought the best way would be to hide the code in the lines.'

'Are you going to tell me what you've already found?' Lara asked.

Will grinned. 'Sorry, am I in "teacher mode" again?'

The waitress reappeared and set two plates of steak in front of them. Will started to eat. Lara eyed him cautiously. 'You were saying?'

Will nodded as he swallowed. 'It's hard to explain, but if Solomon's Seal represents the number five, it could be telling the audience to look at the nearest number in base five.'

Lara thought about it. 'I suppose. So what's the nearest number?'

'I spent hours looking for this one,' Will admitted. 'The poem then talks about the five senses, the five fingers, the five wounds of Christ, the five joys of the virgin and the five virtues of Gawain. I thought it would be a total of twenty-five. Then I realised the nearest number would be the line number, 625. If you multiply that by base 5 then you get the number: one, zero, zero, zero, zero.'

'Ten thousand,' Lara said.

'Well, yes, but it wouldn't be ten thousand because it's in base five. It's the same if you add up the total of the five representations of the pentangle you also get twenty-five, or one, zero, zero, in base five. Either way you get the perfect "one".'

'The perfect "one" what?'

'Pythagoras said numbers represented something else. You add up the numbers so you'd get a number between one and nine. Your name for example, the first letter is "L" so that's worth twelve. Then you'd get one for "A", eighteen for the "R" and another one for the "A". A total of thirty two, and you add the three and two together to make …' he hesitated. 'Five,' he said eventually.

'You're making this up,' Lara said.

'A coincidence,' Will admitted. 'Anyway, the seal represents the perfect "one".'

'So what does five represent? Is there some kind of horoscope behind it.'

'Five symbolises freedom and independence. It's the number of perfection in the poem.' He smiled mischievously. 'Do you feel that describes your character?'

'I guess it's what I've been looking for, even if I haven't found it.' She shifted uncomfortably. 'What about number "one"?'

'Activation. You know, like the first prime number, or the one who was alone to create the universe.'

Lara's eyes narrowed. 'So if you changed your name would your personality change as well?'

'I hadn't thought of that,' Will said. 'Anyway,' he glanced back over his shoulder as if the cathedral would leave if he stopped keeping vigil on it. 'We have to find Solomon's Seal, and find the perfect "one" near it. Hopefully it'll point us in the right direction.'

'This is a lot of speculation,' Lara said. 'You don't know anything about the poet. Why d'you expect to find something in Chester? Why not London?'

'Because the poet wrote in a Chester dialect. He didn't come from London. Chaucer was writing at the same time. Practically a different language.' He took a long sigh. 'It would be helpful if they included an "About the Author" section.'

Lara picked at the remains of her steak. 'If you think the

numbers are important, why not try all the lines which add up to five? 5, 14, 32, 41, 50?'

'I tried it,' Will admitted. 'I thought I was getting somewhere when the poet said "teach me truly with this" in line 401. But when he said, *Who brings us this beverage, this bargain is made,* I realised it might not be so clever.'

'Maybe we ought to ask the waitress?'

'I doubt her training covers medieval codes.' He looked at the two empty plates. 'You wolfed that lot down. Do you feel better?'

Lara nodded. With food inside her she was thinking clearly. 'But this Seal of Solomon,' she said. 'Isn't the five pointed star an occult symbol?'

'Partly true,' Will said. 'Nineteenth-century occultists inverted it, just like the crucifix was inverted to turn the divinity of Christ on its head. Sometimes it's connected with demonology, like in Göethe's *Faust*, but it's older than Christian and Jewish symbolism.' He slipped the manuscript back into his pocket, then politely called the waitress and asked for the bill. He paid cash as he pulled his coat on.

It was cold when they went back outside. A premature darkness had fallen. The streetlights reflected against the wet roads. A blanket of clouds smothered the sky.

'Shopping time,' he told her, leading her into The Rows, the black and white Tudor-style arcaded shops with projecting second storeys. The familiar High Street names seemed out of place in streets that should have been filled with antique and curio shops. He pointed her away from the historic arcades, past the Eastgate and in the direction of Marks and Spencer. 'Just the essentials,' he warned her. 'A couple of changes of clothes and some toiletries. We need to travel light.'

'Will you come with me?' she asked.

He shook his head. 'Women don't like men in the underwear department,' he muttered. 'They get worried if we know what they're wearing.'

Lara found a packet of knickers and a couple of lacy bras. She also bought another pair of jeans and a fleece. She found Will by the toiletries picking up shampoo and toothpaste. He also had a small bag to carry them in. He paid cash again. They had only been in the shop for ten minutes.

Will walked quickly through the streets. Lara found herself struggling to keep up. His shoulders were hunched; the collar of his coat pulled up. *He's been running for a long time,* she realised. *He's learned to look inconspicuous.*

'Will?' she said gently.

He started, as if suddenly believing she was one of the men following him. 'What?' he snapped.

'Do you *really* think there's a hidden code? Or are you chasing rainbows?'

Will smiled at her. '"Thy substance, valued at the highest rate cannot amount unto a hundred marks."'

'"Therefore by law thou art condemned to die,"' Lara said forlornly.

'You're not the only one who was forced to learn *The Comedy of Errors* as a child.' Will grinned. Then his face turned serious, shadowed in the eerie orange of the streetlights. '*Do not be afraid of greatness.*'

'*Some are born great, some achieve greatness and some have greatness thrust upon them,*' Lara completed the quotation. '*Twelfth Night*. So what?'

'Just because you think I might be imagining a code, it doesn't mean it isn't there. And even if you don't believe me, it doesn't mean you're not destined for great things.' He smiled again. 'Your father really forced those plays on you, didn't he? What was he was telling you?'

'Why should he be telling me anything?'

'Come on, Lara, you don't learn two plays and have the rest of Shakespeare's canon excluded. Either your father believed Shakespeare was one of the Greats, or he was a waste of time.

Did you learn anything else?'

Lara shook her head. 'Just to do my best and not to disgrace the family.'

'No pressure then,' Will said noncommittally, turning into Princess Street. He knocked on the door and Mrs Victor greeted them quietly. They mounted the stairs in silence. He walked with her to his room, but didn't speak to her. Instead, he walked to the window and stood looking out at the streets.

'They're close,' he whispered. 'It's like the air's electric.'

'Then they can wait until tomorrow. What's to be done now?'

He didn't turn. 'I know it's only evening, Lara, but I think 'bed' is the best medicine you could take now.'

'I think you're right.'

'Good night, Lara. Sweet dreams.'

'You too,' Lara whispered, closing the door behind her, wondering how long he would stand by the window.

She went to her room and undressed. Lying down on the duvet, she felt her muscles unwinding. Her shoulders ached. She thought about the things she needed to do tomorrow. But tomorrow seemed a long time away. This was her first night of freedom, she thought, as her breath deepened. Her first night of peace.

4

Sleep clung to Lara the following morning, even after she had washed, dressed and come downstairs for breakfast. Will was already sitting at the table, looking surprisingly cheerful and sickeningly alert sipping a cup of coffee, when she had only the ability to point at objects and demand breakfast with single syllable words.

She had learned to get up early. When Michael had been drinking and when he woke with the mother of all hangovers, she had been the one who had to be up early so she could be ready before he needed to go to work.

She wondered if Will needed any rest. When she'd seen him standing sentinel at the bedroom window, contemplating the paths of the future, he'd seemed far from sleep.

'Good morning,' he said as she sat down. His hair was no longer swept back. He'd washed and shaved and now appeared less like an actor and more like a schoolteacher. Lara offered a vague smile as he poured her coffee and buttered some toast. He pushed the plate in front of her. She chewed thoughtfully, slowly pushing the fog from her mind. Will appeared to have forgotten his worries and seemed able to breeze through life without a care in the world.

'Did you sleep well?' he asked.

She managed to nod. She devoured the toast and coffee, not wanting to be drawn into a conversation.

'More coffee?' Lara turned at the sound of a voice behind her. Mrs Victor offered her a wide smile that Lara suspected was false. 'Ah, you're up,' she said and her smile widened. 'Will was wondering if you were going to sleep forever.'

Lara tried to smile. Will grinned, then spoke to Mrs Victor: 'I saw newspapers on the mat as I came down. Could I have a look?'

Mrs Victor hesitated, then nodded uncertainly. She took away a dirty plate and returned a short while later. Will unfolded the tabloid and Mrs Victor retreated quickly.

Will paled. Lara's instincts prickled. 'What is it?' she wondered, her voice still croaky.

'This isn't good,' Will said. He turned the paper towards her.

Two photographs were on the front page. She recognised one of them instantly. It was taken just after her wedding. She was reclining in a wicker chair on the veranda of a hotel near Keswick, where she and Michael had gone for their honeymoon. Her hair had been longer then; she'd had it cut a few months ago as Michael's violence had become more frequent. It was one less thing for him to grab her by. She hated that photograph. It showed he'd once made her happy.

The photograph of Will was a mug-shot with his criminal record number beneath his face. Lara felt her blood running cold. Will inhaled as if about to speak, but she silenced him with a freezing look and returned to reading the article.

"Police are looking for a couple who were last seen in Stamford in the early hours of yesterday morning.

"William Stevens and Lara Greaves were last seen in Stamford as they caught a train towards Birmingham. Stevens is being sought by police following the death of 22 year-old Janet Rose."

She didn't read any more. Whoever was following them would already have contacted Michael. He would have told a series of half-truths about her. In turn, the newspapers would have warped these. Even so, she could not hold back the inevitable question. 'Is it true?'

'What?'

'That the police are looking for you? Was Janet's death under mysterious circumstances?'

Will glared at her acidly. 'That's not what it says. It says police are looking for me, following Janet's death. It's worded so you believe she died under mysterious circumstances to paint me in a bad light.' There was coldness in his eyes. 'Janet died because of bad luck and bad driving. It was her bad luck and someone else's bad driving. It was a tragedy, but there's nothing I can do about it.'

'How can you be so cold about it?'

Will's eyes became stony. 'Don't you think I wish there was a way I could turn back time? Bring her back? Believe me, if there was a way to play out time again, I'd take it. There's nothing I wouldn't do to try and save her.' Now he seemed to be seeking her approval. 'But it's too late for that now,' he whispered in a hollow voice. 'It was always too late. It's natural selection: when your time's come, there's nothing you can do about it. You're going to die whether you're in a bus crash and you're the only one to go, or whether one of your bedsprings bursts through the mattress and kills you because you think it's safer to stay in bed all day. You can't avoid it.' He took a long, drawn out breath. 'You can run from it, like I have, but eventually, it catches up with you.' He smiled, but there was no joy in his face. 'You're not going to believe this, but when I met you, I *wanted* you to come with me because I felt there was a kind of magic about you. *I* had decided it was time to go. I'd, quite literally, laid my life on the lines. *You* prevented it, like an intervening angel, like the Ghost of Christmas Future: when I saw you, my purpose became clearer.' He held up the newspaper and grinned. 'It's hardly a flattering photograph.'

Lara's hands were clenching the table. 'Why are you being so flippant? You didn't tell me you had a police record!'

'You didn't tell me the last time you had sex,' Will countered. Lara was about to retort, but Will cut her off. 'We know *nothing* about each other. What I know about you I've gleaned from vague comments you've made. You've not told me a single fact about yourself. I know you're frightened and you're running from your husband.' Lara gasped, but Will shook his head. 'There's no magic. Your wedding finger: the skin's white and worn, so you've recently taken off the ring. You rub that area because you're not used to the bare flesh there.' He calmed down, taking a long, deep breath. 'This is what they want: they want us to fight amongst ourselves. So, I'll tell you: I was arrested in London a few years ago. It was the stag night of a friend of mine and we'd all got a bit drunk. None of us were actually doing anything wrong, but we were rowdy and charged with breach of the peace. We were all photographed, fingerprinted and thrown into cells to sober up.' He grinned. 'There were five of us and only one policeman. He was shorter than me. But he had this great Doberman pincher with him and that made all the difference.' He looked back at her and there was gentleness in his eyes again. 'Does that answer your question?'

Lara nodded. 'I guess.' But she was not totally assuaged. His answer had been too ready, too prepared. Despite fleeing with him, despite wanting to know if there *was* a code, she realised how little she trusted him. 'This changes nothing,' she grumbled. 'I'm not telling you the last time I had sex.'

Because I can't remember that long ago, she thought.

Will laughed, but his face darkened suddenly. He leaned forward. 'We have to get away now,' he said. He indicated to the kitchen. '*She's* no doubt seen this.'

'Do you think she knows it's us?'

'Sure to,' Will said, but then his voice lowered. 'I bet she's listening at the door right now.' His tone became more conversational. 'We don't have a choice. We've got to get away while we still can.'

Lara shook her head, tapping the newspaper. 'This is serious if we can make the front pages. There isn't going to be anywhere safe.' Now she was leaning forward. 'We follow up what we discussed yesterday and see where it takes us. Your friends in Bath aren't going to give up and we won't ever be able to get back here.'

'We could split up. You can go wherever it was you were

going.'

Her shoulders slumped. 'I don't *have* anywhere else. This is all I've got now. And they're looking for me. They won't stop, whether I'm with you or not.'

'This has become personal,' Will observed.

'Damn right,' Lara said, shaking her head in frustration. Her voice was becoming louder, indignant. 'I don't like their methods. I don't like the fact they can drive someone to suicide. What's at the end of this? Why would someone kill for it?' She realised her voice was raised. And spoke in a whisper. 'This is something Hitler spent a lot of time on. The other thing he spent a lot of time on was the conquest of Europe. Do you see what I'm saying, Will? We have to find this. It's our duty to keep it out of their hands … whoever they are.'

Will smiled as he took a long draught of coffee.

'What's so funny?' Lara asked, frustrated.

'I didn't think I'd find someone as passionate about this as I am.' He peered over his shoulder again. 'All right. We'll play this your way.' He looked down at the paper. 'We *have* only known each other a short while. There's going to be a lot of things we don't know about each other. I'm sorry I didn't tell you I was once arrested: it didn't seem relevant.' He stared past her and his eyes became dreamy. 'When I woke up this morning, I thought, *this is the sunrise I wasn't supposed to see.* Yesterday, I didn't know if I should give up, or catch the other train. You made that choice for me. I trusted you then; I placed my fate in the hands of someone I'd never met. Now I'm asking you to trust me the way I trusted you.'

Lara shifted uneasily. 'Any more dark secrets?'

Will smiled. 'Hundreds, but none are relevant now.' He reached out to her across the table and touched her hand. She did not flinch as she had expected, but she was uncomfortable with the contact. His skin was warm. 'Trust me,' he said again.

When she nodded, Will called in Mrs Victor. 'My guess is she doesn't know whether or not to turn us over, so I'm going to put the ball in her court.'

Mrs Victor entered with another pot of coffee. Her eyes flicked to the newspaper, which Will had laid open so she could see the photographs. She was flustered and embarrassed, perhaps imagining they were crazed murderers.

'More coffee?' she said in a shaky voice. Will shook his head.

'Perhaps you wouldn't mind sitting down,' he said in a calm voice. Mrs Victor looked uncertainly at the empty chair. Will smiled gently. Lara thought he had the air of a doctor about to tell a patient bad news. The return smile was delayed and nervous.

'Mrs Victor,' Will said in a low voice, but there was no menace behind the words. He tapped the newspaper. 'You've read this article.' Mrs Victor made no comment. Will continued. 'I'm not going to explain it. I could deny everything, but that would be lying, because there's a little shred of truth in it. I don't want to lie to you.'

'You know your own business,' Mrs Victor said in a quiet voice.

'Yes, we do,' Will replied. 'You'll be apprehensive if we stay any longer, so we'll be moving on.' He smiled. 'I don't want anyone who has shown us hospitality to feel anxious.'

Mrs Victor nodded.

'The article suggests anyone who sees us should contact the police immediately. Have you done that?'

Mrs Victor opened her mouth to speak. She stammered, then shook her head.

'Thanks,' Will smiled gently. 'I hoped you hadn't.' Lara realised Will's voice had become soporific. 'But I understand you might feel obliged to do so. So, I'm going to go upstairs and pack, while you sit there with Lara. Then she and I will leave so we won't be here if there's an embarrassing scene.' He reached into his pocket and pulled out a wad of notes. 'This is for last night's bill,' Will explained. 'I won't insult you by offering you something for your silence, Mrs Victor. I don't think you'd believe us, whatever we told you. I think even Lara and I find it hard to believe sometimes. Once we're gone it's up to you what you do. There won't be any retribution from us, whatever you do.' He placed the money on the table. Mrs Victor made no move towards it as though the notes had been poisoned by their guilt. He stood up. 'Talk amongst yourselves. I'll be back before you know it.'

He left. Lara shifted, unable to make eye contact with Mrs Victor. What he had said had made sense. Pleading with her not to call the police, would only emphasise their guilt. 'We won't hurt you,' she promised.

Mrs Victor stared coldly at her. Eventually, after a long silence, she spoke. 'You'd do better to turn yourself in, love. If what he says is true and you've not done anything wrong you'd do better explaining yourself, rather than waiting to be caught.'

Lara said nothing, although the woman probably had a point. Whatever trouble Will was in, it wasn't any of her business. Except guilt by association.

But he had piqued her curiosity. She knew she couldn't leave Chester until she had proven Will's theory, one way or another.

Will returned a couple of minutes later with his bag over his shoulder. 'Okay, Lara. Time to go.' He smiled gently at Mrs Victor. 'Sorry for the inconvenience. I'd hoped this wouldn't happen. I guess we don't always get what we want.'

'Just leave,' Mrs Victor said, seeming to find hidden courage.

Will nodded. 'Time to go. I doubt we'll ever come back to Chester, so don't worry.'

He led Lara outside. She stared up disdainfully at the leaden sky. The air was charged with electricity. 'Where are we going?'

'I've not come this far to let some geriatric scarecrow tell me how long I can stay here. We came for a reason. But we need to make it look like we're running away from Chester.' He broke into a run. Lara kept up with him. She'd been on the cross-country team at school. Will, however, seemed to have hidden reserves of stamina.

He stopped suddenly. Lara almost bumped into him. She tried to control her breathing. 'Do you think she'll call the police?' she asked eventually.

Will nodded. 'I think so. Even if she hasn't, we can't chance hanging around for long.'

'Damn,' Lara said. 'She seemed like such a nice lady.'

'Fear corrupts,' Will told her. 'In her eyes we were criminals, she probably feels she has to do something.' He smiled. '*Present fears are less than horrible imaginings*.'

'Is that an observation?'

'No, Shakespeare. *Macbeth*: act one, scene three.'

Lara shook her head. 'Sorry, that wasn't on my Father's reading list.' She looked up at the red stone walls of the cathedral. 'I don't suppose we have time to look around?'

'That depends how long Mrs Victor gives us to get away.'

'It'd be inappropriate for us to go back and ask her, wouldn't it?'

'I doubt she'd thank you.' He stroked his chin. 'I think she'd have given us a few minutes head-start before she called the police. For your sake, not mine.' His eyes were serious. 'Those aren't the police, though. They've been told to hand it over to someone else. This is *ultra vires*: above the Law.' He glanced around them, making a quick calculation. 'As the crow flies, we're about a hundred and fifty miles away from Bath and a hundred from Stamford. Those are two places where I know they are. They could be here in two hours by car.' He shook his head. 'But they won't send the cars. It'll be the helicopters.'

'So what do we do? Hire a car?'

'Too obvious. They'll expect us to run like frightened rabbits, so we've *got* to stay put, stay out of sight, for a while. I'm hoping ... if they don't catch us at a roadblock in the next few hours, they'll think we've got through and extend their search area.' He thought again. 'If they secure the area within the next two hours then they'll have the blocks about eight miles away from the centre of the city.'

'Why eight?'

'The average walking speed is four miles an hour. They'll watch the fields and have the choppers scouring the countryside for us. You can bet any money they're already sitting on the station like hungry vultures.'

'What does it mean?' Lara asked. 'Do we have time to look around?'

Will nodded reluctantly. 'Yes. We can't avoid the roadblocks. We'd be daft to try. If we stay put long enough they might think they've missed us. The blocks will probably be in place for three hours while they look for us, then they'll close in on Chester or extend the search, or both, so let's get inside and see if we can figure out how to get out of this one.'

'Can I make an observation?' Lara asked.

'If you're going to tell me it's going to rain, I already know.'

'It's *you*, Will. You know a lot about the way these people think. What did you say you used to do?'

'I was a history teacher, you know that. I've just been trying to avoid them for a long time. I'm starting to anticipate their manoeuvres.'

'If they've been following *you* for some time, don't you think they'll have sussed out your manoeuvres too?'

'Possibly,' Will said sullenly. He said nothing more and Lara found herself staring up at the red stones and the angular window tracery of the cathedral. She suddenly felt uneasy. She wondered if it was knowing that someone was following them or whether she was overwhelmed by the size of the cathedral and she was stepping back through centuries of history.

The visitor's entrance was in the modern part of the building. Frustration and unease pressed down on Lara as she walked in. The structure made her feel tiny and oppressed. She was pleased when she moved into the cloisters; then she walked into the cathedral itself and stood in the North aisle.

'You look uncomfortable,' Will observed. 'Are you all right?'

'I don't like churches.' Her gaze became vacant. 'I think … I think I saw something once. It's like a bad dream, just creeping in the corners of my mind. I haven't been in a church since.' She shuddered at the concealed memory and glanced around. The cathedral was wide and light, not like the place in her dreams.

'Do you have a faith?' Will asked as he stared up at the high pointed arches.

'None whatsoever.'

'It's important to believe in something,' he said earnestly.

'What do you believe in?'

Will reflected for a moment, as if this was something he had never considered. 'Hope,' he said eventually.

Lara's eyes traced the path of the aisle. 'What are we looking for?'

He shrugged. 'Maybe a seal of Solomon, a five pointed star, or something like that.' He looked embarrassed. 'Actually, I won't know until we find it.'

Lara looked at the wooden carvings at the end of the nave. The woodwork was made up of hundreds of tiny ornate decorations. 'This is like looking for a needle in a haystack,' she said bitterly. 'What happens when we get there? We push the star and a secret passage opens up no one has ever found before? Come on, Will. This isn't a film.'

'*If this were played upon a stage now, I could condemn it as an improbable fiction,*' Will said.

'Don't start hiding behind *Twelfth Night,*' Lara snapped. 'We can't go through every statue and carving in this place. It would take the rest of our lives to do that.'

'Longer, probably,' Will said. 'That's why the poet knew he was safe to hide his secret here.'

'All right,' Lara said. 'Let's think about eliminating some of the work.' She left Will standing in the nave and returned to the cloisters. There was a shop at the end of the cloister garden, and Lara bought a guidebook and map from a girl she thought should be in school. 'All right,' she said when she returned to Will. She spread open the map, 'Fourteenth century is Mid-Gothic?' She ran her finger along the drawing of the walls. 'That's the south aisle, the south transept ...'

'Where's that?'

'That'll be the right hand side of the cross made up by the church. The whole of the choir is pretty much mid-Gothic style and so is the Lady Chapel.'

'Brilliant,' Will said, sarcastically. 'That eliminates a quarter of the cathedral.'

Lara ignored him and started to walk forward towards the choir, avoiding the many rows of chairs. 'I wonder why they stopped building. The north aisle wasn't finished for another hundred and thirty years.'

'The Black Death?' Will told her. 'Famine? No money? Maybe the people were more concerned with staying alive than completing the house of God. Sticking up a building wasn't going to keep the Reaper at bay.'

Lara nodded, looking down at the mosaic. Her heart gave a little leap as she reached the tower crossing. The mosaic on the floor depicted an eight-pointed star. 'I don't suppose the poet lost his ability to count between seeing the star and writing about it?' The echo underneath the tower shocked her. Her words seemed to flee from her then return with added vigour.

'No, he was specific. Five points.' He was reading the guidebook over her shoulder. 'This is nineteenth-century work, anyway. The building is thirteenth-century, but the carvings and tiling have been done in medieval designs.' He sucked on his lip. 'I wonder ...'

'What?'

'We're barking up the wrong tree. The poet would have

guessed carvings wouldn't last forever. He wanted something that would survive for centuries, not something that was probably already riddled with woodworm.' He tapped his foot in frustration. 'The answer's here, I know it. I'm just trying to jump that last hurdle of the poet's logic. The answer's so simple. It's staring us in the face.'

'What is it?'

'I don't know. It's a figure of speech, like not seeing the wood for the trees. Keep looking around, Lara. Five-pointed star, that's what we want.'

She gazed up at the ceiling, and her heart gave another little flutter. The oak bosses had six-pointed stars. 'Still too many,' Lara whispered. With a sigh she started to analyse the medieval carvings. There were misericords telling the life of St Werburgh – the patron saint of Chester. Lara shivered. The parish church in the village where she grew up was dedicated to this saint. There were other misericords in the choir stalls depicting animals. She guessed the carvings were symbolic representations of Christ, although the elephant seemed to be a thick-necked giraffe with a worm coiling from its nose.

Will was standing in the centre of the eight-pointed star, head back, staring at the ceiling. She wondered what was going through his head. His expression was pained, as if he was trying to catch an idea just out of reach.

'The windows!' he said suddenly. 'If we're talking about enlightenment, the poet could have used a double metaphor.'

'Too easily broken,' Lara said. 'How much fourteenth-century glass survives?'

Will took a couple of steps back, then sat in the front row of the chairs. 'Problem is we're assuming the poet knows the same things we know. We've got 20-20 hindsight, as Robert Pirsig would say. *We* know Henry VIII dissolved the abbeys, but this building survived to become a cathedral rather than getting smashed up like some of the others. How could the poet have predicted damage done in the English Civil War? How could he have known it wouldn't have been destroyed in the bombing of the Second World War?'

'I don't think he would have guessed any of these things,' Lara admitted. 'When you consider the destruction this country has faced then it's a miracle the cathedral is still standing.' Her eyes darted around. 'And another thing, we keep calling him "the poet" and "the *Gawain*-poet". Doesn't he have another name?'

'Another mystery lost in the mists of time. We don't really have a name for the manuscript, it was added by later editors.'

'No clues at all?'

Will smiled. 'Just one. At the top of the first folio of the manuscript there are the words "Hugo de". The scribe, or one of the later owners, could have written it. We don't know.' His face creased as if trying to chase an illusive thought. 'What was it you said earlier?'

'Lots of things, what in particular? I started the morning by demanding coffee.'

'You talked about finding the Seal of Solomon and pushing it, opening up a passage no one had found before.'

'Was I? I'm sure it was hypothetical.'

'If you're right, then the poet would have seen the construction of that part of the cathedral.'

'Will, you said that was an improbable fiction.'

'Think, Lara. They stopped building the cathedral around 1350. Most people date *Gawain* as being written between 1350 and 1400 – it contains similar passages to another text, *Winner and Waster*, which dates from about 1352. The poet wouldn't have seen the building of the last part of the cathedral unless he lived to be very old.'

'I thought we'd already established that, that's why I eliminated a quarter of the cathedral from the necessity of inspection.'

'But let's suppose he was influential and could have

convinced the Benedictine abbot that something needed to be built according to his specification.'

'You're saying the whole building could be part of the plan?'

'Why not? He could have been influential. If he had something important to hide and if the abbot was in on it, it's not impossible.'

'That's a lot of "ifs",' Lara said.

The quiet of the cathedral was suddenly broken by chatter: a party of school children had entered. Most gave the impression of not wanting to look at ancient gothic architecture and wandered around, bored. But when they glanced over to see where the noise was coming from, she stared past them.

Four men had followed them. Men in trench coats.

Will saw them too. 'Yuck, we're in trouble,' he said. He walked away from them. 'Don't turn,' he hissed. 'We need to get lost among the tourists. Quickly, Lara. Your map. Where are the other exits?'

Lara fought the urge to look at the men again. With shaking hands she unfolded the map. 'South transept,' she said. 'There's a door in there.'

'Let's hope it isn't locked,' Will said. 'All right, slowly, quietly, let's head that way.' His face was a mask of grim determination. 'You go first. I'll follow in a couple of minutes. They're looking for two people together. Perhaps they won't guess that it's us if we leave separately.'

Lara did as she was told. Will returned to the carvings, trying to look nonchalant. Lara stole a peek behind her. Will was straining to hear the echoing footsteps. She walked like a tourist, looking with apparent disinterest at the huge complex windows which were splashes of colours of red, yellow and blue, then peered at the chapels in the south transept.

Her heart beat in her throat. The south door wasn't far. She fought the urge to run, or to look back to make sure Will was following her. She wondered if anyone could smell her fear. She jumped, hearing a sudden shout, but fought the urge to turn when she realised it was one of the children playing. Then the cathedral was plunged into an unnatural silence, as though everyone had turned as one to recognise Will. When she looked back she could not see him. At first she feared he had been found. But Will had been running for a long time: he would blend in with the other visitors.

Ten steps between her and the door. Ten steps between her and freedom.

She stopped. There would be many people following Will, not just the four in the cathedral. Others might be waiting outside. And she daren't try to open the door in case it was locked, or, worse, alarm bells would ring alerting the entire cathedral to their failed escape.

The cathedral was doused in an uncanny stillness, like time had stopped, and she alone was working outside from it.

Where are you? she hissed under her breath. Perhaps he'd stopped in one of the side chapels in the manner of a casual visitor.

The second chapel beguiled her. The reredos behind the altar was shining gold. Despite every instinct screaming at her to get out, and her heart pounding in her throat, she flicked through the guidebook. Something to do with King Oswald of Northumbria, in a stance of battle against Cadwallon ap Cadfan, the King of the Britons. The stones of the floor glittered yellow and gold, a contrast to the red sandstone of the walls. She read further: the chapel, dedicated to St Oswald, was rebuilt in the middle of the fourteenth century.

Come on, she chided herself. *You don't have time to be a tourist. Get away.*

Where was Will?

She turned away, disappointed. How could they solve the mystery of six hundred years in half an hour? They should have come here before whoever was following Will could have splashed their faces across the front of the newspapers. How could they have thought to find a Seal of Solomon amid this sea of carvings? She doubted the poet would have made it easier by colouring it, exactly as it had been written in the text, a golden star on a gules coloured shield. Or yellow on red.

He heart caught in her throat.

What if the star had been just the symbol and the description of the star, the shield and the line number mixed together to make the perfect 'one'. She gazed around her again, at the red sandstone and the sand-coloured floor.

'Lara.' Will's voice caused her to jump. The hushed whisper was stern and commanding. 'I told you to leave.'

'It's here, Will,' she said. 'We weren't looking for a star at all. It's the colours that are important.'

Will was surprised. 'What colours?'

'The colours on the shield. The stones of the cathedral represent the red. I doubt there's another building in the area that looks like this one.'

'Lara, that's brilliant,' Will said urgently. 'But this isn't going to matter in two minutes when those men find us.'

'Then I've got one minute and thirty seconds to find the seal,' Lara said, her eyes imploring. 'Just something to show us this is the right place.' She crouched on the floor, running her fingers along the stone. 'It's here,' she said, almost giddy with anticipation. 'I know it.'

'Lara,' Will said desperately. He touched her shoulder. 'All right, if you're convinced, I'll make a diversion. I'll try to get out of the cathedral and lead them away from you, and then get them lost in the streets.'

'Wait a second,' she told him.

'We don't have any more seconds.'

She crouched behind the altar, running her fingers across the stone. 'Look at this,' she said. 'There's writing here, almost impossible to make out.'

Will glanced anxiously over his shoulder, then crouched with her. 'It's like they tried to cross it out,' he said blowing some dust away. A figure was cut in the flagstone:

'What is it?' Lara said. 'It's like the Roman numeral for ten, but I've not seen it written like that before.'

'The bar across the top symbolises a thousand,' Will said. 'That symbol means ten thousand. It was easier than writing ten Ms.'

'Will,' Lara's heart fluttered. 'You said that's the figure for 625 converted into base five.'

Will nodded. He peered over the altar to make sure their followers weren't moving towards the south transept yet. 'There's more writing,' he told her. 'Let's see if I can make it out.' He ran his fingers over the letters, as if trying to understand a fourteenth century Braille. 'The first letter is Thorn,' he said with a smile. '*I think we do know the sweet Roman's hand.*'

'Enough of *Twelfth Night!* What does it say?'

'Let's see. *Þe sprynges calle. Þe trauayle biginez.*' He gave a bewildered gasp. 'That's it? No more?'

'What does it mean?'

Will stood up and started to stride towards the south door, oblivious to potential danger. He wrenched it open and walked outside into the cold air. Lara ran to keep up with him. 'Will, what is it? What did it mean?'

'That fourteenth-century clown was having a big joke on us all along,' Will snapped. 'There's no buried treasure in the cathedral, no hidden wisdom. X marks the spot: that was his idea.'

'But what did the writing say?'

'It said "The springs call. The travel, or the work, begins."'

'That's all?' Lara couldn't hide her disappointment. 'There must have been something else, something we missed that told us where to go. Perhaps we need to lift up the stone to see what was underneath.'

'And what d'you think the Dean would think of that? You were right. There's nothing that the renovations of the cathedral wouldn't have discovered. This has been a prank by a medieval trickster, nothing more.'

Lara gave a despondent sigh. She had wanted to believe in Will's idea; she wanted to crack the code with him and do something that no one before had achieved. 'What do we do now?' she asked sadly.

'We go back to the restaurant where we had lunch yesterday.'

'You're kidding, aren't you? We should be getting away now.'

'That's what they expect us to do. I need coffee and I need time to think how we're going to get out of here.'

5

They didn't walk straight to the restaurant. Will walked down several streets, stopping occasionally to use shop windows as mirrors to see if they were being followed.

The restaurant was empty. They sat at a table and Will ordered two coffees. Lara breathed deeply to calm her frantic heart. It didn't work. Her instinct was to run. Will wanted to dawdle. But he didn't want to talk; his eyes were angry slits. She leaned across to him as the waitress left. She spoke in hushed tones. 'Could you return the manuscript, apologise for the inconvenience and tell them it's a big practical joke?'

Will shook his head. 'They wouldn't swallow it. Would you?'

'I suppose not.'

The waitress returned with their drinks. Will picked up the cup and smelled it.

'How're you feeling?' Lara ventured.

For a while he said nothing, staring into space. 'Annoyed,' he said eventually, picking up a sachet of sugar and ripping it open, spilling grains across the tablecloth.

'Just annoyed?'

'All right. Very annoyed. I'd hoped there'd be something there, something to make this worthwhile.'

'There might be if we understood the importance of the spring and the travels.'

'Either that, or he was a fourteenth-century vandal.'

'You're not being very helpful.'

'I'm not *feeling* very helpful. I'm annoyed.'

'And you won't get any further with that attitude.' Lara realised she was raising her voice and looked around to see if she had attracted attention. 'This poet, whoever he was, tried hard to conceal something. If he wanted to hide things, he wouldn't have just given one location; someone could have stumbled across that stone without knowing about it. He'd have expected someone to keep looking, having understood the way his mind worked. He's given us a riddle, something to do with a journey, and a spring. So, let's think about it: does he mean the season or a water source?'

'Either. Or a coil of metal or someone leaping into the air. Is there a place for potential suicides to leap from around here?'

'Will, stop it.'

'Well, you're so clever!' Will said bitterly. 'How could we be so arrogant as to think we could solve a riddle that's been puzzling everyone for six hundred years?'

'Perhaps no one's got this far before,' Lara said. 'We've broken the first code, found out about the seal. Perhaps he's laid a treasure map of sorts, and we have to discover where he's pointing us.' She sipped at her coffee. 'Gawain went on a journey, didn't he? To get from Arthur's court to the Green Knight's chapel?'

'He did.' Will reached into his pocket with a sigh and pulled out the manuscript. 'This what you want? The bit about the journey starts on line 691.'

Lara opened the manuscript and stared at the words. It was hard to read, but she was starting to become comfortable with the alphabet and could get the gist of what the poet was saying. 'This says he travelled into North Wales,' she started, squinting at the faded words. She stumbled over the translation.

'That's good,' Will said. 'You're learning.'

'Don't patronise me,' Lara retorted. 'I'm doing my best.'

Will said nothing. Lara continued. 'Anglesey was on his left, so he was travelling north. Then he crosses the fords and the … what's that word?' she asked. '"Forlondez".'

'Promontories,' Will said.

'All right. He crosses the fords and the promontories, over at the Holy Head.' Confusion furrowed her brow. 'Hang on, how could he have got to Holyhead if he didn't go into Anglesey, but kept it on his left?'

'That's one of the poem's conundrums. We don't know where he actually was. Carry on.'

'Wouldn't he have written about something he knows? If his audience didn't understand, he would have laboured the point, just like with the Seal of Solomon?'

'Absolutely, but we won't find it if we don't know what he means.'

Lara glared. 'A defeatist attitude isn't going to solve this riddle. *You* took a chance with the seal and we found it. We can only go on if we use the same lateral thinking.' She glanced at the manuscript. 'Where does Gawain go from there? "He reached the shore in the Wilderness of Wirral – and there lived few men who were loved by God."' She grinned. 'He didn't like the people of the Wirral very much, did he? I don't blame him: for years I thought Birkenhead was a car park to get to Liverpool.' She gave a long sigh. 'After that it's not specific. This isn't any help. Is there another journey in the poem?'

'Not really, not with the same detail as this passage.'

Lara stared at the text. 'It has to be close by,' she breathed. 'He's referring to things he knows again.'

'How did you work that one out?'

'Because of what he says here.' She pointed to the line. '"*Þe* fordez" and "*þe* forlondez", *the* fords and *the* promontories. It's something else his audience would recognise.'

Will stared at the words. His face brightened. 'You're right. Although we're not any closer to finding out where he goes from there.'

'Yes, we are, because he refers to *the* holy head, not Holyhead in Anglesey. It's not the name of a town or a village or a shrine? Perhaps one which showed a martyr's head on certain festivals.'

'Nice idea, but it still doesn't bring us closer to his location.'

'You got a pen and paper?' Will produced the small notebook from his pocket. 'How much room have you got in there?' she asked, opening the book to a clean page and starting to draw. 'This is the estuary of the Dee,' she explained. 'Chester would be here,' she said, marking a cross inland. 'This is the Wirral,' she continued, drawing to the north of the estuary. 'Now, the poet doesn't say "Gawain travelled through Wales searching for the Green Chapel, then he went into Chester and finding nothing there he went into the Wirral". He doesn't mention Chester at all. He says Gawain forded the river at *the* holy head. *We* have to find a place he could cross.'

'Not easy,' Will observed. 'He travelled in November.'

'But I bet that when this was written, there were stepping stones laid down for a pilgrim route or something.'

'They would have had to have been big stones.'

'It's not unfeasible. We need a map, Will.'

'We need to leave, Lara. I don't know how long we can stay here.'

'Will!' Lara pleaded.

'I'm serious, Lara.' His mouth clenched. 'Damn! We were getting so close. Perhaps we should have waited for this to die down, gone somewhere else. Problem is still getting out. They know we're here, so they'll be watching the station and car hire places too.'

'There *is* a way out of the city, one they won't have thought of.'

'What's that?'

'Well, they think we're in a hurry to get away …'

'… They're right …'

'So they expect us to get out as fast as possible. How about travelling by the slowest possible method?'

'I've told you, they'll have helicopters looking for us if we walk.'

'Slower than walking,' Lara said. 'The Shropshire Union Canal goes from Chester to Wolverhampton and there's a whole network of canals. We could travel anywhere. They wouldn't expect us to try and get away like that.'

'One problem,' Will said. 'We don't have a narrow-boat and we don't have time to hire one.'

'You've never been on a canal holiday, have you?' Lara said with a laugh. 'There's empathy among canal people. They're a friendly lot, with a slow lifestyle, and it can get lonely, so an exchange of opinions and conversation can be a welcome diversion.'

'And if we were heading back to Birmingham, we'd be retracing our steps. They wouldn't expect us to do that.' He grinned at her. 'Lara, you're a genius.'

'It gets better than that,' Lara said. 'If we found someone on holiday, they might not have seen the papers. They won't know who we are.'

Will gazed out of the window. 'How far is the canal from here?'

'Ten minutes if we push it.'

He drained his coffee and left the money for the drinks on the table. 'I hope you're right about this.'

The canal marked the end of the old city at Northgate and the towpath cowered beneath the thick rock supporting the old city walls. Few people walked along the towpath: a few joggers braved the potential rain and a couple were walking their dogs. Lara fingered her hair self-consciously, wondering if they recognised her from the newspapers. She doubted it. Most people would have given the photographs only a cursory scan; even those who scrutinised the papers wouldn't have expected to find fugitives taking a late-morning stroll along the canal side.

'I hope you know what you're doing, Lara,' Will said for the umpteenth time. A helicopter had flown low overhead. They had ducked into the shadow of a rocky outcrop for cover.

'Look,' she said, pointing down the canal. Ahead, was a slow-moving barge. The chugging body was gaudy red. The doors to the cabins were closed and Lara saw a tall man standing proud at the rudder, dressed in a heavy sweater that would once have been white, but was now the same hues as discoloured teeth. He was smoking a pipe.

Lara jogged to catch up with the boat. 'Hello there,' she called out cheerfully. 'Mind if we help out?'

The man turned. He had a kindly, unshaven face. Laughter lines spread from merry eyes. 'Well, we'll be at a lock soon. I'll give you a key, will y'open it?'

'Of course,' Lara said.

The man leaned over and handed her a lock key. 'We'll see you in a minute.'

Lara smiled and walked along the path. At a usual walking speed she and Will easily outpaced the boat.

'I'm not sure about this,' Will said when he was out of earshot of the boat. 'We need to keep moving. That thing can't be doing more than three miles an hour.'

'No more than two at the moment,' Lara admitted. She glanced up, hearing a distant thump of the helicopter's engines. 'Just act naturally,' she said. 'You're not a fugitive. Just someone taking a January barge holiday.'

They walked to the next lock. Lara spent a couple of seconds trying to remember how to turn the key. Soon, the lock was emptying. 'As soon as it's done, the lock gate arm will be easy to push open,' she told Will. 'Don't try before then.'

Will watched the sky apprehensively. The first spots of rain had started to fall. 'How wet do we have to get before he lets us shelter?'

'I don't know,' Lara admitted. 'Here he comes now.'

Lara echoed Will's anxiety, not wanting to linger too long. The gates creaked and yawned open. The boatman smiled and powered the narrow-boat gently forward. A cloud of smoke filled the lock as he threw the barge into reverse and brought it to a stop. Will pushed the lock gate shut and caught a rope that the boatman threw to keep the barge from banging against the walls in the turbulence of the water. Lara opened the second gate.

'You travelling far today?' Will called down.

The man considered this, then peered apprehensively at the skies. 'Not far,' he said. 'It's not fun boating in this weather. Perhaps as far as the next lock until the weather clears.'

From the second lock arm, Lara saw Will's disappointment. She guessed it would also be apparent to the boatman.

They said nothing as the water bubbled in the lock and the boat slowly rose. Occasionally the boatman revved his engine to counter the momentum of the pushing turbulence. Soon Lara pushed the lock gate open. The boatman, however, did not thank them and power the boat away. Instead, he squinted at the sky. 'Helicopter's coming back,' he said nonchalantly, but his eyes flicked from Will to Lara, assessing them for a reaction. Lara wanted to run, but restrained herself. Will might have practised hiding his feelings, but she knew it radiated from her.

The man nodded. 'It'll be raining heavily soon,' he said casually. 'Were you needing to run off, or will you have a mug of tea?'

Will glanced at his watch. 'Not sure if there's time.'

The boatman gave a wry grin. 'I think you have all the time in the world.'

He knows, Lara thought. *He's seen the newspapers.*

At the same time, she detected no trace of a threat in his voice. Will placed a gentle hand on Lara's shoulder. 'Well, little Pearl, what do you think? Do we have time for a quick cup of tea?'

Hearing the rattle of a helicopter, Lara nodded. She forced herself not to run to the end of the narrow-boat. Will helped Lara on board before stepping down.

'The name's Tantris,' the boatman said. 'Not much of a name, I know, but the only one I've got. My wife's Jeanette. She's under deck, so go on down. I'll clear the lock and moor up a while.'

He opened the gaudy cabin doors and Lara and Will went down the small ladder into what seemed to be a long lounge and dining room. A grey haired woman smiled up, although surprised by the visitors, but Tantris called down from behind them. 'Nettie! Put the kettle on, we'll have visitors staying.'

Will shifted uncomfortably. 'We don't want to impose ...'

'Nonsense,' Jeanette said. She had the same *joie de vivre* in her eyes as Tantris. 'It's not often as we have guests. It'll be good to have us some different conversation.'

Will appeared as though he wanted to refuse, but Lara's stomach growled. She gave a charming smile. 'Thank you, that'll be lovely.' Jeanette didn't look like she would have taken no for an answer. She poured water into a kettle and placed it upon a gas stove.

The narrow-boat connected with the bank with a gentle bump as Tantris reversed the engine. Moments later, he came inside. 'Dark in here,' he said, turning on a light. He bid his guests sit down on a long bench at the end of the boat. He made an irritated face at the staccato rattle of rain on the roof.

Jeanette set up a card table between them and placed the teapot, a milk jug and a sugar bowl beside the mugs. 'If you'll excuse me,' she said, 'I'd not been expecting guests.' She took vegetables from a rack at the end of the kitchen.

'Oh please,' Lara pleaded. 'That's not necessary.'

'Nonsense,' Jeanette said. 'You can stay and you will. I daresay it's been a while since anyone showed you any kindness.'

'What d'you mean?' Lara wondered cautiously.

Jeanette smiled at her. 'It's in your aura – the energy your body gives off. It's very negative. You don't trust people at the moment, and you're frightened of strangers. Acts of kindness are virtually unknown to you.'

'I've had a hard few days,' Lara said bitterly.

Tantris poured the tea and added milk to his own. 'Now, my guess is it's something to do with that helicopter.'

'Whoops,' Will said. 'Time to leave, Lara.'

Tantris placed a hand on Will's arm as he rose. 'And where

would you go? Those aren't police helicopters, and it's not army neither, so my guess is you're in deeper trouble than you'd think. Drink your tea, friend, you're safe here.'

Lara regarded him quizzically. 'Why would you do that?'

Tantris's face became serious. 'Let's just say I've no love for any kind of establishment.' He pointed around him. 'That's why I live on a boat.'

Lara relaxed slightly, comforted to find an ally. Will remained tense.

'So, who are they?' Tantris asked Will. 'We're sheltering you. Perhaps you might tell us as much?'

Will's brow furrowed. 'I don't know,' he admitted. He tugged at his chin. 'But you're right, they're not police and they're not military. All I know ... they operate out of Bath. A place where security guards carry guns.'

'Bath, eh?' Tantris leaned forward, his eyes glittering. 'And what might they be guarding?'

Will made a dismissive gesture. 'Antiquities of some sort. Catalogued in German.'

Tantris leaned back in his chair. He seemed satisfied by the answer. He knocked the ashes from his pipe into a metal bin and refilled it.

'The reason ... the main reason I live on the boat is to get away from that. Corrupt organisations with too much power.' His face clouded. 'Once, a dream ago, I worked for an organisation. Our Government never had to say it never existed 'cause no one knew about it. I know about corruption, conspiracies of silence, withholding and leaking information. It's a big game, playing with people's lives. I'll not support nothing like that.' He continued looking at Will, assessing him. It was a long time before he spoke again. 'I'll tell you a story, Will,' he said eventually. 'Hypothetical, of course, because of course, no Government would admit to such a conspiracy.

'After the Second World War, in this story, Berlin's been

occupied and split into four pieces, and the British decided to try and find any surviving war records. The official line was to trace PoW camps. It were the public attempt at displaying a conscience for what had happened at Auswitz and Belsen.' He took a long puff from his pipe. The smoke curled upwards and dissipated across the ceiling. 'In this fictional Berlin,' he said, 'they found other things: occult devices, manuscripts and papers which were supposed to be shared amongst the museums of the allied countries.

'Of course, this hypothetical Government realised it couldn't leave the things in Germany to be used again. So it were all taken to Britain and stored in a place where a select few, in an organisation that never existed, knew about it.' He glanced back at Will again. 'Hypothetically speaking, of course.'

'Why would the Government need it?' Lara wondered.

'The Cold War were brewing. Churchill knew "peace in our time" were going to be short. The Government could use the information Hitler had amassed against the new superpowers, like the Russians.'

Lara started. 'But the Government would be as tyrannical as Hitler's forces.'

Tantris nodded. 'Yes, it would, wouldn't it? But this is a hypothetical situation.'

'You keep saying that,' Lara objected. 'Is this true or not?'

Tantris smiled. 'Maybe I am the immaculate storyteller. But we could add another hypothetical situation, and add the times of the New Millennium, when so many countries were doing their best to initiate the peace programmes, or, at least, blow the living hell out of the Middle East in the name of freedom. Not fighting a country, but an ideology. Supposing there was a way to do that. Supposing the hypothetical Government had promised the documents to the original owners so they could all strike back against the common foe.' His gaze passed from Will to Lara, then back to Will again. 'So if these are the people who're following you, then you've either seen some of the documents. Or maybe taken one. Which one is it?'

Will sucked his lip for a moment. 'You know a lot about this simply from me mentioning Bath.'

Tantris raised an eyebrow. 'It were my job to know these things. But, knowing about the storage areas lost me my faith.' His eyes watched Will, steadily and evenly. 'And before you ask: no, I didn't work for the organisation that's following you.' He settled back in his seat. 'I don't believe an individual should wield power he don't understand,' Tantris said. And for the first time Lara saw coldness in his eyes. The sparkle had become moonlight against frost. 'Power corrupts. One man shouldn't be a conduit for the darker powers.' He looked dangerously at Lara. 'Whatever you may think, my girl, believe me. They *do* exist. But one thing's worse than one man having such power and that's a Government and her allies having that same power to beat their enemies into submission.'

Lara shook her head in disbelief. 'You'll have to forgive me, I'm a bit new to ideas like this. I'm sure almost everything in the universe has a rational explanation. A series of words can't hold that much power.'

'So if I call your name, will you not turn your head to see what I want?' Tantris said dryly. 'So surely it's no different to invoking a demon and bidding It remember things It has known in the past.'

Lara shook her head. 'It's not the same, demons don't exist.'

Will smiled. 'It *is* important to have a faith, Lara,' he whispered.

Tantris fixed his eyes on Will. 'So what is it you stole?'

Will hesitated. 'No occult text. It was a manuscript of *Gawain and the Green Knight*. As an historian, it was like finding that the Mona Lisa hanging in the Louvre was only a first draft. I see it as a poem, not a source of power.'

Tantris nodded slowly. 'Be sure you always see it that way.

There was a reason it were in Bath. Never believe you can command all its secrets or its secrets will one day command you.'

Jeanette called from the kitchen, stating she wanted the table set up. Tantris removed the card table and unfolded another.

When Jeanette entered with four bowls of rabbit stew and dumplings, Lara tried not to wolf down the food and made conversation in an attempt to avoid looking as though she hadn't eaten for days.

'Have you travelled much?' she asked. 'You know this area?'

'All the time since I retired,' Tantris said. He leaned forward seriously. 'The only reason I said what I said is 'cause what I've seen burns inside me.' He turned to Will. I've needed to talk to someone who already knew, someone who wasn't bound by the Security Services Act. But knowing about the storage in Bath – and maybe knowing about things you don't know – that jaundiced my opinion of the Establishment, any establishment. A house is too claustrophobic for me to live in now. A newspaper can't print my story, because they'll abuse the power. We make our lives now by travelling through the countryside and foraging for food.'

Will swallowed his mouthful before speaking. 'Must be hard in the wintertime. This stew is excellent.'

'Nature provides the ingredients. My wife does the cooking.' He scratched his chin. 'Sometimes the canals freeze over, but rarely so bad that we can't move. If things get too bad we'll go into a dry dock so we don't damage the boat, but for the most part we just keep going.' He eyed Lara curiously. 'That wasn't an idle question, young Lara. Were you looking for something in particular?'

'Lara, don't,' Will warned.

'Why not? These people have been all around the place. They know parts of the country we've never seen. Don't be so arrogant to think we could work this without the experience of others who've seen things we haven't.'

Will said nothing but glowered at her. Lara turned back to Tantris and Jeanette. 'Something we've read recently mentions the 'holy head', possibly a reference to a martyred saint where the head would be kept as a relic.'

Tantris considered this. 'Around Chester, you say?'

'We think so.'

'Then you won't find the head. It were put back in its rightful place a time ago.'

'What rightful place?' Will asked.

'Well, back on the shoulders of the person who owned it!' He refilled his pipe and leaned back in his chair as he lit it. 'St Winefride, friends,' he said eventually as a plume of smoke filled the room, and Lara found herself inhaling the thick scent of burning cherry wood. 'She were plain old Gwenfrewi in Wales back in the,' he glanced at his watch. 'Seventh century.' His voice had become lower, gentler and Lara was reminded of the tones her father had used when reading the Shakespeare plays. 'She were a maiden, but the daughter of a local prince. She'd go to a village called Greenfield on the coast of North Wales, where she would listen to her Uncle, St Beuno, and his Christian teachings. The stone where Beuno sat to instruct her still remains.

'Like all the old stories, she were in love with one man, but receiving the unwanted attentions of another, one Prince Caradoc, who followed her around and wanted to marry her.' He smiled at Lara. 'Marriage was a euphemism.' He grinned. 'She said no, and in those days princes didn't like to be refused, so he cut off her head.'

'Not very friendly,' Lara murmured. 'Offering her flowers is much more effective.'

'Prince Caradoc didn't see it that way, lovey,' Tantris said. 'He thought decapitating her would end his emotional suffering.'

Jeanette leaned forward and placed a hand over Lara's own. 'Men sometimes have a heavy-handed way of showing love, don't they?'

Lara wondered if Jeanette had seen something in her eyes, or whether this was just an attempt at humour. She hoped the shadows hid her expression. 'Go on,' she urged Tantris. 'What happened next?'

'The head struck the ground and the ground started to bubble and a well sprung from that place.'

'The spring's call,' Lara breathed. Will nodded.

'Winefride's uncle, Beuno, was at hand. He picked up the head and put it back on to her shoulders. The miracle was performed and Winefride came back to life, completely healed, aside from a thin scar around her neck.'

Will gasped in surprise. 'He picked up the head and it healed again; Gawain also had a thin scar around his neck from the knight's blade.'

'I think we're on the right track,' Lara breathed. 'This could have been one of our poet's sources.' She looked back at Tantris. 'What else happened?'

'Well, of those characters we know nothing now, not even if Winefride was able to marry the man of her choice, but then I doubt it. She was now a venerated saint. Some legends speak of the ground swallowing Caradoc up.'

'Just deserts,' Lara said. 'What about Winefride?'

'Again, there's not much known about her. The legend is she became a nun and later an abbess. That's probably the closest to the truth. After all, most men would find it hard to lie with a woman who has been touched by God. They built a shrine to her and a town grew outside the shrine. It's been visited by pilgrims ever since.'

'I didn't realise Christianity had got to Britain so early,' Will said.

'Officially it hadn't, not until the later part of the seventh century,' Tantris agreed. 'But the first Christians were slaves brought over by the Romans, who settled in Britain right at the end of the second century. You're thinking of Augustine who arrived in Britain at the end of the sixth century. But, the Christian faith had to incorporate many of the ideas of the Old Gods. The pagans' worship the elements and water is one of them: they saw water as having healing powers and that was one of the ideas taken by the Christians.'

'Baptism,' Will said.

'The two ideas must have co-existed,' Tantris said.

'Where was this place?' Lara asked. 'The town that grew around the well?'

'The Chester monk who owned it named it after the well itself,' Tantris said. 'They called it "Treffynon" – "Holy Well". About twenty miles away from Chester.'

6

They stayed with Tantris and Jeanette for three days, chugging along the canal, away from the fear of whoever was following them. Tantris spoke no more about his 'hypothetical organisation', leaving Lara feeling – sometimes – that it really was just a story.

Instead, he told them anecdotes about life on the Canal, which usually ended with someone falling in the water. Lara smiled inwardly, watching Tantris from below deck as he guided the narrow-boat through the canals. Theirs was a peaceful existence, a kind of limbo, neither in one world nor another, only occasionally connecting with society, but generally contenting themselves with their own company.

Tantris had promised to see them down to Nantwich where they would be beyond the boundaries of the roadblocks and search parties. From Nantwich they would have to hire a car. They would be safe to travel to Holywell, providing they took a circuitous route.

They slept on benches in the dining area. Jeanette found them heavy woollen blankets. Every night before sleeping, Will sat at the stern of the ship, keeping his silent vigil. Once Lara thought she heard him talking, but when she peered out he was alone, his mouth moving in an unspoken prayer.

On the first night, as she lay in her bed with the blankets pulled tight around her, she heard Will enter. She didn't open her eyes, but knew he was standing over her, watching her like a guardian. He remained there for a couple of minutes, before going to his bed. She was puzzled, not daring to move again until she heard his breathing become rhythmic.

The engines woke her the following morning. She stared out of the window. The barge chugged on at an unnervingly slow pace, as though it was waiting to be caught. She didn't go above deck, even though she hadn't heard the helicopter for at least a day. Instead, Tantris and Jeanette manoeuvred the boat and opened the lock gates. Occasionally Jeanette returned with vegetables, fresh wild mushrooms foraged from the woods and a handful of fragrant herbs. In the meantime, Will helped at mealtimes using the resources at hand and proving himself to be an imaginative cook of vegetarian meals.

'Where did you learn to cook like this?' she asked.

Will chewed his lips thoughtfully. 'School of life, you get to know these things when you live on your own.'

Feeling as useful as a fifth wheel, Lara spent the day familiarising herself with *Gawain and the Green Knight*, struggling with some of the words and asking Will, who was never out of sight of the manuscript, what they meant. She was confused by the way the poet sometimes referred to the character of Gawain as 'Wawen', and various other spellings of the name.

'It's the way language was developing,' Will explained. 'The French didn't have the letter "W", so when words went over to the French, they were bastardised, so the royal line of "Stewart" was spelled "Stuart", and when French words came over to English, the word "Guerre" became "War", and "Guardian" became "Warden".' He laughed. 'I suppose my own name "William" came from the name "Guillaume". So when you read it, the "W" is often used instead of the "G".'

Having completed a basic translation of the poem, she read one of the other poems in the manuscript, called *Pearl*, which was the story of a man whose daughter, Pearl, died when she was two. The poem described his mourning at her grave in a garden – he described it as losing his precious pearl in the garden – his subsequent dream vision of his daughter's Resurrection in Heaven, and his inability to cross the Rivers of Death to reach her. He awoke, still grieving, but wiser through his experience.

There was something mathematical, formulaic, about the poem, the way lines contained words beginning with the same letter and the way that the poem contained one hundred and one verses – or stanzas, as Will insisted on calling them, – and each stanza a perfect twelve lines long. When she commented on this to Will, he smiled. 'That's why we know *Pearl* and *Gawain* were written by the same person. *Gawain* also has one hundred and one stanzas.'

'But what about this?' Lara said, pointing to the last stanza of the ninth section. 'There's a line missing.'

'Don't know. Perhaps he couldn't find a rhyme to fit. It's the same with the manuscript in the British Library. It's line 472, isn't it?'

She nodded. 'The poem continues as if it's not been interrupted, so it's obviously deliberate.'

'Could it be a year or something?'

'Maybe. And maybe the poet just couldn't think of a rhyme.'

In the evening, after Will had cooked another meal and Lara was unwinding and her head feeling heavy, Tantris produced a small bottle of brandy. 'Our one luxury,' he said. 'Will you take a drink with us?'

Will shook his head. 'Kind of you to offer, but I prefer not to drink.'

Tantris did not appear offended. 'Then we'll find coffee for you,' he said, putting on the kettle and pouring Lara a thimbleful of the drink.

The brandy only touched her lips, but it spread across her mouth like refining fire. She felt her body unwinding, ready for a relaxing sleep.

It was with a heavy heart at mid-morning on the third day that Lara watched the town of Nantwich coming into view. She was sad to leave Tantris and Jeanette. She would miss Tantris's merriness and Jeanette's unfailing certainty that nothing in the world would bother her. Both had had a positive effect on their dark situation.

Tantris helped them from the boat and on to the bank. He stared intently at Lara. 'Remember what I told you,' he told her. 'Remember we're talking about a large organisation. You'll find there are a lot of folk working for them. The web of their deceit and influence stretches far.' He turned to Will, shaking his hand. 'Things get stored there for a reason. Don't try and control *all* the secrets or they'll end up controlling you.'

'I'll do what I can,' Will said and the two of them turned, walked along the canal towpath and then, mounting a flight of stairs by a bridge, turned along the streets of Nantwich that led to the commercial centre. They soon found a car hire firm that would rent them a Ford Focus. Will produced his driving licence and paid cash in advance for the car and a deposit, promising to return it the following day.

They drove west towards Wrexham and then south to Llangollen following the River Dee through the hilly landscape. 'It's not the most direct route,' Will explained, 'but it'll keep them off our tail for a while.'

At Llangollen they turned north to Ruthin and followed the road up to the coast and to Rhyl. Lara felt a stab of excitement as the sea came into view, even though it was grey and tempestuous. She kept looking at it as they travelled east towards Greenfield and turned off at the first sign towards St Winefride's shrine. The journey had taken just under three hours. It was starting to get dark.

'I'm sure there are easier ways of getting from Chester to Holywell,' Lara said.

Will grunted an acknowledgement, 'Yes, when you're not being followed.' He chuckled to himself. 'Do you think Mrs Victor called them?'

Lara glowered, bewildered. 'How can you be so blasé about it?'

'If I wasn't blasé, I'd be angry,' Will replied earnestly. He looked at the grey stone building on the left-hand side of the road. 'I guess this is it.' They peered down the slope into a large garden with a statue of the martyr standing on a pedestal.

Outside the building was a huge rectangular pool. High arches crowned the pool. The two pilgrims' entrances were also dwarfed by the same mid-gothic stonework, reminding Lara of the Arc de Triomphe du Carousel from her visit to Paris. The top of the building was made of a similar stone, but unlike the lower part of the structure, this had been sandblasted down.

'Do we go in?' Lara said expectantly.

Will glanced at his watch. 'It's after four. They won't be open any more. We're going to have to wait until tomorrow.'

Lara rolled her eyes. 'Not again, Will. Not after what happened last time. We should have asked Tantris to stop and let us get a newspaper.'

'And what would that have said?' Will wondered. 'It's unlikely to advertise their movements. Articles like that are meant to throw us out of hiding, which is what happened.'

He pointed a hundred yards along the street, up a steep hill. There was a fifteenth century hospice, built from the same stones as the shrine, and close to the parish church.

'Same thing, over and over again,' Lara said bitterly. 'We'll go in here and they'll have seen the newspapers and then we'll be in trouble again.'

'This is a place for pilgrims,' Will said. 'They're used to runaways. It won't make any difference who we are.'

The door to the hospice was open, and Will entered the main hall. A tall, regal looking woman with flowing cascades of auburn hair stood behind a desk. Her eyes were as gentle as a sympathetic mother. Lara felt herself warming to her before she had crossed the threshold and was not cowed by the crucifix, hanging from the woman's neck.

'Good afternoon,' Will said pleasantly. 'I was wondering if you had two single rooms for tonight.'

The woman scanned a huge diary, but shook her head sadly. 'We have a double room,' she said, and Lara heard an echo of their stay in Chester. 'Lara and I are friends, that's all.'

The woman nodded, as if understanding a silent conversation, she traced her finger through another column in the book and shook her head again. 'How about a room with two single beds?'

Will looked back at Lara. 'It's up to you, Pearl. How d'you feel about that?'

Her reaction was to say 'no' and run, but she remembered they'd shared a room while on the narrow-boat and, aside from that moment he had watched as she slept, Will had not taken any interest in her once she had pulled a cover around herself.

'All right,' she said. She heard the trace of nervousness in her voice, but somehow, in this supposed holy place and, with Will asking her if she was going to be all right in front of someone wearing a cross, she felt comforted.

'It wouldn't be a problem most of the time,' the woman said apologetically as she filled out their details in the book, 'but we've a party of pilgrims visiting this evening, so almost all of my rooms are booked.' She smiled warmly at them. 'Are you pilgrims too?' she asked. 'Are you looking for healing?'

'I think "enlightenment" might be a more honest answer,' Will said.

'Then pray God you find it,' the woman said handing him the room key and a pilgrim's guide to the history of the Well. 'Your room is on the first floor. God bless you.'

'And you,' Will said, bowing his head almost reverently. He made his way up the stairs. Lara followed him quickly.

Will hurried along a corridor and was surprised when he saw the room number. 'It's room five,' he said to Lara. 'Is that a coincidence or what?'

Lara didn't know. 'Does it work?' she asked Will as he unlocked the door. 'The well, I mean.'

'People have come here for thirteen hundred years. There

must be something in it; perhaps it's only mind over matter. Or perhaps it's a place where they can reach out and touch the divine, like the legend of St Macarius where the pilgrims sought the place where heaven met the earth.' He opened the door and peered inside. Two single beds were divided by a small bedside cabinet. 'Is this all right for you?' he asked.

'It's ... cosy,' Lara said and followed him. Will turned on the main light and sat on one of the beds. He started to look at the small leaflet and wrinkled his nose after reading the first couple of lines. 'What is it?' Lara asked.

'The building was built in the early sixteenth century. A hundred and thirty years after *Gawain* was written. Looks like we might have hit a dead end again. We can't go back in time and see a building that's been pulled down.'

'Will ...' Lara said indignantly, but she was cut off by a knock on the door.

Will started. A simultaneous thought crossed their minds. *They've found us.*

'What do we do?' Lara asked. Her eyes flicked to the window to see if they could escape that way.

'We see what they want,' Will said, wiping sweat away from his forehead.

Her heart pounded as he wrenched open the door, braced for an attack. For a moment she saw, actually saw, a grey dog leaping from a man's side, until she realised it was the owner of the hospice raising her hand to knock again.

Will's expression melted from hostility to apology. 'Sorry,' he stammered. 'Caught me by surprise.'

She nodded, appearing to understand more from his tone than his actual words. She smiled pleasantly. 'A company of pilgrims have taken over most of the home,' she said. 'They're communing for supper this evening and maybe some entertainments. They wondered if you'd like to join them.'

Will smiled broadly. 'Thank you,' he sounded pleased. 'We'd

be delighted.'

'Come as you are,' she said. 'They don't appear to stand on ceremony.'

She turned on her heels and Will turned back to Lara. 'Are you coming, or just going to sit there for the evening?'

'I thought we were going to try and keep a low profile,' Lara said.

'If you want to not be noticed, then blend in,' he said. 'We might have thrown off our pursuers for the moment. Even if we haven't, they won't notice two more faces amongst thirty. We can all be pilgrims tonight.'

Lara nodded slowly. She was uncomfortable with being with people she didn't know, but Will had a point. She followed him down the stairs. Music blasted from the hall: the sound of reed pipes and guitars, of drums and flutes. Someone was singing, accompanied by stamping feet and clapping hands.

'Are you sure about this?' Lara asked nervously.

'Don't be such a baby.' Will grinned and opened the door to the hall.

Brilliant lights met Lara. There were nearly thirty people in the room, some dressed casually, some of the women in colourful flowing skirts. Some noticed them and gave them genuine, warm smiles, but the music didn't stop. A group of them were dancing in the centre of the hall, swinging their partners around in a jig. There was also a fragrant smell of cooking, which set Lara's taste buds watering.

Only one of the group gave them special attention. A portly man with a ruddy complexion, bounded up to them. His jacket was a garish patchwork; his face ruddy and his curly hair the colour of wheat; but his eyes were bright with unquenchable warmth. His handshake was strong and enthusiastic. 'Well then,' he said. His voice had a musical Welsh lilt. 'Well then, I'm Tobit, and I have the honour of being your host for tonight.'

'I'm Will, this is Lara,' Will said. 'And thank you for inviting us.'

'It's our way,' Tobit said. 'When we get going, we forget there might be other guests here, so we take the precaution of inviting them before they complain to the management.'

Will laughed, and Lara smiled nervously. Tobit touched her gently on the cheek. 'We'll not bite, Lara. We want you to feel part of the group, so when you leave, if nothing else, you'll say you've made thirty new friends. I'll not introduce everyone – there's too many.' He glanced over to the kitchens. 'We'll eat together, then we can have fun and music, as you like.' He clapped his hands and the music stopped, save for a guitar player in the corner. In a team effort, the pilgrims set tables and chairs in a huge square. Tobit showed them to seats while the others busied around them, laying places.

Nobody sat. Suddenly, the guitar ceased. Serenity fell across the table. They bowed their heads, but no words were spoken. Perhaps each of them was calling on their individual perception of God.

Then Tobit raised his head. 'We have guests this evening,' he said addressing the group. 'Will and Lara, two new pilgrims for the night.'

There was a cheer. They all sat down together. Lara flushed. It was hard not to smile at everyone who made eye contact.

First a huge loaf was passed around and each of the pilgrims tore off a small chunk before passing on the loaf, then glasses were filled with a small measure of wine.

'What's happening?' Lara whispered to Will.

'It's a form of communion. Everyone shares together. It shows we're all equal at the table.' They raised their glasses together and drank, even Will.

Food was brought through. A pretty young woman in a flowery skirt, a tie-dye blouse and wonderfully long hair, brought through platters of spiced meat. She carved it and served it along with a mountain of vegetables.

'Eat,' Tobit urged. 'Else it'll be cold before you know it.'

Lara ate, anxious but hungry. She was partly humbled by the hospitality the pilgrims showed to two strangers.

The meal flashed past. She didn't recall what she talked about, nor with whom. Her tongue was guarded when it came to why they had come to Holywell; but pilgrims didn't need to explain why they travelled. She had spoken of enlightenment, but had made no mention of the poem, nor the trail, nor that they were being followed.

Before she knew it, the tables had been cleared away and the music had started again. She listened to the pretty woman in the tie-dye blouse singing a sweet melody; then some of the men sang songs, first *a capella,* then as a Welsh choir. The songs lifted her heart.

Then Tobit was standing in front of them. 'Well, friends,' he said. 'Pilgrims are notorious for regurgitating old tales.' He smiled. 'We are the old troubadours of yore. We travel and tell our tales, but we travel by cars instead of on foot.' He smiled at Lara, 'Like Athene of the Flashing Eyes, you are. Perhaps you might be able to tell us a new tale?'

Lara shied away from him, stammering. 'I don't know any stories.' She blushed furiously, knowing whatever she did would not compare with what she had already heard this evening. Yet she wanted to entertain them, to thank them for their hospitality.

Tobit smiled gently. He leaned forward and whispered: 'It's all right, we're not monsters. No one's forcing you.'

'I'll stand in for the lady,' said a voice at Lara's side. The hall cheered. Lara was surprised to see Will striding forward. 'I'd like to borrow a guitar,' he said to Tobit.

'Help yourself,' Tobit said, indicating the rows of instruments.

Will picked up a Spanish guitar and sat next to Lara. The hall fell quiet as Will played a chord. He cleared his throat. 'Unaccustomed as I am to public speaking …' he started and the pilgrims started to laugh. 'Here's a bit of a slow one,' he said apologetically.

He played a slow introduction to the song and when he started to sing, he gave Lara a gentle smile. His voice was strong and confident.

I don't know if you can find me, or if my call's in vain,
I don't know if you will see me, and cut right through my pain.
I wonder if you're lonely, and if you can break my chain,
Waiting for you to call me is driving me insane.

I don't know if you want me, but still I make the call
For there is no one else in life, for whom I'd give my all,
Where are you then, I wonder, as my heart just starts to fall?
How can one be on their own, in a busy hall?

Lara's throat had dried. She wondered why his words were affecting her so much. Will changed the beat for the chorus. Lara found herself joining with the pilgrims' slow clap.

Come with me; stay with me, two lost in merry company,
Could take a moment to be found, if we stopped to look around
Come with me; stay with me, two lost in merry company,
Have something better waiting there, if we act in harmony.

We are blinded by glamour, used to forgetting tears
Feeling that surrounded, we'll forget our lonely years,
If I could shout above the calls and shouts and cries and tears
Perhaps I'll find a melody that might reach just your ears.

As a miracle the lights dimmed and at once, I caught her stare,
I called to her, asked her to dance; we danced as if in air.
I reached up and I kissed her, I saw her skin was fair,
"You waited so long to call me," (she said) "I wondered if you'd care."

But I called to you; you came to me, two lost in merry company,
Could take a moment to be found, if we stopped to look around
Come with me; stay with me, two lost in merry company,
Have something better waiting there, if we act in harmony.

Will played the chorus again and this time the pilgrims sang along. He rounded off the song with a chord and the pilgrims clapped and cheered. Will gave a modest smile and took a small bow before returning the guitar to its owner.

'Thank you, friends,' Tobit called. He turned back to his group and, as if an unspoken command had been issued, the musicians broke out into one of their more traditional pilgrim's songs.

'That was really lovely,' Lara said, leaning over to him.

Will shifted uncomfortably. 'Just something I cobbled together. I doubt it was appropriate for this company. I'd thought of singing the song which ends *Twelfth Night*, but it's probably not what these people want to hear.'

'*The rain it raineth ever day,*' Lara said with a smile. 'How appropriate!'

They stayed for a while longer. Lara relaxed, but after a while she found her head was lolling forward and she was no longer able to keep her eyes open.

'Come on,' Will said. 'Let's get you to bed. You're exhausted.'

Lara nodded and allowed Will to take her by the hand. She heard him speaking with Tobit, but all the lights and sound had faded away to no more than a distant buzzing. Then Tobit was standing in front of her. He gave her a gentle, fraternal embrace and kissed her softly on the forehead. 'Go in peace, Lara.'

'Go in peace, Tobit,' Lara heard herself say.

Will did not carry her up the stairs, but he took the most part of her weight. Lara found herself silently cursing that she did not have the resolution to stay awake and assert her own independence. Will propped her up against the door frame as he fumbled for a key, then he pushed the door open and led her gently to her bed.

'See if you can get changed,' he said. 'I'm going to brush my teeth.'

She fumbled with her clothes and managed to drag her night-shirt over her head, slipping between the warm blankets before he arrived. She did not close her eyes immediately, but waited for him to return. He smiled at her before he locked the door and switched off the light. 'Goodnight, Pearl,' he whispered.

'G'night,' she mumbled. She heard the sound of fabric against skin as he undressed, not even able to make out a shadow in the darkness. She heard him sliding between the sheets and then a long and contented sigh as he relaxed.

'Will,' Lara said sleepily. 'Tell me a story.'

'Aren't you a bit old for stories?' Will asked, but there was no disapproval in his voice.

'Every once in a while, I want to be a child, I want to play and lose my adult responsibilities.' She smiled. 'It's like my friends' fathers at Christmas time. They used to give their children toys so that they could play with them. My father wasn't like that. He would buy me books to further knowledge, encyclopaedias and things like that, sewing kits. When Christmas came he was showing me how he wanted me to be independent.'

'Did you miss your childhood, Lara? Did losing your mother mean you had to grow up too quickly?'

'Maybe,' Lara said regretfully. She had often wondered what it would have been like to have time to play, rather than having to learn to cook and clean.

'Well, just for tonight, relax. Just take a deep breath and let go.' His voice was soothing, calming all the troubles she had had throughout the day. Her mind clouded with an almost narcotic confusion. Then she had broken through the fog in her mind. She found herself smiling, cuddling into her pillow. Will's voice had taken a different tone.

'Once upon a time, there was a beautiful girl who lived in a house by the sea,' Will began. 'And her name was Lara.

'Lara liked to walk by the seashore, listening to the waves crashing. It soothed her, because there was something in the house frightened her. She never said what it was.

'One day, while walking along the shore she found a necklace made of precious pearls. She was delighted and put on the necklace. When she did this, she realised she could never return to the house. Whatever was in there had become too much for her to bear. Instead she walked into the water. She realised that with the necklace she could breathe underwater. She explored the underwater kingdom and realised the fear back on the shore couldn't touch her when she was away.'

Lara found herself drifting away from him. She tried to break the grip of sleep, but she found herself falling, falling.

'But no matter how much excitement she found in the underwater realms, she realised one day she would have to go back and face that house ...'

Falling ...

7

Lara started from sleep and peered around. It was light. Surely the alarm clock should have gone off by now? Michael would be angry again if she wasn't ready with his breakfast. She stared around her, disorientated.

Then Will was sitting on the bed beside her. He placed a cool and gentle hand on her forehead and smoothed away her anxiety. She gave him a nervous smile. His hair was wet from the shower and there was a small blob of shaving foam by his ear. 'Good morning,' he said. His voice was as gentle as a spring breeze.

He handed her a cup of coffee. She propped herself up on the pillow and sipped it.

'What time is it?' she asked, her mind still fogged by sleep.

'Half eight,' Will said. 'You were sleeping like a baby. I didn't want to wake you.'

She nodded sleepily. 'I need a shower.'

'Well, listen. I'll go down and order breakfast, while you get up, then you can join me when you're ready.'

Lara nodded and watched him leave. Part of her wanted to turn over again, but she got up when excitement bubbled inside her and her memories of the last two days became clearer – Chester and now Holywell – a place where another clue might be unravelled, inspiring her to leap out of bed and run along the corridor to the shower.

The water was warm and refreshing, prising her away from sleep. She wanted to stay under the powerful jets, but she washed herself quickly and ran down the stairs with wet hair once she had dressed.

Will was drinking coffee in the breakfast room, waiting for the food. They enjoyed an English breakfast together. Lara ate without thinking. She was focused on the holy well.

After breakfast, she waited for Will to pay the bill so they could leave.

The woman who owned the establishment smiled at them as they left. 'God bless you,' she said. 'I hope you find what you're looking for.'

'So do I,' Will said.

There was no sign of the pilgrims with whom they had spent the evening. Perhaps they had already made their way to the springs, to receive the healing they sought. Many pilgrims had already made their way through the waters. Some of them stooped and collected the holy water in bottles; others were murmuring prayers as they walked underneath the massive arches of the grey and brown stones.

Will paid the small entrance fee and they walked around the green to the shrine. Lara stared at the outer pool, running her hands along the iron handrails against steps which led into the pool. There was a large rock in the water, which she imagined was Beuno's stone. It was scattered with coins like a wishing well: the place from which Winefride had received her instruction.

As they passed beneath the arches themselves, Lara's sense of excitement diminished and was replaced by a feeling of reverent fear.

'Are you all right, Pearl?' Will asked after a moment.

Lara nodded, but remained silent.

'It's overwhelming, isn't it?'

Lara nodded again. She wanted Will to stop his commentary so she could enjoy the tranquillity of the shrine. An unfamiliar sensation was pressing down on her, something she couldn't remember feeling before.

Absolute peace.

They moved – almost dream-like – into the inner chamber. Candles flickered in the shrine. A statue of St Winefride stood in an alcove. Her head was intact, although a thin scar ran around her neck from where Caradoc's blade had forced her transition from virgin to martyr. At the base of the statue were vases filled with flowers. Winefride smiled beatifically. She carried an abbess's crook in one hand; in the other she held a palm leaf representing her martyrdom.

Around the pool, slender pillars reached up to the ceiling and for a second Lara imagined pilgrims, unable to walk, being carried upon the back of others, through the waters to receive whatever healing the pool would yield. There was an archway underwater from the pool to the shrine. She shook her head. Present day pilgrims should go to their doctors and not trust their healing to mysticism.

The main pool was a star shape with a bubbling spring in the centre. The basin would have had eight points, but it had been flattened along one edge. Will could hardly contain his excitement. 'On the reverse side of Gawain's shield there's a symbol of Mary,' he told her. 'Sometimes she was represented by the symbol of two interlaced squares. Other people might see this as the old alchemical ritual of squaring the circle.'

'If there's an eight pointed star on the reverse of Gawain's shield, isn't that a total of thirteen angles? Of the stars?'

Will nodded. 'I hadn't thought of it like that. No wonder Gawain was so unlucky.' He considered this. 'The numbers add up to four, of course. That was the poet's number of imperfection.'

Lara stared down at the bubbling spring. The pool was deep, and she guessed she might have difficulty in keeping her head above the water, while still keeping her feet on the floor. There was part of her desperate to test the waters, to see if there was any truth in the tales of healing. But she hesitated. She didn't know what healing she *needed,* whether it was physical or whether the waters would cleanse the deepest pains in her mind. And all the time, Tantris's comments rang through her mind: men found it impossible to lie with a woman who had been touched by God.

'Well, we're definitely in the right place,' Will said.

'Oh yeah? How d'you know?'

'Because the line which mentions *þe Holy Hede* is line 700, and this is a seven sided star, even if it's not perfect.'

Lara's peace grated. Simultaneous thoughts struck her. The first was *how* the poet had commanded such authority and influenced architecture *and* composed his poem to such perfection so the clues tallied with the line numbers. The second was a much darker thought. A dream, forgotten until Will had mentioned it: a seven-sided star, a book, reptilian eyes glaring out from a burning hillside, something primeval … something *evil.*

But the dream fled as she watched the bubbling waters. '*Could* it be coincidence?' she wondered.

'Is anything our poet does a coincidence?' Will answered. 'Even if this basin was built more than a century after the poem was written, the people knew what they were doing.'

Lara's brow furrowed. 'Isn't it possible we're just making the facts fit? Seeing only what we want to see and ignoring everything else?'

'Like what?'

'Like the fact this is a sixteenth century building?'

'*Or in the night, imagining some fear, how easy is a bush suppos'd a bear?*' Will said. '*Midsummer Night's Dream,*' he added.

Lara raised an eyebrow. 'I told you. I haven't read it.' She glanced back at the statue.

'What's up?'

'I just keep wondering if there's something else, something like *promoting* the cult.'

Will shook his head. 'As well as writing one of our national treasures? I doubt it.' He started towards the pool. Lara placed a hand on his arm. 'Think about it,' she said. 'The poet came here from Chester. Monks owned this place. All he sees is a load of decaying buildings that were either going to be pulled down or rebuilt.'

Will nodded.

'And he's got a plan to hide a code. Maybe he thought about something else, tied in with the legend.'

'You might be overstating his importance,' Will said.

'Do you think so? We're talking about someone who could influence the Chester monks to let him leave a piece of graffiti on one of the flagstones?'

'That's one flagstone amongst a million and that stone was pretty well hidden, so unless you knew what you were looking for, no one would have seen it. The legend was written at least a century before *Gawain*.'

Lara pulled a face. She stared out at the spring, hoping for inspiration. Over the pool was a pendant boss. She could make out vague shapes which she assumed were from the life of St Winefride. Time, weather and iconoclasts had made most of the images unrecognisable. She could make out the graven image of a young girl receiving a blessing and she assumed this was Winefride and her abbot uncle, St Beuno.

Will pointed to the seven-sided star. 'If this is the poet's marker, we have to find something engraved in the side, something only the poet would use, just like at Chester.'

Lara peered around. Pilgrims had carved their initials into the stones, perhaps showing dates they had visited the shrine hoping to receive healing, or perhaps they were silent testimonies of healing which had been received.

The gentle sound of the gurgling spring was suddenly lost in the appearance of a new crowd of pilgrims. Lara was distracted. She shook her head in anguish. 'Something's not right,' she said. 'It can't be the star. It's too obvious.'

'Maybe the poet was in a hurry when he was trying to work out his clues.'

'There has to be more to it than that. He hid the clue to Chester behind the colours, not a specific symbol. Why should we immediately assume the most obvious and essential element of the well is the place the poet would have meant?'

'What would you suggest?'

'Something else, something that's not right under everyone's nose, or,' she pointed outside, 'Beuno's stone in the pool. Tantris said Winefride's uncle used to sit on that stone while she received her instruction. Wouldn't it be straightforward to assume that if Winefride received her knowledge from there, then we might?'

Will led her by the hand and pointed to the stone, underneath the shimmering surface of the water. 'That stone's been worn away over the last thirteen hundred years. I think the poet would have taken erosion into consideration if he had also thought the buildings might change?'

'I suppose so,' Lara said. 'But it won't be here. Somewhere else, where you least expect to look for it.' Her eyes widened with delight as she pointed to the symbol of a dragon. 'There,' she said. 'Wasn't Arthur called *Pendragon*?'

Will nodded slowly. 'He was. But Pendragon is a title, not a name. Besides, in Wales the dragon would be a reference to St Cadwalla.' He leaned against one of the pillars and scratched his head in frustration. 'But you're right, the star basin is too obvious. We're looking for something that forms a part of the riddle. Where would you go Lara? If you were going to choose the least obvious place to hide something? Somewhere where time wouldn't touch it.'

She didn't know. She was as frustrated as he appeared to be. She looked at the star basin again, listening to the rippling waters. It wasn't going to yield any answers.

'Look around. See if you can see anything.'

'Roger,' Lara said, giving him the thumbs up.

'What did you say?' Will snapped, his eyes were livid.

Lara was shocked by his reaction. 'Roger …' she stammered. 'Okay …? I'll do it?'

The anger slipped from Will's face. 'Sorry. Thought you said something else.'

Lara walked away from the steps, not understanding his sudden mood swing. She stepped into a small chapel to be away from him. The verbal aggression bubbling beneath his surface unsettled her. She had seen it before, both in Michael and in her father, where the slightest word out of place could make them snap.

The chapel was peaceful. A stained glass window showed Winefride – displaying the scar on her neck – receiving tutelage from Beuno. They sat by the side of the pool. Lara wished he'd give her the same enlightenment he had given his niece.

The window was capped by a picture of a small crown with five stems like sunbeams.

Five ... Lara breathed. She knew the glass was modern, but she wondered if, even now, there was some influence over the imagery.

She thought she could search every stone in the chapel, but she thought it would be futile. But her shoulders sagged, despondently. The flagstones were arranged as a square within a square. To some it would have been an elaborate pattern, to others it might have been a symbol of Mary. But to Lara, the idea of having a five stemmed crown, and an eight sided star so close together was too much to be a coincidence.

But there was no carving on the stones, no clues left by the poet.

She walked away, back into the biting winds, up steps away from the well and towards the chapel. Whatever silent faith Will had, she hoped for the same understanding. She pushed open the heavy oaken door and stepped inside.

The chapel was dark. The air was still and silent and, for a moment, Lara believed she might be alone in the world. The walls were adorned with friezes of animals, worn away by time. She tried to find a link between them and the twelve signs of the zodiac, or the twelve months of the year. Elsewhere was an image of a horse and a rider. These images had nothing to do with the shrine down below and she walked around with casual disinterest, pausing to look at a carved grotesque face. In a moment of irreverent joviality, she stuck her tongue out at it.

She wondered what the gargoyle had looked at for so long. She turned. An angel was carved into the base of one of the vaults. 'There are worse things to look at,' she admitted.

But there was something about the angel, with great-feathered wings and the long flowing robes. Iconoclasts had disfigured her face, but her body, and the shield she carried, remained unscarred by time. Five points were on the shield, not in the shape of the Seal of Solomon, but in the position of a figure five on a die.

When she had been about ten, her father had sent her to Sunday School. She could only remember going once or twice; even then, the village church had been dusty and spooky, like a neglected museum rather than a welcoming place of worship. She'd seen the symbol there: the five points representing the five wounds of Christ.

Her breath caught. *This was the significance of five on Gawain's shield.* She stared at it. Her heart fluttered. She looked at the base of the vault, at the flagstones, at anything in the vicinity, for faded letters scratched into the stone. Eventually common sense ruled over optimism and she realised a carving made more than a century later would not have had any relevance to a poet's visit.

She turned away in disappointment, kicking her feet as she contemplated the nave sanctuary. There was a carving of the Green Man's head, crowned with an oak leaf chain. She doubted it would have borne any significance to the Green Knight in the poem. Foliate heads, she knew, were ubiquitous in church carvings.

Dejected, she sat down at the end of the aisle and realised if the clue had been left in the building, then it would have been destroyed when the chapel was rebuilt, after the poem had been written. There *was* no end to this treasure map. The reason no one had found the true meaning of the poem was that the clues came to a dead end. *Poor old Gawain-Poet,* Lara whispered softly. *You wrote the most complex conundrum in English Literature and this is where it stops. No one will ever know your secrets.*

She wondered why the poet had named *þe Holy Hede*. Why he couldn't have chosen something with more durability, something like the pyramids, or Stonehenge, or something else in the little-known legend of St Winefride that might have pertained to something Gawain had done?

She felt a curious, tingling shock as realisation washed over her. They'd been looking for the wrong thing. She didn't need to see the building or the carvings, but something as abstract as the two colours in Chester Cathedral. The poet might have feared the shrine wouldn't have stood for another century, let alone the test of time. Instead, he'd found a correlation between, or even an influence on, the legends of St Winefride and Gawain. But the poet had mentioned little about Gawain's background. Like Gawain's reputation with women, he had assumed this was something his audience already knew.

She ran out of the chapel, down to the shrine, to where Will was staring absently at the bubbling spring. His disappointment was obvious. 'Find anything?' he asked.

'There's a shield in the chapel with the five wounds on it, but I thought we might be trying to force the facts to fit the formula.'

Will nodded. 'You can't fit a square peg into a round hole. The cult of the five wounds was wide-spread in the fifteenth century.' Frowning, he said: 'This shield, did it show the hands and the feet with the stigmata, and was the heart in the centre.'

Lara nodded.

'But you don't think it was relevant?'

'No. However important the poet was, he might not have been able to demand a certain carving should appear in a certain place. And I don't think we're looking for a symbol.'

'I think you're right. But I was listening to a guide while you were gone. She said the well was owned by the Cistercian monks in Chester. If the poet had influence over them, then they had influence over the shrine and the chapel.'

'Well, it was a supposition that brought us here: the link between the decapitation of the Green Knight and St Winefride.' Lara's brow furrowed. 'I think we need to find another link. Things they both did. But we can't restrict ourselves to the *Gawain*-poet's account. He didn't have time to expand the legends his audience already knew. We need to think about the descriptions in someone like Mallory.'

'Mallory was fifteenth century,' Will said. He considered Lara's ideas. 'I think you're on to something. I wonder if the shrine's custodian can help us.'

There was a renewed fire in his eyes. He led her to where the custodian was selling tickets, guidebooks, postcards and trinkets. He was a tall, gaunt man, with grey hair and eyes as alert as a terrier's. When he smiled, he was friendly and welcoming.

Will explained they wanted to know more about the legend of St Winefride and he nodded, understanding. 'Our own guidebook explains the basic details, but if you're looking for a more historical approach, I suggest you talk to Margaret Whittaker.'

'Where will we find her?' Lara wondered.

'Were you staying at the hospice last night?' he asked.

Will nodded uncertainly.

'Then you've already met the person who would be of most use to you. Margaret Whittaker, the owner, is our local historian.'

Will thanked him and he and Lara walked back to the hospice. Margaret was sitting behind her desk, looking through pages of accounts. 'Good afternoon,' she said softly. 'What can I do for you?'

'The custodian said you might be able to help us,' Will said.

'We need to know more about the well and the history of St Winefride.'

Margaret nodded. 'I can try. What did you want to know?'

'Well, I suppose ... if the Arthurian legends had managed to come this far north.'

She nodded. 'Everywhere in Wales needs an Arthurian link to keep the tourists coming back,' she said and her voice gave the sense of welcoming someone home. '*Moel Arthur*, Arthur's hill, is the place where he's supposed to be buried. And then there's Arthur's court which is supposed to be halfway between here and Nantwich, but sadly there are no actual stories from Holywell itself.'

'There's a poem,' Lara found herself blurting. 'Written in the fourteenth century. It mentions the "Holy Head", but we thought it might have meant Anglesey instead of here.' Will's eyes seemed to claw at her. But she knew they wouldn't find anything if she didn't ask the right questions.

Margaret leaned forward. 'You've come to the right place, of course,' she said with a smile. 'Fourteenth century? He wouldn't have meant Holyhead in Anglesey: that's comparatively new. It was called *Caergybi* until comparatively recently; it means "Gybi's fort". But Holywell has always been known as *Treffynnon*: "ffynnon" is the Welsh word for "well", this place is called "Ffynnon Gwenffrewi".'

Lara nodded. Will had stopped staring at her and spoke again in a shaky voice. 'The guidebook says pilgrims have been coming here for thirteen hundred years. Was it just the Welsh who were interested in the cult, or was it also the English?'

'Both, and for a very long time. Until the railways came there would have been a crossing point to ford the Dee from Greenfield to Parkgate in the Wirral. It was part of a pilgrim's route – they found pilgrims' tokens and, after a storm, they even found a handbell from the Chester monks. Well, industrialised Chester changed all that: the estuary has silted up, but there's a story told in the *Life of St Werbergh* of a local who tried to cross the waters as the tide was coming out and he was trapped. He was saved by a miracle.'

Lara nodded, but she wondered why Margaret was surrounding her answers with exposition. She realised it must be a technique history teachers learned at their teaching colleges, Will spoke in exactly the same way.

'What about Winefride herself?' Will asked. 'Is there any evidence she existed?'

'Not as such. There are two versions of the lives of St Winefride: the first was written by the monks of St Werbergh's in Chester – they owned St Winefride's well – a little before 1148. There isn't much detail about her in those pages. The most information was in the *Vita secunda* by Prior Robert of Shrewsbury, who also talks about the life of St Beuno. But then, Robert, by his own admission, was something of a story teller. The Shrewsbury monks were interested in the well. There's a story of a monk who was dying, and they prayed to Winefride and received a cure, which further promoted the cult.'

'If she was a saint then wouldn't there be some record of her being … sainted in Rome?' Lara wondered.

'The word is "canonised",' Will said kindly.

'I doubt it,' Margaret added. 'The Church would've recognised the customs of the cult. She wouldn't have needed a bishop to petition on her behalf if the cult was already strong. Celts never called churches after Our Lady, but named them after their founders, or someone buried in them: holy graves made holy sites. No, there's only one record of a papal indulgence offered to Holywell in the mid-fifteenth century as a request for alms.'

'What about the old shrine?' Will said. 'Is there any information on what that would have looked like?'

Again, Margaret shook her head. 'We can't tell. Gerald of Wales mentions it in his *Description of Wales*. That's all. We have no idea of what the buildings looked like. Certainly, the shrine must have been quite extensive, else the Pope would not have granted so much in alms for the rebuilding of the church. In the *First life of Winefride,* the *vita prima,* there are a couple of lines which describe how between her martyrdom and her death she went on a pilgrimage to the Pope, but it's fairly unlikely that that happened. It's just one of those conundrums of the legend. Despite being written in Latin, they use the vernacular: the word they use is *pélerinage*.'

'What's so special about that?' Lara asked.

'That is odd, isn't it,' Will said, he looked down at Lara. '*Pélerinage* is Old French. It means "pilgrimage". But it should have been something like *peregrinatio*.'

Pilgrimage, Lara mused, then a series of images connected together. 'You're sure that's what it said?'

Margaret nodded. 'Absolutely certain.'

'Will,' she breathed. 'We have to go.'

'In a minute, Lara,' Will said.

'We need to take the car back,' Lara said. 'We can't stay any longer.' She was tugging on his sleeve.

After a moment, Will took the hint. He gave Margaret a professional smile. 'Thank you so much,' he said. 'For both your hospitality and the information, it's been most fascinating.' He followed Lara outside. 'What was so important it couldn't wait?' he demanded. 'She could have told us something about the shrine.'

'She already has,' Lara said. 'I know where the next clue is leading us.'

Will was surprised. 'You're sure? How do you know? We already know this is a sixteenth-century building. Do you think the custodian came down one day and started to scrawl graffiti on the chapel with a "Choose your adventure" game around the walls? Get real, Lara.'

'When she said *pélerinage* it struck a chord at the back of my mind, and I've just realised what it was.'

'What what was?'

'The chord. You ever read Geoffrey of Monmouth?'

Will nodded. 'A long time ago. Monmouth was probably as much of a fiction writer as Prior Robert of Shrewsbury.'

'Yes, which is probably why one event was in the first life of Winefride, but not in the second.'

'The trip to Rome,' Will said. 'Yes, I saw you get all excited about that. Why?'

'She didn't say "a trip to Rome" she said "a *pélerinage* to the Pope." In Geoffrey of Monmouth, Gawain was sent to Rome as well, it's not sure whether he was an ambassador, or whether he was sent there to receive his schooling, but Monmouth says Gawain was dubbed knight by the Pope himself.'

'I'm listening.'

'Well, I wondered why the word was written in French and not in Latin.'

Will's eyes suddenly widened. 'Lara!' he cried. 'You're a genius! In the fourteenth century the papal court moved to Avignon. *That's* why the word was written in French and not Latin or English. Both Winefride and Gawain would have travelled to see the Pope, but the poet wouldn't have guessed the Papacy would move back to Rome in 1386. That's what he means. The next clue is somewhere in Avignon.'

*

Will took a direct route back to Crewe. There was no sign of a helicopter or the road blocks that Will had anticipated. Lara doubted that – whoever it was – had given up their search. But perhaps they believed Will and Lara hadn't left Chester and were still searching the city for them. There was nothing to link them to Holywell or beyond. Perhaps the stern-looking man in the trench coat believed that the trail had gone cold.

Lara had also been thinking about the healing waters of

Holywell and how much solace they could bring. But, she was suddenly aware of Will speaking: 'The papacy was in France for a century only,' he was saying. 'At the start of the fourteenth century, Pope Clement V moved the papacy from Rome, first to Poitiers, then to Avignon.'

'Why?' Lara asked, disinterested.

'Clement was French. He felt threatened by the civil war that had broken out in Rome. Avignon was strategically situated with the river about it. That's why Prior Robert was so linguistically precise.'

Lara considered this. Then she thought of something. 'How did the story end?'

'What story?'

'The one you were telling me last night, about the other Lara by the seaside?'

Will smiled. 'I don't know. I was making it up as I went along. I stopped when your breath became rhythmic.'

She was disappointed. Her eyes glazed to the scenery as they drove.

'Any idea where the nearest airport to Avignon is?' she asked suddenly.

'Nîmes.' Will spoke without hesitation. 'But I don't think we should go there. They'll work out that we've travelled by plane. We need to expand the number of places they have to look for us. I suggest we go to Marseilles.'

'Marseilles?'

'It'll only take an hour or so to get to Avignon. We might shake them off for a while.'

Lara thought Will was starting to look tired. The strains of the chase were starting to show, especially when she realised he was unable to follow the signposts that directed him into the city. He started to curse when he realised his mistake and snapped at Lara when she tried to pacify him. His face was fixed into a mask that combined determination and frustration.

Soon they were outside the car rental showroom. They walked to the station from there. Will occasionally glanced over his shoulder. He seemed happier when he melted into the emotional and fraught expressions of the other travellers.

He jerked abruptly. 'Something's wrong,' he breathed. 'I can smell it in the air.'

Lara's heart thumped. Adrenalin coursed through her body. Will's fears were manifesting in her brain. Suddenly she wanted to run, but Will's hand was tight on her wrist. He led her to the ticket desk, keeping his eyes fixed straight ahead. He bought two tickets. There seemed to be a pause between his asking for the tickets and the machine printing them, as if the vendor was scrutinising them, examining his face.

The machine spat out the tickets, Lara almost snatched them from the basin under the glass and turned and ran. Will grabbed her by the arm. 'Calm down.'

She felt his hot hands through her blouse. He was as nervous as she was. 'Let's just walk calmly.' He pointed at the *Departures* screen. 'We want the train down to Euston.'

Lara almost didn't hear him, her eyes were wide with anxiety. 'Are they here?' she asked and tried to conceal a tremble in her voice.

He nodded. 'So we're going to have to look as though we're just a couple of holiday makers on our way back south.'

Lara gave a long sigh and let him lead her towards the platform. Suddenly she was exhausted. She wished she'd never met Will. At least with Michael life was … normal.

Her breath caught. How could she have considered that life again? Michael had been brutal. It had taken every ounce of her strength to get away. Whatever fears she had when travelling with Will, they were nothing compared to knowing Michael would have beaten her for any transgression. True, she and Will were running, but she was not living in terror for every bitter day of her existence.

Stepping down to the platform, Will's breath caught in his throat. He pushed her into one of the waiting rooms. 'They're out there,' Will told her. 'They're looking for us.'

Lara instinctively peered round. Will jerked her back. She fought the urge to turn again. She realised she'd never seen their pursuers, aside from the dawn at Stamford station.

Suddenly Will's lips had closed over hers. Shocked, she tried to pull away. His grip was strong, almost brutal. 'I'm trying to hide us,' he growled. She tried to relax, but her instincts took over. She tried to pull away again. 'I'm married …' she protested.

But her shoulders slumped. She wasn't married any more. Not in her heart.

Part of the cover, she told herself. *Two lovers saying goodbye.*

She didn't close her eyes. Neither did he. His eyes were alert.

Will broke the embrace when the train arrived at the platform. 'Walk straight on to that train. Just look ahead.' He gave her a gentle kiss on the forehead. 'For luck,' he told her. 'Let's go.'

Lara didn't look around. They joined the crowds. She fixed her eyes on the train. They were just two bodies amid hundreds.

Someone jostled her.

For a second she believed she had been recognised. Her heart pounded. She looked again. The same man, hauling two suitcases, was pushing past someone else to get on to the train. She glared at the back of the man's head.

Three steps until she could climb on to the train, but each step was an enormous gulf, the queues were moving slowly. Someone had time to scan the crowd, analysing itfor two familiar faces.

'Look for a seat on the other side of the train,' Will whispered to her. 'They'll still be able to watch the train as it's leaving. We're not out of the woods yet.'

Two steps until they would be on the train.

Then just one step. Lara's body was drowning. Every fibre urged her to turn, to see if there was someone standing behind her. The muscles in her neck were taut.

Then she was standing at the door of the train, waiting for other passengers to move inside and find their seats. She scanned the carriages, wondering which she should enter. Will dragged her impatiently by the arm and pulled her into the carriage on the right.

The compartment was busy. They sat on opposite sides of the aisle. It seemed an eternity before they pulled away. Lara finally allowed herself to breathe out once they had cleared Crewe station. Will was far from relaxed. Even so, she saw worry lines clearing from his face the further away from Crewe they travelled. Journeying had a rejuvenating effect for Will. She watched as he finally allowed his shoulders to drop and his breathing became slow and rhythmic. He closed his eyes, as she had seen him do many times before and, for a while, his face became a picture of serenity.

*

From Euston they took the underground to Victoria, and another train from there to Gatwick. Will managed to blend in with the other travellers, yet was on the alert throughout. But even though she tried to stare into space, Lara was aware of her eyes darting nervously, watching to see if someone was watching her.

At Gatwick, they ran to the British Airways desk. For a moment it seemed they were too late, but a member of staff appeared seconds after they arrived. 'You need to go through now,' they were told.

'Suits me,' Will said dryly.

'I suppose it's too late to ask now,' Will said as the plane began to taxi towards the runway. 'How are you at flying?'

'Not too good,' Lara said. 'I only did it that once to Italy. I think it's like going to the dentists. Worrying about it is the worst part.'

Will winced, as if he had remembered a bitter experience. 'Depends on the dentist.'

Lara couldn't relax on the aeroplane. Pain stabbed through her eye from the pressure. She clung to the seat arms. Her stomach muscles had clenched. She needed to make frequent visits to the loo. When she closed her eyes, she heard the blood pounding in her ears.

She just wanted the flight to be over.

'Look on the bright side,' Will leaned across to her. 'We're still ahead of them.'

'We'll lose any advantage as soon as we go through passport control.' She gazed at the mountains out of the window. 'They'll know we're in France. If they know we've left the UK, they may have sent out someone to "meet" us.' She rubbed her temples. 'As soon as we hire a car they'll send the gendarmes to watch out for it.'

'As soon as we clear the airport, we try and blend in. Get to Avignon tonight and see if we can make head or tail of the clues.'

'Do we have to go on?' Lara yawned. 'I'm exhausted. I just want a nice hot bath and a long spell in bed. Anyway, I can't blend in. I'm about as English as they come.'

The plane started its descent, circling over the sea. Lara closed her eyes and prayed the journey would be over soon.

8

Hiring a car in Marseilles, they drove north along the A7 *autoroute*: the inappropriately named *Autoroute du Soleil*. Lara was exhausted. Every sinew in her body protested and her nerves were frayed. Her anxiety was heightened by Will reminding her of something Tantris had said, something about the length of the web of deceit.

'This might be a horrible mistake,' he told her for the umpteenth time. 'The poet could have meant somewhere else. It's a very tenuous link that both Gawain and Winefride both sought out the Pope, whether in Rome or Avignon.'

'It'll fool our followers for a while,' Lara said. 'Let's pretend we know what we're doing.'

She stared out of the window. The dismal sky was an unbroken shield of grey. The windscreen wipers made wide arcs in the light rain. Lara had hoped to see something of the countryside, but the high motorway banks blocked her view. Even when she *could* see something, it was nothing more than a bleak two-tone landscape. The countryside was anaemic as though a vampiric winter had drained it of blood. There were skeletal pockets of forests and desolate fields of grapevines. Occasionally she saw an abandoned farmhouse, the desolate walls daubed with French political slogans. Those settlements still in use had stored wood for the winter; the great piles were like huge funeral pyres.

There were few cars on the *autoroute*. Signs flashed overhead warning drivers about the weather conditions. They arrived at a *péage*. Will leaned out and handed the frozen woman a fifty-euro note and received little change. No wonder the roads were deserted.

He drove along the D225. A ditch at the side of the road was in danger of overflowing with rainwater. They passed a rock formation which appeared like an emaciated jawbone. The stark landscape was unfriendly and forbidding. The distant hills were gaunt with barren shadows, wraiths in the night. At the foot of the hill she saw the welcoming lights of an *auberge*. She thought about a delicious, long shower, then curling up in bed.

'Can't we stay there?' Lara pleaded. 'We're almost at Avignon now.'

Will shook his head, his face remaining firmly resolute. There were dark shadows under his eyes and now it was sheer strength of mind to keep himself going. 'Like you said, we're almost there,' he told her. 'There's no point stopping now.'

She agreed, even if she didn't like it. The idea of a warm bed was becoming more enchanting.

Time slowed, but before too long they were crossing the Rhône. The grey river was swollen and bloated, flowing fast. Will turned off the main road which would by-pass the city and suddenly Lara saw the sand coloured, machicolated elliptical walls of Avignon. Numerous watchtowers surveyed the crenellated glacis.

'The walls are contemporary with the *Gawain*-poet,' Will told her. 'I read somewhere that they were mid-fourteenth century.'

'How do you know these things?' she quizzed.

'I was a history teacher. I specialised in the fourteenth century, although it wasn't on the curriculum. I was interested in the Great Schism, so I read everything I could about it.' He smiled. 'Not that these would be much use as defences. There are parts of the *Rémparts* with no fortification at all. It would have been impossible to defend them, but it had to look good. They served their purpose. They tried to tear them down during the French Revolution, but the craftsmanship was so precise. Even with all their tools, the French soldiers couldn't break the wall, so they gave it up as a bad job and the walls still stand.' He pointed at a hotel just outside the city walls. 'That's where we'll stay. I'm shattered.'

There was a small parking area at the back of the hotel. When they went inside to book two rooms, Lara was surprised to discover that Will's French was fluent. She felt frustrated, not understanding what was going on. Her knowledge of French came from school and what she'd picked up on a school trip which had been over a decade ago.

Then her heart sank: the hotelier seemed to be interrogating Will about something.

Will walked back to her and handed her a key. 'Two rooms,' he said, leading her to the lift. He lowered his voice. 'She wanted to know when we would be bringing in our cases. I told her we were travelling light and staying with my sister in Lyons.'

'I thought maybe they'd …' her voice trailed away, leaving her fears unspoken.

The lift doors opened. They stepped in. The doors closed behind them.

'You worry too much,' Will told her. There was a kind smile on his face. 'I mean, you care about what other people think and try not to tread on anyone's toes in the hopes people won't tread on yours.' He patted her hand gently and Lara was surprised by his sudden show of affection. 'It's a nice trait. Wish I could be as sensitive as you. But it has its downsides. It means you get hurt easily.'

Lara stiffened, indignant. Who was he to talk about 'extreme emotions', when only days before he had been waiting for a train to take his life?

But, the fact she'd been affected by his comment meant perhaps he had a point. In another time, under other circumstances, Will would have been sensitive and considerate: he was intelligent, linguistic, musical and he could cook. What a shame Janet had been so unsure of her love for him that she had had to look elsewhere and paid dearly for her mistake.

'*Do* you have a sister?'

'Why do you ask?' Will said, shocked.

'Just you talking about your sister in Lyons. I wondered if she exists.'

'Not in Lyons. Back in Buckinghamshire. Not seen her in more than a year. We were close once.' He looked away, leaving her with a hundred unspoken questions – what's her name? How old is she? What does she do? Any other brothers or sisters? But she sensed she had touched on to Will's private thoughts and he had built up a wall as impenetrable as those surrounding Avignon itself.

The lift jerked to a stop. The doors hissed open. They walked down a long passage and Will unlocked the door. The room was white and airy. Another door led to an en-suite shower. Lara stepped over to the window to look at the illuminated walls of the city.

'We'll head out for a meal,' Will told her, then smiled down at her. 'If that's all right by you.'

'Why shouldn't it be?'

'You might be exhausted.'

She smiled, but there was no warmth in the gesture. 'I could run a marathon if there's food.'

'That's the spirit,' Will said. 'Let's go.'

They walked outside the city walls until they reached the *Porte de la République*, one of the main city entrances. This led to the main commercial centre of the city. Lara's mind raced from excitement to terror. The buildings were so different to anything she had seen before. She was overpowered by the smells of fresh vegetables, roasted chickens and cheeses from market stalls. At the same time, she wondered what she would do if she was separated from Will. One of the reasons she travelled so infrequently was because she was terrified of being in a place where she couldn't communicate.

She glanced behind her, wondering if someone might have followed them, but all she saw was the milling crowds, walking past the closed shops. Her heart missed a beat as a car appeared from one of the dark side streets, its bass rhythm thumping through her. Crowds bothered her. She stopped in her tracks when she saw a large group of people amassed outside a take-away pizza kiosk, and walked into the road to avoid going near them. In the distance she saw the red flashing lights of a police car.

They entered the *Place de l'Horloge,* a wide market square. There were many restaurants; the visitors were able to enjoy the nightlife by sitting in glass conservatories. It was too cold to sit outside for a drink. The dark skies threatened imminent rain. She started at the sound of the low chimes of a bell and looked up at a white tower to see two automaton figures striking the hour.

'This would have been the Forum when the city was occupied by the Romans,' Will told her. He laughed. '*Place de l'Horloge*: It's almost called "Time Square", I think that sounds better than "Place of the Clock".'

She gazed round at the huge white arches of the theatre, and the Hôtel de Ville, which encompassed the great tower where she had seen the carillon and mechanical figures striking the bell.

She jumped when Will placed a gentle hand on her shoulder. 'Will you calm down?' he whispered gently. 'You're drawing attention to yourself.'

'Is it that obvious?'

'More than you'd realise.' He pointed to one of the side streets. She saw the gaudy and welcoming lights of a number of restaurants in the distance. 'How about getting away from everyone and going somewhere quiet?'

She nodded. Will turned into a dark side street. Lara hesitated, then followed when he pointed to a restaurant that promised traditional French cuisine, sitting in the shadow of a church. Unlike the buildings in the *Place de l'Horloge,* time and traffic had blackened the church's stones. Will walked up the steps to look at the name of the church and the tourist information. 'Saint-Agricol', he told her when he returned.

'Originally tenth century but the façade is fifteenth century. Not what we're looking for. How are you with eating snails or frogs legs?'

'Get real,' Lara said grimacing. 'I prefer not to eat molluscs or amphibians.'

'Just wondering if you'd only be happy with bacon and eggs?'

'I'll find something,' Lara said bitterly. She peered behind her. No one was following.

'The French have got it right,' Will said. 'Their rationale is "if it moves, eat it," whether it's fish or shark, or beef or horse or whatever. They make no bones about their food.'

'Can't ever imagine eating horse,' Lara said.

'It's quite rich, but tastes like beef. The trick is to either marinate it or smear it in a heavy sauce so the unsuspecting tourist doesn't realise what he's being given.'

'How about a salad?' Lara said hopefully.

Will smiled and this time she thought it touched his eyes. 'I doubt you'd be so lucky.' He hesitated by the door. 'You've gone green, Lara. Are you sure you want to try this?'

She swallowed the rising nausea, gritted her teeth and nodded.

The room was dimly lit in subdued red and orange colours. The log fire and gentle piano music made it homely and welcoming. A waiter dressed in a white dinner jacket and a bow tie greeted them with a smile. 'Bonsoir, monsieur, madame.'

'Bonsoir,' Will replied. 'Une table pour deux, s'il vous plaît.'

'Bien sûr, monsieur,' the waiter said and directed them to a table by the window. There was another couple on the other side of the restaurant, starry lovers, drowning in each other's eyes. The waiter took their coats and they sat down. He appeared a few moments later bringing them leather bound menus. 'Vous désirez des boissons?' he asked.

'Do you want a drink, Lara?' Will asked. He stopped and thought. 'Do you drink wine?'

Lara was surprised; it was the first time she had seen him consider anything other than coffee. 'Sure,' she stammered.

Will flicked open the wine menu and pointed to one of the red wines. 'Une bouteille de Côtes du Rhône, s'il vous plaît.'

The waiter gave a small bow and left. 'I ordered a bottle of the local red. Is that all right?'

Lara nodded. 'I'm surprised. I thought you were pretty much tee-total.'

'There's a time and a place for drinking. And with a decent meal, a long way away from anyone who might be following us, it's about the right place. I think we've got some time before anyone realises we're in Avignon.'

Lara settled back in the chair. 'That's comforting. I thought I would have to look over my shoulder all the way through the meal.'

'*Que sera, sera,*' Will promised. 'If they storm the restaurant there's nothing we can do about it, so we may as well relax and enjoy the meal. I've paid cash for everything in France, so hopefully the only hint our friends will have that we're out of the country is that our names will be on a flight record in Gatwick and that we passed through passport control in Marseilles. After that, they won't have a clue. We could have flown to Nîmes. I wanted to make sure we weren't going to the nearest airport.' He stroked his chin, and there was a rough sound of his skin against the stubble. 'Perhaps we should have gone a different way.'

'It's done now,' Lara said, then added, 'And you said I was the worry-guts!'

'I worry to stay alive,' Will said. 'Not about things like calories, cost and complexion.' He smiled then. 'But, to be fair, I think you worry about some of the right things as well. You've never said to me something has too many calories.'

'I've always been naturally slim. It doesn't matter what I eat.'

'I bet other women hate you when you say that.'

'I don't say it very often.' Her eyes glazed as she tried to read the menu. 'I can't read this,' she said uneasily. 'Would you order for me? Only please don't make it snails or horse.'

'How about frogs?'

'Or frogs.'

'You wouldn't know whether I'd ordered you frog's legs or chicken in batter. They taste the same.'

'I don't want to find out,' she said, shifting uncomfortably.

'Suit yourself.'

The waiter returned with a bottle of wine. He showed Will the label and when he nodded he opened the bottle and poured a little for him to taste. Trying to hold back a smile at this sudden burst of culture, Lara watched him nod and the waiter poured two glasses. 'Vous avez choisi?' he asked.

Will ordered for himself, then smiled at Lara 'Et pour madame …' he spoke quickly in French, smiling at her occasionally, knowing she didn't understand. The waiter nodded, gave his little bow and walked away. 'What did you order?' Lara asked, tensing.

'Wait and see,' Will said. He raised his glass. 'A toast, I think. To finding out what the *Gawain*-poet meant.'

Lara chinked her glass with his. 'And not getting caught in the process.' The wine was rich and smooth. She wondered when she had tasted a wine so fruity. It was a long time since she had had alcohol. She wondered when she had last sat in a restaurant of this calibre. Michael had rarely taken her out, and certainly to nowhere like this. She was unused to this kind of relaxed formality and unsure of what to say.

'Excellent wine,' she managed.

'Côtes du Rhône,' Will said. 'It means it's grown in those vineyards by the side of the river.' He leaned back in his chair. 'I don't think I've ever drunk a wine so near to its place of origin. I mean, you don't get closer to the Côtes du Rhône,' he indicated behind her. 'They're about fifty metres that way.' He smiled, then studied the wine label.

'Why history, Will?' she said suddenly.

'What?'

'Why teach history?'

'I guess I have a passion for it,' he said. He thought, then looked past her, eyes glazing over and becoming distant. 'I went to a good school. There wasn't anything that caught my interest. I managed to get by in all my GCSEs, all the things you're expected to do, Maths and English, French and German, combined science, music and twentieth century history. My parents ...' His brow started to furrow and he took a long sip from his wine, '... they wanted me to do A-Levels. I did what I was told because I didn't have a direction. By a process of elimination, I took French, English and History and thought I'd do English at University.

'I managed to bomb my English exam. Didn't know what I did wrong, but managed to get A grades in the other two subjects. It wasn't enough for me to get to University to study English so I took a year out. I did two A-levels by correspondence course in my "year out". I re-took English literature, concentrating on fourteenth century material and did another A-level in history, this time focusing on the Middle Ages. Suddenly history came alive for me. I finally went to University and when it came to writing my dissertation, and under the careful direction of one of the professors, I was allowed to work in the archives with original documents.

'They say hindsight is the greatest of teachers, but the lessons of history are so much more prominent,' he sighed. 'It's written there in black and white. History isn't just an opportunity to try and understand everything that's happened in the past, it's about discovering what'll happen in the future. Coming to somewhere like Avignon is a million times better because you can actually reach out and touch everything that's happened.'

'What do you mean?'

'Sometimes when I look at places like this I can almost feel myself stepping back through time. I can walk through the streets and see the popes and the people in their cap-a-dos and other medieval costumes.' His brow furrowed again. 'Don't you ever feel like that?'

'Sometimes, maybe,' Lara admitted. 'But never with such clarity. Maybe I just lack your imagination.'

'I don't think it takes an imagination,' Will said as the waiter turned up and placed a plate in front of her. 'I think it takes an empathy with the past.'

'Bon Appétit, monsieur, dame,' the waiter said and left.

Lara looked down at the plate, almost not daring to see what Will had ordered for her. She was pleasantly surprised to see prawns set in avocado, covered with French *vinaigrette*. The plate was decorated with a small salad.

'I hope you like prawns,' Will said. 'It was either that or,' he indicated to his own plate, 'snails.' She tried not to grimace at his plate and the smell of the thick sauce of oil and garlic. He broke open one of the shells and speared the meat with his fork. 'Do you want to try one? I promise it won't try to run away.' He was smiling, but she saw he was serious in his offer. She felt her stomach churning, tried to settle it with a taste of the wine, then shook her head and set about devouring the avocado and prawns.

Her taste buds were almost overpowered by the rich food. Will poured her another glass of wine. 'What do you think is out there?' she asked. 'What do you think the poet was trying to hide? And why did he travel all the way out here to hide it?'

'He could have been a knight travelling back from somewhere. Perhaps the poem was written after 1387 and the poet believed in the authority of the Anti-pope, and not the Pope. Perhaps he deposited it here, knowing England was not ready for whatever he had hidden. I just don't know.' He broke open another shell. 'He was possibly a clergyman with an illicit daughter. You've read *Pearl*? He speaks of his "pryuy perle", the "hidden" pearl.' He laughed. 'Perhaps it was the Pope himself, although why the Pope would write in a Chester dialect is beyond me, unless he wanted to see the holy well for himself and dictated something for the local people to write down.'

'And where would he find time to write poetry of that nature? Surely he would concentrate more upon the Christian motif rather than the Pagan images.'

'You think it's Pagan? I thought it was more Christian trying to overcome the Pagan gods.'

'Well, this Green Knight is symbolic of nature, the way it dies in the winter to regenerate in the spring; and the way Gawain decapitates the knight, it's like the pollarding of an old tree.'

'All true,' Will admitted. 'In older legends, Gawain was associated with the Celtic sun god Gwalchmai, who drew his power from the sun and became stronger towards noon and had his strength wane in the afternoon.' He broke open another shell. 'In the thirteenth century, when the Grail legend started to become more prominent, it was Gawain who was sent to look for it. Of course, the later writers realised Gawain had pagan origins and forbade him from looking for the Grail, and so it was left to the more Christian knights, Galahad, Percival and Bors. Are you sure you wouldn't like to try one of these?' he asked, pointing to the few remaining snails.

Lara shook her head and indicated for him to continue.

'Having said that, Gawain wasn't Christian enough to search for the Grail, the poet does give him a lot of Christian ideals, not least the fact that on his journey he comes across all sorts of pagan creatures like giants and fairies. But the poet dismisses all of them in a single line, and says he doesn't have the time to tell a tenth of Gawain's deeds. He has to meet his chivalric challenges with good grace.'

'Do you think it's possible the poet found the Grail and hid it in Avignon?' Lara asked with a smile.

Will shook his head. 'It's unlikely. We'd be following crackpot theories and looking in Rennes-le-Château, Rosslyn Chapel or even under the *Grande Pyramide* in the Louvre. Personally, I doubt the Grail ever existed. It suddenly springs into literature in the twelfth century. Frankly, I think it's a myth created to inspire Christianity when all else was failing.' He leaned back in his chair, having finished the snails. 'But let's not talk about Gawain all night, I'm sure we'll have plenty of time to worry about him when we get to the Papal palace tomorrow.'

'What are we looking for?'

'Same as before, something that's out of place in the design of the building. Something the poet would have seen if he was an ambassador to Avignon. I guess we'll know if we see it.' He took a sip of his wine. 'But enough of that. Let's talk about you?'

'What about me?' She suddenly felt he was prying into those private thoughts she tried to hide. It was a mercy the waiter appeared to take the plates.

'How were the prawns?' Will asked.

Lara was surprised. 'Good. Thank you.'

'Just good?'

'Better than good, wonderful.' She looked at him cautiously. 'What's the next course?'

'Wait and see,' Will said with an enigmatic smile.

She did not have long to wait. The waiter appeared with a plate of flame-grilled lamb chops cooked with garlic and herbs; the flavour had filtered into the meat. She did not dare ask what animal the steak Will was eating had come from. Will ordered another bottle of wine and filled their glasses with the remains of the first. 'Careful, Will,' she said. 'You'll have me under the table in no time.'

'So have you done much travelling?' Will asked.

'Not under the table,' Lara said, giggling. She regained her composure. 'My father was always reluctant to travel. Thought he could see what he wanted at home. The first time I went abroad was with an organised school-trip to Paris when I was thirteen. I guess I was disappointed. It was like being in England with a load of different buildings.'

'In what way?'

'When you're with a large group of English people, you barely hear people speaking French. If you have a problem with the language you look to someone standing next to you and ask what was said.' She smiled uncomfortably. 'It's like being here with you. I don't know what I'd do if I lost you and had to try and find my own way back home.'

'You'd find a way,' Will observed. 'But control is very important to you, isn't it?'

Lara's eyes narrowed. 'I don't know what you mean.'

'Watching you on the aeroplane, you were panicking, not because you were scared of flying, but because you had to trust your life to someone else.'

'That's not fair,' Lara retorted. 'I've had to trust you.'

Will shook his head. 'You've called the shots since we arrived in Chester.' He rubbed one eye as he thought. 'But when you left Stamford you didn't have a plan, you were just interested in going where the tides of time took you.'

'I had to get away. Things really weren't going well.'

'I think "desperate" would be closer to the truth.'

'Well, that's my business,' Lara snapped.

'Of course,' Will said, holding his hands up in surrender. 'So your father never encouraged travel? Haven't you ever wanted to see the world?'

Lara shook her head. 'I think I would like to go back to Paris, if I had more of a command of the language, and just wander around, or befriend a Parisian and have him show me the parts the tourists don't see.'

'*Belle Paris*,' Will said wistfully. 'A romantic city, no place like it in the world. They say the Seine glitters a deep blue if you visit Paris with the one you love.'

'My husband felt the same about travelling as my father ...'

She almost squealed. She hadn't meant to talk about him, but relaxing, the wine had caught her off guard. She wanted to run away and hide somewhere, but Will's expression was one of concern.

She tried to turn her attentions back to her meal, but her hands were clenched into fists and she was stabbing at potatoes in anger, fighting to hold back tears.

'It was really that bad?' Will prompted.

Suddenly she found she wanted to talk. Her unspoken emotions had been eating away at her. She had found no one with whom she could share it, impossible to cut out the cancer eating away inside her.

And yet, here was an offer of friendship. The first she had received in a long time. She was unsure how she should take it, or if she should accept it. Then she was talking, without knowing where to start, without knowing why she was saying these words. 'I just hate him so much,' Lara whispered. She released her tears. She didn't care about anything except getting the hurt out of her.

'Do you want to go somewhere to be by yourself?' Will asked gently.

Lara shook her head and wiped her eyes. 'I don't have enough tears for what he did to me. Too many regrets and only one lifetime to sort them out. He was so perfect when we were dating. Kind, considerate, loving. But all of that changed after we were married. Once we had financial constraints then all the fun was gone. I'm not sure if I loved him, or whether I loved the excitement of having someone to do things with.' She smiled uncertainly. 'Does that sound selfish?'

Will showed no expression, but he leaned forward and gently touched her hand. His fingers closed over hers and Lara was caught in a paradox of taking comfort from the gesture and wanting to flee.

'Things had been going stale between us. I knew that. I was

losing contact with my friends. He was out working and only after a while did I start work to try to supplement our income. I hid a bit of it back every week because I think subconsciously I knew I would need to run. I tried to have a child, hoping that would bond us together.' She avoided Will's gaze and wiped away the tears. 'Mi ... He ... wasn't at the birth. Didn't come and see me for a long time afterwards.'

'What happened?'

'She ... she died,' Lara heard her voice going husky as she remembered the pain of giving birth to Julia and then the maternity nurse placing a gentle hand over hers before trying to explain. 'There was a complication. The umbilical cord had wrapped around her neck and strangled Julia. Nothing could save her.' She looked over at Will, seeking understanding, perhaps even absolution.

Will just shook his head sadly. 'There are no contrite phrases or a magic wand to make everything better,' he said gently. 'Or if there are, you deserve more than that.' He smiled at her and she found her guilt lifting, just a little. But she found no more to say and Will did not press her. 'Did you go anywhere on a honeymoon?' he asked.

Lara nodded. 'The only other time I've been abroad. We went to Tuscany. Saw Pisa, saw Florence, just travelled around for a little while. Didn't have too much problem with the language because we didn't really say anything.' She smiled sadly. 'Or, more likely, that we didn't *have* anything to say.'

There was a long silence as Lara's own words dried up. Will said nothing for a while, then smiled kindly.

'Eat up,' he said, lifting his glass. 'Do you enjoy desserts?'

'Normally yes, but I'm stuffed.'

'Then what do you say we head back to the hotel after this and have a coffee back at home?'

'You'll stay awake all night, although a good brandy by the fireside wouldn't go amiss.'

He shook his head. 'We've had enough to drink. Perhaps I shouldn't have conceded tonight and we should have drunk coffee instead.'

'I'm glad we did,' Lara said. 'It was a fitting complement to a lovely meal. Thank you. All right, coffee it is.'

They finished up and then as the waiter came to take away their plates, Will asked for the bill. He paid and as the waiter returned their coats, Lara asked 'I'm curious. What did you eat this evening?'

Will smiled mischievously. 'Beef in a peppercorn sauce,' he smacked his lips. '*Magnifique!*'

It was quiet outside. The cold air hit her in the face, dispelling any glow she might have felt and sending the alcohol rocketing to her head, but scattering her melancholy. Her fingers tingled in the cold. Shivering, she hunched her shoulders to around her ears and walked quickly through the streets. Will seemed dizzy as well. She smiled: the two of them walking home was reminiscent of a time when she was in college and going home after going to a night-club. She wanted to link arms with Will, walk in silly ways and sing "hey, hey, we're the monkees", but she didn't think that Will's stoicism would cope with a burst of insanity.

As they entered *Place de l'Horloge,* the mechanical figure stuck the bell again. Lara flinched at the sudden sound, and for no reason it sent Will into a fit of laughter. His mirth brought a gentle warmth to her heart and, in her alcoholic euphoria, she knew that with Will by her side, nothing could harm her.

They walked back along the shopping street, towards the city gate, the *Porte de la République*. She looked in the windows as though she hadn't a care in the world. She saw a gorgeous dress in satin. She glanced at the price tag, trying a quick calculation from euros. She gave up. Too expensive anyway.

'Don't you think it's absolutely darling,' she said to Will, taking him by the hand and pointing to it.

Will nodded, but his eyes were tired. At least he hadn't grunted and wandered on. She did not let go of his hand.

'How are you feeling?' he asked, as they walked back towards the main gate.

'Cold,' she said.

'We'll soon be back in the warm.' He pointed up at the gaudy flashing lights outside the hotel, an oasis amid the frozen desert.

She did not worry about stepping into the lift, although time seemed to grind to a halt while she waited to reach the third floor.

She walked with him to her room, opened the door and searched for a kettle. She saw no such facilities.

'No coffee,' he said, disappointed and turned to leave.

'Will, wait,' she said, touching his shoulder. She was breathing heavily. She didn't know whether it was the alcohol or her fears – she dreaded that it might have been her emotions – controlling her. His scent, his very presence, was a command she couldn't refuse. She rose to meet him. He seemed uncertain as to her intentions and halted in front of her, then took a step away. *Take care,* she breathed. *He's been hurt recently, so very badly hurt.*

Will nodded, as if hearing her thoughts. When she stepped towards him again, he did not retreat. His arms folded around her and, before she knew what was happening, his lips were over hers. She tensed momentarily. There was power behind the kiss. She conceded, surrendering herself to him. He kissed her again and this time his tongue probed into her mouth. She relaxed into his arms, pulling herself away from him, yet falling into his embrace. She was smiling; she had no idea how much she was smiling save she must have looked like a Cheshire cat with a coat hanger in its mouth.

'Oh Will,' she said. She wondered if he wanted her like she wanted him, whether he had missed human affection the way she'd missed it. She kissed him on the neck, tasting his clean skin; he had also relaxed in her touch. She took him by the hand and led him over to the bed.

'Lara …' She couldn't trace any anxiety in his words, but when she spoke, she voiced his fears.

'It's all right,' she promised him. Was he still thinking about Janet, and she'd leave him the way Janet had? No more talking. She didn't have the words to tell him she was there for him, would always be there for him, to pour out his troubles when he was ready. She smiled inwardly; there were no words to describe the pure lust she felt. All she knew was that she wanted him. She reached up at him again and kissed him. This time it was he who surrendered. His arms wrapped around her once more, his hand travelled up her back, reaching her bra. He hesitated, as if waiting for permission.

A lone thought broke through the fog of her euphoria. Should she be doing this? When she had married, she'd promised herself to someone else, always and forever. But she dismissed those thoughts, knowing 'he' had pushed her aside and let her go. *Will he think I'm easy?* she wondered. The thought was lost as her bra fell undone and her blouse released from her jeans. His hand rubbed over her stomach, seeming to count her ribs for an eternity, before it rose again, his strong fingers tracing gentle circles on her skin. The hand moved higher, cupping her breast, gently flicking over her nipple. Pleasure nerves she'd forgotten ever existed suddenly exploded into life. She bit her lip to prevent herself from crying out in absolute joy. Her blouse fell open. She wondered how long they had been standing there, how long it had taken him to unwrap the present she was offering him. She tried to undo his shirt. Her fingers were numb with excitement. She could no longer feel her feet, but instead her entire body felt alive with the fire of passion.

Then she was running her fingers over his muscular chest, and she lay back, closing her eyes. She forgot everything except the moment, even forgot her own name, as she was immersed in absolute ecstasy.

9

She woke once during the night. For a while, she was disturbed by dreams that evaded her as soon as she opened her eyes. She squinted in the darkness at the sterile walls, looking up and seeing the tiny red dot of a television on standby. It took her a few moments to remember where she was, how she had got here. Then she saw Will sleeping beside her. Lara exhaled in relief; she was finally and really here.

She watched Will for a while. He was lying on his back, his arms folded across his chest like a mummy. She brushed hair away from his forehead. He smiled gently in the half-light and she turned into him, nuzzling his shoulder, taking comfort from the feel of his muscles, enjoying his musky scent.

When she awoke again, the winter sun was prising through the curtains. She got up, searching for a fresh pair of knickers and a bra. She pulled on her jeans and blouse, regarded the street through the window. It had rained during the night, and now the roads glistened. Tyres hissed against asphalt. Lara glanced at the ancient walls that surrounded the city. In front of her was one of the gates that would lead into the labyrinth of history. She saw arrow-slits and crenellated walkways that would have served as the city's defence. In front of the city were rows of tall spindly-looking trees, lonely in their winter nakedness. What history had the walls and the trees seen? What stories could they tell?

'Awake already?' Will said from behind her. She hadn't heard him getting up. She didn't turn, but let his arms enfold her. He lifted her hair and gently kissed her on the neck. She felt safe within his arms, his muscles encircling her, smelling the scent of his after-shave. She smiled. Had she ever been this happy before? She guessed that she must have, but Will was everything that Michael was not. She gritted her teeth. How long had it been since she had thought about Michael? Why was he intruding on her happiness now?

'Are you all right, Pearl?' Will asked.

Lara nodded.

'No regrets?' he asked.

'No,' she said, turning into his embrace. 'It all happened so suddenly,' she blurted. 'I wasn't sure I was ready, but …'

'You were caught by the moment and let it carry you away,' Will finished. 'That's how it should be. No regrets, just letting go and enjoying yourself.' His embrace became tighter. Lara felt safer.

'I was never unfaithful to my husband before,' she said wistfully.

Will smiled. 'You won't be able to say that again.'

Lara bit her lip, looking up at him, to see if he had rebuked her, but his eyes were closed and his face was a picture of serenity. 'No regrets,' she whispered again. 'I'd just like to know more about you.'

'There's not much else to know,' Will said. His smile was enigmatic. 'You know about Janet, and that my life had been a total shambles before you met me.' He pulled away from her. 'I thought it should have ended on the train lines a few days ago. It just shows that, however desperate you think a situation is, it can resolve itself. You just need that new life, that new challenge.' He kissed her forehead. 'You have been my elixir of youth, Lara. You've given me new purpose. I wouldn't have got this far without you.'

Lara smiled at him. 'I had thought … I was scared you might have been confused in your emotions, that you might have mistaken your feelings of loneliness and gratitude and affection and …'

He shook his head. 'My emotions control me. I don't pretend to understand them. But I know how I feel about you.' He opened his eyes, gave her a little smile. She reached up and kissed him. 'Come kiss me, sweet and twenty,' she said with a coquettish grin.

He kissed her back, gently and continued to hold her, but looked away, out at the coiling streets. He sniffed the air and his eyes twinkled with an excitement she had never seen in him before. 'We're close,' he breathed. 'No one's ever got this far before.' He smiled down at her. 'Do you want breakfast?'

She nodded and he quickly showered and dressed before taking her downstairs. In the foyer of the hotel he found a map and a small brochure about the Papal Palace.

She had expected a continental breakfast consisting of a croissant, a roll and some cheese, but the buffet offered a much more ambitious idea of breakfast. She took a bowl of muesli with natural yoghurt, decorated with slices of fresh banana. Will returned with a roll, some smoked ham and his customary cup of coffee.

'Well, it's been good coming here,' Lara said, 'But, we may have followed totally the wrong clues and be on a wild goose chase.'

Will nodded. 'I thought about that. But everything seems to add up. And I think we would have been disappointed if we hadn't come this far to at least try.'

'But Avignon's a big place. We were lucky with Chester Cathedral ...'

'It wasn't luck. You eliminated the parts of the cathedral that weren't relevant.'

'We were still looking for a needle in a haystack,' Lara protested.

'So we do the same thing in Avignon. We eliminate the buildings that aren't relevant. How many were standing six hundred years ago?'

'A lot,' Lara told him. 'I read it in a guidebook. This place has been around for thirteen hundred years or so.'

'Same length of time as Holywell, then.'

'Things the poet would have seen then might not be standing now. Just think about the soldiers in the Revolution trying to tear down the city walls.'

'The important thing was they didn't succeed,' Will said. 'We can start with the Pope's Palace. If the poet knew Monmouth said Gawain was Arthur's Ambassador to the Pope, then he'd have seen something in the Pope's audience chamber, or the place where the ambassadors stayed. That has to be our first port of call.'

They ate quickly, eager to go out into the streets. The skies were clear and for the first time, Lara was able to predict there was little chance of rain that day. Even so, the wind cut through her.

Her anxiety of the previous evening had abated. Perhaps she was coming to terms with being in France; or perhaps she was secure in the knowledge that Will cared about her and would keep her safe. Every once in a while, Will smiled gently down at her.

The streets were now packed with people going about their daily business. Will walked quickly, excited rather than worried. This was one step closer to their prize. They walked hand in hand like young lovers on a honeymoon.

Having passed through the *Place de l'Horloge,* they saw the great early gothic arches flanking the entrance. High sandy coloured towers with hook-like spires and machicolated walls, which made it look like a fortress to the casual visitor.

The main square in front of the palace was made from cobbled stones the same colour as the palace. A few tourists sauntered down the slopes to the commercial centre of the city; local crowds didn't come here. In the distance, Lara heard the low chiming of the church bells. In the summertime, this would have been a hive of activity. A café, currently shuttered up, would have rows of chairs and tables in the street for visitors to soak up the atmosphere.

Will paid their entrance fee and bought a guidebook. Lara scanned through the pages and realised only a small amount was open to visitors: one part had been converted into a centre for archives and other sections were used as convention halls. 'It'd be just our luck to discover what we're looking for is in one of those rooms,' Will said.

Lara nodded. 'The architecture is from the right time. There are two sections, the Old Palace, built between 1334 and 1342, and the New Palace built over the next decade.'

'So the first palace wasn't big enough for the new Pope? He needed an extension,' Will said with a sarcastic laugh. 'All right, let's imagine we're the poet. He's doing his research, or maybe arranging the clues. So he's a guest, maybe he's met the Pope.'

'Your point?'

'We're not going to find anything in the kitchens or the Pope's bedchamber. The poet would have seen, or put something in, one of the chapels, or the audience rooms.'

From the ticket office, they walked outside into the main courtyard, the *Cour d'honneur*. There was a huge arched window on the right hand side of the wall, about half way up. 'I guess this is where the papal blessing would have been received,' Will said.

Lara nodded, looking at the guidebook. 'But we're not going to find what we want out in the cold, let's go inside.'

She hesitated. For a fragment of a second, she had seen something. The Pope standing at the window, surrounded by cardinals; the courtyard filled with people dressed in old costumes she didn't recognise, their heads bowed in prayer, and the voice of the Pope had sounded with the sonorous tones of a deep, booming bell.

The image was gone as quickly as it arrived, but it left Lara feeling uneasy. The image had appeared to all of her senses. She had felt a warm afternoon sun caressing her skin. She could smell the roasting meats and a thick oily stench of sewage.

Then Will was by her side. 'Are you all right?'

Lara nodded. 'I think I understand now, what you meant about reaching out and touching history.' She shook her head, trying to shake away the image, but it had branded into her mind like a flash-burn on her retinas. 'Come on, Will. Let's get away from here.'

They entered a huge hall. Enormous faded tapestries hung on white walls. At the far end on one wall were portraits of the seven Avignon Popes, and on the next wall, portraits of the two Anti-Popes, resident in Avignon during the Schism.

Will shook his head at the tapestries. 'Those are seventeenth century, the originals must have been destroyed.'

'You're not going to like this,' Lara said, looking up from the guidebook. 'This room was known as the *Salle Brûllée*, the burnt room. There was an accidental fire in 1413, which destroyed all the tapestries, the frescoes and most of the decorations.'

Will made a face. 'Bet the poet didn't take that into account. What do we know about the frescoes?'

'Painted by Italians, they had marvellous colours depicting scenes from the Bible and things like that.'

'Damn, and you can bet one of them was the one we're looking for.' He swore under his breath. 'That's why no one's found the end of the trail. The clues stop here.' He tried to look resolute. 'The fire can't have destroyed everything. Let's have a look around.'

'You'll like this even less,' Lara said. 'During the time of the French Revolution the Palace was turned into barracks and … "renovated" by the soldiers. What the fire didn't destroy, *they* probably had a good go at.'

'We've come too far to give up,' Will said. 'Let's keep going.'

Will became excited when they entered the chapel dedicated to St John the Baptist and St John the Evangelist. 'St John is mentioned twice in *Gawain*,' he said.

'Be careful with those square pegs,' Lara replied.

Her excitement rose as she gazed around the chapel; she had hoped that some of the frescoes, some depicting scenes from the New Testament, would have survived. But Will shook his head in despair. The floor of the chapel was wooden: fire had raged through and destroyed most of the palace decorations. Nothing remained of the tapestries, the frescoes, the floors or the ceilings; they had been replaced with modern replicas.

Room after room they searched, eventually arriving in the north sacristy, with the cross-ribbed ceiling, and animals and fantastic beasts at the base of the vaults. 'We might find something here,' he said, but his voice betrayed resignation triumphing over optimism. 'All the fantastic creatures Gawain encountered on his journey ...'

'And the poet dismisses in a single line,' Lara reminded him. She scanned through the guidebook. 'These are all imitations, just something to show the punters rather than a load of empty rooms. Nothing here is original.'

Finally, they arrived at the Clementine Chapel, the room with the great window from which the Pope would have blessed the crowds in the courtyard. This was larger than any church that Lara had seen. It was light and airy inside, with huge windows in a northern Gothic style, and the cross-ribbed vaults made the ceiling appear higher, although their footsteps echoed noisily around them as they walked through.

There were no decorations inside and Lara saw Will was crushed. Even when she took his hand in her own and gave it a comforting squeeze, he did not look down at her, but kept his eyes fixed upon the window, as if seeking some divine inspiration. 'Perhaps we came to the wrong place after all,' Will said, his voice shallow and forlorn. 'Maybe we were supposed to go to Rome.'

'And where would we start looking?' Lara wondered. 'Rome's a big place and with just the word "pilgrimage", we could spend a lifetime there looking through every building, every document, trying to locate a single Seal of Solomon.'

'We could spend the rest of our lives scouring all the fourteenth century buildings in Avignon,' Will said stiffly.

His melancholy had transferred to her. Her shoulders slumped in dejection. 'Perhaps it was destroyed by the fire then,' she said sadly.

Will had a far-off look in his eyes, but he suddenly snapped back into reality. 'No,' he said forcefully and his words hammered around the walls. 'I refuse just to give up now. Let's look at this logically. The *Life of Winefride* uses a French word, not Latin, not Italian. There were plenty of other pilgrimage sites in France, but both Gawain and Winefride saw the Pope.' His jaw was set. His eyes flicked from one wall to another. 'Where would the poet have gone if he came here? We didn't see the guest quarters, just audience rooms,' he scratched the back of his head vigorously. 'We're missing something obvious.'

Lara shook her head and walked towards the Indulgence window. 'The guest quarters have been turned into storage for the archives now. There'll be nothing in there.' She was already tired. By the window there were stairs outside to go down to the ground floor and into the courtyard. 'He would have made some kind of contingency,' Lara said. 'Something which would have stood the test of time.'

'Let's assume he wasn't the Pope or a cardinal,' Will said. 'Let's assume he was an English noble who made a pilgrimage to Avignon to receive the papal blessing.'

'All right,' Lara said. 'What's your idea?'

'Well, he wouldn't have seen any of these things. He wouldn't have gone into the cardinals' chambers. If he'd been allowed in this building at all then he'd have gone into the big audience chambers. What section of the Palace are they in?'

Lara flicked through the guidebook. 'It's directly beneath us, on the other side of the ticket office.'

They walked quickly down the stairs. Beneath the Great Chapel was a similar sized room with a profusion of intersecting ribbed vaults, the bases of which were sculpted to depict more mythical beasts. There was a fresco around one of the arched windows. It showed a starry blue sky and some of the prophets from the Old Testament. Lara stared at it in disinterest, wondering if she could make a pentacle from the constellations. At the far end of the chamber, a short, dark-haired woman was speaking in a loud voice. 'A guide,' Will said. 'We should have followed her around, or asked her right at the start.'

'You can't just barge in on their tour,' Lara said indignantly.

Will paid no attention. He walked with determination across the room, his footsteps clattering noisily around him. He waited for her to finish speaking before approaching, then giving her a polite smile, he asked: 'S'il vous plaît, madame. Est-ce qu-il y a une peinture ou une statue du Roi Solomon ici dans le palais?'

The woman appeared surprised at the question, then smiled and nodded. She pointed to the arch under which Lara was standing. 'Voilà, monsieur.'

Lara looked up. There were twenty characters from the Old Testament, all of them associated with prophecy, except one. The haloed figure of *Salomon* stood with a forked ginger beard and hair down to his shoulders. His face was the colour of old ivory; his nose was sharp and pointed. His gold-hemmed, long white robe was adorned with eagles or dragons. He carried a phylactery in his hand, a Jewish parchment scroll, bearing an inscription from the books.

'It's him, isn't it?' Will asked, bounding over to her. His eyes were wide with excitement once more. 'How could this have survived?'

Lara read the paragraph in the guidebook. 'It says this has been reconstructed because the painter left a clear description of how it looked.' She stared up 'But I can't read the scroll from here.'

Will squinted at the ceiling. 'You'd not have much hope of reading it if your Latin isn't very strong.' He rubbed his forehead. 'I can make out a few words, but it should be enough.' He pulled out his notebook and wrote the letters as he spelled them out loud: 'Q … U … A … E … R … E, *Quaere lapidem in stella*. That's all it says. ' He sucked on his lip. 'Doesn't sound like anything I've read in the Bible.'

'But what does it say?' Lara was leaning towards him with anticipation.

'It says, "Search for the stone within the star".'

'What star? What did he mean?'

'I haven't got a clue. It's another of the poet's riddles. And it was typical of him to put the clue under everyone's nose. Or over it anyway. Everyone'd expect to see Solomon standing among the Old Testament prophets. No one would think it out of place.'

'So what does he mean, then?' Lara wanted to know.

'That,' said Will, 'will take a little longer to find out.'

10

'All right,' Will said as they walked away from the *Palais des Papes* towards one of the few open cafés south of the square. He sat down at one of the tables outside. Lara sat opposite him, looking up at the decorations on one of the buildings. All of the windows of this residential house had been bricked over on one wall and instead someone had painted in open windows, with characters from nineteen-fifties films conversing with each other. She smiled at the simplicity and effectiveness of the design.

It was a cold morning despite the sun. She pulled her coat tightly around her to keep warm.

'The star is obviously a reference to the Seal of Solomon, the star Gawain carries on his shield,' Will was saying. 'All we have to do is find out what the poet meant by *Hit is a syngne þat Salamon set sumquyle*.' He started to leaf through the manuscript. 'There must be a reference to a stone somewhere nearby.'

Lara shook her head. 'I think we're trying to put a square peg in a round hole again. We've already used the clues from the Seal of Solomon in Chester Cathedral. The same clue can't be relevant to both, can it?'

'Can't it? Perhaps the clues were contrived so just the one clue needed to be hidden within a poem. Then anyone who was looking for whatever the poet was hiding would be scouring the whole of the poem looking for other clues rather than concentrating on the one stanza. 'But then again, you might be right. It's got to be something the poet knew, something important,' Will said. He shook his head in frustration. 'Any guesses?'

'I'd thought about the line where he talks of "þe fordez" and "þe forlondez", talking about something the audience would know. He talks about *the* stone and *the* star.'

Will nodded. 'At least we know we're on the right track. It's the same vocabulary.' A waitress appeared at their side. Will smiled. 'Deux cafés, s'il vous plaît,' he said. When the waitress left, he stared at Lara. 'If someone asked you to think of a star, what's the first thing that comes to you?'

Lara grinned. 'Twinkle, twinkle.'

'All right, aside from nursery rhymes?'

'Something from *Twelfth Night*: *In my stars I am above thee, but be not afraid of greatness.*'

'*Some are born great, some achieve greatness, and some have greatness thrust upon them,*' Will added with a smile. 'What about the other one?'

'*My stars shine darkly over me; the malignancy of my fate might perhaps distemper yours.*'

'*The malignancy of my fate,*' Will mused. His eyes became distant. He looked back at her. 'Anything from *The Comedy of Errors*?'

Lara thought for a moment. 'A few suns, but no stars.' She chewed her lips. 'I keep thinking of when I was in a nativity play. I still remember the words I had to say "Today in the town of David a Saviour has been born to you". I keep thinking of the Star of David and that the sign that led the shepherds to the stable was a star.'

Will thought about that. 'It doesn't follow. The Star of David has six points. The Seal of Solomon is based on the Star of Hermes – only five points.'

'What was so important about Hermes?'

'In Freemasonry, Hermes is thought of as the Great Teacher.' His eyes became distant once more. 'Jerusalem stone was used to build the western wall. It might even have been used to construct Solomon's first Temple.'

'So does this mean we're heading out to Israel?'

'Not unless we can fund an archaeological expedition to find something no one else has managed. The temple was destroyed around two and a half thousand years ago. No one really knows where it is.' He pulled out his notebook and read through his scribbles. He shook his head: 'Solomon's scroll was written in Latin, not Hebrew. The language is important, just like finding a French word in a Latin document. What we're looking for can't be far from here.'

'Or are we just looking at the ecclesiastical language of the fourteenth century?' Lara asked. 'Are we trying to look for too much?'

Will leaned across. 'You'd like to go to Israel?' he asked.

Lara nodded. 'But Avignon's fine as well,' she said with a warm smile.

The waitress appeared with the coffees. Will gave her a smile of thanks and stared at his cup as he poured some cream. He watched absently as the white mingled with the brown, as if it might produce an answer.

'Problem is we could spend a month going through each of the churches and not find the answers we want.' He took a small battered map of the city from one of his coat pockets, circling some of the churches. '*Église Saint-Didier*,' he said, drawing a ring around one of the buildings on the map. 'What else? *Église Saint-Agricol, Église Saint-Pierre, Église et Cloître Saint-Martial, Église et Cloître des Célestins* ... not to mention the *Cathédrale Notre-Dame des Doms*. We could be here all day trying to find out where all the churches are.'

'I don't suppose joining up all the points of the churches would give us a shape of any sort?'

Will looked down at the map, then shook his head. 'It wouldn't work.' They're generally on the left hand side of the city, except one.'

Lara took a sip of her coffee and grimaced at the bitter taste. She gave a long sigh. 'Then I guess we have to do this the hard way,' she said. She ran her fingers over the map. 'Pick a church, any church,' she said with a grin.

'The *Église Saint-Didier* is the closest,' Will said. 'Shall we check that one out?'

Lara nodded. She finished her coffee, making a face at how bitter it tasted. Will left some coins on a saucer and they walked along the *Rue de la République.* The streets were busy: shoppers jostled them as they hurried by. Lara glanced around nervously, wondering if their pursuers had been able to pick up their trail and had already arrived in Avignon. She was relieved when Will ducked down a back street to the church.

It was dark inside the church; almost no light came from outside. Two spotlights illuminated the pulpit making it the focus for the congregation. Flickering candles lit some of the shrines and alcoves. Even the altar at the far end was plunged into blackness.

Lara took a moment to become accustomed to the darkness. There was almost no sound. Somewhere, concealed in shadows, she heard the footsteps of another visitor. She almost didn't dare breathe for fear of breaking the silence. The church felt hostile and unwelcoming.

Will touched her arm and smiled at her. His face looked strange, bathed in the shadows. He pointed at the rows of wooden seats. Midway along the chairs, obscured in the gloom, a couple were sitting. The woman stroked the man's hair. Their faces were close together. He whispered to her.

'Lovers, meeting illicitly, no doubt.' Will's voice was almost inaudible, but a cheeky grin had covered his face. 'What better place to hide than right under the nose of God? No one would think of looking for them here.'

Lara shivered. This building had no heating and the darkness seemed to be closing on her. She cleared her throat and the sound thundered around the building. The lovers did not look up. 'What are we looking for here?'

'A star?' Will said. 'And a stone.' Lara was about to set out to examine the tiny alcoves and shrines but Will caught her arm. 'Don't waste your time. We don't know this is the right place. We could spend hours looking here; that's time we could spend trying to work out about the stars and the stones.'

'Then why are we here?'

'Looking at the church. Seeing if something jumps out at us. We may as well try another.'

Lara looked at Will uncertainly. 'Do you mind if we head to the *Pont St Bénézet*?'

Will gave a dismissive shrug. 'Not at all. Do you think we'll find anything there? Or are you going as a tourist?'

Lara shook her head. 'I've heard so much about the bridge, I thought it might be worth going to see it.'

'As you wish,' Will said, looking bored. They walked back outside. Lara pulled the heavy church doors closed behind her, leaving the lovers to their secrets. They walked along the *Rue de la République* and then through the *Jardin du Rocher des Doms*, a wide park at the rear of the cathedral and the *Palais des Papes*. The winter trees were skeletal and forbidding. The air was still and grey. Lara heard the distant trickle of water. A huge rock towered at the far end of the park, covered with foliage. In a large hollow of the rock, there was a small waterfall. Most of the water had frozen, making bone-coloured stalactites. Vegetation spread over the sides of the hollow, almost enclosing it. Some of the leaves trailed lazily in the water. A small fountain jetted darts of water in the centre of the grotto. A few swans eyed the visitors suspiciously.

'It's beautiful, isn't it?' Lara said, marvelling at the ice cavern.

Will said nothing. She saw the agitation in his face. He wanted to find out about the stars and stones. If she was honest, then she was just as curious, but she needed something to take her mind off the intensity of the journeys, she needed something to tell her that there was a normal world outside of this insanity and once they had finished the trails and could not follow the poet any longer, there would be a normal world waiting for her.

Whatever *normal* truly was.

The *Rocher des Doms* offered a panoramic vision of the city of

Avignon. Lara looked up at the clock tower in the *Place de l'Horloge* and even at the little mannequins ready to strike the bells. She could see the *Palais* and the square in front of it, and behind her, the River Rhône coiled along the side of the walls like an obese grey serpent. The weathered white stones of the four spans of the *Pont St Bénézet* were a brutal contrast of the chainmail colour of the river. A low mist hung over the water and swathed the opposite bank. She stared at the small chapel built into the remains of the bridge. The guidebook said it was called the *Chapelle Saint-Nicholas*.

'Shall we go?' Lara asked.

Will nodded and they descended from the *Rocher* by a series of steep steps that led through the *Rémparts* of the city. At the base of the bridge, she realised they would have to climb a flight of iron stairs and pay to get onto the bridge.

'I don't see why we should pay,' Will said with a mock grudging. 'After all, the bridge doesn't even lead anywhere.'

There were few tourists on the bridge that day. The cold weather kept them away. Lara was disappointed. She'd hoped she might see a number of French people in traditional dress dancing as though they had no cares in the world.

She took Will's hands. 'Come on, Will, dance with me.'

Will pulled away from her. 'I can't. I can't let go when there's so much else to do.'

Lara gave a patient sigh. 'Is that really true, Will? Is finding this so important that nothing else matters?'

'It *is* important. And you want it as much as me.'

Lara stood with her arms akimbo. 'Not at the exclusion of everything else. And I was thinking of something Tantris said: "Don't try and control *all* the secrets or they might end up controlling you".'

'That's rubbish, Lara. I'm not trying to control all the secrets. I just want to find what's at the end of this trail.'

'What if there's nothing at the end of the trail? What if the poet was just trying to get people to visit Avignon: people who believed there was something at the end of the trail? Perhaps, as Feste said in *Twelfth Night*: *Better to be a witty fool than a foolish wit.*'

'Enough with the quotations, Lara.' He turned on her, his eyes blazed. 'Okay, I'll concede. You're right. This *is* important to me. You'll never know how important. But I've been chased across the country by men who'd kill me before the secrets are revealed. I want to know what's at the end of the trail, and I would really like to know soon. If someone thinks it's worth killing for, then maybe revealing what's at the end of this is worth dying for. I'm not much of a gambler, but that's a risk I want to take.'

'Against such odds?' Lara said. Her voice was quieter now. The venom in his voice had taken her aback. 'They might have people in every city. We're just two people.'

'I like those odds. If we can stay just one step ahead of them then before they realise where we are, we'll have moved on again. They've managed to get close to us ... bloody close ... but they haven't caught us, and if we keep moving and if we can work out the clues, then we can be out of here before they ever knew we were in Avignon ... and not waste time by dancing on a stupid bridge.'

Lara nodded. 'I see what you're saying, Will, but if we lose *all* our sense of fun, haven't things just become too serious?'

Will looked at her. Resolution was a bitter mask etched on his face; it was mixed with anger at her defiance. Lara shuddered: it was like looking at Michael's anger. She took a step away when she saw his hands were balled into fists.

Then his eyes closed. He took a deep breath and his shoulders relaxed. He moved towards her and gave her a sheepish smile, then embraced her. He held her tight. She was surprised by his sudden show of affection and the abruptness of his mood swings. But, the strength of his touch made her feel he would always keep the darkness at bay.

'The truth … the truth is I don't like this place,' Will said. 'Like you, I need to be in control of my situation. There's only one way off this bridge and that's back the way we came. I wouldn't fancy my chances of surviving that river at the moment. Even if the current doesn't get us, the cold of the river might.' He gave a nervous smile. 'But this is important to you, so let's do it.'

'We won't be long,' she said, hugging him back. 'Besides, a complete change of thoughts might make us look in a different direction. She took his hands in hers and started to sing *Sur le Pont d'Avignon*.

They danced, holding hands, using each other's momentum to propel themselves. The centrifugal motion seemed to pull all the darkness from her heart. For a short while, she felt all her troubles had faded away. She knew they would still be waiting for her when she left the bridge, but, for the moment, even that did not matter.

Lara's face glowed with pleasure as she broke from the dance. Will was smiling too, but he was agitated, eager to be away from the bridge. His eyes flicked to the building on the shore. She allowed him to lead her away from there. Her heart was pounding, partially with the exertion, partially with pleasure from the dance and partially with fear. Will led her quickly down the iron stairs. They stopped at the roadside near one of the more recent city gates, the *Porte du Rocher*.

Lara's breath caught in her throat. '*Porte du Rocher*,' she whispered. 'D'you think …?'

Will shook his head. 'Sorry to dash your hopes, but the scroll said *lapidem*, not *silicem*. Stone, not rock. And we know he's specific about the words he uses.'

'So there's no point in walking around the outside of the city and checking out the gates?' Lara asked. She peered over his arm at the map. She pointed at the gate in the south western corner. 'What about the *Porte Saint Roch* …?'

Will shook his head. 'No good. For the same reason.'

'Maybe he saw a star in one of the stones on the wall?' she asked hopefully.

Will looked at the map. 'We wouldn't even know if he had a haystack to put that needle in,' Will said. 'Besides, it'd take ages just checking out each of the five main gates, let alone the other gates.' He reached into his coat pocket and pulled out the map again. His eyes widened. 'Five gates …' he said slowly. 'The gates! It's so obvious. The star was right under our nose all the time.' He pointed at the long line of the *Rue de la République,* which ran through the city, through the *Place de l'Horloge,* past the Papal Palace and gardens near the *Pont St Bénézet* and ending at the *Porte du Rocher,* where they were standing. Will took a pen from his pocket and leant against one of the walls, then drew a line from the *Porte de la République* and ended it at the city walls on the northern side of the city, and from that point, he drew a second line down that ended close to the *Porte Limbert,* making an inverted V shape.

'I see where you're coming from,' Lara said. She watched in anticipation as he drew in the other lines:

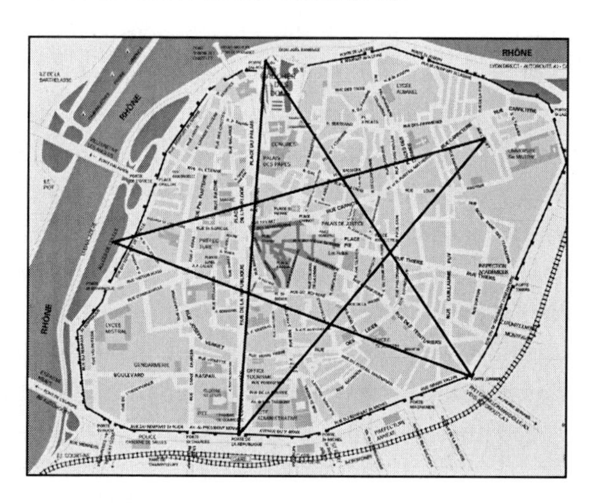

'It's not perfect,' he admitted.

'It's far from perfect,' Lara objected. She pointed to the right-hand point. 'That doesn't go anywhere.'

Will pointed at a point in a square just above the *Rue Luchet*. 'I don't have time to explain that this should be the city walls,' Will said. 'Mostly because I'm making this up as I go along.' His uneasiness was spiced with irritation. 'He was working with the materials he had to hand. He couldn't exclude a part of the city and he couldn't ask the Pope to install a new western gate.'

Lara wasn't totally convinced. 'If you're right ...' she looked at the star again and smiled. 'Once again, the poet's made it obvious so you wouldn't see it unless you knew what you were looking for.' She rubbed her eyes. She was tired. 'But that's only the first part of the riddle. What's the stone at the centre of the star?'

Will looked at the pentagon that was in the centre of the Seal of Solomon. 'We need a more detailed map,' he said.

Lara opened the guidebook. A map was printed on the inside back cover. There were two churches. She stared at the basic map and scoured the guide map for a location. 'The *Église Saint-Didier*, which we've already seen,' she stammered over the word, embarrassed at her attempt at pronunciation, 'and the *Église Saint-Pierre*,' she said, faltering over the French words. 'What's that? The Church of St Peter?'

Will nodded. 'And once again the poet shows us the blindingly obvious.' Lara's eyes narrowed quizzically. Will continued. 'It was Jesus's famous one-liner in the Bible: *You are Peter, and upon this stone I build my church.* The word for "Peter" and "stone" are the same – even in French.' He grinned. 'The poet knew what he was doing. When Gawain gets to the gates of the castle just before Christmas time, the porter utters an oath when he welcomes Gawain stating "By Peter". The clues were in the poem again. Find the church of Peter in the centre of the city by using the gates.'

The *Église Saint-Pierre* was set back from the main commercial road, just south of the *Palais*. The façade was an impressive example of the Flamboyant Gothic style, made from the same sand-coloured, weathered stones as they had seen in many of the buildings of the area. Lara's guidebook said this area had originally been the site of a Roman theatre. A religious building had been on the site for many centuries, but it had been destroyed many times. The main construction of the church had started in the early fourteenth century, and it was finally consecrated in the mid fifteenth century.

Two high towers flanked the tall building. Two dark mid-Gothic windows stared down on them like malevolent eyes, and the great ached doorway looked like a mourning mouth. The heavy doors, twice the height of a tall man, depicted the Annunciation, Saint Michael slaying the dragon, mythical creatures and tiny cherubim carrying cornucopia.

A cloud passed over the sun. Lara was momentarily convinced that one of the chimeras moved slightly, observing her more closely with its snake-like head.

'All right, let's do it,' Will said, pushing open the doors.

Unlike the previous church they had seen, the interior of the church was light. The altar was illuminated in gold, with many wooden arches with painted scenes from the Bible. Lara scanned the faces, hoping to see King Solomon holding a baby in one hand, a knife in the other and with two women at his feet, one indifferent to the death of the child, one pleading for the child's life. It was one of the few stories she remembered from Sunday school.

The door closed behind them, startling Lara. A woman had walked in, dipped her fingers in the holy water, knelt in the aisle in front of the Cross and genuflected. She walked to one of the chairs and her footsteps echoed around the church.

'I don't know how anyone could stay in here,' Lara told Will and lowered her voice as the echo thundered back at her. 'It smells like someone died.'

'Maybe they did,' Will said with a grin. 'You're right though.

They've been a bit heavy handed with the incense.'

'It's not just that,' Lara said. 'The air feels thick, musty. It's like this place hasn't been aired in years.'

'Ambience,' Will told her. He pointed up at the plain, pointed arches. 'These were done a lot earlier than the front. This is an early Gothic style. The front of the building is more Mid-Gothic and a touch of Renaissance as well.' His eyes had a merry twinkle. 'You'll have to forgive me. I'm in history teacher mode again.'

Lara smiled back and returned to her scrutiny of the paintings around the altar. 'Any guesses what we're looking for?' she asked.

'I thought there might be something significant about the word "stone", aside from the joke about Peter, but there doesn't seem to be an important block around here.'

Lara pointed at the last Station of the Cross, engraved from white marble. 'What about the rock that Jesus was crucified on?'

'That's the hill of Calvary,' Will told her. 'We're not likely to find it here.'

'Back to Israel then?' Lara said with a smile.

'Do you have any idea how many inoculations you need to get to Israel?'

'No.'

Will stared at the diamond pattern on the floor. 'Neither do I, but I bet it's a lot.' He gave a heavy sigh, staring into the distance. 'Really important to have the right shots,' he said in a soft and distracted voice.

Lara cleared her throat. 'The manuscript?'

Will suddenly glanced around, as if surprised he was still in Avignon. He opened his notebook. 'It has to be something to do with the clue in the *Palais*.' He read the inscription out loud: '*Quaere lapidem in stella* – it has to mean something.' He rubbed his chin; his face was a mask of concentration. 'Search for the stone in the star,' he mused. 'What other clues would he have provided?' He pulled the manuscript from his pocket and started to read. The Middle English words had become more familiar to Lara. Will was looking at the section where Gawain arrived at his host's castle.

Above the altar was a magnificent golden sun. A huge bird was breaking out of the light, an icon for the Resurrection, no doubt. *A few suns, but no stars,* Lara recalled.

They spent an hour looking at the carvings at the bases of the high vaulted arches, scanning each stone for a tiny engraving. Each statue was analysed in minute detail, with some hope that it might be a reflection from times gone past. Occasionally, Lara called to Will for help, not understanding the relevance of some of the adornments, or hoping he would see something in the images that she did not.

The woman who had come in after them finished praying and left. A few other believers arrived and went to one of the shrines with flickering candles. Some lit a candle and left. Others stayed and waited in prayer, meditating on the flickering flames, reflecting on lost loved ones.

After walking around the church for what seemed like a dozen times, Will slumped dejectedly into one of the pews. He rubbed his tired eyes before he looked up at her. 'What do you say to a coffee and get a break from this place?'

'Lara shook her head. 'A while longer, Will. I can feel the answer's in our grasp.'

'It's the same as the other churches,' Will said. 'No statues of Solomon. No stars, no references to stones.' He peered round nervously. 'Look, Lara, let's get away from here, or go back to the hotel and see if we can find any references to Peter in the manuscript, or see what the porter says Gawain'll find in the castle.' He moved towards the door.

Lara shook her head. 'We're almost on top of it Will, we can't go now.'

'We can't stay, Lara. I'm sensing trouble. Let's get away from here.'

Lara stood resolute. 'You're always sensing trouble.'

'All right, five more minutes,' Will said. 'But I'm going outside. I'm stone-blind here. If I see another Mid-gothic archway, I'll scream. Besides, I'm getting claustrophobic.'

Lara watched Will leaving, wanted to follow him and decided against it. She already knew she wasn't looking for something specifically related to the poem, but something only loosely connected, like a mixture of colours, or a potpourri of legends. A little light fell into the church as Will opened the door. He looked at her back over his shoulder once and then closed the door behind him.

Lara suddenly felt alone, oppressed by the silence in the church. The candles stood erect, sentinels tensing at the same danger that Will had sensed. She shivered with the unnerving sensation of someone walking over her grave.

I refuse to be scared away, she told herself. She marvelled at the great pillars that made up the archways of the church. There were animals carved into the base of the arches. Beneath them, Stations of the Cross were carved in white marble high overhead. She squinted at the Roman numeral of the first Station. '*I think we do know the sweet Roman's hand,*' she whispered.

She realised she'd said those words once before: in Chester cathedral, when she had seen the Roman numeral for ten thousand. Her heart lifted. She was looking for a numeral from the poem; she was looking for the numeral for the star.

She wanted Will to be here, to share the discovery, but she also wanted to prove that the extra five minutes had been worth the wait. She wanted to grin triumphantly, perhaps even to gloat and say "told you so". Perhaps he would then relax; perhaps they could plan their next destination. Perhaps he would take her out to dinner and they would talk as though they had no fears in the world, knowing they would soon be away. Perhaps he would make love to her again with the same intensity as the previous evening ...

She found it hard to wipe the wistful grin from her face. She walked along the aisle. There were two stations on each pillar. She stopped at the third pillar and stared up.

There was a carving of a bear savaging a man at the base of the arches. At least, that's how it appeared: she was unsure exactly what was happening, but the bear appeared happy about it, and the man beneath him didn't. Underneath this were two Stations of the Cross. Here was a depiction of a man helping Christ when he stumbled with the cross. She squinted at the words: *Jesus est aidé par Simon de Cyrène*. She didn't know this part of the Bible. Will would know. She guessed 'Simon de Cyrène' was the name of one of the saints and wondered if her hopes of travelling to Israel would be fulfilled after all.

'I don't understand,' she said. She scoured the carving for some suggestion that this was the object they were looking for. She wondered if she should be looking at the seventh station, because they had seen a seven-sided star in Holywell, perhaps the ninth station as that was the next odd number, or even the eleventh station which was the next prime number. She didn't know.

Her body ached with dejection. She realised she wouldn't be able to walk out with the face of triumph she had hoped to give to Will. Instead, she conceded she needed his help once more, and he would probably be reluctant to return to the church until the following day.

She gazed at the statue of a woman warrior at the fifth station. Her plate armour shone with silver and gold, and the tunic over the armour was the colour of polished ivory, embroidered with golden fleurs-de-lis. Lara smiled inwardly when she saw the tunic had fallen forward to reveal a steel plated thigh – even in the Middle Ages the artists couldn't resist a little eroticism. She wondered if the sword by her side was simply to make it clear that she was a warrior of God.

Her face shone with the radiance of an angel, but her hands

were folded over her heart and her eyes had the concentration of a prayer. She carried a long spear in her hand, with a flag attached at the top. The point of the spear pointed up to the fifth station. She smiled as she realised she was looking at Joan of Arc. She wondered if this was the message the poet was telling her: they should travel to Rouen and visit the place where the English had burned Joan. However, she knew enough history to remember that Joan of Arc was around half a century after the poet would have written *Gawain*.

She remembered the gargoyle in Holywell and followed the line of vision that Joan had been staring at for the last centuries. There was an ornate tapestry against the wall showing the church in times gone by, surrounded by heraldic symbols. It was relatively new, however, and would contain no clues as to the next place that the poet had visited.

She examined the characters on the flag. Most of them were unreadable, obscured by the folds in the long banner, but she was able to make out three characters. Her heart beat excitedly. *G=W*, like the initials that young lovers carved into trees.

'Can't be right,' she said with a shrug. Will had told her that the French hadn't used the letter W: 'War' became 'Guerre'; 'William' became 'Guillaume'. It didn't make sense.

She turned back to the aisle. Her breath caught in her throat. In her excitement, she'd not heard the door opening, or the footfalls in the church. Silhouetted by the light of the door she saw half a dozen men waiting for her, all of them wearing trench coats.

11

Panicking, Lara searched for a means of escape, but the men in the trench coats surrounded her. Her vision started to blacken with fear. Her coat clung to her back. The man closest to her was the man with the round glasses she'd seen from the train in Stamford.

The men in the trench coats took a step closer.

Visitors to the church were startled by the sight of the men. The woman who had been meditating on the candles moved towards the exit, but one of the men stopped her.

'S'il vous plaît, Madame, restez tranquille,' he spoke in a calm voice. 'Ça ne durera pas longtemps.'

The woman took a tentative step away, then fled to one of the shadowy chapels.

The man moved towards Lara. He smelled sour. His expression was unreadable. 'Mrs Greaves,' he said. His tone was flat. Lara gave no answer. 'We need you to return what was stolen from us.'

'I don't have it,' Lara said and winced. She had wanted to say 'I don't know what you're talking about.' Her heart was racing, her chest felt constricted.

'Then who does?' the man said.

Lara did not answer. If they had caught Will outside then they would have searched him, found the manuscript and disposed of him. It meant he was still free. She wished she could have told him of the last clue she had spotted. She might not have been able to work it out, but he would have a chance.

If he was still free.

The man moved closer to her. He towered a foot above her. Now she smelled his breath – the bitter scent of a spray. She saw pockmarks in the skin across his cheeks. She even saw a slight squint in his right eye, making the piercing blue more menacing.

'So, Lara Greaves,' he said. 'Lara Greaves from Stamford. Left from home a few days ago, changes to her maiden name. Seen in Chester, seen in Holywell, seen in Crewe, seen in Marseilles and finally in Avignon. Why would you be in all those places?'

'Sightseeing,' Lara said acerbically. She found a mask of false courage, but he broke it simply by narrowing his eyes. She felt like she was being crushed. Her legs were almost unable to bear her weight.

Like a striking snake, his calloused hand snapped out and grabbed her jaw, squeezing her cheeks together. His fingernails dug into her skin. She tried to pull away, but she was stopped by the man standing behind her. She tried to turn her head, but the fingers dug in deeper. 'Where is Will Stevens?' he snapped. 'Where's the manuscript?'

'I don't know what you're talking about,' Lara said coldly.

His eyes drilled into hers. His face twisted. She looked away, looked at the floor, the ceiling, anywhere but at him. His fingers squeezed harder. He brought her face close to his. 'I only give one chance,' he hissed. 'You could have answered and we'd have let you on your way.' With a sudden burst of energy, Lara snapped her head free from his grip. The two men flanking her grabbed her arms. Her jaw and cheeks stung. Involuntary tears welled in her eyes, but she resisted rubbing her face. That would have given him satisfaction. She stared down at the flagstones again.

'You wouldn't have let me go anyway,' she gasped. Again, she found hidden reserves of false courage. 'So you may as well dispense with false hope and clichéd threats.'

He didn't speak. His silence was an unbearable pressure on her shoulders. She glared up at him.

His lips cracked into a well-practiced, cruel smile.

The woman who had tried to leave returned. A priest followed her. The woman pointed at the men and spoke hysterically in rapid French. The priest glowered at the man. 'Monsieur, s'il vous plaît, vous êtes dans la maison du Seigneur.'

The man gave a placating smile. 'Oui. Et nous allons maintenant.' He turned to Lara. 'They want us to leave. Let's not do this the hard way. Not in church.'

The man standing behind her put a restraining hand on her shoulder. The two others stayed at her side. The one in front turned and walked out of the church. The grip on her shoulder became tighter. Lara gasped. She stumbled forward. She glanced at the priest with desperate eyes. He shook his head sadly.

The skies had darkened. The clouds were heavy with impending snow. Cold scratched her face. Her eyes took moments to adjust to the change in the light: the buildings and streets were covered with an obscuring purple smear. Her eyes flicked desperately, hoping to see Will. If she saw he was safe, she thought everything would be all right.

But Will would have made himself invisible. Her heart sank as she was forced forward. Whatever feelings he might have for her, following the trail was most important. Letting her fall would mean he could buy himself extra days of freedom.

She only remembered fleeting moments of her abduction. She was marched through the narrow streets. If anyone saw her plight, no one came to her aid. She was bundled into the back of a van. A couple of blankets lay screwed up on the floor. Shivering, she pulled one around her and sat on the other.

The engine started. She tried to wedge herself in a corner to avoid being hurled around like a rag doll.

The van soon stopped writhing through the streets: the engine raced as they picked up speed, no doubt on the *autoroute*. She tried to make herself comfortable. She knew it would take an hour if they were taking her to Marseilles. She wondered if she would be able to explain to airport security that she was being taken by force. It probably wouldn't do any good. The men would have concocted a story for her extradition.

Time ceased to have any meaning. She wanted to sleep, but

her mind was racing. Was Will all right? Her thoughts galloped to what she had seen in the *Église Saint-Pierre*: would Will go back, now their pursuers had their prey; or would he leave the church alone, fearing that lightning could strike twice.

Her thoughts flew to the statue of Joan of Arc. She was an anachronism as far as the poet was concerned: a fifteenth-century warrior against the English. And what of the secret she had carried for half a millennium.

But what if the poet was essential to the establishing of the church? she wondered. *Even if he'd died before the completion, those constructing it would have completed things. The poet wouldn't have allowed the trail to reach a dead end, even though he was in his grave.*

This posed another problem. Her understanding of the clues relied on two icons. Any Catholic Church showed the Stations of the Cross, and she was assuming the fifth station was tied in with the Seal of Solomon because of their understanding of the message in Solomon's scroll. What statues had been beneath the other stations, did they also have statues of warrior maidens with a banner? What would she have found then? Perhaps G=L, or even G=G?

Now her mind hurtled back to the barge: Will had already told her the French language had transposed letters. If this was the clue they had been looking for, it seemed the poet had wanted them to see what was, once again, blindingly obvious. All they needed to do was find out what it meant to find out the next location.

Her heart fell. There was no "they" any more. She was out of the game. And Will didn't know what *she* knew.

She listened to the roar of the engine; speeding to an unknown destination. She felt the van urgently weaving through traffic. She wondered if her captors believed she knew more than she actually did. Clearly, they had found her through surveillance rather than working out the clues from Solomon's Scroll.

The engine died. She heard a door slamming, but no one came

to open the van doors. She heard muffled voices talking outside. Then the van started again, but she could no longer hear the sound of tyres hissing against tarmac. She jerked forward: the van was driving up a steep incline.

Then her ears were filled with the sound of roaring engines. Deafening engines. She felt movement. The intensity pushed her back against the van doors. She wanted to place the blanket behind her, but she found the pressure too much even to move. The vehicle lurched once and then she felt her heart leap into her stomach.

My God, she thought. *We're flying, flying back to England … or somewhere else.*

The plane levelled out after a while. Her heart was palpitating; she clung to the blanket with perspiring hands. Rational thought gave way to panic. What if they planned to open the cargo doors and drop the van outside?

She latched on to two thoughts: no department, covert or otherwise, had the budget to drop a van out of an aeroplane. More rationally, however, she knew the men needed to interrogate her, find out what she knew about the manuscript, the clues and Will.

Will, she thought. She wondered if he was safely on his way to the next clue, having found the statue and worked out the relevance of "G=W", or perhaps Will had worked out that there was a different *lapis* in the middle of a *stella*. Or perhaps he didn't realise she'd been abducted and he had gone back to the church to find her. What would he think if he saw she wasn't there? Would he be waiting for her in the hotel room? Would he be waiting with the same intentions as the previous evening …?

Will, she thought again. She wondered why her captors had been in such a hurry to take her away from there. Why had they not left her in a stronghold and forced her to reveal where they had been staying?

She felt another change in the pressure. She didn't know how long they'd been flying. Time had concertinaed. Sometimes she felt she'd been in the van for hours, other times she felt it had been a matter of minutes. The aeroplane banked to the left. She heard the engines powering down. She blocked her ears, trying to control the effects of the drop in altitude. She tried to swallow, to stop the sensation of her blocked ears. She felt her stomach falling; her heart remained in her throat. Then there was a bump, which threw her off balance, another bump and the racing of reversing engines, and then the aircraft taxied to a halt.

She had no idea where she might be. Perhaps she had been dropped in some surreal detention centre, like the Village in *The Prisoner*.

The van's engine started. Someone was shouting orders outside. Lara was tipped backwards as they reversed down the cargo hatch. Then she was jostled as they crossed uneven, perhaps rocky terrain. Then she was forced forward: the van was going downhill.

The sounds of the engine changed to an echo. It was less intense; the van drove slowly before coming to a halt. The sound of the doors reverberated as they slammed.

The rear doors opened. Lara wanted to inhale fresh air, but she found the air was fetid, like breathing in a mausoleum. A blinding torch pierced the back of the van. Lara shielded her eyes with her arm. She tried to see the world beyond the spectral, shadowy figures. It was impossible to make anything out, but the world was black, unnaturally black. Her instinct was to run. A hand restrained her before she had even started to move. She guessed it would be futile to try.

The lights darted, scratching negative images in her eyes. She couldn't focus.

Then someone squeezed into the van beside her. Her coat was pulled away and her sleeve rolled up. A tourniquet was wrapped around her arm. Her fingers started to tingle. She struggled, trying to free herself from the grip, but the man held her firmly.

A quiet, but firm, voice sounded in her ear. 'This is a sedative. You'll be fine if you relax.'

Lara tried to be calm. She had never liked needles, but she didn't fight against whoever was injecting her. She did not trust the voice, but at the same time, she had a terrible vision of the needle breaking in her vein if she fought against it.

'Where am I?' she asked, but her voice sounded groggy and distant, as though a drunk was trying to speak to her from ten metres away.

If her captors had heard her, they didn't answer her question. Grips tightened on her arms, but her arms felt numb and the grips seemed remote. Suddenly she was looking into her lap. No matter how much she tried to straighten her neck, the muscles wouldn't respond. She tried to speak again. Her tongue felt thick in her mouth; her lips felt rubbery. Whatever she said didn't make sense. Her shoulders couldn't take the weight of her head any more. She felt herself plunging into a black abyss.

*

She was aware of the thumping headache before she was awake. It was the kind of headache that followed a late night of excessive drinking, the kind that stabbed at the back of her eyes; the kind where she daren't open her eyes because she knew the room would still be spinning.

Eventually the brilliance of the light prised her eyes open. She clung to the side of the bed, trying to steady the swirling motion of the room. She was disorientated; she thought she was in hospital, but couldn't remember getting here. The whole room was arid of life and smelled of disinfectant. The windowless door was shut tight. The odour of the decontaminated sheets clawed at her throat. She stared up at the long beams of strip lighting and wondered if there was some way to turn them off. Even if there was, she doubted if she had the strength in her legs to get up to do it.

Like a dim memory from an unhappy childhood, Lara was able to claw through the darkness of the past and to recall she'd been in Avignon, at the *Église Saint-Pierre.* After that, everything had become a hazy blur. She wondered what the time was, what the date was, but her jewellery had been removed. There was a pale band of skin where her wedding ring had been once, but she couldn't remember if she'd removed it before she had left Stamford, or whether ... she remembered the men in the trench coats ... they might have taken it. Either way, there was no remorse that it had gone.

She looked down at the starched blanket. She was wearing a bland hospital gown.

Someone undressed me, she thought in a mixture of panic and outrage. *Someone undressed me while I was sleeping ...*

She glanced around the small, sterile room. There were no decorations or hangings.

She strained to hear sounds around her, but her only answer was the faint buzzing of mild tinnitus. No footfalls outside the door, no sound of rain lashing outside, no hum of vehicles on distant roads, no phones ringing or emergency buzzers.

She rolled over and closed her eyes again, trying to calm her headache. Her head was filled with the purple explosions of an oncoming migraine. Nausea clutched her stomach. She needed to sleep, but the disorientation, the headache and the insipid room were not conducive to rest.

Lara had never felt suicidal before. She was terrified by the unknown, but in the past she'd believed there was some doorway in her future that could be opened, some way to escape her troubles – even if that escape led her into the arms of someone like Michael.

But on the wrong side of a closed door, not knowing who was on the other side, she found her choices were limited. She was out of control in this situation. She looked down at the hospital gown again and flushed at the thought of the violation. A blanket of misery covered her.

Her spinning head had lessened. If there were no decorations, it was because there was no intention of making it comfortable. This wasn't a place of convalescence. More like a research centre. It had an aura of death. Lara grimaced, wondering how many times the very sheets upon which she was lying had been used to cover the face of the dead.

Was this where Will had cowered in the dark, battling with the demons of his depression, scavenging for sandwiches? Could he be in a neighbouring room trying his best not to puke up his guts?

She continued her surveillance of the room, trying not to move her eyes too quickly. The walls seemed to melt and re-form, like waves on the shore. She squinted, needing her glasses, as she searched for some kind of spying device. She gave up. They were so small these days they could be hidden in a light fitting.

She struggled to her feet, stumbled once as she tried to walk across the room, but managed to catch herself before she fell.

The walls were soft to the touch. *That's it then,* she thought bitterly. *They've locked me in the proverbial padded cell.*

The silence beat against her like the relentless pounding of noiseless waves. She wanted to whistle and sing, but the room subdued her. Any sounds she made were swallowed by the quiet.

She jumped at the sound of grating at the door: the sound of a bolt being drawn back. At first, she wondered if she had imagined it, wondered if her insanity was starting to eat through her mind like a parasite and she was starting to imagine sounds.

The door opened. A small man peered in cautiously. He wore thick horn-rimmed glasses. His hair was thinning, his face was gaunt. She guessed he was in his forties. Even though he was wearing a laboratory coat, Lara saw his arms were spindly. If she had been at full strength she might have tried to rush him and escape.

Escape to where, though?

He hovered at the threshold of the door like a vampire, seemingly uncertain of what he should do next. Suddenly she felt her energy draining away from her. She staggered and leaned back on the bed. The man stepped forward and caught her arm. His touch was gentle. He helped her back onto the bed.

'I did want to ask if I could come in,' he said in a soft voice. 'I am Eric Marsh, Mrs Greaves.'

Lara said nothing. She clenched the sheets, trying to steady herself. Marsh, however, appeared embarrassed. 'I am sorry,' he said, sounding genuinely contrite. 'I meant to say "Miss Halpin."'

'Just "Lara" will do.' She indicated to the white walls. 'This is a lousy hotel.'

Marsh smiled stoically. 'I do not think you realise the predicament you are in.' Lara noticed he avoided contractions in his speech. Perhaps he thought relaxing his dialogue would undermine his situation. Perhaps it was to punctuate each word with importance.

'Where am I?' Lara asked. She couldn't hold her head up. Her teeth clamped together. Marsh remained standing. Lara turned her head, feeling the tendons straining in her neck. Peering past him, she saw the door was slightly ajar; stark light slipped in from the passage beyond.

Marsh cleared his throat as if trying to drag her attention back to him. 'I must say I am ... very pleased to meet you,' he said eventually. 'I have been following you with some interest over the past years. You have proved to be a most ... unusual subject.'

'Subject?' Lara's voice was incredulous.

'"Subject?"' Marsh mimicked. Only now, Lara realised that a dangerous heart beat inside what had appeared to be a fragile shell. There was an unnatural glint in his eyes, something calculating and menacing. Now he moved towards her. Lara tried to back away across the bed. He stayed at the bedside, standing over her. 'Yes, Miss Halpin. You have been the subject of a little research that was undertaken ten years ago.' He smiled and there was that underlying blade of fear slipping between Lara's ribs. 'You were "selected", Miss Halpin. We hope the next drug tests will provide us with … interesting … results.'

Lara's heart thumped. 'What are you talking about?' Her voice was breathless. She rubbed her forehead with the back of her hand. 'I've never taken drugs in my life.'

Marsh shook his head sadly. 'That is what we all believe, Miss Halpin. True, we never consciously take drugs. But we find them every day, caffeine, nicotine, even pesticides …' His voice trailed away as he reached toward her. Lara pulled away. His hand touched the top of her hospital gown. Expert fingers rolled up the sleeve of her left arm. She pulled away again, thinking he wanted to administer something.

He smiled uncomfortably. He seemed to read her thoughts. 'Nothing up my sleeves, Miss Halpin. You took the drug ten years ago and now you are feeling its effects.'

Lara looked down at her arm: the BCG scar, the immunisation against most illnesses for the future. Just thinking about it threw her back ten years to a time she and her classmates had been forced to queue in cold corridors, roll up their sleeves and endure the pain, not just of the needle itself, but the scabs which had later followed, along with the torments and threats of bruising from others who had already overcome the pain. There were those who told of how painful the experience had been, so as to show their bravery at enduring the agony. There were those who'd declared it had not hurt at all, to show their resilience to pain. Worst of all were those who had refused to speak about it, fearing the silent humiliation of breaking down and crying in front of all their friends.

'Bacillus Calmette-Guérin,' Marsh said, as if stating the full name would place this interview within a more scientific content. 'And our opportunity to administer a series of drugs to school children who knew no better than to do what they were told.' Seeing the look of fear on Lara's face, Marsh continued in a softer voice. 'Do not worry, Miss Halpin. Although the drugs will yield some interesting results, they contained no harmful side effects, and they certainly contained no steroids that would have shown up on a drugs test. The drugs are designed to stimulate the neural pathways we know so little about.'

Lara's mind fogged with incomprehension. 'Neural pathways?' she stammered.

'Brain pathways,' Marsh said, as if trying to explain to a small child. 'They were designed to enhance sections of your brain.'

12

Lara stared at him, incredulous. The violation she'd felt by being undressed was nothing compared to the desecration she felt her body had endured. 'You put drugs into me?' she raged. 'How dare you? Who gave you the authority?'

Marsh gave a hard smile. 'I am sorry.' His voice was laden with sarcasm. 'I am not permitted to tell you who sanctioned it. Let us just say it was at the highest level.'

If she had had the strength, she would have thrown herself across the room, screaming like a banshee, and attempted to claw away his eyes. She managed a feeble push and managed to avoid falling face down on the bed.

'Calm yourself, Miss Halpin,' Marsh said. 'This was something that happened a decade ago. What makes you think you can change the past now?'

'I can damn well have a go at the people who have got me here now,' Lara growled.

'And where would it lead you?' he said. 'My dear, you are one hundred feet underground in some seventy acres of underground tunnels. There is a labyrinth down here. You would never find your way outside without our help.'

Lara pointed acerbically to the hospital gown. 'So that's why you put me in this mega-sexy dress. You're scared I might try a version of Theseus and the Minotaur down here.'

Marsh stared at her blankly. 'No. It is because we want the room to be as sterile as possible.'

A thought crossed her mind, a dark thought. She found a voice for her fear. 'Those drugs,' she said shakily. 'Would there have been any after-effects?'

Marsh shrugged. 'That is what we want to find out. We expect there to be nothing more than enhancements to your brain patterns.'

She did not take her eyes from him. 'Would they have harmed my baby?'

A grin spread across Marsh's face like the rising of the golden dawn. 'You had a baby!' he exclaimed with excitement. 'I had forgotten.'

'Would they?'

Marsh gave a smile that Lara wanted to hit. 'You must excuse me, my dear Miss Halpin. I need to consult other motes. I shall return later.'

She wanted to try to follow him out of the room, but hardly had the strength to move, let alone dodge past him and overpower him.

She slumped down on the pillow and closed her eyes. She needed to urinate, but all she had seen was a chemical toilet in the corner of the room. She contracted her muscles. She could wait.

But there was the added complication that the muscles were clenching in her pelvis.

Bloody men! Why did they abduct her when she had the cramps, the headaches and *needed,* as a matter of urgency, chocolate?

She didn't know for how long she lay there. She curled up on the bed. Her skin felt clammy to the touch. She tried to think of something to take her mind away from the discomfiture, but the antiseptic smell of the walls kept dragging her back to her own problems.

Will, she called silently. *Where are you now?*

She spoke Will's name again and this time it was a searching question, rather than a desire. Something had been nagging at her ever since she had been bundled into the van in Avignon. Marsh had confirmed it. If she had been the object of their search, then why had the men in the trench coats been searching for Will? Was it simply a coincidence that Will had stolen a book from the same people who were about to search for a woman they had experimented on a decade before?

Were there two groups pursuing them for different reasons?

Things weren't adding up.

Without a watch, without any distractions, not even a window to look through and see the gathering clouds, her thoughts glided away from the room, back to the *Église Saint-Pierre*. "G=W". She tried to think of the relevance of the letters, beyond the linguistic application. The poet would have known the poem would be read in England. If they had been in the right place, the letter would have been tied in with the code, somehow.

A part of her couldn't shake off the thought that they were no more than a childish profession of love, like carving initials in a tree.

Her stomach cramps were becoming more intense. Despite becoming hotter, she pulled a blanket around her and circled into a small ball. The discomfiture was severe.

She had fallen asleep at some point. She woke with a start to see Marsh standing over her, grinning his toady little smile.

'Glad to see you are awake, Miss Halpin,' he said.

She managed to find her voice. 'I need some sanitary towels,' she told him. 'And a shower. I need some water and painkillers. I'm not doing anything until I get them.'

Marsh's cruel smile widened. It revealed yellowing teeth. 'On the contrary, Miss Halpin. You are the one who is in pain. I am sure we can arrange these things for you once you have been co-operative.' He sat down in a chair opposite her. She hadn't noticed it before; he must have brought it in with him.

'We have waited for a decade for the opportunity to study you, I am sure we can wait another couple of days. You, on the other hand, look like you want to deal with the matter in hand. The sooner you tell me what I want to know, the sooner I can arrange the things you want.'

'Women are a lot more resilient than that,' Lara snarled. 'I've lived with this for a long time. One more painful period isn't going to floor me. I challenge any of you men to go through the pain of childbirth.'

'Fortunately, we do not have to,' Marsh said. 'But I daresay that you will not want to live in your own filth for the next few days. It is up to you to help us first. Which brings us to the first question: when your daughter was born, did you notice any abnormal thoughts during the latter part of the pregnancy?'

'You mean aside from the craving for Dairy Milk chocolate and mayonnaise? Not really.'

'That is not what we're interested in, and you know it,' Marsh said coldly.

'What am I supposed to say then? I haven't been looking for "abnormal thoughts"? What's the difference between an "abnormal thought" and a daydream?' She heard her voice raising, tried to control it, and then couldn't care less if she expended all her energy screaming at Marsh.

Marsh didn't seem to notice. He reached behind him and poured a small glass of water. 'There is no need to fuss yourself, Miss Halpin. We simply want to know what you have been going through.' He handed her the water. She held it uncertainly, wondering if it was drugged. She didn't know whether to drink it or to throw it in his face. Eventually thirst overcame revenge and she drank quickly. The water tasted stale, but it moistened her mouth. She still had a dry feeling at the back of her throat. She gave the cup back to Marsh. He didn't offer any more.

He sat back in his chair and folded his hands behind the back of his head. Lara stared at him coldly. 'All right, what do you want to know?'

Marsh seemed to hesitate for a long time, making Lara wonder if he actually knew the question he wanted her to answer. Eventually, he fixed his gaze on her. She shifted uncomfortably. 'How did you work out the *Gawain* clues?'

Lara smiled coyly. 'Intuition.' She started to wonder how

Marsh knew about the manuscript and how he knew about the clues. But she imagined he knew an awful lot.

Marsh broke her thoughts by glowering at her. 'Scholars have been looking at *Gawain* for six hundred years, and you are going to tell me you managed to work out everything in a few days? I don't think so.'

She pulled her hospital gown down over her knees. 'Maybe it's because I'm not a scholar. I see things differently.' She indicated to the unknown world beyond the room. 'I assume this is the place the text was taken from.'

Marsh slammed his hand against the end of the bed angrily. 'Stolen from, Miss Halpin. Will Stevens stole the manuscript from us, and you stole it from him.'

Lara raised an eyebrow. 'As a historian, Will had every right to take it. He said you're hiding documents of public and historical interest. I'm sure he saw the justification.' She coiled her legs beneath her and tried to sit up. 'You're not going to believe anything I say, so I may as well tell you the truth. It *was* intuition that sent us looking in Chester. That was Will's intuition. After that, it was simply a case of looking at the facts as they were presented to us and reading the clues in context.' She let this sink in, then continued. 'Until modern transport, what we did would have taken months, even years of travelling. Gawain travelled for a month in North Wales. We did it in an hour. That's why no one's done it before.' She laced her fingers behind the back of her head, mimicking Marsh's posture. He scowled at her, but said nothing. 'I want some answers,' she said. 'I've answered your questions, now you can answer some of mine.'

'I do not owe you any explanations.'

'All right,' Lara said. 'But remember: I'm the one with the answers you want. You may think you've got the monopoly on asking questions, but you don't. If you don't tell me what *I* want to know, these could be really short interviews.' She took a deep breath and felt nauseous with the smell of disinfectant. 'I want to know whether it's me that you've been following, or Will. Will's been paranoid you'd find *him* ever since I met him. But when push comes to shove, I'm the one who's here and he's not. Now, are you telling me all his fears were in vain and you've been looking for me all along?'

Marsh raised an eyebrow. 'And what makes you think he is not here as well?'

'Because I don't think you know where Will is and you're hoping I'll tell you.'

Marsh said nothing. Lara continued. 'You're avoiding my question,' she said. 'My question was, were you looking for me?' When Marsh didn't answer, Lara tried again. 'Okay, what's this drug you've put in me, instead of the BCG inoculation?'

Marsh grinned. 'Oh, you had the BCG inoculation,' he said. 'This was just an optional extra we installed as well.'

'I'm not a computer where you can install "optional extras". Now, what was it?'

'All right, Miss Halpin,' Marsh said coldly. 'Let us start spelling this out for you in words you'll understand. You have been a guinea pig for an experimental serum. It was administered with your BCG inoculation.'

'What does it do?'

'It was designed to open your neural pathways over the course of the last ten years. When we designed it, it was hoped you would develop a certain ... affinity with the past.'

Lara shook her head. 'This doesn't make sense. If you wanted to look into my past, wouldn't it be less expensive to use hypnosis? This is basic psychology we're talking here!'

'People lie under hypnosis,' Marsh told her. 'I am talking about something more prolific. I am not talking about remembering the past. I am talking about an *affinity* with it.'

'To what end?'

'To invoke past memories. To look at it from an academic point of view, to view the past from the eyes of another. The serum makes it possible to look back in time and call upon the memories of that time.'

'I don't follow ...'

Marsh sighed patiently. 'Think of it as *folding* time, time before you were born.'

Lara still didn't understand. 'What's the point of that?'

'For academics it is a tool to discuss what happened in times gone by, to interact with people from a forgotten era, to understand their desires and motivations, to speak with a clear authority on issues that elude us.'

'You don't strike me as a historian,' Lara said coldly.

'One might say I am, from a certain point of view,' Marsh said with a malicious smile. 'You see, beyond science, my field of interest is *military* history. I am interested to know just how much you can *affect* the times gone by with this little serum. We want to see if you can go back in time and change history.'

'You're insane,' Lara said. 'You're absolutely bloody insane. You can't change the past. It's something that's already happened. Even if I did, how would you know? If you sent me back in time to stop the rise of power in Germany, suppose I refused to kill Hitler on the battlefields of the Somme, but devalued the Reichsmark to cripple the country. Didn't that give Hitler the finger of power? Time didn't change, it just made sense. Or what if I killed Hitler and some more brutal dictator took his place and decided not to fight a war on two fronts, but made peace with the Russians until they had conquered Britain and America? How do you know history could be made better with my intervention?'

'Miss Halpin, you are giving a very narrow-minded view of the timelines. From each moment there is an infinite amount of possibilities. We live in only one of them.'

'And what about if I went back and killed *you* as a child? How would you then have developed the serum to give me the ability to send me back in time?'

Marsh feigned a yawn. 'That old chestnut, the temporal paradox. History would have corrected itself. Paradoxes are healed, however the greatest changes can still be performed.'

'This is ridiculous,' Lara said, her words raw and angry. 'I've had no flash-backs beyond my over-active imagination, and even if it were possible, don't count on my co-operation.'

'Have you finished?' Marsh asked.

'No,' Lara said. 'I want to be able to shower. I want sanitary towels, aspirin and plenty of water.' She glared at him. 'And I want chocolate. Lots of it.'

Marsh sighed. He waited until she calmed down. 'All these things can be arranged,' he said. 'But only when you have done something for us first.' He took his glasses and cleaned them, slowly and meticulously. 'Now then, let us look at your friend Will. Was it he or you who broke the codes of the poem?'

Lara smiled sarcastically. '*He did it with a better grace, but I do it more natural.*'

'And what does that mean?'

'It means she's being a stubborn cow, and hiding behind Shakespeare's quotations,' said a voice at the door.

Lara turned. Her heart leapt with joy when she saw Will standing there.

Marsh turned. 'You should not be here,' he said. There was a threatening undercurrent to his voice.

Lara's relief at her rescue suddenly changed to horror as Will did not stride forward to release her but instead stood his ground. 'She'll tell you nothing, not without coercion,' he said coldly. 'She has a small talent for keeping things to herself.'

Pieces of a jigsaw slotted together. Realisation was a bitter pill. 'You've been working with them all along.'

'Got it in one,' Will said with a nasty smile. 'I've been on the payroll of these people for a long time. We didn't need to find out the secrets of the *Gawain* manuscript, we just wanted to see how you reacted to an empathy with the past.'

'So when you were acting as a diversion, letting me go on ahead, you were actually feeding them information?'

'Right again,' Will said. 'By the time you'd got us to Avignon and found the clue in the *Palais*, you'd shown enough potential to start the next part of the experiment.'

'Bastard!' Lara locked his eyes in open warfare. 'And I thought you cared about me.'

Will's shoulders tensed. His face filled with contempt. Then he leaned towards Marsh conspiratorially: 'We've got enough. She's a valuable subject. Hit her with it.'

Marsh moved towards her. Like a magician performing a sleight-of-hand trick, he produced a syringe from nowhere. In her fear, Lara discovered a new source of strength of which she'd never previously been aware. She leapt from the bed.

Will caught her by the gown. His hands were no longer strong and protecting, but brutal and violent. He forced her back to the bed and pinned her against the mattress.

Marsh loomed over her. 'There is nothing to worry about, Lara. This is a kind of BCG injection. It is the same serum you received a decade ago. This will just enhance the brain pathways, so you get a clearer vision of the past.'

Lara writhed on the bed, but couldn't break herself free from Will's grip. 'Stop struggling,' Will hissed at her. His hand closed over her throat. 'Stop struggling or I'll squeeze you till you burst.' She managed to hack in her throat and spit the phlegm at him. He did not flinch when it hit him on the chest, instead he watched it impassively as it dripped back down on to the hospital gown.

She thrashed again as Marsh rolled up her sleeve, but the pressure from Will was too great. Suddenly, her strength drained from her. Fighting against them was useless.

'You'd better hope this fries my brains,' she growled at Will. ''Cause when I get free, I'm going to kill you.'

The needle slid into her vein. Tears sprang to her eyes. Then it was all over. She felt a burst of adrenalin, then with a palpitating heart, she slipped into darkness.

13

She was falling through a void. Her muscles had frozen: her voice had solidified in her throat. There was no light, no sound, not even the wind against her face as she fell. Then, like light at the end of the tunnel, she saw a pinprick of eternity.

I'm dead, she tried to say, but her vocal muscles were long gone. She focused on the circle of light. From this distance, she couldn't see if it was coloured white, or red, wondering if she would be going up … or down.

Her vision swam again. Her pupils dilated, as the pinprick shifted and shimmied in front of her. *It's like being an angel,* her mind whispered to her. *It's like being pure light, infinite, no physical boundaries to hinder me. The only limitation is my own imagination.*

Her mind drifted, floating through an ethereal plane. The pinprick of light expanded into a slim taper of white. She felt neither warm nor cold. The light danced in front of her eyes, like fireflies trapped in a jar. It expanded, becoming a burning, hazy glow. It increased in intensity, increased from discomfort to pain. She tried to turn away, but the light was overwhelming, engulfing. Then sound burst around her, the sound of violent but indistinguishable voices.

Her body froze. It twisted in agony, agony stemming from the biceps on her left arm. The sound exploded again, playing through her memory like a stuck record. Gradually her mind was restricted by the confines of the brain.

'She is waking,' the voice said. It was the voice of Eric Marsh, but it was muffled and contorted, playing at a slow speed. Time, as she knew it, had slowed to a crawl.

But when she thought about what Marsh had said, she heard him speaking again. 'She is waking.' So, in this dream state, time was hers to control. The record, which had been stuck at her point of consciousness, could be sent back. She saw time was like a river flowing from its estuary to its source; ashes turning to wood or coal.

At her command, she heard Will asking, 'Is she going to be all right?'

She saw Marsh walking across the room, shrugging. 'Does it matter? There are more subjects after her.' He placed a hand on Will's shoulder. 'Hush,' he said. 'She is waking.'

Time rolled back, and further back, like raindrops rising to the sky, and becoming clouds; like mighty oaks diminishing into small acorns. The strips of white, she realised, were the light, prising her eyes open. For a moment, she couldn't discern the shapes within the room: the chamber was a grey miasma of twilight. Then she heard a voice, stating, 'You shouldn't be 'ere, Miss'; and the sterility of the room had become a large storage area, and the man who spoke was a uniformed soldier, grimy with sweat, his hands firmly fixed around a large ammunition shell.

Back, and further back, like a film in reverse, clock hands travelling anti-clockwise, numbers decreasing, elderly people becoming tiny babies, back and further back. She was no longer in Bath; her body was not restricted to one location.

She saw wide fields being ploughed, as men urged on great oxen to pull an iron farming frame. The ground was furrowed. Crows cawed and picked at worms in the overturned soil.

She saw a jaundiced timber-framed hall; outside steps led to the first floor. A tall man sat inside. His blue eyes were warm and brilliant with intelligence. The dark room was lit by candles flickering in a breeze. He was hunched over a small desk, scratching a quill against vellum. The air was thick with tallow. The man glanced up, not turning, but looking at her reflection in the window. He nodded an acknowledgement, took a moment to pause and to stroke his grey beard. Then he turned back to his work, undisturbed by the distraction, as if she was expected. She squinted at the page in the candlelight; a huge illuminated letter covered a corner, a large capital S in a box, with the flourish extending to the end of the folio. His eyes narrowed in concentration. He spoke aloud as he composed the first lines in heavy downstrokes and lighter upstrokes: *Siþen þe sege and þe assaut watz sesed at Troye, I-wysse.* 'Old codes,' the man said in an unfamiliar accent. He looked into the glass again, gazing at her as he spoke, tapping the manuscript. 'Codes you should understand. But the times are changing, and so must the *alpha-beta*.'

Lara felt her grip on reality slipping. 'What does it mean?' she said hurriedly.

The man shook his head, and gave an enigmatic smile. His eyes twinkled merrily. 'You already know.'

As if trying to swim against a current, she was swept away. She was being dragged forward. The acorn had fallen from the tree and produced a mighty oak. The river had reached its estuary. Lara refrained from opening her eyes, as she heard Will speaking: 'Is she going to be all right?'

Marsh's voice was distant, but she heard him stepping forward. 'Does it matter? There are plenty more subjects after her.' Pause. 'Hush. She is waking.'

The pretence was impossible to maintain. Her eyes fluttered open, she tried to shield them from the glare of the overhead lighting. Her temples were thumping with an unholy hangover. She fixed her eyes on Marsh. 'I want aspirin, *now*!' The words exhausted her. Her jaw slackened. Her limbs felt like they were tied to the bed, her body was saturated in sweat. The cramps were now crippling her. She closed her eyes, but all she saw were purple explosions of pain: not the pinprick of light, not eternity. When she opened her eyes again Marsh was looming over her. 'Aspirin,' she managed to hiss.

Marsh simply said, 'Not until you tell me what you saw.'

Lara's eyes squeezed shut. Sweat dribbled into them. The salt stung, but she didn't have the strength to wipe it away. 'Nothing,' she said, and the words were like sandpaper against the back of her throat. She half opened her eyes, to see silent conversations taking place between Marsh and Will.

'I'll get the aspirin,' Will said. He turned swiftly and left. Lara tried to unwind, in spite of her pain, but knew the men had been messing with her brain; most of the pain was psychosomatic. The aspirin would exorcise the pain demon from her mind.

Lara's heart sank as she watched Will leave. Part of it was the pain of his betrayal; part of it was loneliness after the love they had made between them.

Then Marsh was standing in front of her again. 'Well, Lara, will you speak to me now your lover has gone?' He tapped his foot impatiently. 'There are things to discuss.'

She breathed in the stale air. Her eyes closed as the room began to spin again. Her head fell back into the pillow. She hoped that time would pass.

When she opened her eyes, Marsh hadn't moved. Will hadn't returned, the pain was still in her head. Any courtesy that Marsh had initially shown was gone. His eyes blazed with impatient temper and his hands wrung together with rage. 'What did you see?' he snapped and then without waiting for an answer, 'Where is the manuscript? Will tells me it was not where he left it. He said you had stolen it.'

'Then Will is a bloody liar,' Lara said with as much venom as she could muster. Her efforts sounded feeble. 'He never let the manuscript go. It was always in his pocket.'

Marsh appeared to consider this. 'I shall investigate that. If you're lying there will be serious consequences.'

'Spare me the macho talk,' Lara said, her voice wheezing like a lifelong smoker. Suddenly, any hope suddenly drained from her. Her vision of the future, any future, was empty. Within the last hours, everything she had believed, everything she had wanted, had been torn away from her. She was walking down that same pathway to oblivion as Will had, when she had first seen him on the railway lines. Facing such bleakness, a part of her wished the drug *had* fried her brain. At least then it would be over. They could have dissected her brain while she was still alive and thrown her still-living body into an incinerator. She would become another missing person. Vanished, having escaped from her abusive husband.

This is how Will felt.

But at the same time that thought crossed her mind, she knew it wasn't true. Will hadn't been suicidal. It had been a means to get to her.

She was sinking in horrible realisation. *Nothing* he'd said had been true. Janet's death, losing his job, wandering aimlessly until he accidentally found this place; it was all lies to let her hear what he thought she wanted to hear so she would pity him, travel with him … even love him.

She closed her eyes, hiding her face like a wounded animal, so Marsh wouldn't see her tears.

She didn't stir when Will appeared a few minutes later. She heard the thud of a plastic beaker on a solid surface and the rustle of foil as a couple of tablets were pushed out of a packet. They could have been a brand name, or illegal drugs, or a placebo for all she cared. She had become used to the pain and, although she was attacked by the occasional sharp stabbing, it had mostly reduced to a dull throbbing.

'She is faking,' Marsh said with an indignant snort. 'This is a waste of time. We need to know what she saw. I am running out of patience.'

She instinctively knew Will was standing over her. This time, she didn't feel safe as she had when he had watched over her on the barge.

'Give me some time with her,' Will said. There was strength in his voice. She opened her eyes. He smiled. It was the same smile he had used on her before. He had a malicious look in his eyes when he spoke to Marsh. 'I might get some answers out of her.'

'She does not have long to cooperate,' Marsh said. He strode away, then turned back. 'Find out where the manuscript is.' He left, slamming the door behind him.

Will pulled the chair to her bedside and sat down next to her. Lara glowered at him. 'I'm less likely to tell *you* anything.'

'I thought you'd say that,' Will said earnestly. There was sadness in his eyes. 'You probably won't ever understand or even accept why I did what I did, but hear me out.'

Lara sat up in bed. She reached for the tablets and the water. Will leaned over to help her. She snatched them away, unwilling to accept his help in any way. She took the tablets and gulped down the water. Her jaw set as she waited for him to speak. 'Come on, then,' she said. 'Let's hear your reasons.'

Will seemed to be caught off guard. Clearly, he hadn't thought she would agree to hearing his explanation. He stumbled over the first words. 'There's a lot I've said that hasn't been true, but there are some things ...'

Lara shot him a pained expression. 'Spare me this much, Will. I'm not interested in you saying, "Poor little me, this is really the reason I suffered." The only truth you told me was that you'd stop at nothing to get your hands on the secrets, and I helped you. I can't believe I helped you on your way.'

'You'll never know how true that is,' Will said. 'But I don't suppose you want to know why.'

Lara shook her head. 'How long have you been working for them, Will? Marsh trusts you with me. He doesn't think we're going to be planning an escape.'

'They had me over a barrel,' Will said softly. 'The bit about wandering and accidentally finding my way in here and finding the manuscript ... that was true. They caught me and they interrogated me.' His voice had become hollow, his eyes became distant as if the memories of his ordeals were too much for him to bear.

Lara's voice was just as forlorn. 'If you're trying to scare me, it won't work.'

'Just answer their questions now, Lara. They've never heard of the Geneva Convention here. They don't just ask questions …'

Her face filled with disgust, and shame burned his face. 'I don't know how long it took them to realise I wasn't a spy. They were like children, asking the same question over and over until they got the answer they wanted. And then they explained to me the seriousness of the situation. I'd seen things I shouldn't have. But they were willing to overlook this, if I helped them to follow you. Gain your trust, find out how much the drug had affected you.' He sat back in his chair, and closed his eyes. 'Besides, they gave me a couple of major incentives, one of which was that I got time studying the *Gawain* manuscript.'

Lara fixed cold eyes on him. 'How many people did you have to sell out just to stay close to that damn book?'

Will said nothing for a while. His eyes fell to the floor. 'They'd been following you for years,' he said eventually. 'If it wasn't me, it would've been someone else. It would have been so easy, just to look away, to not have made friends with you.' His voice dropped again. 'Not to have fallen in love with you.'

'Oh, spare me,' Lara said in sour mockery. 'I'm not falling for that one. If you loved me, you wouldn't have let them stick that needle into me. You don't know that the serum wouldn't have fried my brains.' Her lip curled. 'And even if it had worked, supposing there was some truth in what Marsh was saying, what if I had stepped back in time? Supposing I hadn't been able to come back?' She shook her head. 'This is a ridiculous, childish fantasy. We all dream about going back in time and seeing what life was like. But it's not possible. Time is a constant. You can't get on and off it, like a bus. You can't decide on the passengers.'

Will's face fell. 'I suppose nothing I say or do will make you believe … in me.'

'Nothing at all.'

'Then I have nothing to lose by telling you one thing. I think there are other people looking for the *Gawain* manuscript. The manuscript, not you. At least one group. Maybe more. I don't know who they are. I'm sure I saw someone in Chester and again in Avignon. They were following us, Lara, just not going to make a move until they saw where we led them. I think this is something big, Lara. It wasn't just Marsh, there was someone else.'

Lara shook her head. 'You're a pitiful little man,' she said. 'You try to justify your ... horrible deceptions with these pitiful excuses.'

Will gave a long, stoic sigh. 'So you have no faith in anything I've told you?'

'None whatsoever.'

'It's important to have faith,' Will said sadly.

'Not when the guru leading you is a lying, two-faced son-of-a-bitch, who would sell his grandmother if it got him one step closer to the end of an empty trail.'

'But don't you see, Lara?' Will said suddenly enthusiastic. 'It isn't an empty trail. *You* know what the Gawain poet said in the *Église Saint-Pierre*. You know what code he was hiding. Please, tell me what it was. I can get away. I can follow up that code. I can finish off the trail. Please, Lara, trust me.'

Lara sat bolt upright in bed and stared at him incredulously. 'Is that what this is all about? After all you've done, you want me to trust you? You've got another think coming. You're an evil, scheming little man,' she said. 'And this good cop — insane cop routine you've got with Marsh won't help. I didn't find anything in the *Église Saint-Pierre* and you know that. I was only in there for five minutes while you called for backup.'

Will's shoulders slumped. 'I don't believe you. I think you *did* find something. How can I persuade you that I believe in the code of the *Gawain* manuscript more than anything else in the world?'

Lara smiled bitterly. 'Oh I believe you. I have no doubts you'd stop at nothing to get your hands on whatever's at the end of this trail. That's why I'm stuck in a hospital room and you want to discover what I know. Well, forget it, Will. You sold me out. If I get out then you can leave me the hell alone.'

'I'm sorry you feel like that,' Will said. 'We were good together.'

'"Were", being the operative word,' Lara said, anger seething. 'You know, I hope you find what's at the end of the trail. I hope it's not what you expect. Just a massive disappointment.'

Will stood up, slowly and deliberately. 'I'm sorry you feel like that,' he said again. 'My attempt at peace has failed.'

'I doubt you're surprised, after what you did.'

'You won't be seeing me again.'

'Thank Christ for that.'

'I'll leave you in the capable hands of Eric Marsh.' He strode across the room, then stopped at the door. 'It's a real shame, Lara. In another place, another time, under other circumstances, we could have had something really good.'

'Well, we didn't,' Lara said, and turned over on the bed, so she didn't have to watch him leave.

*

Time had slowed again. She didn't know whether it was the effect of the drugs, or sheer boredom. Her mind wandered, a daydream rather than the drugs. She thought about the man who had been scribing the poem. She had looked into the eyes of the *Gawain*-poet. And what had he said? *Old codes, codes you should understand. But times are changing, and so must the alpha-beta*. Her mind whirled, as she tried to fathom the message he had tried to give her. The *alpha-beta,* the alphabet, was changing, the use of letters such as 'thorn' and 'yogh' was coming to an end. This was the final code he was trying to explain to her.

To the poet, the alphabet wasn't the twenty-six letters that she knew. "I" and "J" were interchangeable. So were "U" and "V". The letter "Z" was barely used. Instead, 'yogh' followed 'G', and 'thorn' followed 'T', to give a series of twenty-five letters.

And, from the message she had seen in the *Église Saint-Pierre,* she knew the poet's code meant that G=W. It was not, as Will had explained to her, the language developing and borrowing from French to English. This was a simple code wheel, like one she had used as a child. "W" replaced "G"; "Y" replaced "A"; "A" replaced "H".

'That's all very well,' Lara said aloud. She had the code for replacing the letters, but she had nothing to which she could relate it. There was no string of apparently random letters for academics to play with in order to find anagrams.

Exhausted, she closed her eyes again. There was nothing else to do, no clock to watch the seconds ticking by. Whatever else Marsh was trying to do, he was succeeding in dehumanising her. Eventually, through sheer boredom, she would beg to tell him everything she knew.

Her mind folded once again; she allowed herself to look back across the past. But this wasn't the effect of the drugs. This was merely a desire to be free from the confines of the room. She dreamed that the past was like looking through a murky window.

Her dreams were interrupted by the sound of a sliding bolt outside. Her eyes snapped open. *Damn it,* she thought, *don't I have any peace around here? No privacy? Won't people knock before they come in?*

She pulled herself up in bed and pulled the sheet up to her chest as far as she could as Marsh entered. He dropped a pair of slip-on shoes on the floor by the side of the bed.

She tried to stand. She lost her balance and steadied herself by the bedside. The muscles in her calves felt like they had contracted. Her ankles throbbed. Marsh did not attempt to help her. 'Can you walk?' he said. He did not smile.

The pain in Lara's legs subsided a little, becoming only a tingling in her toes. 'A little way,' she said. She slipped into the shoes.

'You are to come with me,' he said. 'A shower has been arranged for you.' Lara didn't like the way he said "arranged". It reminded her too much of the fatal showers in Auschwitz. But she summoned her strength and, concentrating, placed one cautious foot in front of another. It was a slow process. She leaned against the door frame.

'Come on,' Marsh said. 'Time waits for no man.' He cocked his head to the left, indicating she should walk that way down the corridor. He followed.

The air was cold. The tunnel, barely illuminated, stretched into the darkness, punctuated by side passages. If this was the underground complex in which Will claimed to have hidden, she understood why the occupants had found it so hard to find him. She imagined she was right in the heart of it, as far from an exit as she could be. It would be folly to try to escape.

Since folly you have sought, you deserve to find it, she thought. She'd read it in the manuscript.

That damn manuscript, she thought, wishing she had never seen it. It should have been burned in the fire, and not left for maniacs like Marsh to use as a source of leverage against her.

She could make out numbers painted on the white-washed walls, indicating storage areas. When she thought back, she recalled something Will had said, about this location being a storage facility in preparation for D-Day. As they walked, she saw the numbers decreasing and, as they passed an intersection, she peered to the right. She was in 'J' corridor, which meant she had to try to navigate herself through ten of these corridors to find her way to the surface. But then that meant accepting all that Will had told her about his confinement in the tunnel as gospel. Given the number of lies and half-truths that he'd already told, she wouldn't trust anything that he'd said.

Narrow iron tracks ran next to the walkway, no doubt a throwback to the war days. The passage had a thick odour of sulphur and stale smoke. Small wisps of stagnant cloud hung in the air. There was a foul stench of damp decay emanating from piles of rubble.

Occasionally the passage broke into larger chambers, supported by white pillars. She saw ladders and wondered if they led up to the world above, or to just another level of this abyssal labyrinth. In other places, when the rails on the ground curved round a corner, Lara saw circular columns and rough walls in the distance. As they moved, the passage became more hospitable. They emerged into a long arched corridor. Rooms with heavy bolted doors were scattered along the way. The rooms without doors were filled with rubble strewn from other places in the complex. Water banged, trapped in long metal pipes. Air growled as it was circulated through a huge rusted convection fan.

They turned another corner. Now the passage had become a semicircle with a low roof. Lara had completely lost her sense of direction. But Marsh didn't seem to be deliberately disorientating her. She thought that Marsh was too self-opinionated to waste time on a sight-seeing tour.

'Watch your head,' Marsh said, indicating low iron girders. Lara ducked. 'You will turn left here,' Marsh commanded. Lara did as she was told.

After a while, she saw the warming glow of distant lights – perhaps the bunks and the mess hall. The rest of the corridors had been so dark, that she squinted against the glare as they moved towards them.

The corridors were empty; no doubt Marsh didn't want her to contact any of the workers in the area. Perhaps they might be sympathetic to her.

He pointed to a small cubicle. 'You will find all that you need,' he said, in a curt voice. He gave a long, drawn-out sigh, as if Lara's washing herself was a personal affront.

'Sod him,' Lara muttered. She pulled the shower curtain around her and quickly checked the cubicle for spy-holes.

Finding nothing, she disrobed. She turned on the taps, not knowing what to expect, but bracing herself against a poison. It did not come. Instead, it was a bracing cold jet of water, which knocked the air from her lungs as it hit her skin. She gasped, but did not cry out. She washed herself quickly, using caustic soap that had a bitter smell of disinfectant. It was fast, but thorough. She enjoyed the moment while it lasted. The act of cleaning herself was more than just a physical act. It seemed to wash away some of the traumas which had etched themselves into her life. She wondered if the waters of Holywell would do the same thing, except that this would be more than a cleaning of her skin, but a cleansing of her inner soul, her inner spirit.

'Come on,' Marsh said, from outside. 'I do not have all day.'

She towelled herself down and found a clean set of underwear and a packet of sanitary towels, which she applied. Then she dressed in the hospital gown again and, wrapping the towel around her hair, returned to Marsh's custody. He did not speak to her as they walked back along the corridor. Instead she was left to her silent observation.

Through the maze of passages once more, Lara tried to trace a path through the darkness, something which would lead her away from her captivity. She glanced down at Marsh's belt; there was no sign of a weapon. Evidently, he felt he didn't need one.

Despondency fell across her. Instead of seeing escape routes, she saw ladders that might lead to a single room in which she'd be trapped; she saw doors to the left and right that might lead into a room with no other exits; she saw passages which went on forever; weakened floor-boards that concealed a pit. Only Marsh could provide her with freedom, unless her fantasy dream-wanderings meant she could move her body as well as her mind.

She wondered if she had been trying too hard and if she could relax a little, then she would be able to roam through time. But she caught the thought and dismissed it as soon as it had appeared. She did not believe in these hopes. She had to believe in something more logical. She had to believe in herself. That was where the problem lay. Will had drained her of any hope. She needed a reason to believe.

Without knowing precisely where she was in the complex, she discovered they had reached her room once again. A large meal was waiting for her. This wasn't the "bread-and-water" rations she'd expected. There was steaming roasted meat and fresh vegetables, dripping with gravy. Evidently, the shower and the walk through the passages had been timed down to the last minute, so the meal would be placed in her room and the carrier could scurry away before Lara turned the corner.

'What's this?" Lara asked with a smile. 'A reward for good behaviour?'

Marsh raised an eyebrow. 'No. It's the condemned's last meal.'

'What?' Lara's voice was incredulous. She tried to speak, but her words had frozen in her throat.

'Since you are unwilling to disclose anything we wish to know, we assume you have outlived your usefulness. You are to be terminated in the morning.' He gave her a malevolent smile. 'Unless you can think of something to tell us. Something useful, something honest.'

'But ...'

'Save it until the morning,' Marsh told her. 'And in the meantime, *Bon appétit*.'

Suddenly, Lara had lost her appetite.

14

The sound of a bolt jarred Lara from her troubled slumber. She shook herself awake, couldn't believe she'd managed to sleep in the face of Marsh's threat.

The door opened. She expected to see Marsh, either for his final inquisition, or with a squad of executioners. Instead, Will rushed in, breathless, panicked, carrying her holdall. 'Come on,' he said. 'Get dressed. We're getting you out of here.' Lara didn't move. Instead, she stared at him quizzically. 'Come on,' he urged. 'We don't have time. They're coming for you soon.'

She sat up slowly, wondering if this was another part of the trap, designed to fill her with a false sense of security, but Will's eyes were full of desperation. He was already by her bedside, pulling out clothes from the holdall. 'Come on,' he urged. Sleep still pinned her down. Will came to the side of the bed, pushing the untouched plate of food on the floor out of the way. When he tried to help her out, she sprang away from him like a startled cat.

'Don't touch me,' she hissed, and her voice was low and menacing. 'Don't you come anywhere near me, you bastard.' Will looked hurt, but he kept his distance.

'I'll turn my back on you while you get dressed,' he said. 'But get a move on.' Her senses were still confused by sleep, but as Will turned his back, she slipped out of the hospital gown and pulled on a pair of jeans and a sweatshirt.

'Okay, I'm ready,' she said. She sat down on the end of the bed and pulled on her trainers. Will reached for her hand, but she pulled away from him.

'All right,' he said. 'But come with me.'

She shook her head. 'I don't trust you. This is a trap.'

Will sighed stoically. 'The other option is you wait until Marsh turns up to interrogate you. You don't have any choice.

Please,' he pleaded. 'I know what their interrogations are like.'

Lara's jaws ached. She was torn. She couldn't stay here. If nothing else, the boredom, the frustration and the fear, were all too much to bear. But she also couldn't trust Will to hold the keys to her freedom. Slowly, she moved towards the door.

Will glanced out into the corridor then led the way. Lara followed. She looked over her shoulder as she hurried away. Her fingernails were digging into her palms. She couldn't see anyone, but that didn't mean they weren't being followed or watched.

Will turned right and then right again into a dimly lit subterranean car park; he opened the back doors to one of the vans parked there. 'Get in,' he said. Seeing her hesitation, he stepped towards her. 'Come on!' he almost screamed in frustration. 'There are blankets in the back. Cover yourself over with them.' Lara clambered in and hid herself among the blankets. The van doors slammed, then the engine started. The van crawled slowly through the compound; then she was tipped back as it went up a ramp.

The van stopped, the engine idled. Lara heard a low murmur of voices. She could just discern Will's voice, explaining that Marsh had sent him on an errand and he'd return shortly. Someone asked what he was carrying in the van. Will replied with a nonchalant grunt. Lara's fear increased. Will *was* selling her out. She imagined him making a facial gesture to explain *she* was in there. Either the van would be searched and she would be discovered, or he was taking her to her interrogation instead of Marsh coming for her himself.

She was shivering uncontrollably, pulling the blankets tight around her.

Then she heard the clattering of electronic gates as they opened; the van started up again, as she heard Will breathing a sigh of relief. 'We're outside ... you can come out now.'

She didn't move, and he didn't speak again until he stopped the van. 'This is Bath station,' he told her. 'I've got you a ticket to

London.'

He opened the door, then stepped back to let her out. She stared out uncertainly, seeing commonplace objects as if for the first time. She would never again dismiss a street light as unimportant, nor would she be able to avoid staring up at the stars without her eyes being filled with wonder. She clung on to her holdall, as if relinquishing her grasp would make this new-found freedom go away. She didn't trust Will, didn't trust his motives, but she knew better than to turn down an offer of help. When she peered up at the stars, she knew she couldn't go back underground like a lab rat.

'Your train ticket's in your purse,' he said. 'From London, you can go wherever you want, as if you'd never heard of me.'

'If only that were possible,' Lara said acerbically. She wanted to turn on her heels and walk away, not saying any more, but a question burst from her lips. 'I don't understand. You went to a lot of effort to get me captured, why are you setting me free?'

Will's face fell. 'Let's just say I've had split loyalties all the way along. I've decided what side I'm on.' Darkness seemed to be pressing down on him. 'The reason why Marsh asked you about the manuscript is because I told him I didn't have it. That was true. I mailed it to my sister, for safekeeping. She's expecting you, if you want to finish off the trail by yourself.'

Lara stared at him coldly. 'I don't know what to say.'

'Then say nothing. I don't expect you to forgive what I did. But one day you might understand.' He closed the back doors of the van and looked at her sadly. 'I'm sorry, Lara, I truly am.' He stared at the ground. 'I'd better go.'

Her heart quivered with shock. 'You're not going back, not after setting me free?'

'One way or another, they'll find me,' Will said with a long sigh. 'I may as well give in gracefully and throw myself on their mercy, rather than keep running. That'll just make them more angry.'

'They'll kill you,' Lara said in an empty voice.

'Maybe,' Will said. 'But I'm tired of running. They'll probably question me first, but I won't tell them where the manuscript is.'

'No,' Lara scowled, 'You'll tell them I've got it and they'll be looking for me instead. That's your way.'

He couldn't meet her gaze. 'They made a promise they couldn't keep, Lara; I wanted to believe them.'

She watched as Will turned and left; and flinched as he shut the door. She wanted to say something, but that would have been the Lara from before they had gone to the *Église Saint-Pierre*. Instead, she steeled herself, picking up the holdall. It was a worthless gesture. She felt empty. How could she try to explain her feelings to him, when she couldn't even explain them to herself?

Inside the station, she quickly scanned the timetables for the next train to London. It would arrive in ten minutes. Will had kept things tight so she would spend as little time lingering as possible.

And as she walked through the ticket barriers down to the platform, she wondered if this was how Will had come into possession of the manuscript in the first place: that he had unwittingly assisted someone, who had then laid down their life, so that he might go free. Perhaps, this was Will's way of returning a favour, and repaying a debt about which she knew nothing. Perhaps this was why Will had always seemed to be on edge.

She realised she was perspiring in spite of the cold. She was constantly looking over her shoulder, expecting to see someone in a trench coat appear at any moment. And who was the man with the glasses? One of Marsh's minions, or a superior?

She kept walking around the platform as she waited for the train, never stopping in one place for more than a couple of minutes. She unzipped her holdall. Her purse was lying on top of her folded clothes. The train ticket was in one of the credit card slots. She took out a couple of coins for the drinks machine – she didn't need a drink, but it was something to take her mind off things. She also picked up a magazine from the newspaper vendor.

Soon, she was sitting on the train and the lights of Bath faded behind her. She ventured up to the buffet car to buy a coffee, hoping to keep herself awake. Only then did she realise her purse was thick with money. She also saw a piece of paper: a note from Will. She hurried back to her seat to read it.

Lara,

I sent the manuscript to my sister. You can go to her if you want to follow the trail to the end.

Don't let it fall into the wrong hands. If you worked out the clues in the Église Saint-Pierre, then you'll know you're close to the end of the trail. Together we found four locations. The poet emphasises the number five.

I don't blame you for hating me for what I did. I had no choice.

W

He had included an address at the bottom of the message: *Home Forest House, Home Forest*. In an additional note, Will had recommended travelling to Amersham and suggested taking a taxi from there to Home Forest House.

There was still the complication that, although she knew *how* to break the last code, she didn't know where that last code would be found without searching through the manuscript itself, which would only remind her of Will and his betrayal.

But when she closed her eyes, she knew she'd go directly to Home Forest, because she wanted to know what the poet had gone to such great lengths to conceal. It didn't matter what she thought of Will: she realised that, like him, she was becoming obsessed with the code. She scowled. She was becoming like him in too many ways.

The train rattled along the tracks and she let her thoughts wander as they approached London. The station clock read that it was approaching half-past ten at night. Her body clock was completely out of synchrony. She wanted to believe that this was because of her captivity, but part of her knew it was something to do with the drugs that she had been forced to take. They'd altered her perception of time, forcing her to amend her preconceptions.

She flicked through the magazine, but couldn't really focus on the pictures, let alone the words. She tucked it back into her holdall as the train approached Paddington.

Stepping off the train, she glanced around cautiously, wondering if she would see anyone following her. She went down to the underground and took the Bakerloo line to Marylebone, then bought a ticket for Amersham.

She sat down, looking at her watch every few minutes. There were a few other people on the platform. No one seemed to be paying any attention to her: a weary commuter read a newspaper; there was a teenager wearing a hoodie; a tired-looking, middle-aged woman.

When the train arrived, she picked a carriage with quite a few people, hoping she might blend in with the crowd. She was anxious about travelling through London, especially at night.

Come on, she chided herself. *How old do you think you are?* She had been willing to run away from a marriage, now she was running again.

But running had been a lot more fun when Will had been around.

She stopped, her heart fluttered. How could she think of Will in anything but the most negative of terms? It didn't matter that he'd tried to make amends. More to the point, she wasn't convinced he *could* make amends. This could be another betrayal.

And, it was *he* who'd got her into this situation in the first place.

She chewed her lips, fighting confused emotions. She had

cared about him once and now she was condemning him. She wanted to understand *why* he had done what he had done. Judging him without understanding was the attitude she'd have expected from her father, or worse still, from Michael.

Suddenly, she felt sick. Was she turning into the same kind of person as them?

Gradually, the number of people in the carriage grew less and less. She regarded the last man suspiciously as he folded up the newspaper he'd been reading all through the train journey, and walked to the same door at which she stood waiting for the train to stop. But once out of the station, he hurried along in a different direction, paying Lara no attention whatsoever.

A lone taxi waited outside the station. The driver regarded her blankly as she asked him to take her to Home Forest and, as she was unable to offer any clue as to where it might be, he grudgingly pulled out a road map. It took both of them a couple of minutes to find the small hamlet of only a few houses. It was no more than six miles to Home Forest, but Lara had been unprepared for the London prices and she blanched when she watched the meter rising.

The hamlet had no street lights. The taxi headlights had flashed across an innocuous street sign. The driver pulled up at the end of a long drive which led into wooded grounds. As Lara walked slowly into deeper darkness, she couldn't make out the shape of the building itself. Her footsteps echoed around the driveway in the silence. It was unsettling. Lara wanted to run before she disturbed anyone. She had expected to hear dogs barking at any moment, warning the owner of her presence, but there was no sound, save the wind blowing through the trees. There was no distant hum of traffic and, even though Lara should have been comforted by that silence, it only succeeded in further unnerving her.

She hesitated at the front door. Who, or what, was waiting on the other side? This could just as easily be another trap. Will was a master of deception and could be telling her once again what she wanted to hear. But a part of her believed Will was genuinely contrite, that he would have done anything to make amends for his betrayal.

As if watching herself in a dream, her fingers closed around the heavy iron-ringed door knocker, lifted it and let it fall. It thudded once, sounding like a gunshot in the night.

She waited in silence, torn between running and staying. The moon passed from behind a cloud, picking out the features of a lion holding the door-knocker in its mouth. She saw the house was a mock Tudor style.

An outside light turned on and Lara was dazzled by the glare. A woman, who was taller than Lara, dressed in a striped rugby shirt and blue jeans opened the door. She did not greet Lara immediately, as she had expected, but instead regarded her with an expressionless face, before slowly nodding. 'You're Lara, right?' she said. It was all Lara could do to force a nod. 'I'm Olivia Simmons. Will told me to expect you.' She stepped back, allowing Lara to cross the threshold. She was shivering, still fearing a trap.

But there was something about Olivia that made deception seem impossible. Her welcome had not been false. Instead, her expression was the confusion of someone who'd been asked a favour, but told not to ask any questions.

She led Lara down a corridor decorated with an abundance of plants, and into a large, palatial kitchen. 'I didn't know if you would come,' Olivia was saying, as she flipped on a kettle. 'Will wasn't very specific.'

Lara stopped by the kitchen table, still clinging to her holdall. 'I need to ask you something.' Her voice sounded distant. 'How do I know you are who you say you are?'

'The same reason I know you are who you say you are. It's an uncommon practice in this cynical generation, but it's called trust.'

Lara dropped her eyes, embarrassed. 'Sorry.'

Olivia grinned. 'Don't be so silly. You had a right to ask. If anything, I should apologise. I forget not everyone has the same sense of humour as me. I had an advantage, Will described you in his letter. I thought he was waxing lyrical about you.' Olivia stepped toward her. Lara backed away. Olivia raised an eyebrow. 'Would you like me to take your coat? I'd like you to stay.'

Lara stumbled over her words. 'Sorry,' she said again, flustered. 'It's ... after all I've been through ...'

'You're fragile,' Olivia finished.

'You know?'

'I don't have to *know*. I can see it in you.' She walked over to the work surface. 'Is coffee okay?'

Lara nodded. She let the holdall fall on the floor and shrugged off her coat before sitting down on a rustic chair. Olivia returned with two mugs, a jug of cream, a bowl of sugar and a plate of biscuits, as if she had been expecting visitors. She sat down opposite Lara at the old farmhouse table.

'Will sent me a manuscript. He didn't tell me much about it. It's in a foreign language to me. He said I should only give it to you; you'd know what to do with it.' Olivia stopped speaking. Her eyes became far away and her jaw tensed. Eventually she spoke again. 'Is Will all right? Her voice was distant. 'I mean, he's not in any kind of trouble, is he?'

Lara tried to avoid Olivia's gaze. 'There's trouble,' she admitted. 'I just don't know how much.'

Olivia sighed. 'I've been worried about him. After our parents died, he was the only family I had left. And then his wife died and he went missing and ...'

'Wait a second,' Lara interrupted, her voice filled with disbelief. 'His *wife*? He was *married* to Janet? The newspapers said she was Janet Rose.'

Olivia nodded. 'She always used her maiden name. Didn't he tell you about her?' She shifted uncomfortably. 'I bet he didn't tell you about his son either?'

Lara shook her head. She suddenly realised she was standing on a precipice of what she knew, or didn't know, about Will.

'Roger was Will and Janet's only child. Will absolutely adored him.'

I was adored once, Lara thought.

Olivia smiled sadly. 'We'd had this big joke that it was the only way our line was going to continue since my divorce.' She looked uncertain. 'I'm not sure I should be telling you this.'

'Please,' Lara said. 'I need to understand.'

Olivia swallowed painfully. 'When Roger died ...'

'He died ...?' Lara managed to gasp.

'Will never spoke about this ... Janet found out he'd cut himself on holiday. Roger was a brave little soldier. Didn't tell anyone ... and he died. Tetanus.'

Lara nodded, fighting back the tears that Will couldn't cry. She imagined Will and Janet sitting helplessly by the bedside, helpless to do anything except to watch him die. She wondered if Janet had blamed him for their son's death, and that had been the wedge which had forced them apart, and when he had tried to reconcile the relationship, Janet had driven away, blinded by anger and grief.

But Olivia was continuing. 'The grief was too much for Will. He withdrew into himself. He actually left Janet for a few days while he tried to sort his head out. And she went to get him.'

'And she never arrived?'

Olivia nodded slowly. 'She went to bring him back safely and then ... his guilt was suddenly multiplied. He *tried* to sort himself out, God knows he did, but it was too much ... and he was drinking ... and then he just vanished. The next thing I know it's a year later and this parcel turns up.' She paused for a moment of sad indecision. 'He hurt you, didn't he? He hurt you so very badly.' Lara didn't answer. A lump had formed in her throat. 'I don't know what's happened between you and him,' Olivia continued. 'It's none of my business. And I don't expect you to swallow this, because it's like I'm defending my brother. But Will rarely does anything without a reason and most of the time only he knows that reason. So please don't judge him too harshly.'

Lara didn't know what to say. She thought Olivia would understand if Lara told everything. She would probably have given impartial advice. But Will was the only family Olivia had. She couldn't tarnish his memory. So she said nothing and hoped Olivia would not infer too much from her silence.

Lara cleared her throat, feeling uncomfortable. But Olivia understood the hint. 'How silly,' she said softly. 'You want the manuscript? Wait a moment, I'll fetch it.' She stood up quickly, leaving Lara to stare around the kitchen with tired eyes. At one end, a back door opened into a conservatory. Beyond, she saw ferns, Japanese maples, bamboos and anemones – something that could have been part of another continent, or another time. For a moment, she forgot everything. As she stared, she would have sworn that, if plants had the possibility of a human ego, then these would have been delighting in the attention. The leaves seemed to expand in a floral embrace. Then she realised she was not looking at them across the room, but across time. If she had concentrated, she could have seen these plants when they were tiny seedlings, watched them as they yielded their first leaves, and then as they became the dense foliage she saw in front of her.

'Are you all right?'

She was suddenly startled by Olivia's voice next to her. She hadn't heard Olivia returning and now her intimacy with the plants seemed taboo. 'I was just admiring your collection,' Lara said, by means of an apology.

'They are lovely, aren't they,' Olivia said. 'I'm lucky with that conservatory. It seems to let in the right amount of light for that kind of plant. Perhaps when it's lighter, you'd like to see round the grounds and some of the flowers there.' Lara nodded eagerly. 'Anyway,' Olivia said. 'Here it is.' She handed Lara a Jiffy envelope. Lara took the package uncertainly. She tipped it and the manuscript slipped into her hands. She scanned the pages cautiously. It was the first time she'd touched it without Will present. She held a small piece of history in her hands and she could follow the trail on her own if she chose. She was humbled by the enormous responsibility.

Olivia was speaking again, unmoved by the momentous occasion. 'You've got to excuse me. I need to get some sleep. You're welcome to stay up if you want, *Mi casa es su casa* and all that, but I'll show you where your room is.'

Lara nodded and followed her into a wide hall with a galleried landing. As she started up the stairs, even though she felt the weights of exhaustion crushing her, she was going to spend as much time with the manuscript as possible. Olivia stepped back and took her holdall from her. Lara smiled weakly. 'I understand Will's interest in *Twelfth Night* now.'

Olivia reached the top of the stairs. 'Olivia: the mourning queen. Look but don't expect to touch.' She grinned back. 'Will can thank his lucky stars he wasn't called "Sebastian" or "Orsino" – the great bear!' She tapped a photograph of Charlton Heston at the top of the stairs. There was a handwritten message in the corner: *To Slix, Happy Birthday, love, Chuck Heston*. 'Will never calls me Olivia. He belongs to an age when everyone called me Slix.' She led Lara along the corridor, without explaining *why* Will used that name, and showed her into a lavish bedroom, the walls painted with pastel colours and the furniture stained mahogany. A large double bed was in the middle of the room and the far wall was made up of mirrored cupboards.

'I hope you'll be very comfortable here,' Olivia said.

'I'm sure I will,' Lara replied with a grateful smile, noticing Olivia had laid out tea and coffee-making facilities, as though Lara was staying in a bed and breakfast. She wished Olivia goodnight and closed the door behind her. She lay down on the bed and opened the manuscript. It took a second to become accustomed to the unfamiliar handwriting, but she was soon able to focus on it. '*Siþen þe sege and þe assaut watz sesed at Troye, þe borȝ brittened and brent to brondez and askes …*' She read the manuscript out loud, listening to the musical flow of the alliteration. 'That's it,' she said, scaring herself with her sudden shout. The alliteration was the code for which she had been looking. But the poet was too shrewd to start at the beginning of the text. She had to find the starting point of the code, a place that would have been obvious to someone who understood the way the poet's mind worked.

She worked late into the night, trying to piece together the codes from half-memories of conversations with Will, she tried to remember his potted history of the manuscript; but her mind was fogged and eventually she was forced to surrender.

She lay in a reluctant sleep, seized by a longing to break that code once and for all; and frustrated that her body was confined by its physical limits.

Her dreams were tormented and twisted, calls from the depths of insanity demanding her attention. She struggled to hold on to sanity and reason, but felt herself slipping away, falling through a clinging mist. She saw nothing and felt no change sweeping over her. Yet her mind was free and the useless clutter of the world was no longer shouting at her. The paths of time had ceased their continual flow and, instead of seeing a relentless river, Lara realised time had become a wide pool through which every instant passed simultaneously.

She heard Will speaking to her, telling her the importance of the manuscript, and then her mind finally clicked upon that part of the code to which the poet had directed her. 'Old codes,' the poet had said; and perhaps, she realised, that was a code in itself. He was talking about the oldest of codes, the one which even he did not fully understand:

And quy þe pentangel apendez to þat prince nobel
I am in tent yow to telle, þof tary hyt me schulde:
Hit is a syngne at Salamon set sumquyle …

Now she saw the *Gawain*-poet working by candlelight, his murky reflection in the glass of his window nodding to her with a smile as he saw she had worked out the code. He was still writing as she watched him, writing in those *lel lettres loken* – loyal locked letters – and on a piece of parchment she could read his notes. He had marked the top corner of the folio with a pentangle, the Seal of Solomon.

She started to float away again, but realised there was somewhere else she had to go before she could rest. The darkness of time unfolded and she was back in the tunnels in Bath, watching Will, bearded, unkempt, cowering for survival as he tried to conceal himself from Marsh and his guards. But even though she knew his capture was inevitable, she still found herself clinging on to the hope Will would escape their clutches. It was like hoping for a film, which she had already seen, to end in a different way. Lost in the labyrinth, Will wandered without purpose, aware that at every corner he might face the foes from whom he was fleeing. She moved forward, drifting through dreams, gaining a momentary glimpse of Will's capture. Then they were questioning him, trying to force out answers that Will did not know. She watched them breaking his already weakening grip on his will to live. In front of Will's face, Marsh had torn up the memories that were Will's reason for living. He had taken the photograph of Janet and destroyed it. Will whimpered like a lonely child caught in a nightmare. When Marsh tore the photograph, Lara felt her own heart tearing with it. Will could have committed no crimes to justify that level of sadism; to have his one fond memory quite literally torn up in front of him.

Marsh, however, had not yet finished his torment. Will slumped to the floor, a broken man, then Marsh cradled Will's head, as though he were his own wounded son.

'You loved her,' Marsh said. It was not a question. Will nodded, almost imperceptibly. Tears were running down his cheeks and into the beard of a man who has lost all motivation to carry on. 'What would you do to get her back?' Marsh wondered. She did not hear Will's first answer and Marsh asked him to repeat it.

'Anything,' Will sobbed.

'I do not expect you to understand fully what I am about to tell you.'

She listened as Marsh outlined the details of an experiment that had already taken place; they just needed to monitor the subject. He explained about the possibility of enhancing communication in the neural pathways, how it could potentially allow the subject to project themselves mentally back in time and interact with, or even influence, characters who had lived centuries before.

'It would mean she could go back to a time before your wife got into the car,' Marsh explained. 'Or even before your son was hurt.'

All Will had to do was to observe the subject, find a way of getting her to stay with him and, when the time was right, bring her in for tests. After that, he would be free to witness the experiment and return to his wife.

Will did not appear to be listening to most of what Marsh said to him. His mind had accepted only one statement: that there was a possibility of getting his family back. Anything else was irrelevant. He did not consider the concept of temporal paradoxes and how there was no force in the universe that could achieve what Marsh had promised. However, now she could understand what Will meant when he said it was important to believe in something. And he believed in hope. He hoped that, one day, his family would be returned to him. And so he had set out, believing in Marsh's false promises and ensnaring Lara with half-truths and a conundrum to keep her interest.

She slipped away from the scene, heart filled with sorrow. She understood something about what Will had endured, hoping his fantasy might one day overcome the stark truth of reality. She guessed that at some point during her incarceration, Will had realised all his hopes were in vain and that reality must rule over optimism.

When Lara woke again, her room was almost light. The sun was trying to force itself through the dense, wintry clouds. She didn't feel as though she had slept, but when she rolled over and felt the hard cover of the *Gawain* manuscript and remembered her dream, then she knew she couldn't stay in bed any longer; and, as she made herself her morning cup of coffee, she reflected on the dreams of the night before. Surely that was all they were: her own thoughts of optimism conquering reality.

Lara scribbled in a notebook as she tried to undo the code, writing first both sets of the alphabets, to act as her code wheel. At first she thought the poet was drawing her attention to the fifth stanza and 'deciphered' the alliterative letters *RAþþAQW*. She hissed in frustration. There was no language in the world that had a word like that.

There was a gentle knock on the door, soft so that it wouldn't have woken her had she still been sleeping. She called for Olivia to come in and greeted her with a smile.

'I wasn't sure if you'd be up yet,' Olivia said. 'If you're anything like me, you probably hate the mornings.' For someone who hated mornings, Lara thought, Olivia seemed far too cheerful. 'Good, I'm glad you've made yourself coffee,' she said, pointing to the cup. Lara realised she'd ignored it since making it and concentrated only on the manuscript. 'The shower's down the hall if you want it, and shall we say breakfast in twenty minutes, in the kitchen?'

'Thank you,' Lara managed to say. 'That'll be lovely.' Olivia left and Lara suppressed a shudder remembering the last time she had showered. She wasn't sure if she could manage a shower for a long time. Instead, she padded down the hallway and washed herself with Olivia's fragrant *L'Occitane* soap and would ask to have a bath later.

She resisted the urge to look around the house as she found her way back to the kitchen. She guessed Olivia valued her privacy and would only want someone to view the house once she, Olivia, had decided they were worthy of the tour.

She had expected something quick and easy for breakfast, and was surprised when Olivia produced a full, three-course breakfast. It tasted wonderful: Lara hadn't eaten properly in a long time.

After breakfast, Olivia did as she had promised and started to show Lara around the land. The trees, stark and skeletal, did not extend to the back of the house. From her conservatory, Olivia had a clear view across a wide meadow; frost had crushed the grasses. Lara imagined it would be beautiful on a warm day, with bees buzzing and a gentle breeze swaying the tall grasses. She heard crows cackling and pigeons cooing, something else she had missed during her time in captivity. They circumnavigated a steep incline with a wooded grove across the top. Lara thought she saw some kind of structure at the bottom of the dip. Olivia walked away from the grove without mentioning the building. It was as though it contained an unhappy memory, something that scared her.

Olivia spoke about trivialities as they walked and Lara was happy to listen. Walking through the fields as though she didn't have a care in the world had the same therapeutic effect as her time on the barge with Tantris and Jeanette.

Leaving the area of the grove, Olivia led her towards an orchard, shaded from the morning sun. She pointed to the first shoots of plants. 'The narcissi aren't out yet,' she said as if apologising. 'They do look so lovely under the apple trees.'

Lara nodded in a non-committal fashion, but suddenly tensed. 'What did you say?'

'Narcissi,' Olivia explained. 'Daffodils.'

Yes, Lara thought. She knew Narcissi were a variety of daffodil. She wracked her brain: lodged in a forgotten corner was the memory of the vain boy who had fallen in love with his own reflection. But she did not see a pastoral, idyllic setting; instead, she saw the poet sitting at his table as he scribed the manuscript, and wondered if writing represented the ultimate form of self-adoration. "Old codes," the poet had said, and now she realised the importance of what she had seen. She had been looking at his reflection. Wherever it was the code started, she had to read the letters in reverse. Even knowing how to change the letters, there was still a further step needed to break the code.

'I have to get back,' Lara said suddenly. 'I know what to do.'

She turned back towards the house. Olivia hurried after her. Then they both stopped. Lara felt a presence nearby and turned.

Will was walking across the field towards them.

15

Olivia squealed in delight. She ran towards him, hugged him tight, then slapped him on the cheek. 'Where have you been?'

Will rubbed his face. 'Good to see you too, Slix,' he said, wincing. He glanced at Lara. She hadn't moved. She took a long, deep, steadying breath, trying to control her whirlpool of emotions. She understood his pain, understood his betrayal ...

And understood he wanted *Janet* back. Not her.

Olivia put her hands on her hips. She raised an eyebrow. 'You had us worried.'

Will said nothing. He was still looking at Lara. Finally he turned to Olivia. 'Any chance of a coffee? I'm freezing.' He wiped his eyes; they were heavy and rheumy. 'And I've been awake since ... I don't know when.'

Will's eyes narrowed. Olivia nodded. They seemed to be communicating without words. Then Olivia turned and led them back across the meadow, back into the warmth of the kitchen. When she switched on the kettle, Will sat down at the table opposite Lara. 'What *did* you find at the *Église Saint-Pierre*?'

Lara held up a hand to stop him. 'Not so fast. I want answers from you first.'

Olivia spoke from over by the work surface. 'Do you two want to be left alone? This sounds like it could get heavy.'

'We'll let you know if it's inconvenient,' Will said.

'Will!' Lara gasped. 'You can't order Olivia around in her own house.'

Will lowered his head slightly and looked at Lara across the table. '*Our* house. We both own it. Slix ... Olivia ... lives here. I don't.'

Lara was surprised, but that was a discussion for another time. 'You left the *Église Saint-Pierre* and let me be captured by Marsh and his men. Why then? Why couldn't you wait until I had told you the final clue?'

'Because I didn't want to know. I figured you'd work it out. And Marsh has a way of finding answers. I couldn't tell him if I didn't know. And I hoped that if you were distracted by Marsh, it might make you think about the clues from a different perspective.'

'But you couldn't do this without me being captured?'

'The advantage of being their man on the inside was that I knew some of what they were planning. But I could only hold them off for a while. They were going to take you in anyway.'

'And you weren't worried about what they'd do to me? Especially having been through it yourself?'

'I hoped I'd get you out.'

'Hoped? That isn't very reassuring.'

'Look, it worked out okay, didn't it?'

'Aside from the risk of having my brain fried? And how do you know he didn't just let us go so he could follow us?'

'I discussed that with him when I went back,' Will said.

'Discussed?'

'Okay, it wasn't quite a cosy chat.' Despite his flippant tone, Will's jaw had tensed. His eyes held a hidden depth of pain. He gave a sigh. 'Marsh said he doubted you'd tell him anything he didn't already know. His threats were only to loosen your tongue a bit.' He smiled sheepishly. 'I think he was counting on your having seen too many spy films, where they disregard human life to achieve their ends. After that, he said my reaction was justified, and there was no point in keeping me now you were gone. And he didn't have the manuscript to wave in front of me like a carrot.'

'And that was it? He didn't threaten you?'

'What was the point? It was *you* he wanted.'

'That's what I mean. He wouldn't let his experiment wander off without knowing the results of his tests.'

'Wait a second,' Olivia interrupted, making a 'T' with her

hands. 'Time out. Marsh who? What tests? What's going on?'

Will sighed patiently. 'Things got a bit … exciting after I last saw you.' He explained about the tunnels and what was stored there. He told her about being captured and interrogated. He explained he'd been coerced into finding Lara, then travelling with her to Chester, Holywell and Avignon.'

'But you were working for them all along,' Olivia said, indignant. 'You snake!'

'It wasn't like that.'

'You betrayed her,' Olivia said flatly. Lara wondered whether this was sibling banter or whether she was genuinely outraged.

'That was an act. I wanted Marsh to believe I was totally loyal to him.'

'What was an act?' Olivia demanded. 'The fact you were working for Marsh, or your love for Lara?'

'Working for Marsh, and you know it.' He flushed. 'I'm not proud of it. I wish there'd been another way of sorting this out, getting to the poet without having Marsh following us all the way, but there wasn't. Besides, I wouldn't have found the manuscript in the first place if I hadn't wandered into Marsh's little metropolis, but now I have, I know there's something waiting for us at the end.' His voice dropped. He looked at Lara. 'But you're the one who's had the worst of this. You're the one who should see this through.' She heard his words breaking. 'I don't know if you want to go on from here. I'll understand it if you don't, and I'll understand if you don't want me to follow you to the end of the trail, but please, understand what this means to me.'

Lara did understand, but it wasn't easy. Will couldn't be trusted: Marsh had let him go once. Then, he had sold out a stranger. Now he could have negotiated his freedom again – Marsh could have bought his loyalty with the promise of access to any of the secret manuscripts. She shook her head in bewilderment.

Will shrugged. 'I guess you'll have to do it on your own, Pearl. But we could have been so good together.'

Olivia glowered at him. 'It's over, Will. You've got to let Lara go in whatever direction she chooses. You can't force her to go any further.'

Will nodded sadly. 'I wouldn't have forced her,' he said in a forlorn voice. 'But then that's it. I have a different path from here.' To Olivia, he said, 'May I see the manuscript?'

'It's in Lara's room,' she said. 'Do you mind if I get it?'

'Not at all,' Lara said. She avoided eye contact with Will. She could not bear to see the despair in his eyes, knowing he could spend another decade looking for the answers she already knew.

Suddenly, she realised she'd asked him to come with her, to come with her to the end of the trail, but she was not speaking, she was singing:

Come with me; stay with me, two lost in merry company,

Could take a moment to be found, if we stopped to look around

Come with me; stay with me, two lost in merry company,

Have something better waiting there, if we act in harmony.

She had been humming the tune all day, but she had not expected to break into song at that inopportune moment. She could barely believe she had sung to Will.

'Are you sure?' Will's uncertain expression waited for her rejection.

Lara said nothing. She tensed her jaw, fighting between heart and head. Instead, she closed her eyes and nodded almost imperceptibly. 'There are a few things first.' Her eyes became hard and serious: 'First, no more chances,' she was surprised by the venom in her voice.

Will bowed his head solemnly. 'I understand.'

So, Lara explained: the means of deciphering the code *had* been in the *Église Saint-Pierre*, and then she had seen the poet working in the reflection so the letters read in reverse. 'I thought it would be the fifth stanza,' Lara said. 'But a *Q* on its own didn't make sense.'

Will shook his head. 'If you were thinking about the significance of the pentangle, the Seal of Solomon, he describes it in relation to five things, and each of those have five elements.' He turned to the twenty-fifth stanza. 'Let's see what he says here …' Will squinted at the manuscript, jotting down the letters, then referring to Lara's chart for substituting the letter. Again, it was a selection of random letters. 'Are you sure about this?' Will asked.

Lara scowled at him. 'I know what I saw.' She closed her eyes, trying to remember. 'I saw the poet, looking at his reflection, showing me the code ran backwards.' She snapped her fingers. 'It's not just the letters, it's the numbers as well. It's not stanza 25, it's stanza 52 – that's halfway through the total of stanzas in the poem.'

Will sighed patiently. 'You can't divide 101 by two.' But, he turned through the folios. The stanza began at the bottom of the right-hand page. Will jotted down the alliterative letters: *netȝyrd*. His eyes widened.

'Doesn't make sense,' Lara said.

'Will raised an eyebrow. 'Yes it does: it's mirror writing! *Dryȝten* – it means "Lord". Then: *eþfoepelseþ*.' When he wrote the letters, he now did it in reverse order: '*þe slepe of þe Dryȝtyn*,' he said. '"The sleep of the Lord."'

Lara stared at the page. She realised she was holding her breath. Will continued scribbling. After a few minutes he spoke again. 'I think I'm at the start of it.' Lara glanced at his notebook. *Þe lynes of þe laye of Perle make þe age of þe aghlich chappel of Kryst, welke to quere þe knyȝt lays ine þe slepe of þe Dryȝtyn.*

'And in English?' she said, but she could work most of it out without Will's help: *the lines of the lay of Pearl make the age of the* … something … *chapel of Kryst. Walk to where the knight lays in the sleep of the Lord*. 'What's this word, *aghlich*?'

'Terrible, fearful,' Will said. He crossed out each of the letters in his pad. 'It's got 101 letters, just like the poem has 101 stanzas. And it's got the alliteration that the poet loved so much.' He sighed. 'It seems too straightforward. I feel like we're being led astray.'

'Perfect,' Lara scowled.

'All we have to do is find the chapel with the tomb of a knight who died in 1212.' He tapped his foot in frustration. 'We can do a search on the internet or scour though every guidebook in Britain to find that out.'

'No,' Lara said.

'It's a lot of donkey-work,' Will admitted. 'But I don't see we have any alternative.'

'We're missing the most obvious point: there aren't 1212 lines in *Pearl*. There's only 1211. The poet missed out line 472.'

'We never did come up with a good reason why he missed out that line.' Will exhaled slowly. 'And again, he's talking about something his audience would have known. He refers to *þe aghlich* chapel. Most likely something he saw in Chester.'

Lara felt the blood draining from her face. She felt cold running down her back and steadied herself against the table to stop herself from falling. Her world was spinning out of her control.

Will was touching her hand and she did not pull away. 'Are you all right?' he asked.

She nodded, still not able to focus. 'He's not just talking about something *he* knows. He's written this for a very specific audience. Someone who'd know what he's talking about.'

'Who?'

Lara's voice was hollow. 'Me. He knows I'll read this. It's the church *I* fear. Not anyone else. It's Beaded church. The village where I grew up.'

*

Olivia had made a time-out sign, observing this had become too heavy. She sent Lara upstairs to have a bath and Lara agreed, taking the hint that Olivia wanted to talk to Will in private. When Lara came back downstairs, hair wrapped in a towel, Will announced that Olivia had agreed to lend them her car.

They left shortly after lunch. Lara sat in the back seat, behind Will. Occasionally, she saw him looking in the rear-view mirror to check to see she was all right. Lara was uncomfortable travelling with him. She repeatedly stared over her shoulder to see if they were being followed.

After nearly three hours, the motorways gave way to the dual carriageways leading towards Chester. Lara fought against sleep, but as the skies darkened around mid-afternoon she found herself dropping off with the hypnotic blurring of the sodium lights, and it was only when she heard the protesting whine of Will shifting down to a lower gear that she woke up and gazed sleepily around her.

The village was dark. A single streetlight lit the road. Lights were on in the few houses and the pub. Fear suddenly clawed at her.

'Stop,' she said suddenly. Her voice was an unnerving interruption following the four-hour roar of the car's engine. Will obediently pulled the car over to the side of the road. Lara glanced out at the pub's lights spilling across the village green. The Parish Church of St Werburgh was no more than a dark silhouette in the distance.

'Why didn't you tell me we were here already?' she said.

'I didn't know. There were no road signs.'

Lara unlocked her door and let herself out of the car. Will dimmed the lights and turned off the engine before he stood with her outside.

The mechanism in the church clock started to whirr. It was a sound that was familiar through the fog of distant memories. It was years since she had last walked into Beaded, but everything about it was familiar, the hum of the clock before the bells chimed, sounds of the aeroplanes overhead, the smells of the pub and the village green. As she stared around her, she saw the low white fence which surrounded the green and the place where a troupe of travelling Morris dancers performed every May-time, a place where the maypole was set up, and where Michael had once led her with his boyish grin, begging her to come with him to the May Pole so he could show her what fertility rituals were all about. She saw the well into which she had nearly fallen as she had tried to balance on the rim. Her friend – Hannah, that had been her name – had run screaming for help, while Lara clung to the rim. And Hannah's father had come running and yanked her out. Here was the place where an old story teller had come and told tales of great imagination to the school children of the area on special occasions, about the history of Chester and what part the area that became Beaded played in the Roman occupation of the county.

And at last, here was her own home. It was the first time she had returned here in years. Will had not moved from the side of the car. She felt herself being forced forwards. She was being manipulated as if she were being controlled by an unseen puppeteer. Fighting the urge to retreat, she knocked on the door.

For a moment she thought there was no one inside. Then the hall light was switched on and Lara saw the familiar stained glass flowers of her own front door, before it opened and an old man peered out.

'Who is it?' the man asked.

For a moment Lara believed her father must have moved without telling her, but as she stared, she realised this man *was* her father. She stared at the aged face. It was a terrible moment to realise time had been so unkind to him, but her own body would have changed much since she had last seen him. Her hair colour had changed. She wasn't wearing her glasses and she had put on a bit of weight following her pregnancy. She gazed at the hooded eyes and the thick grey bushy eyebrows. Much of the hair on her father's head was gone and his muscles had withered away to spindly limbs. She smiled gently, breathing a long sigh of relief. At last she was home.

'Well, who are you?' her father demanded, abruptly, but not unpleasantly.

'It's Lara,' she said and, when there seemed little recognition, she elaborated in a gentle voice. 'Your daughter.'

The man nodded, peering down at her, looking for features he could recognise. 'Yes, she'd be about your age.' He smiled wanly, 'You still had to lose that fat when you left us. You seem to have grown up.' Then his expression changed, his voice became angry. 'But you aren't my daughter. I don't know who you are.'

Lara felt her heart being beaten on a blacksmith's anvil. 'Dad, don't do this. It's been a while, but ...'

'You always had the Devil in you, girl. We always feared it was so. You and the boy you left with both had the Devil's mark. You took your mother as your unhallowed sacrifice.' He turned his back on Lara. 'You aren't my daughter, I don't know you.'

Lara tried to find something to say, but could find nothing. She caught her father's arm, turned him round, forced the old man to look at her, but he shook himself free. 'If you were my daughter you wouldn't have come back here until you'd succeeded. She was such a bitter disappointment to me.'

'That's not fair, Dad. I did my best, you just set impossible targets.'

'Targets which she should have met. Instead she killed her mother and drove her family apart.' His eyes were smouldering with rage. 'Leave.'

The door slammed in her face. Lara stayed there, staring at the stained glass flowers until the hall light was turned off. Then she staggered away, cheeks burning with shame. Her thoughts attacked her conscience. The realisation she had been disowned broke over her like a mighty wave, physically forcing her to her knees. She knelt outside her own home and wept like a baby.

Suddenly, she felt gentle hands on her shoulders. Startled, she looked up into Will's gentle face.

He didn't say anything as he helped her to stand and her tears flowed again. There was no controlling them. She buried her face into Will's shoulder and his arms encircled her, his fingers tracing gentle patterns on her back. 'Perhaps we should leave.'

She nodded and was led by her hand back to the car. She sat on the front seat, staring out at the lone streetlight. 'He disowned me,' she said eventually. 'Like he never knew me.' Her eyes were pleading. 'He said I split my family and killed my mother. I know my mother died when I was born, but there was only me and Dad. He adored me. We'd spend every evening together; he would read to me. He doted on me.'

'And then you left him and he never understood why,' Will offered.

'I couldn't stay here,' Lara said and she stopped suddenly.

'Why not?'

Lara's expression was pained. 'I don't think I'm ready to tell you that.'

Will gently touched her shoulder. She flinched. 'Listen to me, Pearl,' he said. 'You're in Beaded. This is the end of the trail. Maybe you should try to confront some of your ghosts.'

'Not now,' Lara said coldly.

Will regarded her patiently. 'I'm afraid there are more ghosts than you realise. More devils than vast hell can hold and all that. Do you want to talk about your brother?'

Lara jerked. 'What? I haven't got a brother?'

'You sure?'

'What do you know that I don't? What was written about me on my files?'

'Nothing. I was just putting two and two together.'

'And your answer is a brother? That's ridiculous. What reasons could you possibly have to think that?'

'Several. First of all, in spite of your "loving family relationship" with your father, he thinks you've been a disappointment to him. Is it possible that your brother was the disappointment first and your father didn't want you to do the same thing?'

'Rubbish.'

'And let's take the two Shakespeare plays you know so well, so much so that your father read them to you every night. There's one common theme in the plays which is that a missing brother is found. Did you never realise? Perhaps your father was hoping you would prove less disappointing than him, maybe your father was telling you your brother had disappointed him, and was begging you not to go the same way.'

'This is ridiculous, it would mean he would have had to have left around the same time I was born.'

'Is that so hard a thing to imagine? You said your father was a lot older than the other girls' dads.'

Lara turned away from him, but found herself looking at the church. Always there was the church, the one building which terrified her and set her on an active path away from organised religion, and it was the only place to which she had to travel and, as she contemplated the building, she knew Will was telling her the truth. Hidden in a niche at the back of her mind was a memory of an argument, between an angry young man and her father. Staring back across time, she couldn't hear the words, but knew this was a fight which had resulted from pent up, unexpressed grief. The younger man – maybe eighteen years old – had many of her father's features and was refusing to back down in the argument. So was her father. That was the Halpin trait.

She was recalling events that must have occurred twenty years before; she would have been a very small child, hardly understanding her relationship with the older stranger, before she tried to understand why that stranger was no longer there.

'I have a brother,' Lara breathed. 'Why did my father never tell me?'

'Because he'd been a disappointment to the family by never once bowing down with his pride and admitting he was grieving as much for your mother, just as your brother was. Their grief became anger and there was no one else in the circle to direct the anger.'

'He kept telling me he didn't want me to disappoint him because my brother had already done it, and he didn't want to be let down.' She gave a sorrowful sigh. 'And thinking he was doing nothing but berating me, I left and disappointed him further.'

'It explains a lot,' Will said gently. 'So, what will you do now, Lara Halpin?'

Lara glanced at the house, then at the church, then back at the house, then back at the church. She felt the frustration of a child being forced to do homework that was too complicated; she felt the terrors she had excluded from her mind wrapping themselves around her.

She got out of the car. Her feet felt weighted. 'I have to face my ghosts,' she said with resolution. 'And then I'll prove to my father that I was "good enough".' She began to stride towards the church.

16

St Werburgh's church stood beside a large field. It was silhouetted against the leaden sky, gaunt and foreboding. The moon glowered, shining a vague jaundiced light through the windows, like malevolent eyes glaring at them. The sun had set behind a small hill. The landscape was cold. The ground had frosted. Ice cracked underfoot.

A gnarled old horse-chestnut tree stood in the graveyard. As children, Lara and her friends had gathered conkers, throwing sticks up to knock down the fruits from the higher branches. A few birds' nests clung grimly to the branches of the conker tree. Crows, startled by the intruders, flew through the branches, cawing noisily. Beneath, the tombstones were scattered through the graveyard like rotten teeth.

'Cheerful place,' Will breathed. 'No wonder you've no fond memories from here.'

Closer to the church, Lara saw the all-too familiar granite walls. They were cold and unfriendly.

A chilling wind whipped up. Lara pulled her coat tighter around her. The wind seemed to be mocking her, taunting her to run and never return.

Lara gave a tentative look over her shoulder; the distant sodium of streetlights spread a red and orange stain across the sky, like a spreading pool of blood. One of the lights flickered uncertainly. Her breath misted in front of her. She kept her hands in her pockets, hoping to bring some circulation back into her fingers.

She wanted to tell Will that this was a hostile place and they shouldn't be here. The very name filled her with a fear that was more than just a childhood memory: Beaded ... *Be Dead*. How could anyone want to live around here? It was insipid, yet sucked people in so they could never escape.

But she couldn't leave now. While their quest might be a lost cause, and they might find nothing in the darkness, there was a possibility someone might see her if she came here during the day, someone who might recognise her and speak to her father. With the blanket of dusk came anonymity.

They stepped through the lych-gate outside the graveyard. The grass was withered, like a dead man's hair. The air was filled with a stench of rot – decomposing funeral flowers. The sound of turning clockworks cut through the silence. The clock chimed. The resounding bell seemed to be warning the locals of their presence.

'Will,' Lara breathed. She didn't know what else to say, but drew comfort from his name. He did not reply, did not turn to look at her. He simply continued his relentless march towards the church like an automaton, or a man possessed.

She glanced behind her, feeling they were being watched, that Marsh was following so close behind he was treading on their shadows.

She stared at the church walls again and the fearsome gothic windows. It wasn't a surprise she'd been put off religion when she had spent her childhood faced with such terrible images. She tried to control her laboured breathing, but the air seemed to stick in her throat, suffocating her, before it flowed into her lungs, the cold of the evening freezing her internal organs.

The crows had silenced and the echoes of the bell tower had receded. Even the ground seemed to have softened, so the cracking of ice was reduced to a sludgy step.

Then she was standing in front of the door. It had been left open for evensong. She guessed one of the churchwardens would be around somewhere and would not be averse to a couple of tourists, or pilgrims exploring the church. *Is my father still a churchwarden*? she wondered.

Will waited patiently by the door. 'Are you sure you want to go through with this?' he asked. But there was something in the way he asked that made her feel she had no choice but to go on.

Even so, standing in front of the church was confronting a past that she'd tried to suppress for so long. The church was the bank vault that stored her memories.

If she turned away now, there wouldn't be another time. In her brief visits into what her father termed 'forbidden Shakespeare', she had learned to screw her courage to its sticking place. If she left now, she would never again find the strength to come back. She would never return here if she could help it, and she knew she couldn't endure the further disappointment of her father.

'When was the last time you were in this church?' Will asked as he held open the door for her.

Lara shifted uncomfortably. 'Years ago,' she whispered. Too many to count. Before she had met Michael, but after she had rebelled, when she decided that enduring the beatings from her father was preferable to sitting in the cold, listening to the vicar accusing the congregation, accusing her, of guilt in a blood-and-thunder style.

Lara had eventually realised that what the vicar called guilt was no more than child-like curiosity and working through feelings and emotions like any other girl of her age, along with the pressure of growing up without a mother. Instead of shaming her for having natural feelings and instincts, the misogynist bastard should have been giving her words of support.

'Pearl?' Will's voice was beside her, filled with concern. 'Are you all right?'

So that was the ghost: lurking for her outside the church where she was not expecting it, rather than inside, waiting to jump out from the shadows. She turned away from the doors and walked towards the conker tree in the graveyard. Eight stones from the conker tree, four stones up. She crouched down in front of the black stone and stared at the gold letters. There was the name, Rowan Elizabeth Halpin, her mother.

The stone was her only connection to the woman of the past;

here was her name, the epitaph "Beloved Wife and Mother", the date of her death and her age. There was no date of birth. She had wondered if her father had been economising, or whether he had considered it unimportant.

A small pocket of snowdrops grew next to the grave. She picked one of the flowers, looking at the white petals in the distant orange light, before placing it, child-like, on the gravestone. She had never known her mother, but she still found it hard to hold back the tears when she was next to the stone, feeling the stark realisation there was a body which had been her mother's shell during her time on the earth, resting six feet under her.

She glanced over to where Will was waiting patiently for her. 'That's my friend Will, Mum,' she said in a soft voice. There were no other words to say. Then, standing up, she returned to Will. He said nothing and she did not want to assuage his curiosity.

Stepping over the threshold of the church, she was swallowed by the shadows.

It was like remembering a distant nightmare: entering the church; looking at the arches inside; the regiments of pews; the foreboding of the pulpit; and the darkness around the altar. She had been convinced that spectres were concealed by the shadows of the church. This place inspired fear and misery. There was no joy, no love, no devotion, just the desolate duty of coming to a place she did not love, to sing songs she did not like and to meet with people who wanted her to be something she was not.

'Did they get many people here?' Will said, looking around and apparently not noticing she was no longer fearful, but sombre instead. He flicked on his torch and directed it over the seats.

'Perhaps fifty on a holy day,' Lara sounded bored. 'Generally not more than twenty-five who were there for the regular services. Most of them came for the bingo.'

'I thought the Church didn't advocate gambling.'

'And neither did the minister who came along afterwards.' She cast her mind back. 'Timothy Outram. He was younger, but still a traditionalist. Most people said gambling was okay if it was done to bring in funds for the parish. Rev Timothy put his first cat amongst the pigeons by asking if murder was all right if it was done in the Lord's name.'

Will whistled in amazement. 'Bet he was popular.'

Lara shook her head. 'Father Timothy was very different. He made me see the other minister was a hypocrite. He saw the church as the centre of the community and it didn't matter if people were members of the congregation or not, at least that's how I remember him. It was a long time ago.' She drew a shuddering breath. 'He came to speak to me once. Told me the value of having a church wedding. Michael and I … we listened politely and then had a civil wedding at Tatton Hall.' She looked at him cynically. 'Frankly, I want to have more wit than a Christian does,' she said caustically, then her tone changed. 'He's moved on now …' She shivered, realising she'd talked herself on to a precipice of remembrance and Will's next question was going to push her over.

'Lara,' he said softly. 'What are you trying to keep from me?'

'Please don't ask me.'

He placed a hand on her shoulder. 'You were here once before,' he probed. 'When you were in Chester Cathedral you told me you'd seen something that had frightened you. You said there were ghosts in your past. That was here wasn't it?'

She stared out at the desolate graveyard. A branch had fallen from the conker tree, the wood was like a blackened spinal column and the thick twigs were the rib cage. A small animal scuttled from the ribs, looking for shelter against the oncoming weather.

The memories broke through the barriers of Lara's subconscious. It pained her to speak, like squeezing a septic wound, but the poison flowed from her.

'I was eleven or twelve,' she said. 'My father had started drinking. I used to hide until he'd drunk himself into a stupor. There aren't many places for a teenager to hide in Beaded. I'd thought I'd sit in the graveyard all evening. But it started to rain. I didn't know where else to go, so I sheltered at the front of the church. Then I saw people coming. I thought they might be looking for me, so I hid inside. I crawled under one of the pews and waited there.'

'Who were these people?'

'"Supernatural investigators", they called themselves. Father Timothy hadn't been here long. People in the village were convinced there was a malevolent spirit, or even a cult using the church for rituals. One of the cleaners started a panic. She found excrement over the doors and ash over the altar. Rev Timothy said it was vandals, someone trying to scare them. But, he called in someone he knew … he'd known one of the hunters from years back, so he asked him to do a preliminary investigation before he spoke to the bishop.'

'Not usual protocol,' Will observed. 'What did this supernatural investigator do?'

'He came into the church, searching for evidence of a haunting.' Her eyes became misty, but fearful. 'There were two of them, a man and a woman. He was the more level-headed of them. He sought reasons why it couldn't be a "supernatural manifestation", that was what he called it. The woman, she wanted to find a spirit and make contact.'

Will's face betrayed his tension: tendons protruded from his neck. 'That sounds dangerous.'

Lara scoffed. 'It would've been if she wasn't a nutter. I mean … psychic links with spirits?'

'Unless they're real,' Will said darkly. 'There are more things in heaven and earth than are dreamt of in your philosophy.'

Lara touched the pew, as if it would offer some stability to the present day, but touching the wood was like reaching back across time, as if the pews contained the memories she had tried to suppress. She lurched, trying to pull herself away, but the whirlpool of memories seemed to drag her back.

*

The man pushed open the door and examined the lock with intense eyes. 'That's our first problem solved,' he said to his companion, a shorter woman, dressed in jeans and a dark sweatshirt. 'There's no question about how they got in and out. Time and the weather's warped the doors. The lock doesn't fit any more.'

'They don't lock the door anyway,' the woman said patiently. 'Reverend Outram wants St Werburgh's to be an "open church" so people can come whenever they want, day or night.' She dropped a large holdall by the door and followed him in.

'If you leave your church open all day, you can't complain if people come in.' He glanced around, then walked behind the pews to the central aisle. 'At least the Father knew to move anything of value, or, at least, to nail it down.'

The woman shook her head. 'Reverend Timothy doesn't like the "trappings" – he called it Papal nonsense. He wants the church to work on a shoestring budget.' She smiled. 'I liked him. He focuses on charity rather than trying to make the Church a middle-class institution.'

The man's eyes flickered playfully. 'You like a priest? That has to be a first.' He sniffed and wrinkled his nose. 'Smells artificial around here.'

'Incense spray.' The woman ran her finger along the back of the pew, then rubbed her thumb and forefinger together. She pointed to the line she had made in an almost invisible white film on the wood. 'See?'

He didn't answer. He walked further into the church, standing at the altar. The woman sat down in one of the pews and closed her eyes. Lara wasn't sure how much time passed. She thought she saw a white aura emanating from the woman's body, shimmering, spreading out in a beatific radiance. Her breathing became shallow, bronchial. Her face became serene.

The man continued undeterred and turned his attention to the altar.

'Something's here,' the woman said suddenly. Lara froze. Somehow, the woman had discovered her! Perhaps she was using telepathy to reach out and discern everything that was in the church, or simply listening so intently that she had heard another presence. Either way, Lara was blushing. She was suddenly aware she was holding her breath, attempting to avoid discovery.

The woman's expression was vacant. Her eyes had opened but they weren't focused. 'Reverend Timothy is only half right about this place. Something's here. It isn't what he thinks it is. What he sees is vandalism. It isn't a supernatural force.' Consciousness returned to her eyes. The lustre around her body had faded. Her face became busy again. She seemed suddenly drained of energy. 'How long did you say he'd been here?'

'Month at the most,' the man said, making his way back.

'There's your answer then. It's his new approach to the church. Ruffled a few feathers. People complaining they didn't do it this way before. They're trying to frighten him off. Shit across the walls? Ash in the communion wafers? Pissing in the Holy Water? Jesus, can't these people think of anything original?'

'Then it's not our problem,' the man said. 'We'll tell Reverend Outram to have the police take care of it.' He shook his head, trying to clear it. 'I need to get out of here,' he said. 'I hate that air-freshener stuff. Always gives me a headache.'

'You'd have preferred the smell of shit then?'

The man scowled at her, and made his way through the church towards the vestry door. Lara found herself peering around from under the pew to get a better look at him. There was something familiar about him: like remembering the faces she'd seen in dreams but never truly recognised. She liked him. He had an honest face, but it was fixed with a tired, stoical grin.

He stopped in front of the vestry door. Shivering, he spoke to the woman: 'You said Reverend Outram was only half-right about this place. What's the other half?'

The woman closed her eyes and shivered as though she had eaten something bitter. She had paled. 'There's something else here. Something powerful. Something ancient.'

'Evil?' the man asked.

She shook her head. 'No malice at all. It's like a guardian. It's harmless as long as you don't disturb it.'

The man sighed stoically. 'Guess what we're going to do next?'

The woman considered this. Outside, the clouds had yielded to the weight of the raindrops. The sound against the slates was like bullets fired against tin. The man peered up uncertainly. The woman rose from where she sat and tapped the stone on the wall near the vestry. 'Hollow,' she said. 'And it isn't some kind of priest-hole. It's the way down to the crypt.'

'Don't like crypts,' the man said. 'Imaginations can run riot. Not good for our profession at all.' When he was at her side, he ran his fingers across the stones, then reached into his pocket and produced a small Stanley knife. 'It's not sealed,' he said. 'They just painted over the stone.' He sliced through the paint with the blade. Small white flecks fell down to stones beneath. He worked quickly down one side, then across the top. His blade was obstructed on the left side. 'I think this is a hinged door,' he said. He pointed to where he had been cutting. 'Do you see how this has been integrated into part of the wall? Whoever did this certainly knew what they were doing. This is real craftsmanship.'

*'Craft*spersonship,*' the woman objected. The man shot her a mock glare, and continued to work his way around the frame.*

Lara felt her legs cramping. She shifted her weight. She tensed as she banged her knee against the back of the pews and bit back a cry of pain.

But the two investigators didn't turn, too engrossed in their work to notice anything else. The man seemed slightly nervous, as if he were a master in his art and was suddenly coming into new territory. He stepped away from the door, wiping his forehead with the back of his hand. 'I could murder a pint.'

The woman shook her head. 'Not while we're working. This is big.'

'No pint?' The man sounded disappointed. He touched the wall gently. 'Let's see if this baby gives.' He pushed and appeared surprised when he heard the sound of a catch dropping. 'Sounds like it's spring locked.'

'A bit anachronistic for a church of this age. When was it? Thirteenth century?'

'Around then. The spring could have been added at a much later date, in the hope of concealing, but not actually sealing it off altogether.' He released the door and it slowly opened towards him. 'Has all the hallmarks of someone concealing it at a later date.' The door grated against the flagstones. The sound echoed through the church, thundering back from the ceiling. Lara took the opportunity to shift herself.

'Good acoustics,' the man said as the noise died away. He peered down into the darkness. 'I need a flashlight.'

'I'll get you a torch, if you want one,' the woman replied. 'You know I hate that American shit.'

The man shrugged and watched as she went back to the main entrance. She returned with a Maglite and switched it on before handing it to him.

A wide pool of light spread across the opposite wall. Stairs led down into the darkness. There were strange letters on the stone. She couldn't read them from where she was and, even if she could, she doubted she'd understand them. She squinted and could just make out the shapes of some of the characters.

The man crouched down and winced as his knees cracked. He traced a finger along the line of characters. He blew across the letters. A cloud of dust swirled away. 'This isn't good,' he said. 'I've seen this language before. It's Glagolitsa – Slavic – used in early occult and demonological texts. It was used when they wanted to hide something from Latinate scholars.'

'I know,' the woman said sounding bored. She stumbled as she spoke

some of the words aloud, they were rough and guttural. The man's eyes flashed in anxiety. The woman stopped. She snapped her fingers at him. 'This is it. This is the source.'

'Is it possible this presence is what's motivating someone to get rid of Reverend Outram?'

The woman shook her head. 'There's great power here, but it's not a motivating power.' She smiled. 'Besides, who'd trust the word of a couple of ghost hunters who said there's something in the church telling the people to get up and do things? We'd be run out of town in no time.'

The man rubbed tired eyes and tried to stifle a yawn. 'What about these words?Do they say anything of any note?'

'It's like an inscription from the Egyptian "Book of the Dead" – she ran her finger along one line of characters, then cursed as the walls started to crumble. 'Better not do that again,' she said. 'It's like a reference to eternal life. It's a riddle of sorts. It says: "The Darkest paths are those easiest to follow. The desire for life is greater than the hope of Death. Those who would walk on the path of life for all eternity must first lose the soul of the living, but the darkest path, the greatest wish, may be more than an eternity. But cursed be he who thinks evil of it."'

'Honi soit qui mal y pense,' the man said. 'It's the motto of the Order of the Garter. Doesn't fit. The Order was formed in the mid-fourteenth century. These letters are a lot older. Wonder why it's here?'

'We need cameras,' the woman said, but Lara shuddered. There was an unpleasant edge to her voice. Her eyes had widened with avarice. Perhaps it was the way the torchlight cast shadows across her face that made her no longer a friend, but a malicious enemy.

The man shook his head, sensing something in her voice. 'If this language is what I think it is, we shouldn't mess with it. Leave it to the professionals. Better still, seal it up and leave it well alone.'

The woman started to argue, but her colleague cut off any objections with a cold glare. 'We need polyfilla and emulsion paint. We can cover this place over as if we've never been here. Then I'll have a word with

Reverend Outram and recommend he goes to the police about the "haunting".'

'Filler's in the car,' he said.

They left together. The woman stopped, turned and scrutinised the church. Her eyes fell on the hidden cavity in the wall. Her face seemed twisted and unfriendly.

Lara knew they wouldn't be gone for too long. She needed to find another place to hide, perhaps in the pulpit. When they came back again she might not be so lucky to be undetected. She squeezed herself from her hiding place and started to run towards the altar.

But she was compelled to look back at the entrance to the crypt. She tried to back away from it, fearing the darkness, fearing the way the ancient characters seemed to be calling her, and at the same time being forced to walk along the cold flagstones towards it. Her footsteps echoed. The crypt gave off a stale musty odour.

She hesitated by the heavy stone door, trying to find an excuse to leave, but not having the strength to resist. She heard herself whimpering as she stepped over the threshold and into the darkness.

Spiral steps coiled into the darkness. Something was calling to her from the base of the stairs. She took another step, oblivious that the supernatural investigators might return at any moment.

Something prevented her from going any further. She remembered the story of the children who never shut the wardrobe door behind them for fear of being trapped inside. She turned away from the hypnotic darkness and back to the writing on the walls.

The letters were calling her back, demanding to be read. There was more written on the wall behind her. She panicked, feeling like an animal caught in a snare. She tried to pull away, but couldn't resist. Instead, she was drawn towards the writing. She could make out the characters written in the Latin alphabet, but there were others: a blend of characters from other languages. She couldn't work out any of the words.

In the dim passage, perhaps no more than a metre wide, her back brushed against the wall to get them into focus. She realised she had already destroyed some of the flaking characters. The sudden exposure to the elements was sealing the fate for the rest of them. As she watched, she realised there was something else, a figure behind the writing, etched into the stones. The letters had concealed the angles.

The inscriptions faded away. All that remained was a glowing Seal of Solomon.

*

Confusion flashed across Will's eyes. 'How could you see all that when you were hiding *under* the pew?' He sucked his lips as he thought. 'You said you were aged eleven or twelve. Is it possible you'd just had your BCG inoculation and …' he hesitated. '… All the other added-extras?'

'Could have been,' Lara said. 'It was so long ago.' She started to walk away from Will. 'I don't know what I saw there, other than the Seal,' she said. 'But the woman was right, there *is* something in here.'

Will nodded. 'It sounds like our poet,' he said with a bitter smile. 'Always trying to be the mysterious man with the riddles. The clues hidden in *lel lettres loken* – locked in letters.'

Lara shook her head. 'This wasn't the poet at all. I think he knew about the inscriptions, but they weren't his words. He was a man of few words. *Þe sprynges calle. Þe trauayles biginez* was one of his. *Quaere lapidem in stella* was another. In Holywell, he didn't say anything at all. He believed in understating everything.'

'What happened after that?' Will asked.

'They came back and sealed the crypt. I came down from the pulpit once they'd left and tried to find the cracks, but I couldn't see them. But I don't think it was *them*. I think the woman, reaching out with her mind, she opened the door. When she left, it closed by itself.'

'Why her?' Will wondered. 'I don't deny she was very psychic, from what you said, but why couldn't it have been *you* who opened the door?'

'Not me,' Lara said. 'The oppression was gone when *she* left. I didn't feel I was being dragged anywhere. Whatever was in the crypt was like a magnet when I was standing at the top of the stairs, but once the door was shut, there was no way it could hurt me.'

'But you never went into the church again?'

'Can you blame me? I didn't realise what it was at the time. I don't think I do now. I don't believe in higher powers or anything beyond the sphere of normality …'

Will nodded. '… But there was something in there that challenged your thoughts on "Other Worlds".'

'That's pretty much it. Of course, I went home and dragged my father to bed and all those thoughts were gone by the morning. But I knew I didn't want to go back into the church again.'

'How did your father react to that if he was one of the church-wardens?'

'Sometimes he beat me and called me a heretical bitch. Sometimes he told me how much I disappointed him. And there were times when he was just too drunk to notice. That's the mercy of drink.'

Will peered apprehensively at the high arches. 'If you go in, you might be dealing with the same thing again.'

'Don't patronise me,' Lara glowered. 'I can deal with whatever's in there.'

'All right,' he said, holding his hands up in submission. 'This place is making me a bit nervous as well,' he admitted.

They stepped inside and Lara led the way along the aisle, towards the vestry door, to where she had seen the supernatural investigators open the door to the tomb.

Will switched on his torch and directed the beam at where Lara was pointing. Now the lines of the crypt door were more prominent. 'Looks like our friends didn't do such a good job of concealing this thing after all.'

Lara shook her head. 'You wouldn't have known it was there when they left.'

Malaise was growing inside her, or seeping through the stones. She stepped back to let Will get closer.

He handed her the torch and pulled a Swiss army knife from his pocket. 'If that bloke could get through with a Stanley knife, then I'm sure this will do the job.'

He flicked open the blade and inserted it between the stones. 'It's like going through wax with a hot knife,' Will said, as flecks of paint, plaster and stone fell to the ground. 'Problem is people will know we've been here. I wish you'd told me about the supernatural investigators before we came. We could have been prepared.' He cut at the shape of one of the stones, then stopped, thinking about what he was doing. 'I don't like this. They had permission to vandalise the church. What we're doing here is just short of sacrilege.'

'Scared for your immortal soul?' Lara asked acerbically.

Will looked at her coldly. 'More than you'd ever realise.'

Lara turned on him. 'And what's the difference between this and selling me out to those people. If you had really cared about me why didn't you give me some hint something was amiss?'

'And what would that have achieved? This has been going on for more than a decade. If I hadn't followed you then it would have been someone else.'

'Is that the only reason? You wanted to be the one to betray me?'

'That's not all, but that's all you're going to believe, isn't it?'

'Try me.'

Will shook his head. 'This can wait. This isn't the time or the place. At the moment I have another fish to fry.' He positioned his blade in the small cracks, but simply touching the stones made the hidden door click.

There was a hiss as the tomb gases escaped as the door

opened. Will stepped back, holding a hand over his mouth. A graveolent stench filled the church. Lara felt her stomach churning. 'You can see why they use incense in churches,' she said miserably. Her head was spinning. She glanced at the entrance nervously.

Will waited for the invisible noxious cloud to dissipate, then pulled the door open. The effluvium passed into a stale nausea. Lara shuddered; whatever evil lay beyond, that source of her fears, would be free.

When she heard the door grinding, she also heard the thundering of her heart. Then Will was shining his torch into the darkness. She knew this was not an irrational fear; it was not the confrontation of a nightmare she had had when she was younger. This was a very real presence that was overpowering her.

In the same moment that she wanted to leave her memories well alone, she realised she could not leave Will alone with whatever lay at the bottom of the stairs. He'd betrayed her once, why shouldn't he do it again now?

She couldn't read his expression when he turned back to her. His features had been swamped by the shadows. He turned back again and stepped on to the first of the stairs. The torch light flashed across one of the walls. She saw places where the obscure, profane symbols had once stood, tainting the church with their foul occult corruption. Beyond that was the Seal of Solomon. It seemed etched deeper into the stones, as though her first visit to the tomb had been no more than an invitation to understand the secrets contained within the crypt.

Now it was a demand.

She braced herself against the loathsome putrescence and stepped down.

17

The spiral steps coiled into the darkness like a twisted snake from a terrible legend no one dared tell any longer. The air was cold and musty, a putrid emanation from the darkness. Small eddies of dust circled around, wisps of the Devil woken by her intrusion. Lara started to step forward, then stopped, startled at a sound behind her. She held her breath until she realised it was the echo of her own footsteps. She stepped forward again. The stairs were narrow, winding tighter and tighter and the dank air squeezed around her heart and lungs. This time when she stopped, it was the realisation, the horror, of her actions. It was the same fear that had prevented her from going any further years before. She could not take her eyes from the Seal of Solomon.

'What's the matter?' Will asked. He turned, pointed his torch down the stairs. The beam cut through the darkness. It created more shadows in which evil could hide.

'We're going into someone's tomb,' she whispered. It was a lie. The glowing lines beguiled her. Tiny currents of electricity passed between the points.

Will nodded seriously. 'You're right. It's a family crypt. But we're going to be the first people to go in there for centuries. The world doesn't know that this place exists. If that supernatural investigator is still alive I doubt he'd have gone further; he's probably tried to erase Beaded from his mind.' He smiled comfortingly at her, seeming to understand her fear. 'But there are no ghosts or demons down here. This is a shrine to the memory of those long gone.'

'Then what right do we have to desecrate it?' Still those lines, as if passing by them would break the five-pointed star and suck away the energy from her body.

'Because we were invited. The poet left a long series of clues how to find this place, even if it was a round-about route.'

'Why would he have gone to such lengths?'

'He needed to be sure whoever was looking for him was dedicated to their quest. In the fourteenth century, such a journey would have taken a very long time.' He saw her looking fearfully into the shadows again. 'I know. You've probably seen a thousand horror films where something nasty is waiting at the bottom. To be honest, this place gives me the screaming heebie-jeebies. I'm terrified of going down there, not because I think there's a malevolent force at the bottom, but because I don't want to fall over in the dark.' He seemed embarrassed. 'And because I read about the curse of King Tutankhamen, where the curse pretty much wiped out everyone who went looking for the tomb' He shook his head and his face seemed to steel with resolution. '*Death will slay with his wings whoever disturbs the peace of the Pharaoh*.' He laughed. 'But I realised the curse was fake: in Egyptian mythology Anubis, the god of the Dead, was a jackal. Death doesn't have wings, except in Christianity – avenging angels and all that.'

'But this isn't King Tut,' Lara said nervously. 'Surely English people didn't have enough occult power to create a curse that exists six hundred years later.'

'Don't you believe it,' Will said gravely. 'I'm not trying to scare you. This was a time of superstition. *They* believed in curses and sometimes belief was just as powerful.'

Lara shuddered. She couldn't tell him the true source of her fears: the Seal of Solomon unnerved her – she didn't know why it was there. But even that was not what truly terrified her. She was afraid of *him*, afraid of his betrayal. How did she know their freedom was not just another attempt to regain her trust, and to lead her on to another dark path and to who-knew-what danger?

But all of this was wrong. She saw he was as frightened as she was. She *had* to trust him. They could work together and overcome their fears.

She stepped back. 'I can't do this,' she admitted. 'Can you go first?' She tried not to let her eyes stray back to the Seal.

He hesitated, but then nodded. He stood at the top of the steps, trying to peer into the darkness. She realised Will was attempting to summon his resources, his inner strength, to overcome his fears. Taking a deep breath, he stepped down. Lara glanced back at the heavy stone door. It was firmly wedged open. There was no chance of it being blown shut by the wind. She wondered if Narnia might have been a completely different story if the kids had been trapped inside the wardrobe and starved to death, rather than making their way to another world.

He took another step forwards. His shadow fell across the wall. It eclipsed the Seal. She watched the lines breaking, the light failing. Then it was like it had never been there.

'Will?' Trepidation filled her voice.

Will turned once, but she found no words to explain what she had seen. He continued into the darkness.

Taking a deep breath, she stepped after him.

The cold hit her immediately as she passed the place that the Seal had been. It seemed to devour her very core. Then she had passed it, stepping on the centuries of dust that had gathered on the steps. Will was a few steps further down. He reached into his pocket and pulled out a handkerchief to cover his nose and mouth. She wished she had one as well.

Silence enfolded them. Lara paused, wishing to hear a sound from above, footsteps outside the church, a passing car, even an aeroplane flying overhead, but there was nothing. These stairs could have been a portal between one realm and the next, a limbo where none of the senses functioned. Will was no more than a half dozen steps in front of her, but he had been swallowed by the spiral, so all that remained of him was his flickering shadow against the walls. She dared not linger any longer. If she waited, those shadows would also vanish, and Will would be swallowed by the darkness.

She held her breath, reached out to the wall. The stone beneath her was worn and uneven: the dust and bones made the steps precarious. The wall appeared to crumble as she touched it, but squinting in the failing light she saw she had dislodged more dust.

She stumbled, tried to steady herself as she fell. She heard herself calling Will's name. She was blinded as he turned to her and the torch shone in her eyes. 'Sorry,' he muttered. 'Are you all right?'

She said nothing, but he must have seen the terror in her face. His own mask of fear melted. He reached out to her. 'Come on, Lara. We're nearly there. Take my hand.'

She wanted to refuse, as if accepting his help would be an admission of the trust he demanded of her. Adrenalin pumped through her. She didn't move.

Will climbed back up two steps and reached out to her again. 'Lara,' he said in a gentle voice. 'No one is forcing you to come down here. Whatever it is, I want to share with you. I want you to be a part of it.'

Share death? Lara wondered. *Be a part of the decay down here*? Slowly, she reached out for him. It was like calling for the help her father had never offered, knowing she would never call on him to fulfil the father's role that he had failed so much. Even now, his bitter comments, that she had failed the family and dishonoured their name, rang in her ears. Surely, this was more madness, weaving herself deeper into a pattern of insanity that would further incur her father's wrath.

'What's the matter?' Will asked. His hand closed over hers.

Tears trickled down her cheeks. Will took a step closer to her. His face was level with hers. 'Pearl?' he said softly. 'You don't have to go on if you don't want to.'

Lara shook her head, wiping the tears away. How could she explain she wanted to be away from Beaded and never to return? How could she explain that her feelings were only enhanced by the darkness, not created by them? How could she explain that her mother had been buried in the graveyard and somehow she felt her presence? How could she explain any of it to Will when she couldn't explain it to herself?

Will reached up to her; took her in his arms. She flinched at his touch, not knowing whether to pull away, or allow herself to be engulfed; to accept the likelihood he would betray her again, or to continue listening to his lies. She didn't know which one she had the strength to face.

Suddenly she tensed again, recoiling from his touch, retreating a couple of stairs. Will did not move. She was unable to read his expression; his face was a shadow.

'Lara,' he spoke softly. 'No one's going to make you go anywhere *you* don't want to go, but I *have* to go on.'

She said nothing. The brutal silence froze her heart. She heard a bell ringing, like a warning of distant memories. She squinted down the stairs at him. The coils were becoming narrower and narrower. The deathlike stillness chilled her blood. 'I can't,' she said, squeezing her eyes shut. Her voice sounded hollow and warped. It seemed to hang in the air. 'I can't trust you, Will. I can't go on.'

Will bowed his head gravely. 'I thought you'd say that,' he said and his voice plumbed the depths of sorrow. 'I can't change what I did. I didn't know I'd fall in love with you. I didn't want it to happen, but we can't help the way our feelings change, can we? I realised things could never be the same between us afterwards. We live with the consequences of our actions, however hard it might be.'

Lara peered back up the stairs, her escape to salvation. 'I don't think we were supposed to find this place. Not us. Someone better.'

'Do you really think that? Why would the *Gawain*-poet have left such a clear map if it wasn't going to lead us here?' He gave a long sigh. 'Problem is we can't always control who finds our hidden secrets.' He turned away from her. 'I would have given anything to not have betrayed you, Lara. I wish there was some way of changing what's been done, but it seems the serum didn't lead to what I was promised.'

'If it *had* worked, you wouldn't have been with me. If I'd changed the past, you'd have stayed with Janet and your son. You'd have never met me.'

Will nodded. 'If you could change one thing in the past, what would it be? Seeing if there was a way of bringing your mother back? Seeing if there was a way to keep your family together? If you can change one mistake then you're rich!'

Lara shook her head. 'We learn from our mistakes. I may have made some serious mistakes in my life but I've come through it. I got away from Michael. I can get by on my own. Who said, "what doesn't kill us makes us stronger"? I'd hate to think I'd spent my entire life in a protective bubble and learned nothing in my time on this earth.'

Will had screwed up his fist, emphasising his resolution. 'But if you could change one mistake from history – warn Archduke Ferdinand that Sarajevo was dangerous? Tell Abraham Lincoln to stay in and read a book rather than going to the theatre? Or warn the Soviets they needed to spend more money on Chernobyl? Wouldn't you do it?'

'They wouldn't have listened,' she said eventually. 'Time can't change. History can't change, it'll find a way to get back on course again.' She sighed unhappily. 'And even if it won't, maybe I *did* sort something out. Maybe I've already done it. Nothing to do with Lincoln or World War Two or Chernobyl, because we *know* that those happened, but something that was worse than JFK's assassination and Hiroshima or 9/11. But who'd know, because time has gone on from the point I changed it?'

He did not answer. She watched him walking down the steps. The torchlight became hidden by the spiral staircase. She stepped out into the darkness; it was a leap of faith. Just one false step would break her ankle and Will might not be there to catch her when she fell. It was the cloud of unknowing that shrouded her and she was clawing desperately to free herself from the miasma.

Behind her, above her, she heard a sound. It was strange, unidentifiable, like a footfall in a forest, or the cackling of the wind. She was hyperventilating. She pulled her damp collar away from her neck. She stepped again, stumbling on loose fragments of the stone and steadying herself against the cold stone. She saw the light in front of her again, a beguiling shadow of a will-o-wisp.

She continued onwards, steadying herself against the wall. Will stopped. Lara almost ran into him and he turned and looked at her coolly.

Will shrugged. 'I'd have given anything to find out what those supernatural investigators had really seen. I bet she saw … or felt … something important and that was why they left.' His gaze became distant. 'I wonder why they chose to hide what they found instead of confronting it.'

'Maybe there was nothing there.'

Will snorted. 'You know she saw something real. But *you* were the one it was calling to.' He gave a long sigh. 'No. It was something else. Maybe it was just too big for them.'

The shadows had taken a life of their own as they flickered across the wall. Cold hands squeezed at her heart. She thought something would burst in her chest. The paths of terror were clogging up her brain. She struggled against the surrounding darkness. Realisation dawned on her. 'It was the Seal. *He* must have seen the seal at the top of the stairs, and knew that if anyone went past it …'

Will looked at her incredulously. 'What seal?'

'Gawain referred to the seal on his shield as "the endless knot". It was at the top of the stairs. It wasn't broken until you went past it.'

'*What* seal?'

She spoke with sudden realisation. 'That was the Seal of Solomon on the wall by the entrance: the seal of wisdom. It wasn't supposed to be broken.' She took a deep breath and her lungs were filled with a sickly stench, like rotten cheese. She retched, but didn't vomit. 'Do you realise what we've done? We untied the endless knot.'

'I don't believe this,' Will said aghast. 'You let me walk past a Seal and you didn't even tell me?'

'I didn't know what it was.'

Will's hands were livid. Then, as quickly as his rage had come, the anger flowed from his face. 'You wouldn't have known. It's not your fault.'

'What wouldn't I have known?' she demanded, annoyed at his presumption of her ignorance.

'That a Seal would've been put at the top of the stairs to keep some force in, or out ... my guess is the woman you saw ... she sensed something beyond the seal, but it was psychic emanations from whatever's down here. Nothing else. She reached out with her mind and touched it, woke it. I'm hoping that we haven't done the same.'

'Woken what?' Lara said. Her imagination conjured unspeakable creatures in her mind. Will gave no answer, instead he continued down the stairs. She followed.

When she expected to have to go down a further step, her foot met solid stone. Her footfall echoed around the small chamber. Will's torch pierced the darkness. She saw rows of composite pillars, joined to the ribs of the vaulting across the ceiling. Will's breath coiled in front of him like the breath of a sleeping dragon. Shadowy alcoves adorned the walls, each containing a tomb. Marble effigies of the deceased lay across the top of some of them. Carvings of knights in their battle armour lined the sides.

Is this what's meant by stepping back in time? Lara wondered. She tried to follow Will's torchlight. The vast unknown was a precipice in front of her and she was teetering on the edge. One single misplaced step would force her into the Abyss.

She stepped forward, ducking under a partially-decayed arch. Her movement echoed around the vault. It was slow and uncertain. She did not want to stumble and fall. In the torchlight she made her way towards the nearest of the tombs, running her fingers along the stone statue of a great knight at rest. She traced through the dust on the epitaph; the torchlight glanced across the tomb. *Thomas de Masci,* she read. Through the torchlight she saw seven great stone vaults in the crypt. Seven tombs, all that remained of the house of de Masci.

'Seven,' Will said. 'And arranged like the points of the star in Holywell.'

Lara jerked. The distant sounds had become more prominent, like someone following them down the steps. Her heart thumped violently in her chest. Dust clung to the nervous perspiration on her hands. For a moment she imagined a mason chiselling the stone; then the vault was filled with grieving relatives. She saw their sombre expressions and their funeral weeds. An elderly woman was being comforted by a younger man, presumably her son. She heard the minister reciting the Latin mass, commending the soul of '*the most faithful of brethren*' to the cradle of God. This was no pauper's funeral.

She gazed at the tomb and at the effigy of the deceased. The hands were livid, as though he had valiantly fought death and almost succeeded in his struggle. The proud face was wan, with thick hair and beard. Age had traced lines into his gaunt face, but the muscles were those of a warrior, even in old age and death. The armour glinted with the lights from the mass's candles and she even thought there was a trace of incense in the air.

For a moment, she was a part of the funeral, one of the mourners. Her heart fell, like when she had realised her friends at school had a mother and she had not. She drew some comfort from having a family briefly, even if it was not her own. But she was also unnerved about these glimpses across time and she needed to be away, back in her present.

She felt a touch on her arm, waking her from her dream. Will was looking at her, his face lined with concern. 'Are you all right?'

Lara nodded. 'It frightens me when you drift off like that,' he admitted. 'I don't know what you're thinking.'

'All this death,' she murmured softly. 'These people were loved. They had folk to mourn them when they died. This man was someone's husband, he was someone's father.' She did not tell him about her insight into the funeral. She didn't trust him with any of her thoughts. There was still time for him to turn against her. 'One thing I don't understand,' she said. 'We've just followed clues to a man's grave. How did he know where to lead us if he was leading us to his tomb?'

'This is a family tomb, Lara,' Will said. 'All of the names here are from the de Masci family. Here's Gerard. Then there's Thomas, William,' he scurried round the tombs. 'That's John de Masci.' He stopped, overawed. 'This is Hugo. He must be the poet.'

'How do you know?'

'The first page of *Gawain*, has the name "Hugo" at the top of the folio.' He reluctantly moved away from the sarcophagus. 'There's Alison. She must have been his wife, and next to her.' His voice fell, 'Margery de Masci, the subject of *Pearl*.'

'The little girl?'

Will nodded sadly. 'Alison must have been her mother and at the end of the line of tombs, Margery's father. Hugo.' He touched the stone lovingly. 'At last we know who the poet truly is.' He returned to Hugo's tomb and pointed to a clasp at the top. The metal was rusted and flaking. 'It's on a hinge. He was expecting someone to find him and to open the tomb without breaking it.' He reached for the clasp, but Lara held his hand. 'What's the matter?' Will said. His voice was edgy.

'Just something you said on the stairs about "death with wings",' she said softly. 'We've come this far. Do you really think the poet will give all of his secrets without a final little surprise?'

'What are you thinking?'

Lara tried to answer, but she was momentarily silenced. An infinity of thoughts crowded into her mind. Her heart thumped in her chest. She shivered again. 'I think the name on the manuscript, "Hugo", might be a red herring, or maybe a dedication to the poet's father, or something. It floats on the first folio like a spectre; it doesn't have any relevance. I think there's something we've missed. I need the manuscript.'

Will pointed to the tomb once more. 'But it's a *hinge*,' he said irritated.

'The manuscript,' Lara said, holding out her hand.

Will surrendered it reluctantly. Lara turned through the pages to *Gawain*. 'Something's been bothering me,' she said. 'When the poet talks about the Seal of Solomon, he keeps talking about the symbolism of the five points.'

'Yes,' Will said patiently, as if Lara was pointing out the obvious.

'Five senses, five fingers, five wounds of Christ, five joys of the Virgin, five virtues ...'

'Yes,' Will said again. 'We worked that out. Stanza 25 is reversed to 52, which is where the code starts.'

'Five, five, five, five, five,' Lara said. 'He's really labouring the point.'

Will rolled his eyes. 'He's not the only one. What's *your* point?'

'So obvious,' Lara said. 'Suppose he's pointing us to the fifth stanza.' She turned to the folio describing the Court before the arrival of the Green Knight.

Bot Arthure wolde not ete til al were serued,
He watz so ioly of his ioyfnes, and sumquat childgered:
His lif liked hym lyȝt, he louied þe lasse
Auþer to longe lye or to longe sitte,
So bisied him his ȝonge blod and his brayn wylde.

And also an oþer maner meued him eke
Þat he þurȝ nobelay had nomen, he wolde neuer ete
Vpon such a dere day er hym deuised were
Of sum auenturus þyng an vncouþe tale,
Of sum mayn meruayle, þat he myȝt trawe,
Of alderes, of armes, of oþer auenturus,
Oþer sum segg hym bisoȝt of sum siker knyȝt
To ioyne wyth hym in iustyng, in iopardé to lay

She translated aloud: 'But Arthur would not eat until all were served. He was so jolly in his joyousness, and childlike in his excitement. He liked the carefree life and loathed the thought of lazing or sitting around, so he busied his young blood and his wild brain. And, in another way, he was also moved, that through nobility, he had undertaken that he would never eat upon such a dear day until he had heard of some adventurous thing, an unknown tale, of many marvels that he might hear of princes, of prowess or other adventures, or that a knight would seek them out to join with him in jousting, to lay his life in jeopardy …'

'This is fascinating,' Will said impatiently. 'But I don't see what you're getting at.'

Lara squinted at the characters. 'It's the alliteration and the stresses on the letters, Will. Look what it spells out.'

Will squinted to read the manuscript. He spoke uncertainly. '"*W*olde" … "*w*ere" … "ser-*w*erd",' he glanced over at Lara. She nodded, her eyes glittering with excitement. He continued: '"*i*oly" … "*i*oyfulnes" … "ch*i*ldgered".'

'That's it,' Lara said, almost jumping.

Will spelled out the letters: 'W … I … L … L …' He went to the next line. '*b*isied'… '*b*lood.'

Lara put a hand on his arm. 'No,' she said, urgently. 'Look at the stresses in the words. "B*i*sied … h*i*m … h*i*s … bra*y*n … w*y*lde". The "I" sound is repeated.'

Will gave an unconvinced snort. 'Let's assume you're correct.

And by that rationale, the next line is "A" ... "*A*nd *a*lso *a*n oþer m*a*ner".' He looked at the next lines: 'The "N" is repeated, and the "D", then the "A", then "M" ... "A" ... "S" ... "I".' He stared at her in astonishment. 'Willia*n* da Masi,' he breathed. 'It's not perfect, but ...'

'When has anything the poet did been "perfect"?' Lara said. 'The seven sided star? The pentangle in Avignon? The whole point of the poem is to show that even the most perfect knight *can't* be perfect.' She pointed again to the line of imperfection: 'He þurȝ nobelay had nomen ...'

'"Through nobility he had undertaken ..."' Will started.

'But that's not all it says. "Nomen" in Latin means "named". It *could* read "he had been nobly named".'

Astonishment washed over Will's face. 'And that's the name of the poet? It was there all along? William de Masi?'

She moved over to William's tomb, tracing her fingers over the top, brushing the dust away. The inscription read: *William da Masci – Kt.*

There was a simple emblem on the stone. Two knights sharing a horse, with the inscription: *Sigillum militum Xpisti.*

'Now,' she said, returning the manuscript to Will, who placed it in his pocket. 'Sir William's a clever man. He worked out how to write in a way only someone with ... lateral thinking ... is going to realise there's a code. Anyone else is going to think it's a clever piece of literature.'

'It *is* a clever piece of literature,' Will said.

'But even now,' she said. 'He wants to make sure we've been paying attention. He isn't going to leave the answer in his own grave. He can't *do* that. And it'd be too obvious. He's going to make sure the clue is where he wants it.' Lara reached into her pocket and pulled out her own notebook. She turned to a page where she had written out letters substituted by numbers. She peered at the inscription on Sir William's grave. 'His name is written as William d*a* Masci – with an "A" as in the manuscript.

All the other names are spelled with an "E".'

Will took the notebook from her. 'He doesn't use a "C" in the manuscript either,' he said. He substituted letters for numbers: *23, 10, 12, 12, 10, 1, 14*. He did the same for the rest of his name, then added them together. "One hundred and thirty-two," Will announced. He moved over to the rows of tombs. 'I guess we need to start counting.'

Lara shook her head. 'That's not what it says. It says "William da Masci – Kt". I think it means you have to deduct the sum of "K" and "T" from the total.'

Will used her notebook to find the numerical values of the letters. 'Deduct 20 and 11.' He paused. 'Total: 101.'

'*Now* we start counting,' Lara said.

Will started with Sir William's tomb, then moved clockwise: John, Hugo, Alison, Margery, then Gerard, Thomas, back to William and onwards, round and round, like a wheel of chance, until he counted, 'ninety-nine, one hundred, one hundred and one.' He stopped, pointing at Margery's tomb. The statue on top was of a small child. A cap covered her hair, her hands held together in prayer over a long white gown. The epitaph written for her was simply *þe pryuy perle*. There was a flower engraved in the lid: a rose.

'I'd have thought it would be a daisy: a marguerite,' Will said. 'The rose has thorns.'

'So does the poem,' Lara said.

Will became quiet. 'Margery …' His eyes became both sad and anxious. 'Lara, you can't expect me to defile the tomb of a three year old girl?'

'What's the difference between that and a seventy year old man? It's still defiling a tomb.'

'I don't understand this, why would he leave his secrets in the tomb of his daughter? I'd have thought he'd have wanted to give her eternal rest.'

'It's not his daughter's tomb,' Lara said, snapping her fingers.

'In the story of *Pearl,* he says he "lost her in a garden", she wasn't buried in the family tomb, she must have been buried on the family lands, after all, that's where the dreamer goes to sleep.'

'All right,' Will said slowly. 'You've convinced me, but I really don't like this.' He walked over to Margery's tomb, placing his torch down onto the floor. The light made a wide yellow arc across the side, highlighting the carvings of ancient angelic faces set to guard the child while she slept for eternity.

'Here goes nothing,' Will said, tracing his fingers along the side of the coffin. Then, trying to gain purchase on the stone, he tried to heave it up. His face contorted with exertion and he exhaled loudly, thumping the top of the coffin in frustration.

'This isn't going anywhere,' he spat. He looked around, as if searching for something to smash open the tomb.

Lara moved to his side, looking down at the slab and the effigy of the little girl. She could make out a few words: *Hic jacet.* Her eyes ran over the rest of the words, *obiit 1398.*

Lara's eyes narrowed. Something was wrong, something she couldn't quite put her finger on.

Then she saw it. The date. It should have been in Roman numerals.

She traced her fingers over the numerals. They were slightly indented. She pressed down.

As if on a spring, the number gave way. Lara gasped, releasing it. The number returned to where it had been. She touched it again. With a little pressure, she was able to slide the number along until the number 7 was showing.

'Will?' she breathed, as she pushed the number next to it to reveal the number 8. Will watched, his jaw hanging open as Lara pushed the next number, but in a slightly different way: the number 3 slid downwards to become the number 4. When she touched the number 1 it remained fixed in position.

'What do you think?' Lara said.

Will moved closer, pushing one of the numbers himself.

'There'll be a sequence. Something the poet would expect us to know.' He leaned over, squinting in the gloom, sliding the numbers up and down. When he clicked the last one into place, he stepped back. Lara saw that the number sequence now read *1212* – the number of lines of *Pearl*.

Nothing.

'The first number doesn't move,' Lara observed. 'It's not part of the combination. This is something more subtle.' She squeezed her eyes closed, sifting through her mind. 'It's something we would have noticed.' She gently placed her hands over his and began to move the numbers.

'It'll take forever to try all the combinations,' Will protested

'We'd better make a start then,' Lara whispered. She reached out with her mind. A thought fluttered just beyond her grasp. A feather caught by a gust.

'Something's missing,' she breathed. Then, something clicked in her mind. 'Everything that the poet did was flawed,' she said as she moved the first number to 4. She laughed to herself. 'It's like he was perfect with his imperfections.' She pushed the second number up to 7. Finally, she slid the last number down to 2: *472*.

There was an audible click.

'The missing line from *Pearl*,' Lara explained.

Will nodded slowly. He gripped the end of the tomb and heaved.

Hinges protested, grinding with centuries of neglect. The sound of grating stone. There was a hiss of dark vapours as the lid opened. A foul stench filled the room: decay and disease. Will stepped back, gagging on the foul clouds of death gases clawing at his mouth, as he tried to prevent himself from vomiting. The stone lid crashed down. The sound thundered through the crypt like an explosion. Tiny shards of stone and dust fell from the ceiling. Lara felt the floor trembling. She rushed to Will's side, regretting it as the nauseating odour of decomposition and putrefaction became more intense. Will was choking, coughing. His eyes were rheumy.

'Are you all right?' she asked.

'Don't think I breathed too much in,' Will said. 'I'll be okay.' He looked down at her, steadying himself against the side of the tomb. 'Can you give me a hand with this thing?'

Lara nodded. Both taking a deep breath, they heaved up the tomb lid.

The torchlight did not reach the interior of the tomb; instead the heart of the sepulchre was bathed in shadow. Lara leaned down and picked up the light. She dreaded to look inside, knowing the skeletal face of a child might be leering up at her. She squeezed her eyes shut as she pointed the beam inside, cutting away the shadows.

'My God,' Will said.

Lara did not want to open her eyes, but, like Lot's wife, she felt compelled to look. She squeezed one eye open.

Parchments, leather-bound manuscripts, vellum documents. This tomb was a hive of information from a time long forgotten. Will leafed through them like a child in a sweetshop, not sure what he should try first.

'This is brilliant,' he said, his eyes glowing. 'This must be the largest find of medieval papers ever.' He started to look through a leather-bound manuscript and examine the pages. 'This is a history of the Order of the Garter, these are sermons and ideas of early Christian philosophy, and this' – he held up another set of pages – 'this looks like another manuscript written by Sir William.' He grinned at Lara. 'Do you think he had another code buried in this one? Do you think our journey has just started?'

Lara shook her head. 'For you, maybe. It would take the rest of your life to sort through these. I don't see it has anything to do with me anymore.'

'Disappointed that we didn't find any gold?' Will asked. 'This is bigger than any hoard.' He lifted the vellum and parchments carefully from the tomb, then rummaged at the bottom. 'What's this?' he said.

Will held a small piece of metal in the torchlight. Looking closely, she saw it was a golden signet ring. The pentacle from Gawain's shield was engraved in the metal. 'Looks like Sir William took his idea of Gawain's virtues very seriously,' Will said.

'That little trinket?' Lara said. She didn't want to stay in the crypt any longer.

Will offered her the ring, so she could examine it more closely. But it seemed to be calling to her, challenging her. She backed away. '*I will show you fear in a handful of dust,*' Lara said softly.

'That's not *Twelfth Night*.'

'No, it's T.S. Eliot. I think he was telling us not all treasures have a monetary, or even a physical value.'

Will dropped the ring into his pocket alongside the manuscript. He turned back to the vellum.

Lara stared around the room. The darkness seemed to be closing in on them. She wondered if the strange apparitions lurking in the corner of the rooms were their own shadows, or spectres of the past who had come to protect their treasures. More than once she thought she saw glowing eyes, then two pairs, stalking them, surrounding them, cutting off their escape to the world above.

'Will, do we have to stay any longer?' she breathed. 'Can't you read them outside?'

Will did not appear to hear her. He had escaped into a forgotten world to which he had been granted limited access. It was as though the papers would melt away from him like a dream once he left the crypt.

'These manuscripts were buried for a reason,' Lara said. 'Do we have the right to bring them to light?'

Will moved his head towards her. He seemed reluctant to tear his eyes away from the papers. Eventually, he nodded. 'These papers are of vital historical importance. They explain the importance of the Order of the Garter. This is big news.' His eyes widened. He held up a large piece of vellum with a wax seal attached. 'This is a Papal Bull. It says the Pope absolved the Templars of all heresies in 1308.'

'What's the big deal?'

'Most Templars were accused of being heretics. It means there was some serious pressure on the Pope.'

Lara shook her head, not really understanding.

Will began to gently leaf through the parchment. Some of the pages were brittle; fragments were falling away with his touch. Suddenly he stopped. His eyes widened.

'Oh God,' he managed to breathe.

'What is it?' Lara was at his side. He had turned to a page of vellum. The ink had faded, but Will was tracing his finger along the lines, and was mouthing the words.

'What is it?' Lara said again.

'This is the document everyone's has been looking for,' Will said. 'It's written by Sir William.' He traced along a few more lines.

'What does it say?' When Will did not answer, she asked again.

Will was annoyed at the distraction. 'Hold on,' and he read out loud:

> *'I, William de Maßci, surrendre my wisdom to þe, who haþ followed þe paþ of my laye Sir Gawayne, & which haþ brought þe to þis, mi last reßting place.*
>
> *Siþen þe deþe of mi dauAter, þere shal be no mor of þe lyne of de Maßci. Mi family is deßcended from þe grete crußader who founded wiþ Richardus Rex Cor-Leonam þe miȝtie temple of* שדקמה תיב'.

Will stumbled when pronouncing the Hebrew writing: *Beit HaMikdash.*

'What's that?' Lara asked.

'The Holy House. It's how the first Temple of Solomon at Jerusalem is described,' Will said. 'Destroyed two and a half centuries ago by the Babylonians. It was the place where Solomon kept the Ark of the Covenant.' He continued to read:

> *'Sir Gerard returned from þe Holy Londes with a great priß – þe legendary Ring of Solomon – for which þe ordre of þe Poore Fellowe Kniȝtes of Krist and of þe Temple of Solomon was founded.'*

He breathed in astonishment. 'The Ring of Solomon,' he explained. 'Lara, this "little trinket" is what King Solomon used to control the demons ...'

'And that's why it cannot be left in your control,' a voice said from behind them. Lara and Will turned as one. Will's torch beam found a face at the foot of the stairs: Tantris.

18

The relief that washed over Lara at seeing Tantris, a familiar face, quickly subsided. There was something in his gait, his posture, his very presence, that made her feel uneasy. Will must have felt it too. His hand covered his pocket containing the manuscript and the ring. Tantris's hands were in his own pockets as if concealing something.

'How do?' Tantris said pleasantly, but there was a bitter edge to his smile. He turned to Will and held out his hand. 'The ring, if you please. It belongs to us.'

Will clutched his pocket tighter, shielding it from Tantris. 'Not a chance. Not after what we've been through.' He stabbed a finger at Lara. 'What she's been through.'

Tantris took a step towards them. Will backed away into Margery's tomb. 'You don't have any choice, Will,' Tantris said. 'The ring is an object of absolute power. Power corrupts. It can't be left in the hands of one man.'

'It can't be left in the hands of one Government either,' Will said. 'There's no way we'd let you take this and let armies use it against their enemies.'

'I never worked for the Government,' Tantris said flatly.

'Wait a second,' Lara said. His voice was desperate. 'What's so important about it?'

'If this is what Sir William says it is, then it's the ring Archangel Michael gave to Solomon to discern the names of demons in order to control them to help construct the temple of Jerusalem,' Will explained, looking anxiously at Tantris.

Tantris nodded, '*The Testament of Solomon* also tells of someone who cannot control the power he is given and loses it all for the love of a woman.'

'So what's your interest in this?' Lara demanded, finding new reserves of defiance.

Will didn't wait for Tantris to answer; nor did his gaze flicker from him. 'You remember I told you there were two organisations following us in Avignon? Tantris here has been a member of one of them all the time.' He shook his head. 'That was pretty sharp, getting to us at the canal in Chester. It's like you knew what we were doing before *we* did.'

Tantris nodded slowly. 'It certainly could appear that way.'

'I thought it was strange how you seemed to know all about the tunnels in Bath,' Will continued. 'At least you didn't tell us "trust no one",' Will said bitterly. 'That really would have been a cliché.'

'You were doing a good job of trusting no one by yourself.' Tantris smiled. 'It may have been clichéd, but it would also have been good advice.'

'And your name isn't really "Tantris" is it?' Will said. 'I should have spotted that right from the beginning.' He glanced at Lara. 'In Béroul's *Tristan*, Tristan arrives in Ireland and calls himself "Tantris" to avoid giving away his true identity.'

'Not a very good pseudonym,' Lara muttered. 'Don't suppose you're going to tell who you work for?'

Tantris shook his head. 'But it's not the Government of any country, nor any terrorist organisation.'

'I'm sure you wouldn't admit to it, even if you were,' Lara said acerbically. 'Then who's left?'

Tantris removed his hands from his pockets and held them out, palms facing them, to show there was no threat. His head bowed slowly. 'This is outside of the remit of a Government, or NATO, or even the United Nations. There are other powers in the world to which even these great organisations must bow.' He stepped away from them and leaned against Gerard de Masci's tomb. He looked at them, as if he were a storyteller, waiting for the children to settle before he began 'There are some forces not bound by political rules.'

'Such as?' Lara asked.

'Start with the weather,' Tantris said. 'No Government can stop it.'

'Will!' Lara said with sarcastic enthusiasm. 'Tantris is an agent of the North Wind!'

Will shook his head, suddenly serious. 'You're not talking about the wind. You're talking about something more ... supernatural.'

Tantris raised an eyebrow and nodded. 'The storm clouds are gathering.'

Lara gave a cynical laugh. 'And the earth shall shake and the ocean floors shall crack asunder, and the oceans will pour into the chasms. And nameless abominations shall ravage the earth. And the rest of the day will have light winds with scattered showers.' She laughed, in spite of herself and was surprised when Will shot an angry glare at her.

'This is important,' he hissed.

Tantris pointed to the pocket concealing the ring. 'This is another weapon to help our war against chaos. From chaos, order will come, and from order, life will come.' He closed his eyes for a moment, then reached into his pocket. Lara flinched. Then he took out a battered packet of cigarettes. He offered them to Will and Lara, who silently refused. He lit the cigarette with a flame-less lighter and inhaled deeply. As he breathed out the smoke coiled away from his mouth and hung in the still air like morning mist.

'Have you read the *Book of the Apocalypse*?' Tantris asked looking directly at Will.

Will nodded. 'It was called *Revelation* when I read it. I was fourteen. It scared me to death.'

'But you'd have read it again since then?'

Will grunted an acknowledgement.

'*Hit is a syngne þat Salamon set sumquyle,*' Tantris said, not faltering over the Middle English. 'The seals of the Apocalypse are those which signify not the end of the world, but a "new" beginning as well as the fifteen signs before Judgement.' He indicated up the spiral stairs with his head. 'Here in the church is a seal. It is not one of the seals of Revelation, but the stone in which it is infused is ancient indeed.'

'Infused?' Will said, puzzled.

Tantris nodded as he drew on the cigarette once again. 'It was infused in Babylonian times, brought back by Gerard de Masci who was with the crusaders when they took Jerusalem in 1099. He also took the ring you now hold; it is called the *pentalpha*. Sal ad-Din fought to take Jerusalem almost a century later, solely to reclaim the ring.'

'But he didn't find it,' Will said, reaching into his pocket and taking out the ring. His eyes took on a nasty shine. 'You realise I could use this to discern your name?'

'Would it do you any good?' Tantris asked innocently. He pointed to the ring. 'Of course, it was already in England, already under the careful guardianship of the de Masci family. But when Margery died, the line and the hopes of the de Masci family died with her. That's why it was such a lamentable tragedy that led Sir William to write *Pearl*. It was a practice before he wrote *Sir Gawayne*.'

'You knew this all along,' Will accused. 'Why did you need me to trail around and follow the clues? Why not just come and find it yourself?'

'We cannot interfere with the course of time. *You* broke our predictions and stole the manuscript, *you* started to follow the path. You had to believe you were doing this yourself, doing this in defiance of us, not because of us.'

'This doesn't make sense,' Will said, holding up the manuscript. 'There are a million copies of the Gawain manuscript available, even facsimiles of the original. What makes this one so important? Why couldn't someone else get the Clarendon Press version and follow the clues?'

'Because the manuscript you hold is not the B-text as you

suggest, but the first that was written, the only one in the author's own hand, not a copy like the one stored in the British Library. It is ... *infused* with the poet's knowledge. It is, as you would say, Lara, "the sweet Roman's hand".'

'I'm not following you,' Lara said. 'Why should that make a difference?'

Tantris's kept looking at Will. 'You can empathise with items from the past simply by touching them. You can see through Sir William's eyes by holding the manuscript; feel his thoughts around you so thick that you have to push them away.' He took a step towards Will. 'If you concentrated,' Tantris continued, and Lara wondered if she could see a look of trepidation in his face, 'you could even see the things that Solomon saw.' He took a long, deep breath. 'I don't advise it.'

Lara stood straight. 'Hold on. *I'm* the one who was injected. I'm the one who can supposedly do this.'

Tantris slowly shook his head. 'You were *both* injected,' he said in a quiet voice.

Will did not answer for a long time. His mouth fell open, flapping in soundless speech. His eyes were wide, and Lara wondered if she saw fear etching its way across his face. His shoulders slumped as he eventually found his voice. 'Bastards.'

Tantris cocked his head and took another long draw on the cigarette. An eternity passed before he spoke again. 'I'm afraid you're as much a part of this experiment as she was, Will. Your circumstances had to be manipulated for you to get to Bath.'

Realisation crossed Will's face. 'They killed Roger.' His voice was like air escaping from a tyre. 'Then Janet. They killed them just to get me to play their games.'

'It was necessary,' Tantris replied. There was no hint of apology or remorse in his voice. These three words where his way of offering an explanation.

Will screamed as he lunged across the room. The torch clattered to the floor. It bounced once and the light failed. Lara heard the sound of scuffling where Tantris had been leaning. She fumbled across the floor, trying to find the torch, hoping the fall had only dislodged the batteries, not broken the bulb.

Her hands closed over something small and cold. Bolts of pain seared through her hand. With this came the realisation that Will had dropped the ring as he had leapt at Tantris. She held the ring of Solomon.

The ring called to her, more than that, it was *commanding* her. She twisted it between her thumb and forefinger. This was an artefact of unspeakable power. She tried to resist it, but knew she had neither the strength nor the will. She wanted to throw it away, but the more passionate part of her mind wanted to see why it was so important.

There was no light. In the distance she heard the two men struggling. It seemed so far away, they could have belonged to a different time. Surely no one would notice if she was quick. Deftly she slipped the ring onto her finger.

For a moment she felt no different, but when she tried to remove the ring she felt it fighting her, challenging her. *Now I know how Frodo felt*, she thought unhappily.

A great void opened in front of her, and she knew she was no longer in her view of present day, but in a time before history was recorded.

The chamber melted away. She no longer felt the cold; instead she felt the abrasive sandy winds of the desert buffeting her. In front of her the great King Solomon was standing, holding aloft the ring of power. She smiled, realising that Solomon did not have ginger hair and a forked beard as he had been depicted in Avignon. He was a handsome black man, his hair and beard streaked with grey. She heard him shouting; his voice was powerful and it rose high above the winds. The words were a foreign language to her, but at the same time they seemed familiar.

She did not hear the words. She tried to block them from her mind. She squinted through the shimmering heat haze of the desert, seeing unnameable shapes as they manifested themselves at Solomon's command, bowing to his power. When they spoke, they spat and growled at him, begrudging his command of them. They each told him their names and the celestial body that ruled over them. She saw one of the demons refusing to co-operate. Solomon sealed it in a small earthenware vase. The stopper was marked with the same seal, but with four letters: הוהי

Solomon commanded the demons to construct the Temple, spinning hemp for the construction ropes, cutting blocks of Theban marble and moulding clay for the Temple vessels. An Arabian Wind demon moved an immense corner stone that could not be lifted by all the workers and the demons together. Then the Twelve Tribes joined with the building, until the temple was complete. It was a construction of brilliant beauty and perfect geometry. Lara could barely take in the details: pillars with bases of gold, silver and bronze; courtyards full of trees, flowers and fountains; lamps glittering with emeralds, hyacinth sapphires and lapis lazuli, and graven seraphim and cherubim guarding the altar.

Then she saw a woman, beautiful as the night, demanding that Solomon sacrifice beetles in the name of Molloch, in return for sexual pleasures. He did this, not realising it was not the value of the life that was important, but the action of sacrificing to a demon. The Wisdom of Solomon was lost. He had fallen from favour from the Almighty and the demons he'd commanded broke free from the invisible chains that had shackled them. They lost the allegorical imagery that Lara had first perceived. They were nothing like the denizens Milton described with red cloak, horns and a pointy tail. These were terrible creatures from unremembered nightmares. She caught momentary flashes of a leathery hide and wings, a prehensile tail, snatching claws, snapping jaws. She saw them attacking Solomon, not to kill him, but to blind him.

Then their eyes turned, as one, to her who now carried the ring. She saw salivating maws, some with needle-like teeth, others with teeth the size of a building. She tried to scream, but the sound froze in her throat, burned away by the desert sun. She tried to run, but the sand clawed at her, dragging her down. She screamed again and this time she found a voice for her fears. Time froze around her, and her ears were filled with the single high-pitched wail of her death cries.

She felt a gentle hand on her shoulder. She felt the ring being removed from her finger. She did not fight Tantris. She was laying on the hard flagstones in the tomb, shivering in the cold, eyes straining in the darkness. The sole light was the glowing tip of Tantris's cigarette that had fallen to the floor. In the silence, she heard the crackling of the tobacco as it burned.

She leaned her head into him and cried. He stroked her hair and spoke in a language she'd never heard before. The language of comfort.

'You understand now, Lara,' Tantris said, his voice was a stark contrast to the silence, even though he spoke gentle words. 'The ring calls to you. It is too powerful for any one person to hold, the desire to try and control it is too great.' His voice dropped. 'Give the ring to me. There is an organisation in Ephesus who specialise in the study of magical antiquities. I promise you no Government shall have this power.'

Will had been fumbling in the dark. He finally found the torch and turned it on. It was an explosion in the darkness. The image of the crypt burned into her retinas. She blinked, trying to clear the purple stains on her eyes. She could make out Will. He had abandoned them to their discussion and was hurriedly looking through the parchments, manuscripts and scrolls. He picked up Sir William's testament and continued to read.

She twisted her neck and looked up at Tantris. 'Who *are* you?' her voice was hoarse. It felt like she had been swallowing burning sands.

'It's better you don't know,' Tantris said quietly. 'There are things even the Governments of the world shouldn't know. Some avenues are better left unexplored.'

'Are you a Templar or a descendant of that Order? Is that how you know these things?'

'No,' Tantris said. 'Your poet may have misled you. The Holy Crusades were not about finding the Ring of Solomon. That was merely an added bonus. There were other reasons, darker reasons.' His gaze became empty; for the first time she thought she saw a trace of humanity in his eyes.

Not humanity. Fear.

'The storm clouds had gathered and the Templars had to disperse them. For centuries they've rooted out the evil. Decades ago they finished their quest, but still they stand, watchful, in case they discover another line, yet to be … finished.'

'I don't understand,' Lara said.

Tantris shook his head. Lara wondered if he was embarrassed. 'Nor should you. Forgive me. These are the ramblings of a nostalgic old man.'

'But all these things, the ring, the demons I saw. Surely that's just fiction. These things don't really exist.'

'Believe that if you will,' Tantris said. 'It is closed minded, but you'll be kept safe with those thoughts.' He stared into the corner of the chamber. 'But never under estimate the power of the unknown.' He looked at Will apologetically. 'I need the ring, and I need to take two of the parchments. One of them is the one you're holding.'

Will held it close to his chest. 'This one? No way! You can't take the only proof we have that William de Masci wrote *Gawayne*. This is the first shred of evidence that's been unearthed since the Cotton library burned down.' She heard his voice cracking, like a witness breaking under cross-examination. 'Don't take this away, please.'

Tantris smiled gently. 'I must. The *Testament of Solomon*, the book that contains the detailed account of Solomon's command over the demons, was removed from the Bible in the third century, because the Council of Nicaea knew it amounted to a tome of practical demonology. The Christian Church didn't advocate the discussion of demons, except as allegories. It was too close to the Truth.

'But Solomon was real. The demons were real. Solomon's seal

was given to the King by the Highest of Powers. God gave humans instructions on how to build other artefacts, Noah's ark and the Ark of the Covenant – which was stored in Solomon's Temple. But that was not the case with the ring.' He held it up. The torchlight danced in the circle of the band of gold. Lara found herself reaching forward, dream-like, desiring it. Her left hand scrabbled around on the flagstones, searching for a loose rock, or anything else to use as a weapon.

But with a simple conjurer's slight-of-hand trick, the ring had vanished from Tantris's hands. With the temptation removed, Lara realised her shoulders had dropped in relaxation.

She felt sick to her stomach. 'Keep it away from me,' she said in a voice filled with self-loathing. 'Take it.'

'What's the other manuscript?' Will asked.

Tantris moved to Will's side and took a single sheet of papyrus, and read it slowly. Lara heard her heartbeat in the silence. Eventually, Tantris spoke again. 'This is the paper which I have sought. The Apocalypse speaks of the seven Seals. Four have already been broken over the last century, this paper outlines the location of the fifth.'

'The fifth seal of Revelation,' Will whispered. 'No wonder you wanted this place to be hidden until the time was right.'

'The fifth seal promises salvation for those slain in the name of God. The fifth angel holds the key to the abyss and promises armies of scorpions across the world.'

'*And quy þe pentangel apendez to þat prince nobel, I am in tent yow to telle, þof tary hyt me schulde,*' Will said softly, finally understanding. 'The text doesn't refer to the Pentangle that Gawain had on his shield. The corruption of the spelling: *Pent-angel*. He's talking about the fifth angel from Revelation.'

'Now perhaps you understand why I have to take all references to the Angel and the seal with me. It is too great a secret for man to unearth. There are some things that are better left unknown.' He crushed the cigarette underfoot. 'Now it's time for me to leave. Please don't follow me.'

Lara wanted to scream. In her mind's eye she saw Tantris re-sealing the crypt with them still inside.

But Tantris's voice had a calming effect. Now he held the ring and the parchments, serenity bathed his face.

'Just answer me one thing,' Will said as Tantris turned away. 'Why did the Cotton library burn down? Was it an accident or was it deliberate?'

Tantris looked at him and the torchlight cast sinister shadows. '*We* were not responsible.' He stared skyward for a moment, as if seeking inspiration, or listening to an answer, then he gave a long sigh. 'But as you correctly observed, there are at least two groups looking for the trail at the end of the *Gawayne* manuscript. Be thankful that it was I who found you first.' With that, he turned on his heels and left.

*

The footsteps retreated from them, fading away as he mounted the stairs. Moments later, it was as though Tantris had never been there.

Will's shoulders sagged. The light dropped lethargically, like a knight lowering his lance when he knows he is beaten. He tried to smile, but he was fighting to hold back tears. It wasn't so much the tears of grief or frustration. Instead, as his shoulders slumped, Lara realised this was his moment of release. He was finally allowing himself to let go now he knew the truth about Roger's death.

When he spoke, his voice grated in his throat; the sound of a voice that had not spoken in centuries. 'They used me.' There was no anger, just the disappointment of realisation. 'They used me to use you, to see what influence they could have over short term events, to see the impact of halting the turning of the Wheel of Fortune and to see how the future might influence the past.

They used the things I loved the most to get to me. Roger, Janet, you, the manuscript.' He looked up at her. Shadows covered his face. 'I had the secret of the *Gawain* manuscript in my hands. I *knew* what the poet wanted us to understand and it's all been stripped away from me.'

Lara didn't speak. She was consumed by the sorrow that had already overwhelmed Will. Losing his wife and son had taken his torment beyond breaking point: he had followed the trail to the point of obsession because it had given him a direction in life. She nodded slowly, beginning to understand a part of her own role in his life. Will had lost his reasons to live and he had set himself the most difficult of tasks to exaggerate his feeling of failure, to give himself a motive to return to the railway lines and end everything properly. Each time she offered him a lifeline, he grabbed it, because it was all he had.

And, now he had achieved it, they had taken it away from him and left him as nothing more than an empty husk. No more purpose. No more hope.

She took a step towards him. Then another. She had expected him to flee, but now she saw a broken man, drained of all energy. Then her arms enfolded him. He didn't move, didn't return her embrace. Nor did he pull away.

'You loved her so very much,' she said. Even now, despite her efforts, she knew her words sounded insincere. 'I can't imagine what you're going through,' she admitted, 'But I understand why you needed to cling to the hope you could call her back.' She felt him becoming limp in her arms. 'Forsaking all others, isn't that what you promised?'

Will pulled away, only a fraction, so he could look at her. He nodded gently.

'What now, Will? What do you have if you don't even have hope to hope for?'

Now he pulled away, turned from her and glanced down at the piles of parchment and vellum. 'Reality,' he said eventually.

'No matter how horrible it is, I still have reality.'

There was no strength in his voice but, in that moment, Lara imagined the puppet master who had been controlling him had cut the strings and set him free. He slumped down against one wall and was hugging his knees to his chest. His hands were trembling. 'Someone once said it's better to have loved and lost, than never to have loved at all. He said if you'd loved and lost, you had the advantage of having loved once.'

'But then you know exactly what you're missing,' Lara said. 'If you've never known company, you have no concept of loneliness.'

Will's eyes became vacant. His spirit had broken. His torment was a sphere of agony around him. It tore Lara's heart to see him there. In that moment, she realised if she could have changed one thing in history, it would not have been to warn of an imminent assassination attempt, or impeding disasters because she knew she would have been seen as Cassandra – able to predict the future, but never believed.

Instead she would have done anything to spare Will this suffering; her decision would change the course of time from a moment where she and Will had never met. Marsh had told her that paradoxes healed themselves. He would find a way to apprehend her without even needing to manipulate Will. She looked back at him once. She would never see him again, he would never know who she was, but at least he would be at a time before all that he loved had been taken away from him.

Not everyone needs to lose in this, she told herself.

She closed her eyes, and was aware of the chamber becoming insubstantial around her. Time became a shimmering pool. It became eternal instead of perpetual. Every instant of time existed in the same moment; then floated past her. It had become easier to step into the pool; easier to find the tiny droplets she needed.

She began to wade through Will's past.

Like shuffling through a deck of cards, she selected a point before she had ever met him, before he had ever *needed* to meet her.

At least a year ago ... Olivia had told him that was when she had last seen him. Roger's death would have been before then. How long did it take for him to be broken on the rack of grief? Two months? Six months? Was eighteen months all it took to turn a happy, successful man with all that he wanted into a wretch determined to end everything?

There were three of them staying in the farm cottage: Will, Janet and Roger. Will appeared a decade younger. Anxiety and trauma had not taken their toll on him. Janet was a slim, pretty woman in her early twenties. She had treacle-coloured hair, tied back in a ponytail, and almond-shaped eyes. Will was exhausted after the long drive; he lay on the sofa with his eyes closed. Janet was busy unpacking and making the beds. Roger was out exploring.

Lara took a mental step away from them, back into the main courtyard of the farmhouse. There was a square of rutted tarmac. The nearby buildings were in a state of near dereliction. Nettles and long grasses grew around them. A red battered wooden door with slats missing from it, warned in slurred white paint 'Danger – Keep Out'. Above the places where the windows had been bricked up were huge gaps in the slating and, like a huge mound of coins in the 'Penny Falls' games at the seaside amusement arcades, the slates piled up against the guttering, ready to fall.

A huge grain chute ran from this building into one of the stables. It was to this that Lara felt herself being drawn. One gate at the stable's entrance was missing and the other hung on rusted hinges, almost hidden behind the foliage. Lara stepped over patches of clover and dandelions and on to the concrete floor. Swallows chirped overhead. She paused at the threshold, hit by the scent of the damp hay, but was surprised there was no odour of animals. Much of the stonework had been started in the fashion of a dry-stone wall, but conventional brick had replaced the places where it had fallen into disrepair.

All she heard was the bleating of the sheep, mocking chirps of the swallows, the creaking of the roof overhead, the occasional proclamation of a cockerel and the gurgle of distant water. She saw a trailer which carried sacks of grain; here was a metal container on its side, covered in bird droppings and spilling out hay. On one side of the barn were vicious looking hooks, but the menacing gleam that they might once have had was replaced by the dull warning of the rusting metal.

She walked past farming tools: rakes, scythes, shears and hayforks. They hung on rotted wooden pegs: it would take a little more than a strand of gossamer to break the supports and bring them crashing down on an unsuspecting innocent who happened to come this way. She made her way past sheets of iron and piles of sticks, cut down to the size of firewood. The barn had fallen into neglect. The clear sheets of corrugated plastic overhead let in light, but could not take away the sense of foreboding.

She gazed back at the entrance, seeing only the red door and its ideograph, and the diving swallows. Occasionally the birds swooped up to the rafters, but they seemed reluctant to stay once they were aware of her presence. Were these the guardians who would take away Roger's soul and lead him to the next life?

When she had reached the far side of the stables, she had to step over two railway sleepers that had been used to block off the entrance to a small walkway over a stream. The sound of the water was soothing and for a moment Lara forgot the reasons why she was standing there. She crouched down, allowing her fingers to trail through the cool water. She touched her lips and the water was sweet and refreshing.

Upstream was a tangle of foliage. She could see only a couple of metres, but, looking downstream, something about the straight path of the water and the overhanging willow branches reminded her of the tranquillity of the central aisle of the cathedral.

She paused, waiting here, leaning against a rickety fence and allowing herself to relax. She smiled. She had to remember this was not her time, but at this moment, she wished it was. Eighteen months ago, she would have still been subjected to the torments from Michael. She made a rough calculation. In this time, while Will was relaxing on a farm and had no idea of the shadow of impending disaster which loomed over his future, she had been crying and begging to see her stillborn daughter. That flower of hope was crushed in one second under the violent foot of despair.

She was distracted by the sound of a small boy running through the long grasses. This must be Roger, she thought, as he entered the stables. He wasn't a particularly tall boy for his age, but Lara instantly warmed to him. He was wearing brand-name trainers, shorts and a white T-shirt, as he walked in. There was a spray of freckles across his nose, which would no doubt be a source of much ridicule when he was at school. His pale skin had already caught the sun and had started to peel. His eyes, the same blue as those of Will, were wide with curiosity and excitement and life.

Lara felt nauseous. He would be dead in a matter of weeks and there was nothing she could do about it. She glanced around at the rusted hooks and the jagged shards of metal. She paled as she realised he could cut himself on any one of these things and, because he was of the age where it was important to be "strong" and "brave", he wouldn't tell anyone about his wound, nor tell them it had become infected, and he would die.

She knew there was no way she could save her own daughter's life; pleading to the doctors that the umbilical cord had wrapped around the baby's throat and demanding a caesarean would have been dismissed as the anxieties of a woman in labour. But she could at least give Will the gift of his family by changing the past. He would never know what she had done for him. When she finally returned to her own time, she would never have met him and would probably have no recollection of how time had altered, but for this one second, she felt good about herself.

She moved away from the railings, but felt herself momentarily losing her balance. She reached out to the wood to steady herself and instead of finding support she heard the wood protesting under the weight and then cracking. She did not fall, but the sudden sound had startled Roger. His curiosity had been overwhelmed by his realisation he was in a place where he possibly should not have been. He gave a yelp of terror before turning and running blindly from her, knocking into the metal box with the hay spilling from it. She heard the sound of ripping fabric and didn't need to see the red stain on his T-shirt to know he had cut himself.

And that *she* had been the cause of the accident.

'No,' she fought for breath, but oppression was crushing her chest. Her face had creased in horror. Her vision was swimming. There had to be a way to travel back in time and play through this scene again, but the pool of time had drained away from her and she was trying to claw her way through the arid landscape of the present. Her throat was clogged with dust from the crypt; her vision was blurring with tears.

Will was not looking at her when she opened her eyes. He was gathering the documents from Margery's tomb. She didn't know how much time had passed. Perhaps only seconds. Her face flushed with the knowledge that she had to explain her actions, had to explain her guilt. She suppressed a sob, found herself choking on the dust. Lara coughed until her eyes watered, her head span and purple fireworks exploded in front of her eyes. She gagged and wheezed. All strength left her. She staggered and held herself up against Sir William's tomb.

'Will?' Her voice was filled with a forlorn desperation.

Will did not answer immediately, instead he placed the parchments in a careful pile on Sir Gerard's tomb, balanced the torch on top of them, then walked across to her, patting her firmly but not painfully on the back.

He started to embrace her, but she pulled away. 'I've done a terrible thing …' she started.

'It's all right,' Will said. 'I know. I've always known. Marsh told me a long time ago that you caused Roger's death. At first I only believed it because I needed someone to blame. That was why it was so easy to agree to betraying you. But then I got to know you, watching you sleeping. I realised you couldn't carry that on your conscience. You weren't that kind of person.' He looked away. ' How can I condemn you? You were trying to change it so I wasn't part of all this.'

She cried into his shoulder. 'How can someone get it so wrong when they're trying to do the right thing?' she wailed.

'Time doesn't change,' Will said softly. 'It just makes sense.' He looked down sadly, '*Thus the whirligig of time brings in his revenges.*'

She tried to pull away, to be free of the love that he was giving her, love she didn't deserve. 'How can you even look at me?'

Now he did pull away, just a little so he could look down on her. She tried to look up, not knowing what she would see in his eyes. 'What you did, you did out of love. No matter what anguish it would have caused you. You wanted *me* to be happy.'

'I killed your son,' Lara whispered.

Will shook his head. 'No you didn't. *Fate* killed my son. You didn't put a gun to his head and pull the trigger. He was in the wrong place at the wrong time. I should have been there supervising him. Janet should have noticed he was hurt, except that he changed his top and hid the one he'd torn because he was embarrassed.' He started to gather up the documents, unable to look at her. 'Whether you were there or not, something would have happened to Roger. Tantris told me that. We've both been pawns in a game where we don't even know the rules.' He held her again, so she could cry into his shoulder. 'I can't hate you for what you did,' he whispered. 'That'll just make the future more difficult.'

'I'll go back,' Lara said with sudden determination. 'I'll go back and change everything again. Find a way of warning myself I shouldn't go back and change the past. Things can still be all right.'

'They won't, because I'm here, now,' he said, shaking his head solemnly. 'We can't change the past. We can only learn from it and hope we can change the future.' He sighed. 'I *did* try to tell you not to change things on the day we first met.' He kissed her gently on the forehead. 'I'm sorry I let you down, Lara, but maybe you understand all my reasons *why*. They told me you'd help me by changing things that have already happened, but instead it was *that* which caused me to be in the mess I was in.'

'But why me?' Lara said. 'I'm nothing special. I'm not the kind of secret agent who could use the serum for military powers. I'm just me.'

'Perhaps we should ask the person who allowed you to be administered with the serum in the first place, someone who also wanted to change the past.'

'Who?' Lara said, but realisation was already dawning on her. 'No,' she said, jaw clenching in a mixture of terror, anger and understanding. 'Not my father.'

19

Lara ran from the chamber. She became blinded on the spiral staircase, seeing neither light from above, nor below. Will's footsteps clattered behind her, but she paid no attention. Her mind was set on retribution against her father for using her as a guinea pig. She grazed her arm against the wall as she ran. Light echoed off the walls as Will drew closer. Then he was holding her, preventing her from extracting her revenge.

'I want to tear him to pieces,' Lara said struggling to be free from his grasp. 'I want to rip him in half.'

Will nodded. 'I'm sure you do. But let's just take it easy for a second. I'll tell you what: take a few really deep breaths; help me get the documents into the car; and *then* you can go and rip him to pieces.'

Lara still resisted, but with less effort. Her eyes were livid, her hands twisted into claws, but she inhaled deeply. Even at this point on the stairs, she could smell the church incense.

Will took her hands, peeled back her fingers, then led her back to the crypt.

They did not stay for long.

Will loaded up Lara's arms with some of the documents, but took the majority of them himself, then wedged the torch under his armpit and led her up the stairs. Lara followed, silently raging, but careful not to crush the fragile parchment.

The air of the church, although heavy with incense and polish, was sweet compared to the stale air of the tombs. Will laid his manuscripts and parchments on one of the pews as he pushed the stone door to the crypt shut. It grated across the flagstones, and that grating turned into a rumbling, echoing down the staircase and returning to the high ceiling. Lara set down her own documents and went to Will's side. She saw no telltale white scratching across the floor. Nor was there any apparent join in the stones where the entrance for the crypt should be. It was as if the stones had healed themselves. If she had not known what was concealed within those walls, she would have sworn there was nothing there.

Then Will was at her side. He gently took her elbow as if guiding an invalid. He pushed open the heavy oak door and peered outside. Seeing no one about, he led her away.

She stopped when they reached the threshold, taking a tentative glance over her shoulder. She took a moment to look at the crypt's entrance and then at the great arched windows over the altar. This would be the last time she came here. She no longer had anything to fear. She had confronted her memories, the ghosts that had wandered down the aisle. She could leave, knowing she had exorcised a small piece of her past. She swallowed, then looked at the distant street lights and the shadows created by the gravestones. Her eyes flashed involuntarily to her mother's gravestone – she could pick it out, even in the darkness, then she marched down the pathway, leaving Will to pull the door shut behind him. It slammed shut and the metal door-ring clattered and echoed in the darkness. He trotted a few steps to catch up with her.

'Are you all right?'

She nodded, but she did not smile at him. Her feelings for Beaded had changed. Instead of fearing what was in the church, her emotions had twisted into anger, directed at her father. She walked with determination towards the lych-gate and the pub. She was always a few steps ahead of Will, impatient to find the answers she needed to hear.

'I need you to sit here for a moment,' Will told her.

She shook her head. 'The last time you left me on my own, Marsh's thugs took me. You're not leaving my sight.'

He sighed stoically. 'I need to get the documents,' he told her. 'We don't want to be here any longer than we have to. And you need a couple of minutes to calm down before you see your father.'

She didn't like it, but it made sense. He handed her the car keys then turned and scuttled back towards the church. She unlocked the car, sat down in the passenger seat, then locked the car again. Her teeth and jaws hurt from where she had been clenching them. Her fingernails had scored into the palms of her hands. She hugged herself tight, shivering with both cold and pure rage.

She didn't know how long he was away. She adjusted the rear-view mirror and kept glancing behind her. Eventually, he appeared again, weighted down with medieval documents. His steps were slow and precise. He stopped at the car, waited for her to unlock it and to open the boot, then he lovingly placed the manuscripts on a blanket and covered them over, before shutting the boot once again. 'All right,' Will said, looking at the sky. 'I don't want to leave those in there for too long. They'll get damaged. We have a choice: we can either rest on our laurels with the manuscripts we've got, and go back to Olivia's to try to decipher them, or ...'

'Or,' Lara cut him off, 'We can go and see my father, get some answers and see if I still want to tear him to pieces.' She started to march towards the house.

Will hurried after her. 'Be careful,' he warned. 'You might not like what you find.'

She stared at him coldly. 'I've had a lifetime's worth of not liking what I'm finding in the last week, so why should it be any different now?'

As she stormed forward, she wondered if she had made the final connection: her father had agreed to her being injected, because he owed something to Eric Marsh.

Because Eric Marsh was her long-lost brother!

She stopped when she reached the front door, trying to assimilate these suppositions. Marsh was about the right age. Her brother had not simply gone missing when he had reached the age of consent. Instead, he'd taken his leave and gone to the secret military establishment. He'd informed their father he'd been working on a secret formula and needed a test subject. This was the argument she'd remembered as a tiny child: Eric Marsh had wanted to use *her* as his experiment and her father had refused. But all it had taken to convince him was the knowledge that Lara had been the cause of her mother's death and the world would be a better place without her.

She saw her reflection in the glass of the front door and realised her face had contorted into a snarl. She realised how much she loathed him, loathed the fact that any failure to conform to *his* wishes resulted in beatings and erosion of her self-esteem. How could she have idolised her father because he had spent time reading Shakespeare to her, when all the other girls were going to the zoo or the fair with their family. And if their fathers read to them, it was from a book of their choice, not some archaic play she could barely understand.

Will had no doubt seen the way her face was twisting. He placed a hand on her shoulder. She did not flinch away from him, but she did not feel comfortable with the touch either.

'You ready?' he asked.

She shook her head, but knocked robustly on the stained glass of the door. 'Let's get this over with.'

She tapped her foot impatiently and found herself staring at the door. It was strange how even the door could conjure memories: here was the scratch in the wood where she had run her bike into the frame. She remembered playing *Trick or Treat* one Halloween with one of her friends from the village, and even calling at this door, hoping her father would not see through her disguise and would give her sweets. She smiled inwardly. Her father had spent three weeks helping her make her costume. How could he fail to recognise her …

No! She recoiled from this prosaic memory and allowed herself to admit the truth. *She* had spent three weeks working on the costume and all the time her father berated her for wasting her time with frivolities when she could be doing something useful. And at the bottom of the door, there was the dent from when her father had come home from the pub absolutely out of his tree. She had been asleep when he'd knocked and, before she had been able to answer, he'd started kicking the doorframe and cursing her for being a lazy, good-for-nothing bitch, even though it had been two in the morning. The argument had ended with Lara retreating from her father when he had slapped her. She had screamed 'Bastard!' at him, which he had taken to mean that she had invited the Devil into her soul, and only a beating would drive the Evil One away. But Lara was no longer the naïve girl her father had expected and she had defended herself, clawing at him: huge rakes of blood ran down his cheeks. In this instance, the drink had been merciful, forcing him into a sea of unconsciousness before he could lay a finger on her, but she never, ever forgot what had happened that night. Even now, she was convinced there had been a sparkle of drunken lust in his eyes. Despite everything else she'd endured, once she had seen that, she no longer felt safe. For the next couple of months she made sure she was awake when he came home to avoid his increasing anger. Sometimes it was the early hours of the morning, on one occasion it was six o'clock the following evening, because the pub had had a lock-in and no one had told her. And at the same time, she had started seeing a young man called Michael, and she was doing everything she could to plan her escape.

When the door opened, her father looked at her with the disinterest of someone who knew a visitor was coming, and with the expression that she was not at all welcome. Lara was about to launch into a tirade against him, but Will placed a gentle hand on her shoulder. 'We'd like to speak to you, Mr Halpin,' he said. His voice was soporific. Lara felt the rage draining from her. Halpin nodded slowly and stepped back to let them into the hallway. Will gently nudged her forward.

Lara was hit by a sensory bombardment. The house had its own, unique sounds and smell. There was the heavy ticking of the grandmother clock on the stairs, the reeking of beeswax and Brasso for the fireplace ornaments, the thick smell of the coal fire, her father's soap and aftershave. The hallway was the same lurid orange that her father had been promising to re-paint since she was fifteen. There was her father's distinct odour, lingering through the hall, and the stench of wine congealing in the bottom of a bottle. Her stomach churned and she wondered when the hall had last seen a vacuum cleaner, or if the disinfectant had even moved from the place in the cupboard under the stairs, where she had left it years before.

Halpin walked into the lounge without even looking at them again. They were not offered a drink, for which Lara was grateful. The glasses in the display cabinet were stained brown. She did not sit down and, following an infuriatingly long silence, her father eventually spoke.

'Somehow I knew you'd come back to haunt me.'

She was surprised there was no despair in his voice, just the tone of someone who had been caught, and who knows it is useless to deny the charges put against him. Lara was about to retort, but again she felt Will's hand on her shoulder.

'Do you understand why I had to do it, Lara?' her father spoke in a soft voice.

Lara thought for a minute 'No,' she said eventually. 'All of my life, I've believed one thing, believed in you, believed the stories you told me. Even when you were drinking and bullying, I believed there was good in you and you'd protect me no matter what.' The words were tumbling out in an unstoppable torrent. 'Now I find there's a brother I knew nothing about, and rather than protecting me, you're the one who sold me out.'

Her father nodded, but did not show any repentance. 'I did what I needed to do. And if you've ever believed in something so much you'd sacrifice anything for it, then you'll understand what

I mean.'

'But your own daughter ...' Lara started.

'A daughter who took away the only person I truly loved,' Halpin said. There was fire in his eyes now; it was the first time he had focused on her. 'You would only understand that if you had loved anyone as deeply as I had loved her.'

'The only person you ever loved was yourself,' Lara spat. 'Did you really hate me so much you had to sell me to Eric Marsh to be one of his experiments?'

'I took no money,' her father said earnestly. 'I make no apologies. I have no regrets.'

'He promised you something,' Will said. 'He said he'd help you get her back.'

Halpin raised an eyebrow. He turned back to Lara. 'I needed your mother, and you were in the way.' His gaze became stony and unwavering.

Lara was about to speak, but Will interrupted. 'And what if the serum had fried Lara's brain?' he asked coldly. 'Would you have said the experiment was a success then?'

Halpin turned to him. 'I don't know who you are, sir, and in my house I don't answer to you. This is between my daughter and myself.' He turned back to Lara. 'But to answer your man's question: you were expendable. But what I did, I did out of love, love for your mother. Your presence here smells strongly of a desire for revenge, revenge for something you know nothing about.'

'This isn't revenge,' Lara said. 'It's justice, and for you to take responsibility for your actions.'

'Don't patronise me,' her father said. 'Your intentions are nothing but a self-centred, glossed-up euphemism for revenge.'

'This is getting us nowhere,' Lara said.

'Whose fault is that?' her father snapped. 'I didn't invite you into my house. You were the one who knew it all and was quite happy to leave me here to fend for myself.'

'Yeah,' Lara said. 'That's what you'd have liked me to believe, but there was always my brother, wasn't there? I'm sure he made sure you didn't want for anything.'

'What are you burbling on about?' her father said.

'You're not going to insult me by telling me that I haven't got a brother, are you?'

Her father shook his head. 'No. It took you long enough to work it out. But I haven't seen him in about twenty years.'

'But …' Lara started.

'How clearly do I need to spell it out to you, girl? Your brother left twenty years ago. He left Beaded after a traumatic time at home, for which I was largely responsible, but *you* were the cause.'

'Stop blaming me!' Lara shouted. 'I was four years old. How can you blame a four-year old for ripping the family apart?'

'Because you killed your mother!' Halpin glowered. 'And neither of us had anywhere to direct our grief. It ate at us, ate all the good bits and left the rest to rot.'

Lara wanted to retort, but suddenly her fight was gone. Halpin continued. 'Your brother went away, joined the Merchant Navy. I didn't hear from him again.'

He looked away from her, for which Lara was grateful. He wouldn't see the relief flooding across her face as she realised she'd been wrong to believe that Marsh was her brother. Instead, Marsh had played upon her father's weakness.

Halpin continued: 'The famous Halpin pride was our undoing. He left, and I spent the next years trying not to talk as though you would live in a shadow if he came back, because he disappointed me. He disappointed me by not resolving our misunderstanding. But *you* had been the wedge between us. But I *tried* to love you. I *tried* to tell you about him through the stories. I didn't want you to disappoint me the way he had. There were two things you could have done. You could have brought your mother back to me, or your brother.' He shook his head sadly. 'But you failed on both scores.'

Then Will was speaking. 'Mr Halpin. I read Lara's file. Her mother died in childbirth. That's not the kind of guilt you can pin on a child.'

'I'll thank you for not interfering with my family,' Halpin snapped. He turned back to Lara. 'You failed to realise any of my hopes. So now I look at you and say you were a disappointment, and I would willingly change history for a time when you didn't exist.'

Lara was floundering, burning with shame. This was more than the paradox of changing time so she and Will never met, so he couldn't have betrayed her to Marsh, so she could go back and change time. This was the old conundrum of someone going back in time to kill their own grandfather so they could never be born. This was the paradox of willing herself out of existence. 'This would have affected everyone else in the world,' Lara said hopelessly. 'What gave you the right to decide how history was going to change?'

'Your brother had the right to the love I couldn't provide. He had the right to a mother. I had the right to a wife. And you, you just let yourself be defeated and crawl into the corner, rather than be a part of the most important scientific experiment of all time.' His eyes blazed. There was no sign of the old man now. There was power behind those eyes, power that had victimised Lara in the past. She found herself cowering from him like a child. 'You're pathetic,' he said, and didn't try to disguise his contempt.

Lara's determination sagged. There was no fight left in her. Halpin sensed his advantage and played his trump. 'Of course, your whole marriage was a sham, too.'

'It didn't work out,' she admitted. Her voice sounded pitiful. 'It happens.'

Halpin smiled at her. There was no humour, just baring his teeth in the malicious knowledge that he had won. '*Michael* was working for Eric Marsh. He was employed to keep an eye on you when I felt I could no longer do so without arousing suspicion.'

Game, set and match.

Lara gasped. She almost doubled over in the agony of shock, as if Halpin had physically hit her. *Michael was a part of this too?* It had only been days since she had left Stamford, but she was having difficulty in remembering what Michael looked like. Then she glanced at Will and, finally, her father. Every man that she thought she could trust had been a part of this conspiracy. Every man she thought she'd loved had lied to her.

She looked up at Halpin. She suddenly saw him for what he was: a sad, pathetic old man who'd never found the courage to confront his tragedy. She had expected to be angry at his mocking, condescending tone. She had expected to be upset by his vehemence towards her. But, as she straightened herself and refused to break her stare, she felt nothing. She had left here three years ago, and soon she would do it again. 'You've consoled yourself with a story of time-travel and you only loathe me because you don't have the courage to loathe yourself. Face it: my mother's death was a tragedy. I may not have seen the signs that I had a brother, but at least I didn't spend my entire life trusting in a serum that didn't work. And if it *had* worked, I wouldn't have brought my mother back. What makes you think she'd want to spend another second with such a ... cruel man.' She smiled confidently. 'The serum doesn't work. It never did.' This was a gamble. She didn't look at Will, but time seemed laden as she waited for him to speak.

'She's right,' Will said eventually. 'There's no secret serum that can take you back in time. Even if there were, it wouldn't change things. It's all to do with cause and effect. No action of the future can affect the past. The past is a written book that cannot be changed.' Lara saw beads of sweat on his forehead, and she placed a gentle hand on his arm. 'Accept it, Mr Halpin. Our business is concluded.' He leaned forward. His face was steely; there was darkness in his eyes. 'Lara no longer has to watch out to see if you, or Marsh, or Michael, or anyone else is following her,' he said. His voice was powerful. For a moment, Will reminded her of the way Tantris spoke with hidden power. 'It's over.'

Halpin maintained an almost perfect poker-face. The only betrayal that he was feeling *anything* was an almost indiscernible narrowing of the eyes.

She turned and walked away. There was nothing more to say. She didn't want him to see the tears burning her eyes. She gently slipped through the front door, the door that evoked so many memories, and walked towards the car.

Will did not follow immediately. She wondered, briefly, if his statement that Marsh's experiments had been a failure was only a carefully constructed lie to deceive her once more, and to deliver her to him once again. But when he returned, he was sombre, as though he had to pass on bad news. 'Your father won't bother us anymore,' Will said. 'I explained to him you should be left alone in terms he'd understand.'

'What did you say?' Lara asked.

Will gave a nonchalant shrug. 'I told him I'd break his fingers if I found anyone following you. He seemed to understand.'

When Lara sat in the car, a spring of triumph started to bubble inside her. But it was quickly substituted for rage. She thumped against the dashboard. 'How could he?' she screamed. White hot anger flashed across her eyes.

Will shrugged. 'I can understand what he was doing, even if I don't agree with it. He loved your mother so much that he couldn't bear the thought of life without her, and would have stopped at nothing to bring her back.'

Lara felt like she had been forced to take a bitter pill. 'I understand that,' she said. 'I just hate the thought that my father saw me as an expendable pawn, just a stone to kick along the roadside.'

Will nodded. 'Yeah. Talk about casting pearls before swine. He never saw your true worth, did he? After all, you'll always be my precious pearl.'

*

Lara was glad that Will drove away from Beaded and didn't suggest stopping somewhere *en route*. Exhaustion was driving skewers into her back. Her arms and legs felt limp. Her neck screamed at her every time she yawned. Even so, she needed to get away from here. And even though they had reached the end of the trail, she had a nagging feeling her journey *wasn't* completely over. She had been running, and she still had nowhere to go. She needed to find a place where she could start again and establish herself. *Then,* she thought, *only then will it be truly over.*

There was little traffic at this time, except for a steady stream of haulage lorries, but Lara needed to look over her shoulder. She was suspicious of any car that followed for more than a short distance.

She felt safer once they had passed the RAC building and the slip-road for the M5. After all, it had been in Birmingham where she had joined the chase. Now everything had turned full circle. Will must have sensed her relief as he turned and smiled at her. She glanced behind them at car lights, but Will placed a gentle hand over hers.

'You still worrying about Marsh?' he asked softly. 'You don't need to.'

He didn't say any more; Lara had learned that Will would tell her in his own time. The rhythmic flash of the motorway lights was beguiling. Lara closed her eyes for what seemed to be a few moments, but then she heard the change in the engine's pitch and Will was driving along the road towards Home Forest House.

'Slix'll be in bed,' he told her as they got out of the car. 'But I know where she keeps the spare key.'

'She won't mind us being here?' Lara said.

Will frowned. 'A big house like this, all to herself? No, she'll welcome visitors.' Then he grimaced and rubbed his cheek. 'Most of the time.'

She waited while Will hunted under plant pots for the key, then he unlocked the door and returned to pick up some of the manuscripts. 'Besides, I told you, it's *our* house.'

The plants seemed to prickle as if sensing intruders as Lara and Will walked through to the kitchen. Lara was almost certain she heard something whispering amongst the foliage as the plants reassured themselves that these visitors were friends. Despite the welcome she had received from Olivia, Lara still felt this was a spooky place; there was something … primeval … about it.

Will set the kettle to boil, then sat her down with a cup of coffee before he left her for only a few moments. When he returned, his arms were full of the remaining parchments. Lara watched him, fascinated by his childlike innocence. His eyes widened with excitement as he scoured through the pages. He traced his finger along the lines of script, reading under his breath the words in Latin and Middle English, and in other languages she didn't recognise.

She tried to stay awake, but the pressures of the day were taking their toll and her vision started to swim as her head dropped lower and lower towards the table. 'That came over all sudden …' she thought, as her eyes closed. It was as if she'd been … drugged.

She began to panic, trying to fight the overwhelming urge to sleep, but it was a useless struggle. She might as well have been chasing a rainbow. Her last thought before her eyes closed was the realisation she shouldn't trust Will. He had sold her out to Eric Marsh once again.

20

She woke to the sound of clattering: rain upon the conservatory roof. Lara half-roused herself. She had laid her head on the table and not moved. Her eyes were still heavy with sleep. Will was still sitting in front of her, his eyes had the same rheumy sheen as someone who had been drinking, although Will had probably spent the entire night focused on the minuscule letters of various documents. He didn't even glance up at her when she moved. He was obsessed with what he was reading, working like an automaton, taking copious notes, marking pages in documents with torn slivers of paper.

Gradually, she became aware of her surroundings: she was sitting in Olivia's kitchen. Olivia was sitting outside in the conservatory. When she saw Lara had opened her eyes she smiled and gave a little wave. Lara smiled back uncertainly and brushed the last of the sleep from her eyes and staggered over to where Olivia was sitting.

'I can't believe he left you there all night,' Olivia said. 'I mean, he didn't even see you safely to your room before starting his single-handed cataloguing of the entire collection.' She shook her head in mock despair. 'Men!' She smiled again. 'You have two choices: coffee with me, or getting some proper rest and I'll go back to reading my book.'

Lara smiled weakly. 'I think I'll try coffee and conversation.'

'That's more than he's tried,' Olivia said, indicating to Will. 'I can't get a coherent thought out of him at all. It's like those papers are going to run away if he takes his eyes off them.' She got up and went over to the kettle. 'I'll drip-feed him caffeine every hour and see how long he goes until he collapses with exhaustion.' She smiled, remembering. 'That's Will for you. Always the obsessive and always got his nose in a book.'

Lara chatted with Olivia for the rest of the morning, although she realised she was doing most of the talking, and Olivia had hardly said anything about her own life.

Eventually, like a long-distance underwater swimmer, Will came up for air. He seemed bewildered when he gazed around, as if surprised that so much time had passed and the sun had risen. He eventually focused on Lara and smiled, rubbing tired eyes and massaging his temples. 'Anything interesting?' Lara said.

'You wouldn't believe it,' Will replied. 'There's something here which explains why the poet made the clues.' He rummaged through the papers and pointed to one of the parchments. The ink had faded in the light; the pages had become brittle. He winced. 'These need to be stored in the right conditions,' he said in a hollow voice, realising that in order to preserve the documents, he would have to surrender them to someone else. 'The plan to write *Sir Gawayne* was conceived by the monks in Chester. They felt that writing a poem showed religion in a new light; it's a constant trial and testing against an unknown foe. It's an allegory for life itself. The Church was divided with the Papacy moving to Avignon, and there were the further worries over Wycliffe's paper which rejected the Biblical basis of papal authority.'

Lara yawned. 'All very interesting. What does it mean?'

'It shows that for the times of William de Masci, the papal struggles and the Protestant reform attack were rocking the Catholic Church. You've also got long periods of war. The idea of the Chester monks was to establish a backdrop everyone would understand: Arthur's court, and so, they created an antithesis of the troubles of England at the time. You've got a depiction of a stable and noble monarchy, the brotherhood of religion, a devotion to God without the questions of papacy and Protestantism and a noble knight who is prepared to lay down his life to protect the honour of his King.'

'And what about the trail?'

'Sir William wrote the poems with the guidance of the Benedictine monks, and so they had enough influence to include a discreet stone in the building of the south transept, containing the kind of language the poet himself would have used. The Cathedral also owned the site of Holywell, and so they were quite capable of tying in the legends of Gawain; they could also influence some of the building of the chapel there: the Star Chamber is an example of that. When the Pope realised that something was going on, he summoned Sir William to Avignon. He went and explained that his family were descended from Sir Gerard, a Templar, that the family had been guardians of the Ring of Solomon for a century and he needed to keep it hidden. Clement V wanted to ensure the survival of the Templars despite the pressures from the French King, and Clement VI, a Benedictine himself, understood the urgency of the mission, so, instead of commanding him to leave the Ring in Rome, he agreed to include part of the clues in the *Palais des Papes*. He ensured the complete details of the fresco would be saved and the depictions restored when age took their toll on them. He wasn't to know it would be Napoleonic soldiers, rather than age, that would destroy the frescos – or maybe he did, because he was known to have consulted astrologers.' Will considered. 'Or maybe the ring had certain other powers. Anyway, Clement VI enjoyed his comforts, and he turned the Palais into a palace for princes, a place where he could entertain the ambassadors to the Christian Church, rather than the cold fortress it had been before. He also oversaw the building of the *Église Saint-Pierre*, with a special directive as to which statue should stand beneath the fifth station of the cross, and what it should represent. Sadly, those papers must be lost, or held in some Vatican archive where we'll never find them. One thing is for certain, the de Masci family were respected by the highest orders of the Church, if even the Pope would bow to his almost childish treasure-trail.'

'If the Pope knew about the ring and the location of the Seals of Revelation, then how could he allow them to fall into anyone's hands?'

'Perhaps because they believed in predestination, and that the seals would be found when the time was right. Perhaps it was because even the Pope has to answer to the powers Tantris spoke of. I just don't know.' He looked back at the documents. 'Sir William also says he planned to include a trap in his own tomb just so the unwary – grave robbers – wouldn't stumble across the manuscripts, and that was why he had Margery buried in the garden, rather than the family vault. Anyway, the de Masci family owned significant amounts of the land around Beaded. Peasants who worked on the land raised the Village and the Parish Church was established as a focus of Village life, exactly what Father Timothy wanted from it. It's too bad that there's been a steady decline in moral standards, and the people were so resilient to change.'

'All these years and Beaded hasn't known what a great heritage it's had. The only thing we knew was that it was a thirteenth century church.'

Will regarded her seriously. 'Hardly a great heritage, when you think about it. It was established through treasures stolen from Jerusalem. Some of the Templars were noble knights, Gerard de Masci is an example of that, but others were downright bloody butchers.'

'I was talking about the fact that Sir William – and the whole of his family – lived in Beaded, and we never knew anything about it. I assume he must have lived in a manor or something. I wonder what happened to it?'

'I think I can answer that. In one of the diaries, de Masci spoke of the rivals to the family, the *Tempestarii*, who, if they couldn't get their hands on the ring itself, wanted to ensure the secrets were never used by some other organisation.' He leaned forward. 'The literal translation of *Tempestarii* is "Storm Bringers". Tantris said a storm was coming. My guess is that they burned down the manor, not realising the manuscript had already travelled to a safe place. I guess they also burned down the Cotton Library in 1731 and destroyed so many of the medieval manuscripts. The British Library manuscript of Gawain was one of those that survived.'

'They destroyed a library in the hopes of destroying just one book. That's barbaric!'

'It's as barbaric as wiping out entire villages hoping to find the one enemy of the faith hiding within. That's what the Inquisition did. And the Templars for that matter. We can take some comfort from the manuscripts that were saved. We nearly lost the only copy of *Beowulf* in that fire, along with a load of other manuscripts. That would have meant studying Anglo-Saxon or Medieval literature would have been a much shorter, but less rich, task.' He picked up a cold cup of coffee from the table and sipped at it. 'The *Tempestarii* apparently didn't know about the original, the one that Sir William wrote with his own hand. It was sent to Avignon for safe-keeping and the German army must have found it when they occupied Avignon in 1942. Then it was taken to Berlin and then to Bath, once Berlin had been occupied.'

He looked away from her, at the rain that was sheeting against the window. 'But even now the manuscript's secrets have been unlocked, this isn't the end of the trail. There's been one attempt to cover up and destroy the evidence that the *Gawayne* manuscript ever existed. Now it's exactly the same thing again. We have no evidence that William de Masci wrote the poem and no evidence that there was ever a Ring of Solomon.'

Olivia rushed into the kitchen brandishing a copy of *The Times*. 'You've got to see this.' She had folded the paper open and pointed at an article at the bottom of the page.

EXPERTS DISMISS UNEARTHED MANUSCRIPTS AS HOAX

Medieval manuscripts, presumed to date back to the fourteenth century, have been dismissed as hoaxes, leading experts have stated.

The papers, said to have been discovered in St James's Church, Gloucester, were supposed to have contained religious tracts, letters and poetry. They were allegedly discovered in the crypt 'by accident' by a group of amateur treasure-hunters.

Experts from the British Library suggested that while the vellum pages and parchment were consistent with the period, and have been carbon dated to the late fourteenth century, the penmanship is definitely from more recent times. Michael Goddard, Head of the Department of Antiquities at the University of London, claimed that the documents were 'convincing, clever fakes'. He concluded that 'These manuscripts are no more than an improbable fiction.'

'What's this got to do with us?' Will asked.

Olivia raised an eyebrow. 'I think it's hardly a coincidence that the newspapers run this story on the day after you find your treasure trove. This is a way of telling you not to go public with what you've found, otherwise you'll be laughed out of town.'

'That's them shutting the gate before they've even got a horse,' Lara said.

'What makes you think it isn't an unhappy coincidence?' Will wondered.

Lara cocked her head. 'I'd start with the fact that it ends with a quotation from *Twelfth Night*, saying this is all an "improbable fiction".'

'They're not even going to let me catalogue them,' Will said. His shoulders slumped. 'Bang goes my idea for a few articles and some translation work.'

'And why should they?' Olivia asked. 'The more you protest now, the more it sounds like you're trying to prove a spurious point. It would be like trying to prove that the Hitler diaries aren't fake now.'

Will slammed the paper down on to the table in frustration. 'God, if only we had the documents Tantris took away with him. We could show this article up for the joke that it truly is.' His eyes were cold. 'Someone's coerced this Goddard bloke, just like Pope Clement V was forced to disband the Templars.'

'Still, at least we know the trail and the ring are real,' Lara said stoically. 'Besides, you can spend your time translating them and producing books on medieval life with references that no one else has seen …'

'Or believes,' Will concluded. 'These papers are worthless now.'

'Only to the narrow minded,' Lara snapped. 'If you're smart, then you can still use them to understand more about the way of life from times gone by. As I said before, not all treasure has a monetary value.'

'Well,' he said, with a long sigh. 'Let them have their little victory.' He looked down at the article again. 'I wonder who did this?'

'Marsh,' Lara said. 'If he can't get to us, he can make sure we never go public about his little setup.'

'I'm afraid it's probably Tantris.'

'It's the sort of thing Marsh would do,' Lara protested.

Will shook his head, giving her a gentle smile. 'As you say, not all treasures have a monetary value, and here's one you might appreciate. You don't need to worry about Eric Marsh again. When I said he'd let me go, it wasn't quite the truth. What happened was that there was a small explosion in those underground tunnels, which sadly means Mr Marsh is incapable of following us.' He gave her a cocky half-smile. 'See, not all gifts need to have a monetary value.'

'What sort of "small explosion"?'

'A sort of …' Will thought about it and made a circular wave with his hand. '*Big* small explosion. It collapsed a few of the walls. Not enough to cause any permanent damage to the structure overall, just enough to seal off some of the rooms.'

'And you caused it?'

Will made a non-committal gesture. 'I didn't say that. Neither will the newspapers.'

'Be fair, Will. The newspapers won't say anything.'

'Well,' Will said nonchalantly. 'That's the problem with being a top-secret organisation. You can't prosecute anyone, even if you suspect they might have had something to do with … an explosion in one of your tunnels. Problem is that it was somewhere near one of the storage areas.'

'Storage areas?' Lara said, shocked. 'But that means all the manuscripts …'

Will nodded sadly. 'But I suspect that even if those manuscripts had come to light, they would have been dismissed as fakes, just like our findings in Beaded were.'

'But you could have learned so much,' Lara said.

Will shook his head. 'I think I would have learned *too* much. The point is that there are no absolutes in history. The fun in history is *speculating* why certain people acted in certain ways. If I had a load of papers which had never before come to light, or even the definitive document with all the answers, then it would take out all the fun of going to history conferences and watching so-called experts bickering over their petty little points. Sometimes it's much more fun to speculate.'

Lara looked down sadly. 'So where do we go from here?'

Will pushed the documents to one side and hummed gently to himself: '*Trip no further, pretty sweeting, Journeys end in lovers meeting.*' He laid his hand over hers. 'Maybe it's time we stopped thinking about the past. Maybe it's time to start thinking about the future.'

Epilogue

At a time when English men and women were speaking a vernacular Teutonic language, unrecognisable in the present day, there were few written records. Instead, hearts and courage were stirred by the strings of a lyre, accompanying songs and legends. Most of these old *laïs* have passed into the forgetful mind of history, but the legend of the Abbess, St Winefride, has survived with such importance that her shrine gave its name to the town.

Standing beneath the huge arches, Lara knows this is a fifteenth century structure to celebrate the saint's life, but the significance is not lost on her. People have come to the rejuvenating waters for fourteen hundred years.

Lara wears a bikini underneath her T-shirt. She looks at Will by her side. She is anxious, but he smiles encouragingly and gently squeezes her hand. He then lets her step forward on her own. She walks underneath the vast arches and into the Star Chamber. Pilgrims have already been here today, lighting candles in prayers for healing. Some of them will have already bathed, either for themselves, or vicariously for those who need healing but cannot make it to the shrine.

In spite of the noise of the nearby roadside, tranquillity washes over Lara. All sounds have been muted, and even uncertainty retreats from her. Lara feels she is being held in a protective bubble, distancing her from reality. She wants to look for her lover again, but she knows this is a journey she must make by herself. Looking for him would be a sign of weakness.

She has been warned about the temperature of the water with almost scientific accuracy. She stiffens and gasps as she walks down the first steps of the bathing pool; the cold water is almost unbearable. It numbs her ankles, then her shins and calves. She bites back the urge to squeal with the shock of the cold, but does not manage to suppress a shiver.

The water smells clear and pure. It reminds her of clear morning dew. She feels her lungs swelling with the sweet scent. As she reaches the bottom of the steps, she lowers her body so that her shoulders are immersed. The cold forces the air from her lungs with sweet pain. It is all she can do to bring herself to kneel on Beuno's stone for a second. There are knee-shaped grooves in the stone, worn away by centuries of pilgrims.

She is momentarily blinded by memories. This place has been a focus of worship and prayer for centuries. It is a place filled with hope and anticipation of answered prayers. The emotions are positive; they are as powerful as the waves that crash on the shore not far from here. It is small wonder that pilgrims come across the world to be here. It is a well of favourable emotions, as real as the water itself, honourable and virtuous emotions that Lara feels are as physical as the water in which she is kneeling. It is only the cold that forbids her to stay any longer. She tries to leave the pool as quickly, but reverently as possible. Her skin is frozen, but her body begins tingling, revitalised, as blood flows through her.

She walks around the Star Chamber as the blood flows through her veins, compensating for the cold. When she immerses herself the second time the water still bites, but she can endure it longer. Kneeling on the stone, she remembers a time when she was with Michael, another lifetime ago. She also remembers Julia, the daughter she had always wanted, but couldn't keep. She also thinks about the mother she never knew. Her grief will always be there, but now, instead of mourning their deaths, she feels able to celebrate their lives.

Will has told her that baptism by triple immersion comes from a Celtic ritual. She considers the ancient traditions as she walks around the Star Chamber once again. Then, in her third immersion the waters seem to be playing with her, jostling her, pushing her off balance. Now she is able to kneel for longer, considering the healing she needs, and also others, particularly her father.

She wonders about others who have kneeled here. Her mind wades through the pool of time. She sees a crowd of folk from every century, praying for her, reaching out to her. The memories still unnerve her, but she knows she has been given a great gift. In time she will understand how to control the gift, in time she will become used to the invasion into her mind.

Will waits near the statue of Winefride in the Star Chamber. She walks to him, smiling, refreshed. He wraps a towel around her and holds her. She becomes aware once more of the noise of the traffic. She shivers, but not because it is cold. She cannot remember when her mind has felt so clear. The healing she hoped for has started. She has taken the first step on her new journey.

Will hands her a second towel and then walks away to the pool. He is bathed in shadows as he steps into it . He needs the healing more than her, she thinks. He has lost the two people he loved the most.

She looks away. The healing is a private process. It should not be watched. Instead, she looks at the statue of St Winefride who has witnessed these proceedings. Lara wonders if the stone palm leaves are rustling in the slight wind. The thin line on the statue's neck seems to glow in the morning light, but it might be the sun breaking from behind a cloud.

Will returns after a short time. It does not seem like he has had the chance to immerse himself three times. But he has.

She hands him the towel. When he holds her, she can smell the purity of the water, mixed with his musky scent and his wet hair. She feels safe in his arms. She wonders if any tourists have noticed the two strange bedraggled figures, wrapped in towels, embracing on a wet morning. She looks up at him through her fringe and gives him a shy smile.

'Come with me, stay with me, Pearl,' Will whispers to her, but Lara hesitates.

'What about Michael?' Lara says. 'I was married. I can't dismiss that.'

'I'd listen to the voice of the past,' Will tells her. 'The oldest fragments from Anglo-Saxon times tell us *One easily divorces what was never truly united*. You were never married to Michael in your heart. But your healing here is a symbol of your stepping away from your own past. You're free to make your own choices.'

He holds out his hand and she takes it. As they step forward together, Lara realises that the past has released its grip on them. Their misguided attempts to resurrect their memories are replaced by their hopes for the future.

Honi soit qui mal y pense

About the Author

Jon Mackley has worked in Film Production, Public Relations and Journalism. He has completed a degree in English at the University of Stirling, and a PhD at the University of York. He is currently a Senior Lecturer in English and Creative Writing.

If you prefer to spend your nights with Vampires and Werewolves rather than the mundane then we publish the books for you. If your preference is for Dragons and Faeries or Angels and Demons – we should be your first stop. Perhaps your perfect partner has artificial skin or comes from another planet – step right this way. Our curiosity shop contains treasures you will enjoy unearthing. If your passion is Fantasy (including magical realism and spiritual fantasy), Horror or Science Fiction (including Steampunk), Cosmic Egg books will feed your hunger.